Contemporary Fiction and the Uses of Theory

Also by Michael Greaney

CONRAD, LANGUAGE AND NARRATIVE

Contemporary Fiction and the Uses of Theory

The Novel from Structuralism to Postmodernism

Michael Greaney

First published in 2006 by
PALGRAVE MACMILLAN
Houndmills, Basingstoke, Hampshire RG21 6XS and
175 Fifth Avenue, New York, N.Y. 10010
Companies and representatives throughout the world.

PALGRAVE MACMILLAN is the global academic imprint of the Palgrave
Macmillan division of St. Martin's Press, LLC and of Palgrave Macmillan Ltd.
Macmillan® is a registered trademark in the United States, United Kingdom
and other countries. Palgrave is a registered trademark in the European
Union and other countries.

ISBN-13: 978–1–4039–9146–1 hardback
ISBN-10: 1–4039–9146–4 hardback

This book is printed on paper suitable for recycling and made from fully
managed and sustained forest sources.

A catalogue record for this book is available from the British Library.

Library of Congress Cataloging-in-Publication Data
Greaney, Michael.
    Contemporary fiction and the uses of theory : the novel from
    structuralism to postmodernism / Michael Greaney.
        p. cm.
    This book examines the representation, or "novelizations" of literary
    critical theory (structuralism, poststructuralism, postmodernism) in
    contemporary fiction, and traces an alternative history of the "theory
    wars" in the pages of contemporary fiction.
    Includes bibliographical references and index.
    ISBN 1–4039–9146–4 (cloth)
        1. English fiction – 20th century – History and criticism. 2. American
    fiction – 20th century – History and criticism. 3. Criticism – History –
    20th century. 4. Literature – History and criticism – Theory, etc.
        5. Structuralism (Literary analysis) 6. Postmodernism (Literature) I. Title.
    PR808.C93G74 2006
    823'.91409113—dc22   2006045217

10 9 8 7 6 5 4 3 2 1
15 14 13 12 11 10 09 08 07 06

Printed and bound in Great Britain by
Antony Rowe Ltd, Chippenham and Eastbourne

Contents

Acknowledgements   vii

1. Introduction: Theory in(to) Fiction   1

2. The Structuralist Novel   9

    Christine Brooke-Rose, *Thru*
    Anthony Burgess, *MF*
    John Fowles, *The French Lieutenant's Woman*
    David Lodge, *How Far Can You Go?*

3. From Structuralism to Dialogics: David Lodge   24

    David Lodge, *Nice Work*; *Small World*; *Thinks ...*

4. The 'Culture Wars' and Beyond: Theory on the
    US Campus   41

    David Damrosch, *Meetings of the Mind*
    Percival Everett, *Erasure*; *Glyph*
    Sandra M. Gilbert and Susan Gubar, *Masterpiece Theatre*
    John L'Heureux, *The Handmaid of Desire*
    James Hynes, *The Lecturer's Tale*
    Richard Powers, *Galatea 2.2*

5. The Vanishing Author   59

    Gilbert Adair, *The Death of the Author*
    John Banville, *Shroud*
    Malcolm Bradbury, *Doctor Criminale*; *My Strange Quest for
        Mensonge*; *To the Hermitage*

6. Foucauldian Fictions   83

    A. S. Byatt, *The Biographer's Tale*
    Patricia Duncker, *Hallucinating Foucault*
    Hervé Guibert, 'Les Secrets d'un homme'; *To the Friend
        Who Did Not Save My Life*
    Julia Kristeva, *The Samurai*
    Toby Litt, 'When I Met Michel Foucault'

7. Feminism *versus* Post-structuralism   99

    A. S. Byatt, *Possession*
    Angela Carter, *Nights at the Circus*

8. Criminal Signs: Murder in Theory   123

    Umberto Eco, *The Name of the Rose*
    Norman Holland, *Death in a Delphi Seminar*
    D. J. H. Jones, *Murder at the MLA*
    Julia Kristeva, *The Old Man and the Wolves; Possessions*

9. The Novel in Hyperreality   140

    Julian Barnes, *England, England*
    Christine Brooke-Rose, *Textermination*
    Mark Z. Danielewski, *House of Leaves*
    A. N. Wilson, *A Jealous Ghost*

10. Conclusion: Fiction after Theory   156

Notes   161

Bibliography   172

Index   181

Acknowledgements

I am grateful to the Arts and Humanities Research Council for funding the period of research leave during which this book was completed.

I would also like to thank Neil Bennison, Fred Botting, Arthur Bradley, Jo Carruthers, Mary Eagleton, Alison Easton, Anne-Marie Evans, Sarah Gibson, Tim Johnson, Richard Meek, Linden Peach, Jane Rickard, John Schad, Catherine Spooner, Andy Stafford and Andrew Tate.

1
Introduction: Theory in(to) Fiction

Creative writers are scarcely renowned for their enthusiasm for critical theory. 'Novels come out of life', says Julian Barnes, 'not out of theories about either life or literature'.[1] On the face of it, this seems like an eminently reasonable claim, since fiction so frequently urges us to appreciate that lived experience is infinitely richer and more complex than anything dreamt up in the mind of a cold-blooded intellectual. From George Eliot's Casaubon to Woolf's Mr Ramsay to Joyce's Stephen Dedalus, intellectuals tend to fare badly in fiction; they are usually too busy grooming their pet theories to engage meaningfully with their fellow human beings or soak up any of the practical wisdom that everyday life might have to offer. The novel has always been a proudly anti-theoretical genre, one that attaches more significance to the moral adventures of its unpretentious *hommes moyens sensuels* than to the misguided intellectual projects of its introverted system-makers and maladjusted bookworms. Novelists never tire of sabotaging the mental labours of theorists, exposing every ambitious new quest for some key to all mythologies as just another journey down an intellectual blind alley.

Nor does the remarkable rise of critical theory in modern literary studies seem likely to allay novelists' long-standing suspicions of all theories of literature and life. The terms 'critical theory', 'literary theory', or just plain 'theory' have served in recent years as more or less interchangeable flags of convenience for a very loose coalition of interest groups who have found a common cause in their impatience with the intellectual and ideological limitations of traditional literary criticism. 'Theory' has become a sweeping but indispensable shorthand for the state of permanent methodological revolution that characterizes contemporary literary-critical debate, with its apparently endless supply of new -isms and -ologies: structuralist and post-structuralist conceptions of language, difference and textuality; Marxist and Foucauldian demystifications of state power and ideology; Freudian and Lacanian explorations of desire, subjectivity and the unconscious; feminist critiques of patriarchal reading habits and male-dominated canons; postcolonial challenges to western cultural imperialism; postmodernist questionings of the official post-Enlightenment narratives of culture, truth and value. What we have here is a set of controversies that promise to keep critics occupied indefinitely but seem to offer precious little in the way of inspiration for the creative writer. This is partly because theory tends to operate as a form of what Paul de Man calls 'negative knowledge', a remorseless cataloguing of the ideas that no longer work, the intellectual categories that have outlived their usefulness, and the literary-critical myths that need to be exploded.[2]

Theory's favourite *eureka* moments have usually been negative epiphanies: the author is no longer an inspired genius who creates the work *ex nihilo*; the self-conscious, self-determining human subject has become the plaything of impersonal discourses and desires; the universal truth claims of political, religious and scientific ideologies have dissolved into interchangeable micro-narratives; language has become a self-enclosed system with no purchase on any non-linguistic reality; indeed, 'reality' is nothing more than a copy without an original. Reports of the 'death of the author' (Barthes), 'death of the subject' (Foucault) and 'death of the real' (Baudrillard), together with the news that grand narratives are obsolete (Lyotard), and that there is nothing outside the text (Derrida), can only reinforce the suspicion that theory specializes in obituary-writing and general debunking. As well as its famously sceptical treatment of notions of literary imagination, creativity and originality, there is also the often rebarbative language of theory, a style so thick with pseudo-scientific neologisms that Mark Currie – by no means a defensive traditionalist – has branded it 'the ugliest private language in the world'.[3] If this is true then it seems unlikely that theory is ever going to endear itself to fastidious literary stylists as anything other than an irresistible object of parody.

For all its reputation as the *bête noire* of the creative writer, however, theory has played a significant role in the development of recent literary fiction – not simply as a butt of anti-theoretical humour, but as a formative influence and imaginative resource, a repertoire of embryonic stories and radical ideas that contemporary novelists have been ambitiously re-writing since the late 1960s. The possibilities for creative dialogue between theory and fiction are perhaps most obviously visible in the literary careers of novelist-theorists like Christine Brooke-Rose, Umberto

Eco, Julia Kristeva and Sandra Gilbert and Susan Gubar, professional academics who moonlight successfully as creative writers. Such authors have produced numerous *romans à clefs*, like Kristeva's *The Samurai* (1984) or Philippe Sollers' *Women* (1988), featuring thinly veiled portraits of leading personalities from the theory wars, including Althusser, Barthes, Derrida and Foucault. Campus novels by figures like Malcolm Bradbury, A. S. Byatt, James Hynes and David Lodge have followed suit by offering comic portraits of the upheaval produced in literature departments by the arrival of French theory. Some novels, like Gilbert Adair's *The Death of the Author* (1992) or Patricia Duncker's *Hallucinating Foucault* (1996), explicitly announce their investments in theoretical debates, whereas the unsignposted Foucauldian intertextualities of a novel like Angela Carter's *Nights at the Circus* (1984) are smuggled in for the cognoscenti. The range of verdicts that these novels cast on theory encompasses everything from Anthony Burgess's enthusiastic engagement with structuralist anthropology in *MF* (1971) to the roundly satirical treatment of poststructuralism in Raymond Tallis's *Absence* (1998).

On reviewing the literary careers of novelist-theorists like Eco or Kristeva, it seems reasonable to ask whether what we are dealing with here is a question not of *influence* of theory on fiction, but of a new *confluence* between the two – a creative intermingling of discourses that dissolves the traditional boundaries between literary text and critical metalanguage. 'Knowing how to deal with a topic that preoccupies us is an ever-recurring problem', says Kristeva. '[S]hould we treat it theoretically or fictionally? Is there a choice?'.[4] For many commentators on the contemporary literary scene, the answer would be that there is no choice – or, rather, that the opposition between theory and fiction is a false one that has been comprehensively undermined in recent years. For a time in the 1970s the term 'critifiction' seemed poised to come into its own as the name of a new hybrid discourse that would flourish between texts and their critical and theoretical contexts.[5] More recently, Mark Currie coined the term 'Theoretical Fictions' in his discussion of the literary credentials of post-structuralist theory and the theoretical credentials of postmodern fiction, a chapter that concludes by asserting that 'the wall between academic literary studies and fiction has been demolished from both sides'.[6] Theorists have certainly been eager to lay claim to literary status for their writings. '[M]y deepest desire', Derrida has said, '[is] to write literature, to write fictions'.[7] Barthes describes *Mythologies* and *Empire of Signs* as 'romans *sans* histoire' and *On Racine* and *S/Z* as 'romans *sur* histoire'; his autobiography, meanwhile, describes itself as '*almost* a novel'.[8] Foucault categorizes *The Order of Things* as 'a novel' that he did not make up, whilst Baudrillard mischievously suggests that we read his notorious writings on the Gulf War as fiction.[9] There is something curiously ambiguous about this generation of theorists outing themselves as closet novelists. On the one hand, it is a gesture that downplays some of their more provocative or outrageous lines of argument; when Baudrillard describes *The Gulf War Did Not Take Place* as a work of fiction, for example, he is implicitly reassuring us that the book is *only* a fiction. Like his fellow theorists, Baudrillard evidently wishes to style himself as an intellectual storyteller rather than an authoritative truth-teller or system-maker; he is angling for the same immunity from falsification that fiction traditionally grants itself, the same freedom from the rigorous standards of proof commonly applied to non-fictional writings. On the other hand, there is also something notably self-aggrandizing – Steven Connor calls it postmodern 'Post-Modesty'[10] – in bids by contemporary theorists for the kind of cultural prestige enjoyed by, say, Joyce or Proust. These literary aspirations are also writ large in the *style* of the post-structuralists – in the idiosyncratically 'autobiographical' style of the later Barthes, for example, or in the labyrinthine wordplay of Derrida's philosophical commentaries. Indeed, Derrida's 'antibook' *Glas* is the central exhibit in Geoffrey Hartman's argument that 'Literary criticism is now crossing over into literature'.[11] In 'The Literary in Theory', Jonathan Culler tells a similar story of cultural crossover, though in his version it is the 'literary' that has 'migrated from being the object of theory to being the quality of theory itself'.[12] Niall Lucy takes this story one step further when he nonchalantly asserts that 'literature' is just another name for 'literary theory'.[13]

However, before we accept any such easy conflation of literature with theory, it is worth taking on board one or two reservations. In an astute discussion of 'Literary Commentary as Literature', Seán Burke argues that Hartman makes *Glas* 'a canonical text but only at the price of declaring his own work secondary, parasitic, sponsorial'.[14] The border between theory and literature thus survives Hartman's best efforts to erase it – which is hardly surprising, since you cannot cross a border that does not exist, any more than you can erase a border simply by crossing it. Following Burke, I would argue theory and fiction have survived recent efforts to collapse one into the other; if novelists and theorists have been stealing one another's clothes, it is more a reflection of what Patricia Waugh calls the 'mutual anxiety of influence'[15] between the two, rather than a simple merging of identities.

Of course, self-conscious authors have always been aware of the potential for crossover and subversive mutual imitation between literature and criticism, and if we are looking for significant literary precedents for the contemporary 'novel of theory', then we will find them in texts like Oscar Wilde's *The Portrait of Mr W.H.* (1889), Henry James's *The Figure in the Carpet* (1896), Vladimir Nabokov's *Pale Fire* (1962), and in the literary fables of Jorge Luis Borges, such as 'Pierre Menard, Author of the Quixote' or 'Averroes's Search' (both 1945). These narratives focus on the unending power struggles between authors, critics, reviewers and translators for the control of literary texts. Returning continually to the textual and institutional relationships between criticism and creativity, they ponder the lot of the critic as a second-class citizen in the republic of letters, harbouring envious designs on the prestige enjoyed by the professional author. These narratives abound in cranky mis-readers and fanciful over-readers who constantly threaten to become belated and illicit 'co-authors' of the literary texts they so obsessively consume. The critical fictions of James, Wilde, Nabokov and Borges thus constitute a series of powerful pre-emptive strikes in the debates about the death of the author that would massively preoccupy both post-Barthesian theory and post-theoretical fiction.

My study of the development of post-theoretical fiction opens with a chapter on the reception of structuralism – in its literary, narratological and anthropological guises – in John Fowles's *The French Lieutenant's Woman* (1969), Anthony Burgess's *MF* (1971), Christine Brooke-Rose's *Thru* (1975) and David Lodge's *How Far Can You Go?* (1980). For Burgess and Brooke-Rose, structuralist theory seems to license the kind of knowing theoretical writing that is pitched squarely at a professorial audience, whereas Lodge and Fowles are more concerned with assimilating it to a traditional realist aesthetic. Lodge has always responded to theory with measured enthusiasm, and my next chapter will examine his ambivalently comic versions of the theory revolution from its first rumours in *Changing Places* (1975) and *Small World* (1984) to its last gasp in *Thinks ...* (2001). Chapter 4 offers a different version of the same story by reading the work of the American campus novelists, including Perceval Everett, Sandra Gilbert and Susan Gubar, James Hynes and Richard Powers, for its satirical reportage from the front lines of the 'culture wars' and for its speculative accounts of what a post-theoretical republic of letters might look like.

Chapter 5 examines the theme of the death of the author as it is taken up in novels by Gilbert Adair, John Banville and Malcolm Bradbury, and reads Adair's *The Death of the Author*, Bradbury's *Doctor Criminale* (1992) and Banville's *Shroud* (2002) as cautionary variations on the theme of Paul de Man's posthumous disgrace. The reconstruction of the author is one of the primary sources of narrative drama in post-theoretical novels, which frequently envision literary scholarship as a sometimes dangerous game of hide-and-seek between hyperactive critics and self-effacing authors. The 'death of the author' is one version of the larger post-structuralist theme of the 'death of the subject' that has been most influentially articulated in the writings of Michel Foucault. In Chapter 6 I examine the remarkably diverse responses to the life and work of the charismatic French post-structuralist in fiction by A. S. Byatt, Patricia Duncker, Hervé Guibert, Julia Kristeva and Toby Litt. In particular, I focus on the extent to which these authors comply with the desire for facelessness that's articulated so often in Foucault's work.

In Chapter 7 I read A. S. Byatt's *Possession* (1990) and Angela Carter's *Nights at the Circus* as challenging feminist responses to the post-structuralism of Barthes, Derrida, Foucault, and Lacan. The possibility that theory is simply another manifestation of patriarchal thought, a masculine discourse through and through, has troubled feminists as different as Elaine Showalter and Hélène Cixous,[16] and Byatt and Carter's novels endeavour in different ways to map out a non-theoretical space from which patriarchy might be critiqued. If theory is figured as a culpably patriarchal discourse by Carter and Byatt, it is implicated in cases of theft and murder in fiction by Norman N. Holland and D. J. H. Jones. Chapter 8 examines Holland and Jones's campus whodunits alongside theoretically self-conscious murder stories by Umberto Eco and Julia Kristeva in order to explore the ways in which theory has been 'criminalized' by creative writers. My final chapter reads a cluster of texts – Christine Brooke-Rose's *Textermination* (1991), Mark Z. Danielewski's *House of Leaves* (2000), Julian Barnes' *England, England* (1998), and A. N. Wilson's *A Jealous Ghost* (2005) – for their critical and creative engagements with postmodern theories of hyperreality. As they chart the changing status of 'reality' in the age of mechanical and electronic reproduction, these texts haver between nostalgia for lost authenticity and cheerful acquiescence in the endless simulations that now circulate in place of what we used to believe was 'reality'.

Overall, these post-theoretical novels represent a remarkable efflorescence of literary creativity in the graveyard of the humanist verities. They also serve as an 'alternative history' of the theory wars from the structuralist controversies of the 1960s through to the post-structuralist and postmodernist debates of the 1980s and 1990s which makes for engrossing reading at a time when 'theory' seems to be busy organizing its own funeral. The term 'post-theory' has been in circulation since at least the early 1990s, and a recent spate of books on the themes of 'life after theory' have given significant impetus to the post-theoretical turn in literary studies.[17] Not that this means that theory can been quietly forgotten; there is certainly no going back to some naïve, pre-theoretical way of engaging with texts. One of the commonplaces of introductions to critical theory is that there can be no non-theoretical approach to reading literary texts, and that those critics who claim to get by armed with just native intelligence or instinctive good taste are naïve or simply in denial. But if it is true that you cannot *not* have a theory, then the question of my own theoretical position seems unavoidable. It is certainly true that theory cannot simply be the object of my discussion, and must figure also as a significant element of my critical approach to the texts in question. In the pages that follow it will be clear that my primary interest is in what John Sturrock terms the 'word from Paris':[18] the writings of Barthes, Cixous, Derrida, Foucault, Kristeva and Lacan, and the discourses of structuralism, post-structuralism and postmodernism. To some, this might seem to represent a suspiciously convenient symmetry between text and approach, since these of course are the very authors and discourses that loom so large in the novels under discussion. For example, what could be more redundant than a Barthesian reading of *The Death of the Author*, a semiotic reading of *The Name of the Rose*, or a Foucauldian reading of *Hallucinating Foucault*? We can conveniently read off the theoretical content of these texts from the surface of the narrative; but such an act of reading amounts to little more than a re-statement of the text as it stands. This might even seem like an exemplary case of what Barthes calls theoretical 'blackmail' whereby texts demand critical recognition by obligingly reflecting the theoretical predispositions of their readers – effectively, by saying 'love me, keep me, defend me, since I conform to the theory you call for'.[19] Indeed, it seems as though the recent attempts to topple Angela Carter from her position as the most celebrated contemporary British writer have been prompted by a sense that her novels have blackmailed themselves into critical recognition by obediently reflecting all the fashionable theoretical ideas of our time. Commenting on the extensive literature on Carter and Bakhtinian carnival, Dominic Head voices his suspicion that 'Carter is being used to illuminate the theory, rather than vice versa'; similarly, Valentine Cunningham puts Carter's immense popularity as a thesis-topic down to 'the spread of feminist Theory'.[20] It seems to me, however, that none of this means that we should stop reading Carter; rather, we need to start reading her more carefully – as her more astute critics have already done – as a writer whose fiction powerfully *critiques* many of the theoretical ideas in which she was obviously so well versed. And from the case of Carter I would extrapolate a more general lesson that the 'novel of theory' is often distinguished by its resourceful *resistance* to theory, and that any tactful reading of these texts needs to be mindful of the ways in which they pre-empt theoretical analysis.

To take just one example, there is a brilliant spoof of Lacanian analysis in *The House of Sleep* (1997), Jonathan Coe's comic novel about the tangled emotional lives of a group of students in the 1980s.[21] Towards the end of this novel, the psychotherapist Russell Watts organizes an impromptu seminar for colleagues at which he presents a paper entitled: '*The Case of Sarah T.: or, an Eye for an "I"* ' (283). Sarah T. is Sarah Tudor, the novel's central character, and one of Watts' patients; her strange sleep disorders and painful emotional problems provide the raw material for his paper. Drawing liberally on Sarah's confidential statements about her dreams, her sexual history and her narcolepsy, Watts conducts his sceptical audience on a tour of her 'strange, private, opto-erotic sexual universe' (293), laying particular emphasis on slippages of meaning in Sarah's language that betray her unconscious needs and desires. Watts' Lacanianism is presented in an obviously satirical manner by Coe; it is one of the many forms of false knowledge with which his novel is concerned. But his analysis of Sarah nevertheless has a preposterous plausibility, resonating suggestively with what we know of her from the remainder of the novel: the novel has let an obviously bad reader deliver a suspiciously good reading of its central character, consciously entrusting its secrets to an ostentatious charlatan in a bid to disarm any would-be psychoanalytic reader. It may well be possible to generate a psychoanalytic reading of *The House of Sleep* that does not simply reproduce Watts' Lacanian pyrotechnics, but such a reading would have to find ways of negotiating the novel's forceful *resistance* to psychoanalysis.

In a well-known essay Paul de Man identifies two forms of 'resistance to theory'. There is an 'external' resistance, which takes the form of institutional objections to new-fangled terminology and unfamiliar methods; this kind of 'humanist backlash' discourse has no truck with theorizing of any kind and clings stubbornly to pre-theoretical ways of doing things. But de Man argues that there is also an 'internal' resistance on the part of theory itself – a necessary element of built-in scepticism that prevents theory from trying to assume the privileged status of the 'logocentric' discourses that it debunks. Theory, as de Man sees it, is a 'self-resisting' discourse that probes the limitations of other discourses without ever making special claims for its own truthfulness.[22] To adapt de Man's terms, we might therefore regard the 'novels of theory' that I examine in the chapters to follow not as fogeyish acts of resistance to theory but rather as literary expressions of theory's powerful self-resistance.

2
The Structuralist Novel

The idea of a 'structuralist novel' sounds like an oxymoron, or even a joke. You can see how creative writers might find inspiration in the subversive wordplay of deconstruction, the uncanny secrets and desires of psychoanalysis or the glossy, hyperreal landscapes of postmodernism, but it is hard to guess how a theory as cold-bloodedly scientific as structuralism could ever quicken the novelistic imagination. Spreading from the linguistics of Ferdinand de Saussure and Roman Jakobson via the anthropology of Claude Lévi-Strauss into the semiology of Roland Barthes and the narratology of Gérard Genette, A. J. Greimas and Tzvetan Todorov, structuralism made criticism the home of the *-ology*, replacing the genteel language of literary appreciation with quasi-scientific talk of *langue* and *parole*, diachrony and synchrony, syntagm and paradigm. Even the New Criticism, once a byword for unsentimental analytic rigour, began to seem quaintly belletristic by comparison with a theory that had critics of the 1960s and 1970s converting exquisite verbal icons into so many algebraic formulae, semiotic rectangles or catalogues of functions. If theory is indeed the world's 'ugliest private language', then structuralism, with its cheerfully rebarbative crimes against fine writing, must surely bear a significant part of the responsibility.

Which is not to say that structuralism's disconnection from the world of literary creativity is exclusively a question of style. Theoretical scepticism about authorship, human nature, the creative imagination and the privileged status of literature can be traced directly back to the structuralist lesson that meaning is created by systems rather than by people: 'Language', Saussure famously claims, 'is not a function of the speaker.'[1] According to the logic of structuralism, language is a set of conventionally meaningful signs rather an innate human capacity: even the most spontaneously heartfelt utterance is ultimately the effect of deep structures or signifying systems that govern what it can and cannot mean. And if language is, as Saussure puts it, a 'type of algebra',[2] then so too is literature. To write a sonnet, for example, is not to spill one's heart out onto the page in an access of powerful feeling, but to manipulate elements from an existing repertoire of literary conventions; any 'new' sonnet always-already exists as one possible permutation of those conventions. As Roland Barthes puts it, in the literary text the originating voice is always ' "lost" in the vast perspective of the *already-written*'.[3] Or, to put it another way, the sonneteer does not write the sonnet, but is *written by* it. Nor are the implications of Saussure's insights restricted to literature. His intellectual successors – most notably the Barthes of *Mythologies* (1957) – have shown that just as every verbal utterance is the effect of an under-lying linguistic system, so the phenomena of everyday life are the effects of underlying cultural systems. There is a 'language' of food or clothes or architecture or family ties in which we acquire fluency even if we are oblivious to its hidden 'grammar'. The structuralist model of human experience is a precise inversion of the story of Adam naming the animals in the Garden of Eden; for Barthes, the world is never innocently pre-linguistic or patiently waiting to be named, but always-already satu-rated with names, texts, signs and codes. For this reason, structuralism has become a major resource of anti-humanist thought, because its emphasis on the primacy of *langue* over *parole*, of signifying systems over individual speech-acts, not only paves the way for the 'death of the author' but also powerfully suggests that human nature itself is an effect of linguistic and cultural systems. Men and women are no longer the spontaneous authors of their own personalities and actions, but rather 'subjects' sleepwalking through predetermined roles scripted for them in the deep structures or signifying systems that orchestrate human experience.

What freedom – if any – do human beings enjoy in such a world? Loewe, a lawyer in Anthony Burgess's *MF* (1971), breezily concedes that 'Nobody's free. I mean, choice is limited by inbuilt structures and prede-termined genetic patterns and all the rest of it'. But not only are we not free to act as we please – we are not even free to *think* differently: 'Nobody can help thinking these things these days. The French started all that'.[4] If Loewe is to be believed, it seems that we are all structuralists now. And Burgess has indeed described *MF* as a 'structuralist novel', one that pitches into the debates that the French have started over inbuilt structures, predetermined patterns and freedom of choice.[5] Of course, the late-twentieth century scarcely enjoys a monopoly on such debates – the freewill *versus* determinism question is as old as philosophy itself.

But not only does structuralism represent a formidable new version of the determinist side of the argument, it also specifically threatens to snuff out *artistic* freedom, to relieve the author of his or her claims to original creativity and liberty of expression. Unsurprisingly, then, those novelists who have engaged with structuralism have done so in a broadly adversarial fashion. This chapter will examine Burgess's novel alongside a cluster of other works – David Lodge's *How Far Can You Go?* (1980), John Fowles's *The French Lieutenant's Woman* (1969) and Christine Brooke-Rose's *Thru* (1975) – that engage creatively but sceptically with the discourse of structuralism. Two key questions preoccupy each of these novels: Is it ever meaningful to think of novelistic characters as creatures of choice and free will? Can experimental novelists ever truly grant themselves freedom from the dead hand of tradition or the prison-house of the already-written? The problem is that the more a novelist parades his or her freedom to conjure up and meddle in a given fictional world, the more the inhabitants of that world come to resemble puppets rather than people, whereas if characters begin to exercise freedom of choice, then the novelist is demoted from authoritarian puppet-master to impotent onlooker: the struggle for 'freedom' between authors and characters is clearly a zero-sum game.

David Lodge's *How Far Can You Go?* is a darkly comic exploration of the paradoxes of freedom and determinism in the context of the authoritarian belief systems of Roman Catholicism.[6] The novel takes as its primary theme the decline of the 'traditional Catholic metaphysic – that marvellously complex and ingenious synthesis of theology and cosmology and casuistry, which situated individual souls on a kind of spiritual Snakes and Ladders board' (239). As a corollary, Lodge's text self-consciously explores the decline of faith in fiction itself, the sense that the illusions of 'reality' conjured up by a supposedly omniscient author may be nothing more than moves in a game of literary snakes and ladders. When structuralists contemplate fictional narratives, their first move is to suspend any suspension of disbelief. Novels or stories that strike us as recognizably 'life-like' are simply giving off a powerful 'reality-effect'[7] generated by self-disguising literary codes and conventions. In the age of structuralism, the 'realism' of a text and 'omniscience' of its author are no longer sacred items of faith but relics of a discredited literary theology.

A prevailing mood in *How Far Can You Go?* is a certain anxiety of freedom in the face of the erosion of the old textual and theological certainties. On one level the novel's title translates as 'What can I get away with?', and refers to the nervous amorous fumblings of Lodge's sex-starved Catholic undergraduates in 1950s London. But the title is also a question that the novel asks about itself and its limits. How much unalleviated pain is permissible in a comic novel? How far can comedy go before it tips over into tragedy? And does the novel's freight of ideas – its theoretical asides on contemporary metafiction and its embittered critique of Catholic doctrine on sexuality and birth control – pull it into the territory of non-fiction? Throughout *How Far Can You Go?* realistic narrative is interrupted by authorial games-playing, and middlebrow storytelling by highbrow theoretical discourse. For example, one of Lodge's undergraduates scours the newspapers in his scruffy student union lounge for images of women's cleavage, which the narrator describes as 'that fascinating *vide*, that absence which signifies the presence of the two glands on either side of it more eloquently than they do themselves (or so the structuralist jargon fashionable in another decade would put it)' (6). The intrusion here of a jarringly discordant and anachronistic theoretical voice world plays momentary havoc with the novel's illusion of 'realism', as though Lodge is playing snakes and ladders with one of his own characters.

'Structuralist jargon' makes a more obtrusively sustained appearance later in the novel, once again into relation to sex. Lodge's narrator alludes to a 'treatise on narrative' by a 'contemporary French critic' – the book in question is Gérard Genette's *Narrative Discourse*[8] – to make a point about storytelling and routine: 'a novelist can (a) narrate once what happened once or (b) narrate n times what happened once or (c) narrate n times what happened n times or (d) narrate once what happened n times' (150). The narrator adapts this point to comment dryly on the sex lives of the novel's Catholic couples:

> The permutations of sex are as finite as those of narrative. You can (*a*) do one thing with one partner or (*b*) do n things with one partner or (*c*) do one thing with n partners or (*d*) do n things with n partners. For practising Catholics faithful to the marriage bond, there was only the possibility of progressing from (*a*) to (*b*) in search of a richer sex life. (152)

In part, the point here is that structuralism is not remotely sexy – but then again, neither is routinized sex. Genette's blandly itemized narratological permutations thus provide an entirely appropriate language in which to review the disappointingly monotonous sex lives of the novel's characters. In the most intimately personal aspects of their lives Lodge's Catholic couples seem to be going through the structuralist motions. But whereas his characters seem to be unconsciously subject to

Genette's laws, the novel itself is reluctant to play into the hands of structuralist analysis. By discoursing in theoretical terms on its own characters, *How Far Can You Go?* pre-empts the moves of the would-be theoretical reader: the novel inoculates itself against theory by internalizing it in limited quantities. Lodge's gamble is that his overall realist narrative is sufficiently resilient to withstand minor doses of structuralist demystification. If the novel's reality-effect can survive periodic sabotage at the hands of its own narrator, then it would appear to be perfectly safe from the attentions of structuralist critics.

The question that haunts *How Far Can You Go* – that of whether the novelist can still play God in the age of structuralism – has been most influentially posed by John Fowles's *The French Lieutenant's Woman*, which has acquired landmark status as one of the first postmodern novels in English fiction.[9] Its flamboyant array of metafictional strategies – its playful interbreeding of documentary history with romantic storytelling, its meticulous pastiche of nineteenth-century prose, its questioning of the privileged ontological status of its own author-narrator, its multiple endings – bring off a brilliant reconstruction and deconstruction of English realist fiction in its Victorian heyday. If we want to identify Fowles's source of inspiration for this bravura performance we need look no further than the opening page of the novel. On the sea-wall at Lyme Regis the novel's hero, the amateur palaeontologist Charles Smithson, is looking landward, to England; its heroine, the disgraced governess Sarah Woodruff, at the 'seawardmost end' of the wall, is looking enigmatically out to sea – apparently to France.[10] The novel sites itself on a physical, cultural and textual margin: between land and sea, home and abroad, England and France. Staking out the marginal territory between English realism and French postmodernism, this scene can plausibly claim to represent the inaugural moment of contemporary English fiction.

'I do not like the French' (33). This summary verdict on England's neighbours across the channel is delivered by Mrs Poulteney, the ferociously narrow-minded *grande dame* of Lyme Regis, on hearing of Sarah's acquaintance with the French lieutenant. Her aggressive Francophobia extends to that nation's literature – 'I will not have French books in my house' (37); indeed, 'French' has become a byword in Mrs Poulteney's imagination for scandalous immorality of any kind. When she contemplates Ware Commons, the traditional place of illicit courtship for Lyme's young lovers, she imagines 'French abominations under every leaf' (83). 'France' thus occupies a special place in the mind of Mrs Poulteney as the disreputable home of indecent literature and unbuttoned sexual morality; it represents, as it were, the sexual and textual unconscious of English propriety. But it is an unconscious that can be visited: the young Charles Smithson, who has been penitently contemplating Holy Orders after a night of debauchery in London, is dispatched by his father to the fleshpots of Paris, where his sexual adventures soon erase any thoughts of his new-found vocation. More worryingly for the Mrs Poulteneys of this world, it is an unconscious that threatens to visit itself upon England – most obviously in the person of the French lieutenant himself.

Monsieur Varguennes remains a tantalizingly indeterminate figure throughout the novel; hard information about him is very thin on the ground. What we can be fairly sure of is that he is the lieutenant of a French merchant vessel shipwrecked on the Dorset coast who, convalescing in the home of one Captain Talbot, strikes up a relationship with Talbot's French-speaking governess, Sarah. Beyond that, nearly everything we learn of him is unreliable. If we choose to believe local rumours and clergymen's gossip, then Varguennes's plausible manners and ingratiating charm have reduced the naïve governess to a state of mournful, half-mad infatuation; and, if we are to believe Sarah's own version of events, her relationship with Varguennes was consummated in a Weymouth inn prior to his return home to France – and to his wife. The lieutenant's sexual and verbal duplicity represent everything that is dangerously seductive about France in the novel, but his function is not simply to confirm the worst suspicions of Mrs Poulteney about philandering Frenchmen. He also stands as a fictive nineteenth-century avatar of those other Frenchmen, Alain Robbe-Grillet and Roland Barthes, whom Fowles cites in chapter 13, and whose seductive and subversive theories of narrative appear to have cast their spell over his traditional English novel. Not only does France seductively overpower England at the level of character and plot; it also appears to be doing so at the level of narrative technique: Mrs Poulteney's paranoid fantasy of an English landscape harbouring 'French abominations under every leaf' thus threatens to come true in the leaves of Fowles's Francophile English novel.

From chapter 13 onwards, as the novel unfurls its range of metafictional strategies – questioning the author's omniscience, speculating on characters' levels of freedom, inserting 'scholarly' footnotes – it would appear that it has fallen for Monsieurs Robbe-Grillet and Barthes as wholeheartedly as Sarah fell for Monsieur Varguennes. Except of course that Sarah *was not* seduced by Varguennes: the story she tells of her 'seduction' at his hands is precisely that, a story. The Frenchman is constructed as a source of lies, of fictions – 'all he said was false' (147) – but Sarah proves to be every bit as unreliable. Fowles's heroine lets people believe that she was seduced by Varguennes because one of the few freedoms still available to her in a world of Mrs Poulteneys is the power to dictate the terms of her own rejection. In this way, she manages to cling on to the position of narrating subject in a society that attempts to treat her as nothing more than a narrated object. In other words, you could say that Sarah is secretly trying to rewrite *The French Lieutenant's Woman* as *The Woman's French Lieutenant.*

This tale of an English woman's non-seduction at the hands of a mysterious Frenchman has far-reaching implications for Fowles' own relationship with structuralism. Just as Sarah has her own reasons for letting the Lyme townsfolk believe she is a fallen woman, so too does Fowles foster the impression that he has fallen under the spell of French intellectual culture. Consider, for example, his two cameo appearances in the novel: in the first, he appears opposite Charles in a railway carriage as a 'massively bearded' figure, possibly a lay preacher (346); in the second, he appears strolling outside Dante Gabriel Rossetti's house in Chelsea, 'As he really is', with his 'full, patriarchal beard ... trimmed down to something rather foppish and Frenchified' (394). This cultural makeover, from bearded English patriarch to Frenchified fop, seems to reflect the 'Frenchification' of a novel that began life as a belated piece of Victorian English realism. But just as Sarah frees herself from the pro- prietary grasp of the French lieutenant, so Fowles is out to free himself from the grasp of Barthes and Robbe-Grillet.

It is customary to treat *The French Lieutenant's Woman* as a companion- piece to Barthes's most notorious essay, 'The Death of the Author', which appeared the year before Fowles's novel.[11]However, when Fowles was working on the novel, Barthes would have been chiefly known as an exponent of the *nouvelle critique,* and as an influential commentator on the 'degree-zero' style of Robbe-Grillet's *nouveaux romans*; he also achieved notoriety in the mid-1960s during a high-profile altercation with the distinguished French *littérateur* Raymond Picard that was sparked off by his iconoclastic study of Racine. But it is Barthes's *name* that matters most in the context of Fowles's novel. The fleeting appearance made by 'Roland Barthes' in *The French Lieutenant's Woman* is in the guise of a seductive bogeyman of modern European letters, an enemy of literary tradition and champion of experimental writing. The challenge that Fowles sets himself is to resist the blandishments of the *nouvelle critique* and write a novel that stays loyal to the best traditions of English realism. This challenge comes into sharp focus at the novel's climax, where it subdivides itself into multiple, apparently interchangeable endings. The first of these, which pairs Charles off with Ernestina, would have pleased Jane Austen. The second, which unites Charles and Sarah, is an altogether more Hardyesque piece of matchmaking. The final ending, meanwhile, leaves Charles wholly isolated, the existential hero of a modern French novel cut adrift in 1860s London. On the face of it, then, Fowles's sturdy realist novel seems to be falling apart at the seams, rewriting itself as a *nouveau roman* before our very eyes. But even in this 'collapse' it is not difficult to discern the invisible hand of the author-God stage-managing the text's disintegration and firmly nudging the reader towards the novel's final ending as the most appropriately 'realistic' of the three; the 'Austen' and 'Hardy' endings are written off as conventional, novelistic and therefore not genuine options. So the 'break' with linear narrative and the 'empowerment' of the reader are the empty promises of a text that grants us only the choice to agree with its final vision of Charles as a courageously isolated modern Everyman. Which is to say that *The French Lieutenant's Woman* is never more conspicuously in the author's hands than when it purports to relinquish control to the reader. Despite those siren calls from across the Channel, then, this 'Frenchified' text never truly surrenders its traditional English virtues.

If Fowles regards structuralism as something to be resisted, Anthony Burgess seems to have been happy to embrace it in his vividly strange experimental novel, *MF*. The narrator, Miles Faber, is a rebellious young student who, after being thrown out of college for public fornication, travels to the Caribbean island of Castita in search of the artistic works of the neglected genius Sib Legeru. Miles eventually discovers the Legeru archive in the course of a string of bizarre adventures that culminate in him killing his own *doppelgänger*, marrying his long-lost sister, and being challenged to a life-or-death game of riddles with a flock of talking birds. The novel is filled with riddles, but is also itself a kind of large-scale riddle – by turns outlandish, farcical, violent, surreal and cryptic. Its themes become a little clearer towards the very end when the circus owner, Dr Zoon Fonanta – who also happens to be Miles's grandfather – helps to make sense of these outlandish events, and supplies the notably useful information that *siblegeru* is the Anglo-Saxon for '*incest*' (233). At this point we can begin to see how the initials 'MF', which obviously refer to the protagonist's name, and perhaps to the male–female opposition, may also designate the novel's incestuous hero as a 'motherfucker', a postmodern Oedipus.

So this riddling novel is richly interested in incest; or, to put it more accurately, in the enigmatic relationships *between* riddles and incest. Burgess has disclosed the origins of his novel's preoccupation with the 'incest/riddle structure'[12] in Claude Lévi-Strauss's inaugural lecture as chair of social anthropology at the Collège de France in January 1960.[13] In this lecture Lévi-Strauss notices the curious association in literature and myth between incest and riddles asked by talking animals. The association is famously there in the story of Oedipus and the Sphinx, but also in the myths of people 'separated by history, geography, language, and culture' (22), such as the Iroquois and Algonquin Indians of North America. It is from the North American myths discussed by Lévi-Strauss that Burgess takes many of the central images and situations of his novel – the murdered *doppelgänger*, brother–sister marriage, talking birds that pose life-or-death riddles. *MF* is thus a 'novelization' of this piece of structural anthropology, conveying an obvious sense of excitement at Lévi-Strauss's ideas, but also resisting the more deterministic conclusions that might be drawn from the lecture. Like Lévi-Strauss, Burgess is fascinated by the incest/riddle conjunction because it seems to provide tantalizing evidence that human experience is governed by deep, unchanging structures that we are only now beginning to uncover. But he also realizes that the idea of freedom of choice would be the first casualty of any thorough-going structuralist world-view. *MF* is thus, as Burgess describes it, an attempt to 'juggle with the free will of fictional characters and the pre-destination of an imposed structure' (179).

'Free will' and 'imposed structures' confront one another in the novel's opening scene, where Miles recounts to his father's lawyer the act of shameless public fornication that got him expelled from college. In this confrontation between an anarchic taboo-breaker and professional representative of patriarchal law, the novel initiates its theme of an ongoing struggle between the impulse to human freedom and the regimes of legality and order. These regimes are represented both in terms of personnel – policemen and lawyers form a complacently unsympathetic chorus in *MF*, always ready to admonish and harass its hero for real and imagined transgressions – and in terms of the object-world of the novel. It is well stocked with the paraphernalia of incarceration: locked doors and hidden keys, padlocks and chains, police cells and confined spaces, birds in cages and detainees in solitary confinement. Even Castita's colourful circus is represented as a prison cell waiting to be occupied by the novel's hero. Miles's double, Llew, comes up with an enthusiastic proposal for a new circus escape trick using props that once belonged to 'The Great Bondaggio': Miles will be 'cruelly manacled and chained and locked' in a cabinet from which 'Llew the Free' will then triumphantly emerge, carrying duplicate chains and manacles (104). This escapological illusion is like a spectacular parody of Miles's quest for freedom, since the act would leave Miles securely enchained behind the cabinet's inner wall. He would also be professionally manacled to his egregious twin, and obliged to conceal his identity in public behind dark glasses and a false moustache. In an uncanny anticipation of Angela Carter's treatment of similar themes in *Nights at the Circus*, Burgess uses this circus trick to disclose the paradoxical interdependence of freedom and captivity. And even though Miles chooses not to join forces with Llew, there is a sense in which the novel makes him play the role of 'The Great Bondaggio' whether he realizes it or not.

Though a phenomenally quick-witted solver of riddles, the novel's hero is remarkably slow on the uptake when it comes to grasping this key revelation about the relationship between freedom and captivity. Miles is in thrall to a naïve undergraduate dream of pure or absolute freedom – the kind of comprehensive break from structure, pattern and order that he imagines will characterize the surrealist masterpieces of Sib Legeru. For Miles, structure, meaning and cohesion can only be oppressive, which is why he attaches such value to the liberatingly un-structured or de-structured art of Legeru. *MF* is thus is a strikingly offbeat example of what Suzanne Keen calls the 'romance of the archive', the life-changing scholarly quest for some vanished author, lost text or hidden cache of documents.[14] But it particularly invites comparison with the misguided voyages of intellectual discovery undertaken in texts like Malcolm Bradbury's *Mensonge* or A. S. Byatt's *The Biographer's Tale*, where the object of the quest is a mirage conjured up in the feverish imaginings of readers and critics. Like *The Biographer's Tale*, Burgess's novel is an 'anti-romance of the archive',[15] an impassioned quest down a long and winding intellectual blind alley from which the naïve scholar-hero emerges empty-handed. When Miles finally tracks down Legeru's artistic legacy, what he discovers is an archive of verbal and visual gibberish: oil paintings in which loaves become blood, and blood becomes white pudding; a Shakespeare Folio walking on a sea made of buttons, sleeves and silk; an epic novel in which a radio broadcaster is guided by a talking fly through impossible sequences from history and myth (151–3). What is more, there is no neglected genius behind all of this: 'Sib Legeru', it turns out, is a collective pseudonym for Dr Zoon Fonanta and his patients, all 'victims of incest' (235), who produced these deranged words and images as part of a therapeutic exercise. 'Incest' in this novel thus ultimately serves as a shorthand for what Fonanta calls 'the breakdown of order, the collapse of communication, the irresponsible cultivation of chaos' (235), and for what Burgess calls the 'stupidity of so-called total freedom in art'.[16]

The Legeru archive also functions in *MF* as a bad double for the novel itself. Whereas Legeru's supposedly profound paintings and writings are unmasked as chaotically surreal gibberish, Burgess's chaotically surreal narrative proves on closer examination to be a carefully orchestrated 'structuralist novel'. If anything, the novel is perhaps *too* heavily and parasitically dependent on its Lévi-Straussian source, trapped in its structuralist intertextualities like a failed escapologist. When Frank Kermode reviewed *MF* for *The Listener* he was congratulated by Burgess for being the only reviewer who cottoned on the Lévi-Strauss connection, and therefore the only one to make any kind of sense of the novel. Though Kermode has said that discovering the 'master key' to *MF* was one of the most pleasurable moments of his career, it seems possible that his unique success points to a distinctive kind of imaginative failure in Burgess's text.[17] If, as Kermode remarks, there is 'a model exterior to the text which must be known if the book is to be explained or closed',[18] then the book seems curiously incomplete, like *The Waste Land* without the footnotes. It seems reasonable to argue that if a text denies access to those who do not possess some arcane theoretical skeleton key, then that text has become self-defeatingly exclusive, more a book-length riddle than a novel proper.

However, Burgess's riddling structuralism is not quite so exclusive as that: albeit with a certain malicious Joycean pleasure, he does lace his narrative with clues to its 'hidden' meaning. Some of these – notably 'Sib Legeru' – are glossed by Burgess's own characters; but elsewhere it is up to the reader to grasp the symbolic import of Miles's residence in the Algonquin Hotel (3), or to notice the novel's casual neighbouring references to Levis jeans and Richard Strauss (13–14), or spot the tell-tale acrostic spelt out when food orders are called in a Manhattan diner – Indiana nutbake, chuffed eggs, saffron toast (16). At times it is as though the novel wants to infect the reader with its own mania for puns, secrets and hidden meanings, to convert him or her into a crack riddle-solver, another Oedipus or Miles Faber. However, if *MF* tempts us to read it as the sum of its clever in-jokes and covert allusions, it does also work to free itself from its mythical, literary and theoretical sources – most notably through what in the end looks like a very striking *absence* of incest in the novel's action. Among Fonanta's revelations is the fact that the woman with whom Miles copulated on the steps of his college library was not – despite what the novel's title has led us to believe – his mother; nor, in the end, does he consummate his marriage with his sister. Incest clearly runs in the hero's family, and it is something that *apparently* happens or *almost* happens throughout *MF*, but in the end history conspicuously fails to repeat itself – Burgess's narrative 'swerves' decisively away from those master-narratives of classical myth and Lévi-Straussian anthropology where incest is a kind of structural inevitability. *MF* ultimately resists the 'exterior model' that aims to explain and close it: the novel's potentially 'incestuous' relationship with structuralism is, like Miles' wedding night, a case of *coitus interruptus*.

If the structuralist origins of *MF* are teasingly camouflaged by Burgess, the theoretical intertextualities of Christine Brooke-Rose's *Thru* are blazed across the novel's notoriously difficult surface. *Thru* is perhaps the most theoretically literate novel of our times; its range of reference includes the central figures of structuralist thought – Barthes, Brémond, Genette, Greimas, Hjelmslev, Jakobson, Lévi-Strauss, Propp, Saussure, Todorov – but also numerous figures associated with structuralism's complex aftermath: Bakhtin, Bataille, Deleuze, Derrida, Eco, Irigaray, Kristeva. The novel is a kind of reading list or *Who's Who* of the rising stars of 1960s and 1970s theory, the structuralist and post-structuralist thinkers whose work Brooke-Rose imbibed at the Université de Paris VIII at Vincennes, which she joined in 1968, writing criticism during termtime and fiction during the summer vacations.[19] Obviously the intellectual range of this novel stretches well beyond structuralism: as one of its characters remarks, as it were on behalf of Brooke-Rose, 'of course I am not a structuralist I never have been I merely played with it besides one has to pass through it to understand modern linguistics' (84). Similarly, structuralism is something that *Thru* playfully passes through in the course of its journey of theoretical discovery.

Written between 1971–72, *Thru* dramatizes Brooke-Rose's keen sense of her self-divided literary identity at this time – the 'painful and exhilarating' split, as she describes it, between 'author and theorist'.[20] It seems fair to point out that in the reception and reputation of this novel, pain has figured more prominently than exhilaration: *Thru* is the work of an 'anti-novelist'[21] at her most uncompromisingly and unapologetically experimental. What is more, it regularly enjoins us to read up on the theory that both explains and compounds its difficulties – 'Read Todorov' (40), 'You should read Kristeva' (69), 'You should read Lacan' (72), 'Read Bakhtine!' (133; *sic*). Brooke-Rose has claimed to use 'critical jargon as poetry',[22] but the 'critical poetry' of *Thru* is dauntingly modernist rather than attractively lyrical. This intimidating display of state-of-the-art erudition – or 'intertextual overkill',[23] as Patricia Waugh describes it – makes precious few concessions to those readers unschooled in the ways of theory; indeed Brooke-Rose, though she usually refers to this novel in affectionate and vigorously defensive terms, once mentioned in an interview that it was 'written almost tongue-in-cheek for a few narratologist friends'.[24]

One of the central challenges of *Thru* is that its theoretical inter-textualities are not interruptions of an accessibly realistic narrative but intensifications of its existing difficulty. The 'world' of this novel, its characters, and the unfolding story of their relationships, are taken beyond the boundaries of coherent intelligibility by a narrative of dizzying ontological fluidity. Its 'story' charts the troubled relationship between Armel Santores, a teacher of creative writing at an unnamed American college, and Larissa Toren, an academic specializing in theory at another academic institution. Creative writing and critical theory, as personified by Armel and Larissa – whose names are near-anagrams, with 'I' missing from the former and 'me' from the latter – thus enjoy a strange kind of *doppelgänger* relationship: they are both interdependent doubles and ontological rivals. What is more, the novel is haunted by the suspicion that each of its protagonists is a product of the other's imagination: 'if Larissa invents Armel inventing Larissa', the narrating voice reasons, then 'Armel also invents Larissa inventing Armel' (108). This chicken-and-egg paradox ingeniously captures Brooke-Rose's sense that no simple cause-and-effect model can accommodate fiction–theory relations: theory is a by-product of creative writing to precisely the same extent that creative writing is a by-product of theory.

A central difficult in reading *Thru* is that of ascribing narrative and dialogue to identifiable sources. The question that taunts us throughout the novel – 'Who speaks?' (1, 22, 42, 59, 110, 116, 127), or '*Qui parle?*' (107, 145), or '*Chi parla?*' (128) – is doubly unanswerable. *Thru*'s narrative can never be confidently ascribed to a single voice: there are various potential candidates for the position of 'narrator' – Diderot's Master from *Jacques the Fatalist*, an anonymous unreliable narrator, Larissa, Armel, the Creative Writing students *en masse* – but no basis on which to adjudicate between them. And in any case the question 'Who speaks?' is itself incapable of simple attribution, since it is one of the great (non-)questions of Barthesian and Foucauldian theory. Though it is far from easy to give up on the old humanist belief that voices have speakers, narratives have narrators, and texts have authors, we need to accept that this novel stages an unwinnable competition for 'ownership' of an intertextual narrative that belongs to everyone and no-one. And there is one cheerfully upbeat voice in *Thru* that greets this news in terms that sum up the novel's revolutionary post-Barthesian aesthetic: 'We're all in this together aren't we? There's no more private property in writing, the author is dead, the spokesman, the porte-parole, the tale-bearer, off with his head' (29). In the world – or worlds – of *Thru*, 'inventing' narrators become 'invented' characters, figures from other novels acquire a strange new lease of life, and ostensibly 'real' narrative episodes are unceremoniously revealed as creative writing exercises. Every major transition in the novel represents not a shift of perspective on the same coherent fictional world, but a disorientating knight's move into a different order of reality. In these ways *Thru* opens up the 'radical ontological hesitation' that for Brian McHale makes it a 'paradigmatic postmodern novel'.[25]

In place on the smooth controlling discourse of an omniscient author or reliable narrator, the text of *Thru* is extravagantly variegated with anagrams and acrostics, polyglot voices and unattributable dialogue, informative technical diagrams and tables, and unconventional typography that often resembles concrete poetry. At times its pages also look like they have been defaced by a kind of theoretical graffiti. Among the most notable of these is a reproduction of Roman Jakobson's diagram of the six linguistic functions – emotive, referential, poetic, phatic, connative and metalingual – from his essay 'Metalanguage as a Linguistic Problem' (1957).[26] The diagram is followed with the comment: 'There should be placards saying: Danger. You are now entering the Metalinguistic Zone' (51); the complex irony here is that whilst *Thru* is self-evidently metalinguistic – it would be hard to find another text that theorizes more openly on the behaviour of language – it simultaneously denies the possibility that any discourse (theoretical or fictional) can obtain a secure critical distance from the fluidity of language. Shlomith Rimmon-Kenan argues that *Thru* 'employs the reader's metalanguage as its own object language'; which is to say that *Thru* pre-emptively seizes the very theoretical tools that we might think of applying to it. One of the recurring revelations of the novel, as Glyn White argues, is that it is 'impossible to fence in narrative with theoretical metalanguage'.[27] Or, to put it another way, in this novel the 'Metalinguistic Zone' is a no-go area.

Also central to the novel is Gremais's semiotic rectangle, the elementary diagram of contraries and contradictories taken from his 1968 essay, co-written with François Rastier, 'The Interaction of Semiotic Constraints'. The rectangle appears in numerous guises in *Thru* (7, 12, 20, 49, 56, 89, 112, 117), as though the text is repeatedly coughing up its own structural unconscious. One of *Thru*'s narrating voices trembles with intellectual excitement at the compelling simplicity of this structuralist model: 'Maybe it's the grammar of the universe' (83); but elsewhere these hidden grammars create a certain unease. On one occasion the crossed diagonals of Greimas's model appear across a passage of text, an act of over-writing through which the discourse of structuralism seems to place the language of fiction *sous rature* (20). And there is a deeper anxiety that human subjectivity itself has been theorized into abstraction: 'the more thoroughly we understand deep structures the more man is reduced to a cybernetic sigh to cypher into psychic invisibility a statistic two-dimensionally static on a page' (107). Brooke-Rose does not answer this by some nostalgic recuperation of three-dimensional human subjectivity, but by dragging theorists and their theories into the two-dimensionality of her novel's pages. Tellingly, *Thru* ends with a roll-call of its dramatis personae in which everyone from Adam through to Yorick is 'marked' for his or her performance in the text. Some of the structuralists acquit themselves reasonably well – Barthes, Genette and Greimas are all awarded a $\beta+$, though Lévi-Strauss under-achieves notably with a $\gamma+$. But the text's star students are not theorists but creative writers and fictional and allegorical figures – there are alphas for Lewis Carroll, Elizabeth Browning, 'the man with the blue guitar' and Snoopy, whilst Death, Eros and Thanatos all achieve an $\alpha+$. This end-of-term report thus plays with the idea of 'marking' theory – both in the sense of formally appraising its academic achievements, but also of marking it out, inscribing it onto the body of the text where it has to compete on equal terms with other discourses. Even as it flamboyantly foregrounds theory, then, Brooke-Rose's novel puts it firmly in its place.

One name that does not appear in the novel's final roll-call is 'Christine Brooke-Rose', and you are left wondering how the novel would 'mark' its own achievement. Brooke-Rose's most extensive commentary on *Thru* is an essay that offers a close reading of the novel's first twenty pages. Though it ends by extending an hospitable invitation to the reader to 'script the *texte scriptible* with me', the essay only tends to confirm the impression that *Thru* is a novel that can be explicated but not read.[28] Overall, the novel brings to mind Umberto Eco's sceptical remarks about the illusion of readerly freedom created by supposedly 'open works' like *Finnegans Wake*: 'You cannot use the text as you want, but only as the text wants you to use it'.[29] *Thru* has surely earned its place as the *Finnegans Wake* of British postmodernism – a recognized but rarely-visited landmark that has achieved the unlikely feat of being even less accessible than its structuralist sources.

3
From Structuralism to Dialogics: David Lodge

David Lodge has probably done as much as any British writer to bring continental theory to the attention of a non-specialist audience. Many students would sample the writings of key thinkers in the field for the first time in his two major anthologies, *Twentieth-Century Literary Criticism* (1972) and *Modern Criticism and Theory* (1988). Many would also have been given their first sense of how theoretical ideas might translate into critical practice by Lodge's scrupulously accessible deployment of ideas from Shklovsky, Jakobson, Bakhtin and others in his critical writings on nineteenth- and twentieth-century British and American fiction. Of course there will be thousands of general readers whose education in 'post-structuralism' has been gleaned not from the pages of *S/Z* or *Of Grammatology*, but from the lectures, conference papers and shop-talk of Professor Morris Zapp, Dr Robyn Penrose and the other garrulous critical theorists of Lodge's campus fiction. Over the course of his career, Lodge has proved himself the most conspicuously 'ambidextrous' of the contemporary generation of novelist-critics. In what looks like a calculated reproach to the traditional division of labour between authors and critics, his major campus fictions, *Changing Places* (1975), *How Far Can You Go?* (1980), *Small World* (1984), *Nice Work* (1988), were produced in systematic alternation with his works of theoretical criticism, *The Modes of Modern Writing* (1977), *Working with Structuralism* (1981), *Modern Criticism and Theory: A Reader* (1988), *After Bakhtin* (1990). Fiction and theory are, for Lodge, complementary, even symbiotic modes of writing that speak productively to one another in an ongoing two-way exchange. His novels participate imaginatively in the intellectual debates that preoccupy his criticism, dramatizing the ideas, controversies and personalities of the theory wars; and his criticism draws liberally on his fiction as a source of illustrations and case studies.[1]

24

During the 1980s, Lodge would find in the writings of Mikhail Bakhtin powerful theoretical corroboration for the 'dialogic' principle that seems always to have governed his literary career. In his book of post-Bakhtinian essays, reflecting on the different ways in which the discourses of structuralism and its successors have been processed in his writings, Lodge remarks that he has 'learned from them, applied them, domesticated and cannibalized them in criticism and literary journalism, and satirized and carnivalized them in ... novels'.[2] What Lodge has never done, however, is champion 'pure' or 'high' theory. His preference is for theoretical ideas that emerge from hands-on contact with literary texts – from Barthes on Balzac, say, or Bakhtin on Dickens – as opposed to ones that originate in contexts remote from literary study, such as psychoanalysis or philosophy. And he has always been conspicuously unenthusiastic about the attempts of *engagé* materialist critics to unmask and interrogate literature's guilty ideological secrets. One of the hallmarks of Lodge's dialogism is his obvious reluctance to grant theory the 'last word' on literature or life.

Unhappy with what he characterizes as the modern literary politics of 'confrontation' and 'terrorism',[3] Lodge has tended to position himself as an honest broker or trustworthy middleman between the traditional and theoretical schools of criticism. This has not always been a comfortable position for him, since he has frequently been caught in the crossfire between the two camps. The title of *Working with Structuralism*, for example, was something of a gift to his detractors: its tone of lukewarm pragmatism reminded Bernard Bergonzi of World War Two collaborationists who resigned themselves to 'working with the Germans', whilst Terry Eagleton likened it to 'a circus trainer's autobiography entitled *Living with Leo*'.[4] Leaving aside Bergonzi and Eagleton's jibes, the interesting point about the expression 'Working with Structuralism' is the extent to which it might be taken as the motto of Lodge's fictional technique as well as of his critical methods. We have already seen that *How Far Can You Go?* is a rare instance of British structuralism, and it seems plausible to assign Lodge's other campus fictions to the same category. Just as in his criticism he likes to co-ordinate his arguments using pairs of opposed terms – metaphor and metonymy, *lisible* and *scriptible*, monologue and dialogue – so in his fiction binary structures provide the framework for comic interplay between supposedly antithetical ideas and incompatible people. The primary binarism is usually constructed in fairly bald terms – Rummidge versus Euphoria (*Changing Places*), town versus gown (*Nice Work*), art versus science (*Thinks ...*) – before being deconstructed and reconstructed in the course of the dramatic stand-offs, ironic reversals and strange convergences of Lodge's fast-moving comic plots. On the one hand, Lodge confronts these binary oppositions in a brisk problem-solving manner, eager to discover the common ground between radical extremes of opinion; his novels might be read as broadly humanist attempts to overcome difference in a quest for unity and identity in a society bedevilled by ideological division. But on the other hand, he writes with a Saussurean awareness of difference as the very condition of meaningful signification – which is why the moments in Lodge's fiction where differences are synthesized, reconciled or transcended are invariably hedged around with ironic reservations or plagued with a nagging sense of unfinished business.

The influence of structuralism on Lodge is also visible in his fascination with cultural systems; he describes the language and customs of a given group, say, middle-class English Catholics or modern literary intellectuals, like a postmodern anthropologist reporting back on his work in the field. Nor do Lodge's novels restrict themselves to their 'official' topics: in *Small World* this inquisitive mindset takes in pantomime in Rummidge, Karaoke bars in Tokyo and the red-light district in Amsterdam, displaying a voracious curiosity about 'the amazing variety of *langue* and *parole*, food and custom, in the countries of the world' (233). Lodge is fascinated by the cultural systems and practices that confer structure and meaning on life, and is fond of reporting his findings in terms of extended analogies, like the snakes-and-ladders theology of *How Far Can You Go?* or the richly developed parallel in *Small World* between modern conference-goers and the questing knights of medieval romance. He delights in resemblances and correspondences, and is a modest virtuoso of the kind of imaginative lateral thinking that lets illuminating connections spread pleasingly across disparate regions of experience; or, to borrow his own favoured terms from Jakobson, his writing is always on the point of shifting from the axis of selection to the axis of combination – that is to say, from metonymic realism to metaphorical transformation.[5]

The anthropological gaze of Lodge's fiction has turned most frequently and powerfully on the '*langue* and *parole*' of the contemporary literary intellectuals whom he affectionately satirizes in his campus novels. In the Prologue to *Small World*, he indulges in a brief but revealing fantasy about how Chaucer might react if, like Troilus, he were to look down from the eighth sphere of heaven on '*This litle spot of erthe*' and its frantic traffic of globe-trotting scholars. 'Probably', Lodge surmises, 'he laughs heartily at the spectacle, and considers himself well out of it'. The image of the great medieval poet gazing benignly down on the frenetically inconsequential activities of twentieth-century literary critics provides an ironic prelude to a novel in which theorists are fêted whilst creative writers are merely tolerated. And whereas Chaucer is 'well out of it', Lodge enjoys no such privileged exteriority: though his novel may crave some heavenly vantage-point from which to survey its territory, it is self-consciously written from *within* the cultural system that it represents. Of course, this 'insider's anxiety' is simply one version of the dilemmas that plague all campus novelists. The problem of the campus novel has always been its own insularity, its status as a product of the very small, elite worlds that it satirizes. Produced and consumed by professional intellectuals, this is a genre whose narrow social horizons and cosy in-jokes constantly threaten to drown out any rumours of the existence of a world beyond the seminar room.

One obvious function of the title of Lodge's novel is to flag up an ironic awareness of the novel's generic limitations. *Small World* is an expansive novel about insularity. It opens with a conference attended by some 57 delegates in Rummidge, pays flying visits to London, Amsterdam, Lausanne, Vienna, Heidelberg, Ankara, Honolulu, Tokyo, Seoul and Jerusalem, and completes its breathless circumnavigation of the small world of academic conference-going with a 10,000-strong 'megaconference' (313) in New York. As we follow this round-robin of social, professional and sexual transactions between a clique of authors, critics, theorists, publishers, teachers, reviewers and translators, you could be forgiven for thinking that Lodge believes himself to live in a world inhabited exclusively by literary intellectuals. Certainly he seems to rejoice in the intellectual squabbles and acrimonious rivalries of the globalized literary scene; but he also deplores the increasingly arcane theoretical idioms that threaten to cut the new literary intelligentsia off from traditional critics, creative writers and ordinary readers.

Lodge's fiction is, of course, generously accommodating to readers who are not well versed in theoretical debate. *Small World* is saturated in theoretical intertextualities: the footnotes to an annotated edition of the novel, glossing and every reference to Barthes, Derrida *et al*, would run into the hundreds – but they would be largely unnecessary. Theoretical positions are lucidly articulated from first principles in lectures and conference papers delivered by Lodge's academics, or are helpfully glossed during the *ad hoc* intellectual exchanges between his characters; the novel thus smuggles in substantial quantities of expository theoretical writing for the benefit of the readers for whom structuralism and deconstruction are baffling novelties. The reader's surrogate in this respect is the young Irish poet and critic Persse McGarrigle, whose ingenuous questions – 'What is structuralism? Is it a good thing or a bad thing?' (14) – are uttered as it were on behalf of the non-specialist reader. Persse's ignorance of structuralism occasions a series of mini-lectures in which its basic tenets are outlined – both for his benefit and for the reader's. McGarrigle, who contracted tuberculosis during his graduate education and worked on his dissertation in the sanatorium, has been literally quarantined from structuralism and related developments in critical theory. The irony of Persse's earnest declaration to his Head of Department – 'I want to study structuralism, sir' (150) – is that structuralism was a bit *passé*, even in 1979; the cutting-edge theorists had moved on to various versions of post-structuralism. But though McGarrigle picks up a smattering of knowledge about such developments in theory, the education he receives in *Small World*, as is often the case in campus novels, is largely non-academic: geographical, cultural, financial and sexual. *Small World* thus provides the amateur reader with an education in the basics of contemporary theory whilst ironically questioning the value and limitations of that education.

One notable sign of critical theory's ascendancy in Lodge's global republic of letters is its ability to attract the kudos that once attached to creative writing. In purely financial terms, it is instructive to compare the relatively meagre £1000 Anglo-Irish Poetry prize awarded to Persse with the handsome $100,000 salary attached to the novel's professional holy grail, the UNESCO Chair of Literary Criticism. This dwindling of creative writing's prestige is reflected also in a general defection among the ranks of Lodge's critics from literature to theory. The Rummidge conference has its soporific papers on Chaucerian metrics, on editing Shakespeare's *Pericles*, and on animal imagery in Dryden's heroic tragedies, but it is only Morris Zapp's controversial paper on deconstruction that enlivens this torpid affair. Zapp, who was once '*the* Jane Austen man' (24), has transformed himself from an author-centred specialist into a theoretical generalist in precisely the same way as his former colleague Sy Gootblatt, who has switched opportunistically from 'Hooker to the more buoyant field of literary theory' (234). The prevailing critical trend plotted by Lodge's novel is a drift from author-centred criticism (Chaucer, Shakespeare, Dryden, Hooker, Austen) to thematic or generic criticism, or from literary texts to the *idea* of literature. The fact that the novel demotes its creative writers to the role of minor characters is of course a wry comment on the eclipse of the author in the age of the theorist as global celebrity. Lodge's creative writers, like Zapp's ex-wife Desirée Byrd and the unfashionable British realist Ronald Frobisher, are also reduced to chronic writer's block by an intellectual climate that seems anything but conducive to creativity. Though Lodge depicts his novelists' anti-theoretical scepticism with obvious fellow feeling, he does not extend the same sympathy to his traditionalist critics. Typical of the latter group is Persse's Head of Department, Professor Liam McCreedy, who has taken refuge from the world of structuralism and postmodernism behind the 'battlements' and 'fortifications' (149) of his Anglo-Saxon texts. Perhaps the novel's least sympathetic character is the supercilious Oxford *bellettrist* Rudyard Parkinson, whose ignorance of continental theory does not prevent him from dismissing it wholesale in a waspishly nasty review of a Morris Zapp book. Rummidge's Philip Swallow, meanwhile, is clueless rather than vindictive: incapable of telling the difference between structuralism and deconstruction, he is a decidedly feeble champion of the liberal humanist cause.

If creative writers and traditionalist critics feature in *Small World* as variously beleaguered, demoralized and out of touch, the novel's cast of critical theorists appear as vivid, affectionately caricatured representatives of their respective theoretical positions: Morris Zapp stands for deconstruction, Michel Tardieu for narratology, Siegfried von Turpitz for reader response, Fulvia Morgana for Marxism. It is possible to read *Small World* as a kind of fictionalized anthology of contemporary theory whose *dramatis personae* comprises idiosyncratic personifications of major positions in the theoretical debate. 'Losing not their souls but their identities', says Robert A. Morace, 'the academics have successfully reduced themselves to the theories they propound'.[6] This strikes me as only partly true. Lodge's novel certainly scores a number of satirical points at the expense of the reductiveness of theory, for example in its focus on Tardieu's ludicrous efforts to formulate 'a complex equation representing in algebraic terms the plot of *War and Peace*' (113). And the 'merging' of a theorist into his own theory is exemplified when Von Turpitz is exposed as a plagiarist, having stolen Persse's idea about the 'influence' of T. S. Eliot on Shakespeare: what Lodge implies here is that plagiarism is the *reductio ad absurdum* of a theory that permits the reader to assume total control of a given text. Elsewhere, however, Lodge's academics are represented not as creatures of their own theories, but as opportunistic quick-change artists: Zapp, for example, appears 'in Amsterdam as a semiologist, in Zurich as a Joycean, and in Vienna as a narratologist' (234). But what really matters for Lodge is the telling *disparity* between a given academic and the theories s/he propounds. Fulvia Morgana may be blind to the contradictions between her Marxist principles and her millionaire lifestyle – not to mention her links with extreme left-wing terrorists – but these contradictions are the keynotes of her character. Morris Zapp, meanwhile, discovers the limits of his faith in theory when he's kidnapped by those same terrorists – an experience that leaves this sadder and wiser post-structuralist observing that 'the deferral of meaning isn't infinite ... death is the one concept you can't deconstruct' (328). Lodge's technique in this novel is to use a given character to ventriloquize a given theory – say Marxism, narratology or deconstruction – before problematizing that theory by converting the ventriloquist's dummy into a flesh-and-blood character. For Lodge, the 'humanization' of the theorist – his or her exposure as a complex bundle of flaws, contradictions and vulnerabilities – is a necessary polemical response to the algebraic abstractions and monologic slogans of theory.

Lodge's 'ventriloquial' approach to theory also enables him to strike the kind of radical intellectual poses that he studiously avoids in his own criticism. Whereas the Lodge of *Working with Structuralism* or *The Modes of Modern Writing* is diligently cautious, selective and balanced in his use of theory, the Lodge of *Small World* or *Nice Work* gets to play at theories in which he does not officially believe, to perform set-pieces of *bravura* theorizing in the safe confines of the fictive. Perhaps the most important acts of theoretical ventriloquism in these novels are Morris Zapp's conference lecture on 'Textuality as Striptease' (*Small World*, 24–8), and Robyn Penrose's undergraduate lecture on the Condition of England Novel (*Nice Work*, 71–83). In a sense, Zapp and Robyn's talks can be read as the 'keynote lectures' of their respective novels, formidably clever attempts to theorize pre-emptively the fictional narratives in which they appear. But although these lectures are conspicuously rich in clues about how to read *Small World* and *Nice Work*, these novels are constructed so as to resist and exceed the theoretical frameworks laid down by Zapp's deconstruction and Penrose's materialist feminism. Zapp's lecture, which is obviously indebted to Roland Barthes's well-known essay on striptease, argues that literary discourse tantalizes us with the promise of a final unveiling whose postponement in an 'endless cycle of encoding-decoding-encoding' (25) can yield only 'masturbatory' (26) pleasure for the frustrated reader. The lecture thus sets the tone for a novel that will trawl through brothels, adult cinemas and strip clubs in Birmingham, Soho and Amsterdam, but also foreshadows Persse McGarrigle's perpetually frustrated quest for Angelica Pabst, the beautiful but elusive Spenserian. However, when Zapp repeats this performance in Amsterdam he is roundly heckled and when he repeats it again at the *MLA* he has become a distinctly half-hearted deconstructionist: his lecture seems to be subject to a frustrating law of diminishing returns, as though what seemed revolutionary in Rummidge can only appear as tired and obvious in

New York. Significantly, the MLA conference also provides the venue for Angelica's sophisticated feminist interpretation of romance, which argues strongly for a female erotics of reading, and which therefore implicitly challenges and revises the unacknowledged phallocentric bias of Zapp's model of textuality (322–3). Taking its cue from Zapp, *Small World* presents critical reading as a saga of disappointed phallocentricism whose hero is a questing male subject in pursuit of a duplicitously elusive female object that both provokes and resists masculine fantasies of consummation and possession. But with the emergence of Angelica as speaking subject rather than sought-after object, the novel both feminizes Zapp's model of reading and makes partial amends for the very striking absence of feminism from its own repertoire of theoretical interests.

Not that it would be at all plausible to claim that *Small World* comes into its own as a feminist novel at the very end. Although Angelica's MLA paper significantly balances and answers Zapp's Rummidge lecture, feminism is still excluded from the novel's more public representations of the future of theory. There is no feminist candidate for the coveted UNESCO Chair, the vacant throne of critical theory. This empty chair signifies the open question that increasingly haunts this novel: the future belongs to theory – but which theory? One of the novel's best running jokes concerns the conference delegate whose paper-in-progress has stalled agonizingly on the question of how literary criticism can survive in the age of deconstruction. Deeply vexed by the same question, Lodge's novel struggles with the responsibility of making some authoritative pronouncement on the condition and future of critical theory. In the event the best answer to this question is provided not by one of Lodge's theorists, but by Persse, who dumbfounds the illustrious speakers at the MLA forum on 'The Function of Criticism' with the liberatingly ingenuous question, 'What follows if everybody agrees with you?' (319). Such a moment of perfect critical consensus would, of course, have fatal implications for a process of literary interpretation and debate whose very lifeblood is controversy and disagreement. As Arthur Kingfisher puts it, in impeccably structuralist terms, 'what matters in the field of critical practice is not truth but difference' (319).

However, if Persse's affirmation of critical pluralism seems to resolve matters all too comfortably, the novel does nevertheless differentiate pointedly between the differences that flourish productively in theoretical circles, and the gulf of incomprehension that yawns between theorists and non-theorists. Like many campus novels, *Small World* is notably short on non-academic characters, beyond the odd taxi driver or exotic dancer; and it is exceptionally short on non-academic *readers*. In this context the subtitle of Philip Swallow's book on Hazlitt sheds valuable light on the novel's problematic limitations. Greeted by the novel's theorists as a laughably unfashionable piece of anti-theoretical polemic, *Hazlitt and the Amateur Reader* is Swallow's elegy for the fate of the non-specialist reader who has been disenfranchised from literary debate by the hyper-specialized language of theory. However, there might be a basis for arguing that the 'amateur reader' is the absent hero of *Small World* – ignored and forgotten by the novel's cartel of theorists and critics, the amateur reader is an apocryphal creature on the margins of this 'Professor's Novel'.[7] The only real amateur reader in this book is Cheryl Summerbee, the British Airways check-in clerk whom Angelica Pabst converts from 'Bills and Moon' romance to the real thing – Ariosto and Spenser; she even embarks on some taxing secondary reading about the genre, and is soon discoursing in psychoanalytical terms on its conventions. The novel ends with Persse, having transferred his affections from Angelica to Cheryl, embarking on a new romantic quest in pursuit of the latter. If *Small World* is indeed a professor's novel, it is one that argues that literature is too important to be left to the professors and one that attaches considerable symbolic importance to this isolated non-specialist who reads for the love of reading. Persse's new quest, for the lost amateur reader who has improbably connected herself with both Renaissance literature and contemporary theory, promises to be even more daunting than his bid to fathom the mysteries of structuralism.

When Cheryl Summerbee vanishes from her post at the British Airways check-in desk, *Small World* runs up against the built-in generic limitations of the professorial novel: Lodge cannot follow his sole amateur reader on her new adventures without violating the boundaries of campus fiction and striking out into the *terra incognita* of the non-academic world. However, in *Nice Work* Lodge decisively extends the horizons of his fiction beyond the small worlds of university life. He does so by forging a problematic alliance between university fiction and an older genre, variously known as the 'Industrial Novel' or the 'Condition of England novel'. *Nice Work* is steeped in allusions to and echoes of this tradition: it contains a series of epigraphs from Victorian texts by Dickens, Gaskell and Charlotte Brontë; its dramatic content deliberately echoes scenes and situations from such texts as *North and South* and *Howards End*; and its heroine, Dr Robyn Penrose, is an expert in the Victorian social problem novel. Of course, the very idea of a 'postmodern Condition of England novel' is something of a structural joke, since the texts that *Nice Work* playfully emulates represent English fiction at its most stubbornly realistic. With their focus on the plight of the urban poor and the evils of the factory system, and with their vision of England hopelessly divided between a privileged rural gentry, a cultured intelligentsia and a philistine bourgeoisie, these novels function as hard-hitting documentary records of contemporary social problems. Dickens, Gaskell, Disraeli and Forster belong to a novelistic tradition that takes its social responsibilities altogether more seriously than seems the case with postmodernism, where metafictional games-playing rather than documentary realism is the order of the day. In the case of *Nice Work*, rather than choosing between traditional realism and postmodern metafiction, Lodge makes this tension the implied subject of the novel. Similarly, this is a text that deliberately cannot decide whether it is a 'Condition of England' novel or a 'Condition of EngLit' novel, since it functions both as a panoramic survey of Thatcher's England and as an introspective examination of the state of Lodge's discipline in the latest phase of the theory wars.

The England of *Nice Work* is, to cite the famous subtitle of Disraeli's *Sybil*, still divided into 'Two Nations'. But the Two Nations of this novel are not the rich and the poor, nor even utilitarianism and liberal humanism, but capitalism in its Thatcherite phase and an academic culture whose theoretical obsessions have placed it further than ever from the socio-political world on which it likes to pontificate. Lodge's device to bring these two nations together is an Industry Year Shadow Scheme that requires the Rummidge academic Robyn Penrose to observe the working practices of Vic Wilcox, a hard-nosed senior manager at the local engineering firm Pringle's. Robyn and Vic thus personify any number of stark binary oppositions that the novel strives to resolve or overcome – theoretical knowledge *versus* practical know-how, highbrow culture *versus* philistine commerce, radical feminism *versus* patriarchal authority. According to one sceptical critic, however, *Nice Work*'s repertoire of worryingly 'irreconcilable' social binaries are merely pseudo-problems of its own invention. Steven Connor takes the view that 'The apparent split between two worlds, two nations, two forms of novel and readership is really the mechanism that the novel employs to fantasise its own power to encompass and analyse'.[8] It is certainly possible to argue that the schizophrenic England of *Nice Work* may simply be a product of the novel's governing binary structures. Which is to say that the 'Two Nations' of *Nice Work* need to be understood as effects of its formal organization rather than as external realities caught in the novelist's field of vision. Of course, to put it this way makes *Nice Work* sound like a rather mechanical exercise in binary thinking, but what brings this novel to life is its dialogic – and recognizably Bakhtinian – negotiation of the apparently frozen polarities around which it revolves.

Lodge has professed deep admiration for the work of the Russian postformalist Mikhail Bakhtin, describing it as inspirational evidence of 'life after poststructuralism'.[9] *Nice Work* registers this impact, in a comparatively minor way, in its variations on the carnivalesque themes developed by Bakhtin in his books on Dostoevsky and Rabelais. Lodge has never been squeamish about following his characters into the toilet or the bedroom, and his earthy comic interest in the body and its sexual and excretory functions can be seen as a milder English version of Bakhtin's work on the gross materiality and irrepressible vulgarity of the 'grotesque body'.[10] Similarly, if we are looking for a text-book illustration of the relationship between carnival and authority, then we need look no further than *Nice Work*'s kiss-o-gram scene (251–3), where a lunch-time meeting between management and shopfloor slips into temporary anarchy when a scantily-clad young woman, egged on by the salacious chants of the Pringles workforce, approaches Vic singing a suggestive variation on 'Jingle Bells'. But this scene of festive topsy-turvydom is over almost before it begins when Robyn recognizes the kiss-o-gram as one of her own undergraduate students, Marion Russell, whom she promptly recalls to her 'official' identity. Whether she realizes it or not, Lodge's radical theorist is thus weighing in on the side of order and authority as they clamp down on the riotous vulgarity of popular festivity.

As well as echoing Bakhtin's carnivalesque themes, *Nice Work* also displays a sophisticated awareness of the spatial dimensions of fiction that merits comparison with his work on the characteristic time-spaces or 'chronotopes' of different genres.[11] *Nice Work* is a novel that moves restlessly through a range of vividly imagined cultural spaces – the impeccably landscaped grounds of Rummidge University; the affluent South Coast home of Robyn's parents; the oppressively dark, noisy and dirty machine-shop and foundry at Pringles; the variously affluent and run-down suburbs of Rummidge; the City of London at the height of the yuppie era. The novel might almost be read as an atlas of the cultural geography of 1980s England, one that attempts to map out connections between these different spaces that are more meaningful than the sprawl of ring roads and flyovers that weave their way in and out of its action. But it is only when Robyn leaves England to jet off with Vic to a trade fair in Frankfurt that we are granted a vision of England as a unified cultural space rather than a collection of disconnected localities. This passage, which gestures towards a famous scene in Waugh's *Vile Bodies* where two airborne socialites gaze nauseously down at English suburbia, provides an excellent illustration of what might be called the 'England-from-a-plane' chronotope:

> Robyn looked out of the window as England slid slowly by beneath them: cities and towns, their street plans like printed circuits, scattered over a mosaic of tiny fields, connected by the thin wires of railways and motorways ... Factories, shops, offices, schools, beginning the working day. People crammed into rush hour buses and trains, or sitting at the wheels of their cars in traffic jams, or washing up breakfast things in the kitchens of pebble-dashed semis. All inhabiting their own little worlds, oblivious of how they fitted into the total picture. The housewife, switching on her electric kettle to make another cup of tea, gave no thought to the immense complex of operations that made that simple action possible ... The housewife gave no thought to all this as she switched on her kettle. Neither had Robyn until this moment, and it would never have occurred to her to do so before she met Vic Wilcox. (269)

This lofty perspective on England offers a brief return to the heady days of untroubled authorial omniscience when we could gaze with the all-seeing eye of the author down onto an integrated whole. But what holds the 'total picture' together for Robyn is, crucially, an *economic* system – the hugely complex process of human endeavour that has gone into designing, creating, marketing, advertizing and selling the emblematic kettle in the hands of her tea-making Everywoman. When a humanities lecturer can begin to think like a captain of industry, Lodge seems to imply, then England can once more be seen as a whole. But this vision of a united England is necessarily a brief glimpse, a receding panorama. The anonymous, unthinking housewife is clearly a kind of double for Robyn, and as Lodge's airborne critical theorist looks down on her non-intellectual *alter ego* the novel once again encounters a profound disjunction between the rarefied atmosphere of theory and the experiential realities 'on the ground'.

Though there are obviously grounds for reading *Nice Work* for its carnivalesque moments and distinctive chronotopes, its strongest and most sustained affinities with Bakhtin lie in its handling of notions of dialogue and polyphony. The significance of these notions for Lodge is spelt out in his collection of post-Bakhtinian essays, where he identifies the two most appealing elements of Bakhtin's thought. First, there is his creation of a 'linguistics of *parole*' that frees us from the airless textuality of post-Saussurean linguistics by locating meaning in real-life interaction between language users rather than in the play of differential relations between signifiers. This interactive model of language use forms the basis for Bakhtin's hugely influential dialogic and polyphonic models of literature. Second, there is Bakhtin's reinstatement of the author – whom post-structuralism had threatened to consign to oblivion – as the necessary ventriloquizing presence behind the polyphonic text. As a practising creative writer, Lodge is pleased to see language released by Bakhtin from the Saussurean vacuum, and is obviously delighted to see the author rescued from the attentions of Barthes, Foucault *et al.* But what Lodge does not convincingly address is the potential tension between Bakhtin's model of polyphony, which represents language as a multi-voiced free-for-all, and his reinstatement of the author, which implies that texts do after all have a centre of gravity, a privileged individual voice behind their polyphonic babble. Though we can hardly blame Lodge for failing to resolve this unacknowledged tension between monologism and polyphony in Bakhtin's critical thought, it is intriguing to note just how deeply *Nice Work* – particularly in its complex representation of Robyn Penrose – is characterized by the same tension.

Robyn Penrose, as sketched by Lodge, is a rising star in the fields of feminism and Victorian studies, extremely well versed in the debates of contemporary literary theory, and passionately committed to radical causes. Her brand of 'semiotic materialism', which harnesses Marxism and feminism to the anti-humanist thinking of post-structuralism, represents a powerful synthesis of the theoretical voices that compete so fiercely with one another in *Small World*. When Lodge's narrator introduces Robyn, he makes much of the fact that he is about to introduce a character who herself does not believe in the concept of character: for her, it is an article of faith that there is no self, no author, no origin. At this point in the novel, the narrator's prose becomes noticeably inflected by Robyn's theoretical lexicon – in an abrupt shift of register, this section is suddenly crammed with talk of postmodernist deconstruction, subject positions, modes of representation, bourgeois myths and intertextual webs of discourse (39–40). Rather than simply adopting a style of 'zero degree' neutrality, the novel evokes Robyn's character by dialogizing the narrator's pleasantly unassuming commentary with her theoretical pieties.

This 'dialogue' between the down-to-earth narrator and his highbrow heroine becomes particularly noticeable in the politely bemused account of Robyn's austere anti-humanism:

> It might seem a bit bleak, a bit inhuman ('antihumanist, yes; inhuman, no,' she would interject), somewhat deterministic ('not at all; the

truly determined subject is he who is not aware of the discursive formations that determine him. Or her,' she would add scrupulously, being among other things a feminist), but in practice this doesn't seem to affect her behaviour very noticeably – she seems to have ordinary human feelings, ambitions, desires, to suffer anxieties, frustrations, fears, like anyone else in this imperfect world, and have a natural inclination to try and make it a better place. (40–1)

What is striking here is the novel's willingness to grant a fictional character the right of reply: Robyn is given the opportunity to challenge the way she is being characterized by a supposedly 'omniscient' narrator. This excerpt thus invites comparison with the qualities that Bakhtin praised in the fiction of Dostoevsky. Bakhtin credits Dostoevsky with the invention of the 'polyphonic novel' in which characters become virtual co-authors in the sense that their voices merge with, or bounce off, or challenge, or even drown out the author's voice. No longer the passive objects of the author's discourse, Dostoevsky's heroes are *'free* people, capable of standing *alongside* their creator'.[12] On the face of it Robyn seems to enjoy a similar kind of freedom: her interjections are brisk, confident and forthright, whereas the narrator's voice is altogether more tentative ('a *bit* bleak', 'a *bit* inhuman', *'somewhat* deterministic'), impressionistically rendering what Robyn *seems* (another key word here) rather than dogmatically asserting what she *is*. However, although the omniscient narrator appears to be deferring to the superior wisdom of one of his own characters, the deference is obviously ironical. In part the joke here is that despite their radical credentials, theorists have become altogether more dogmatic, monologic and authoritarian than the all-knowing narrators of traditional realist fiction. But for all his self-effacing modesty, Lodge's narrator does in the end claim to know Robyn better than she knows herself: and crucially it is his reference to what she is like in *practice* that is designed to trump all her purely *theoretical* self-knowledge.

This is not to criticize Lodge for failing to live up to the Bakhtinian ideal of creating *'free* people, capable of standing *alongside* their creator'. As we saw in Chapter 2, there is no meaningful sense in which a fictional character can ever be described as 'free'. But it is worth noticing how frequently Lodge cuts his theorists down to size by pointing out this kind of discrepancy between their theoretical principles and practical behaviour. In *Thinks …* (2001), Robyn – who is now Professor of Communications and Cultural Studies at Walsall University – delivers a guest lecture at the University of Gloucester entitled 'Interrogating the

Subject'. Among her audience is the University's Writer in Residence, Helen Reed, who finds Robyn's theoretical arguments against the humanist subject both uninspiring and demoralizingly pessimistic. In person, however, Robyn proves to be perfectly likeable and sympathetic – an old-fashioned human being rather than a deconstructed subject.[13]

Like Morris Zapp, Robyn is presented by Lodge as a professional monologist, a purveyor of eloquent half-truths that sorely need to be challenged and invigorated through dialogue. Part One of *Nice Work* finds her lecturing with great panache on the Condition of England novel, effortlessly and entertainingly dissecting *Hard Times* and *North and South* for an audience of undergraduates. Touching as it does on a whole range of issues raised by Lodge's novel, Robyn's lecture presents itself as a possible 'reading' of *Nice Work* – and a rather unsympathetic one at that, given her emphasis on the ideological failures and limitations of Condition of England texts. But the monologic force of Robyn's lecture is challenged even as it unfolds, since excerpts from the lecture are intercut with scenes in which other characters from the novel go about their daily business at home and work. Not only does this break up the flow of her argument, but it also invites us to question the extent to which her monologic authority might extend to the world outside the lecture theatre. The remainder of the novel, meanwhile, concerns itself with the re-education of this monologic spokeswoman for the discourse of radical literary theory. At one level, the story of *Nice Work* is the story of Robyn and Vic acquiring fluency in each other's languages. Robyn's time with Vic endow her with the vocabulary to envision England as an economic system of production and exchange, while Vic acquires an unexpected appetite for Victorian literature, and chips in with some canny remarks on Tennyson during one of Robyn's undergraduate seminars. By the end of the novel he is also making admirable progress on the distinction between metaphor and metonymy. The education they gain from one another is pointedly contrasted with the sterile circularity of Robyn's debates with her sometime boyfriend Charles, over dialectical materialism and Lacanian phallogocentrism.

The 'dialogic' method of *Nice Work* is thus designed not to demolish Robyn's intellectual position, but to undermine her confidence that she has a monopoly on the truth. Robyn's weekly visits to Pringle's open her eyes to the reality of heavy industry that had previously been for her only a figment of the Victorian imagination; Wilcox proves to be an essentially decent human being, not the brutal capitalist she had expected; and when she is pestered by a smitten Wilcox after what she hoped would be a no-strings-attached one-night-stand, she finds herself mired in a messy human reality that the abstractions of theory cannot explain away. Though she once regarded Derrida's *il n'y a pas de hors-texte* as gospel, Robyn ruefully acknowledges that she has been 'dragged into a classic realist text, full of causality and morality' (304). In short, Robyn fondly imagined that she inhabited Derrida's world, but finds herself in Dickens's.

One of the 'lessons' of *Nice Work*, then, is that literature contains wisdom that cannot be found in theory. Indeed, the relationship between creative writing and critical theory in this novel is ultimately hierarchical rather than dialogical. Though the novel is rich in intertextual references from both fiction and theory, its epigraphs are drawn from only the former – George Eliot, Disraeli, Charlotte Brontë, Gaskell, Dickens; this way, continental theory is decisively subordinated to English literature. And whilst Eagleton's complaint that theoretical ideas in *Nice Work* are 'travestied as so much foreign flim-flam'[14] is clearly exaggerated, it is certainly true that the voices of the Victorian sages are formally privileged by Lodge's text above those of the gurus of post-structuralism.

An even more intriguing problem for *Nice Work*'s status as a would-be dialogical text is its failure to acknowledge Bakhtin's existence. In the highbrow conversations between Robyn and Charles, and in the mini-lectures on literary theory that Robyn delivers to Vic, Lodge releases a welter of allusions to and quotations from literary theorists into his text: Saussure, Freud, Marx, Lacan, Derrida, Kristeva, Irigaray, Cixous, Hillis Miller, Barthes, Gilbert, Gubar and many others provide a running theoretical commentary on Lodge's humdrum Rummidge drama. But the one conspicuous absentee from this chorus of illustrious theorists is Bakhtin himself: Lodge's theoretical guru is nowhere to be seen in *Nice Work*. This is a striking omission – partly because you might expect two start-of-the-art academics like Robyn and Charles to be in on the Bakhtin revival that swept through Anglo-American academe in the 1980s, but mainly because you might expect Lodge to take this opportunity to generate more favourable publicity for a theorist whose work he was championing in his critical writings of the time. Perhaps we might speculate that it is precisely Bakhtin's *importance* to Lodge that accounts for his absence from the novel. Bakhtin is in a sense the novel's patron saint, and Lodge was evidently reluctant to drag his name into the knockabout comedy of *Nice Work*, where it would be spoofed, carnivalized and robbed of its special privileges. By not taking the opportunity to bring Bakhtin's words into a dialogic relationship with the many other theoretical and non-theoretical discourses of the novel, *Nice Work* grants the great advocate of dialogism the dubious honour of a position *outside* dialogue.

In his essay on the 'Prehistory of Novelistic Discourse', Bakhtin famously observes that 'Novelistic discourse is always criticizing itself'.[15] Few contemporary novels have managed to be as entertainingly self-critical as *Small World* and *Nice Work*; and not only do Lodge's novels constantly criticize themselves, they also criticize any number of critics and theorists of novelistic discourse – with the conspicuous exception, in the case of *Nice Work*, of Bakhtin himself. The crucial irony of Lodge's portrait of the theory wars is that his decision to come down on the side of vibrant literary polyphony as against the many versions of dogmatic theoretical monologism is made possible by a theory that, in the end, dare not speak its name.

4
The 'Culture Wars' and Beyond: Theory on the US Campus

This chapter will examine the place of theoretical controversies in fictional representations of the 'culture wars', the acrimonious debates over political correctness, multiculturalism, feminism and affirmative action that have divided US academic culture since the 1980s. Such debates are by no means confined to departments of literature, or even to academic culture at large, but campus novelists of this period frequently use the professional in-fighting of literary academics as a convenient shorthand for wider controversies. Often explicitly harking back to the academic comedies of David Lodge, prominent US campus novelists of recent years – including Sandra Gilbert and Susan Gubar, David Damrosch, James Hynes, Richard Powers, John L'Heureux and Perceval Everett – find that the small worlds of literature departments are both the best and worst microcosms for culture at large. On the one hand, debates about the literary curriculum and professional tenure, about what gets taught and who gets to teach it, raise questions of value, tradition, power and inclusivity that resonate far beyond the small worlds of academe. It is only a small step from debating the fate of the 'western canon' – as influentially championed by Harold Bloom – to debating the fate of western civilization. On the other hand, to put it this way is to risk taking literary intellectuals almost as seriously as they take themselves, and recent US campus fiction roundly satirizes those academics who imagine that the future of the west hangs on their next conference paper or job interview. Departments of literature in these novels can thus appear as apocalyptic intellectual battlegrounds or as talking shops with delusions of grandeur, depending on the novelist's changing angle of vision.

Many of the leading combatants in the culture wars – including Alan Bloom, Harold Bloom, Jacques Derrida, Henry Louis Gates Jr, Gerald Graff,

Geoffrey Hartman, Julia Kristeva, J. Hillis Miller, Camille Paglia, Edward Said and Helen Vendler – appear as 'characters', alongside the authors themselves, in Gilbert and Gubar's *Masterpiece Theatre: An Academic Melodrama* (1995).[1] Sprawling across the boundaries between fact and fiction, critical and creative discourses, high culture and crowd-pleasing populism, *Masterpiece Theatre* brazenly defies easy generic classification. Kenneth Womack tentatively identifies it as a 'postmodern closet drama' though you would be hard pressed to come up with any other examples of this genre; alternatively, if we are looking for literary precedents or companion-pieces, then we might set *Masterpiece Theatre* alongside Ihab Hassan's 'Prometheus as Performer' (1980) as examples of that tiny genre, the 'university masque'.[2] But whatever generic label we ultimately decide on, it is crucial to acknowledge that Gilbert and Gubar's text somehow manages to be both derivative and *sui generis* – a paradox that is designed to shake up our protocols of reading in a world where texts are increasingly being *processed* rather than read.

Masterpiece Theatre features real-life theorists alongside media celebrities and fictional characters in a seriously comic exploration of the fate of books and reading in the culture wars. According to the authors' introduction, the culture wars were sparked off when right-wing ideologues like William J. Bennett and Allan Bloom sought to scapegoat liberal academics for the social and political ills of a Reaganite society – the blame for declining literacy standards could be pinned on 'deconstructionists', for example, while changes in traditional family structures could be laid at the door of academic feminists. Bennett and Bloom function here as leading spokesmen for what Gilbert and Gubar call the 'Back to Basics' group, a rearguard defence of universalist ideals of disinterested wisdom, literary greatness and timeless truth from the onslaughts of politically correct ideologues. Yet despite their obvious disdain for the 'intellectual captains of conservatism' (xi), Gilbert and Gubar do nevertheless find themselves in sympathy with the conservative case for 'the joy of reading, the pleasure of writing, the historic centrality of the book' (xiii). Such arguments are, of course, scarcely fashionable among the coalition of radical academics whom Gilbert and Gubar brand as the 'Forward into Instability' group. At the outset, then, they find themselves caught in a dangerous no-man's-land between the entrenched positions of the culture wars.

Gilbert and Gubar's 'academic melodrama' also strikes boldly into the no-man's-land between criticism and fiction, advertising as it does so the fact that, whatever the powerful tensions between radicals and conservatives, both camps are 'alienated from the real practices and producers of the art' (xix). Accordingly, *Masterpiece Theatre* aligns itself with those 'real practices and producers' of art as against its fractious professional consumers. Only creative writers and writer-critics – Carolyn Heilbrun, Ursula K. Le Guin, Toni Morrison, David Lodge, Isabel Allende, Buchi Emecheta, Bharati Mukherjee – are exempted from its scattergun satire, by virtue of their commitment to producing texts rather simply interrogating them circulating, them or profiting from them. Not that Gilbert and Gubar present themselves as potential members of this illustrious company. Self-deprecatingly presented as 'SG1' and 'SG2', Gilbert and Gubar are the Rosencrantz and Guildenstern of this drama – marginal and interchangeable to the point of anonymity. Nor does this piece present itself as an instance of high art or a candidate for literary immortality. Fashioned according to a cut-and-paste aesthetic that promiscuously samples both the trashy discourses of popular culture and the serpentine prose of post-structuralist theorists from Kristeva to Derrida, *Masterpiece Theatre* is self-consciously *not* a masterpiece but a rather a deliberate 'vulgarization' of the culture wars, a carnivalesque send-up of the high-minded polemic that rains down from both sides.

In the best traditions of melodrama, *Masterpiece Theatre* follows the ordeals of an unworldly innocent at large in a society of designing scoundrels and cloak-and-dagger intrigue – though Gilbert and Gubar's hero is not a guileless youth but an unidentified Text that gets into a series of deadly scrapes with unscrupulous readers and critics. The drama begins when a 'Murderous Villain' forces the Text at knifepoint onto a railroad crossing near Boondock State University, chaining it to the track to await a freight train. Led by Assistant Professor Jane Marple, crowds of literary intellectuals soon descend on the scene, though in all the uproar it becomes increasingly hard to differentiate those who wish to save the Text from those intent on destroying it. In the helter-skelter action that follows, this traumatized Text is variously abducted, stolen, hijacked by special interest groups, replicated in multiple clone versions, converted into computer files, auctioned off to the highest bidder, and even, at one point, 'crucified' (137) by being impaled on a bulletin board. This melodramatic ordeal allegorizes the multiple vulnerabilities of the literary texts in an era when books are subject to countless forms of moral and ideological censorship, and are in constant danger of being de-canonized or deconstructed, overwhelmed by theoretical discourse or eclipsed by the attention-seeking controversialists among their readers.

For Gilbert and Gubar, then, the Text is the primary casualty of the culture wars, trampled underfoot by combatants who prefer to engage polemically with each other than to engage sympathetically with literature. When the Text is stolen by a pair of sinister media agents named the McGuffin Brothers, Gilbert and Gubar release a valuable clue if not to the Text's literary content, then at least to its structural function. *Masterpiece Theatre* exposes the ways in which the culture wars reduce texts to the status of content-free McGuffins, empty pretexts for the thrills and spills of intellectual controversy. The Text is valuable to Gilbert and Gubar's culture warriors not in its own right but as a *tabula rasa* on which they inscribe their own ideological obsessions. The 'Back to Basics' loyalists automatically assume that it's a timeless canonical masterpiece under threat from resentful multiculturalists; whereas in the ranks of the 'Forward into Instability Group', it is variously supposed to be a working-class text, a gay text, a black text, a subaltern text or a woman's text. Everyone is eager to champion the Text in the name of their cause, but with the exception of Jane Marple, the culture warriors are conspicuously reluctant to *read* it – though a number of them piously intone Paul de Man's dictum that 'the resistance to theory is in fact a resistance to reading' (24, 115, 179). In the present intellectual climate, it seems that even theories of reading can serve as alibis for not reading.

As Karen R. Lawrence points out, however, quite what would represent an appropriate style of reading in a context where every theory seems ripe for satirical debunking is anything but clear. A pre-theoretical 'zero-degree reading'[3] of the Text is what *Masterpiece Theatre* seems to advocate but cannot practically demonstrate. The unread Text is thus condemned by *Masterpiece Theatre* to the demeaningly inconsequential McGuffin-role from which Gilbert and Gubar hoped to save it. It is not, however, completely silenced by this role, and does manage to get a word or two in edgeways. Confronted with irreconcilable versions of its own identity, it deliriously babbles excerpts from Shakespeare, Keats and Beckett, parrots chunks of critical theory, and mimics the language of popular newspapers, lifestyle magazine, and student papers – in short, it resembles nothing so much as cultural mélange of *Masterpiece Theatre* itself. It is as though the Text, with its chameleon-like changes of style and register, is *Masterpiece Theatre*'s proxy in its own fictional world. Gilbert and Gubar seem to use the Text to conceptualize their drama's own multiple literary identity – and also to rehearse its own reception, to preview its ordeal at the hands of those who will take it hostage in the name of canonical tradition or multicultural radicalism. That Gilbert and Gubar's melodrama seems destined for the same fate as its hapless textual hero could indicate that the culture wars are here to stay. Or, as seems more likely, it could be that its authors are too busy stoking the controversies and enjoying the spectacle of the culture wars to imagine terms on which a truce might be called.

It might be added that some influential commentators are perfectly happy at the prospect of the culture wars continuing indefinitely. After all, you could argue that the very term 'culture wars' simply melodrama-tizes the intellectual argument and debate that ought to be the lifeblood of the academic profession. As Gerald Graff shows in his history of American literary studies, those who mourn the demise of scholarly consensus are harking back to a past that never happened: the nineteenth century witnessed titanic struggles between classicists and modern-language scholars, while the 1940s and 1950s saw running battles between the New Criticism and the 'old historicism'.[4] Valuable though Graff's historical perspective is, it offers little in the way of con-solation for those scholars who harbour more utopian ideas of academic culture. David Damrosch concludes *We Scholars* – a sober critique of the 'academic aggression' and competitive individualism that bedevil modern academe – with a plea for a new culture of genuinely collaborative writing and research.[5] Damrosch's campus comedy *Meetings of the Mind* (2000) – which is laced with rueful comments about the indifferent reception that greeted *We Scholars* – represents a playful attempt to imagine solutions to the problems diagnosed in the earlier book.[6]

Meetings of the Mind focuses on the shifting relationships of rivalry, friendship and collaboration between the literature professor 'David Damrosch' and three fellow veterans of the conference circuit – the erudite dilettante Vic d'Ohr Addams, the feminist Marsha Doddvic and the Jewish deconstructionist Dov Midrash, DCA. As their paths cross and re-cross over a period of six years at conferences in Japan, the United States and Mexico, this argumentative quartet debate the condition and future of literary studies from every conceivable angle. In its depiction of their various conference papers, the novel contains some of the most strikingly 'realistic' and uncaricatured reconstructions of theoretical dis-course in recent campus fiction. When Doddvic speaks on Woolf and materialist feminism (18–20), say, or when Midrash critiques the 'traveling theory' (51–5) of Edward Said, you get the sense that their arguments are being taken seriously and given a fair hearing, rather than simply being held up as choice examples of professorial gobbledegook. It is not theory but the relationship *between* theories that provokes searching satirical critique in this novel. What troubles Damrosch is not so much the truth or otherwise of different theoretical positions as the apparent impossi-bility of establishing consensual dialogue between them. Typically, his post-paper discussions degenerate quickly into *ad hominem* polemic and bad-tempered one-upmanship; none of the novel's conference panels produces anything like a 'meeting of the mind'.

If conferences have become 'sad parodies of collaborative work' (43), it is not because of theory *per se*, but because critical methodologies have become so extravagantly variegated that consensus has been sacrificed to limitless pluralism. Such a situation is exciting but also intimidating for consensus-building liberals like Damrosch. Throughout the novel, he cuts a diffident and awkward figure alongside his friends, as they banter confidently about critics and philosophers from Adorno to Žižek. Not only does their easy fluency in the language of theory leave him nursing a mild inferiority complex, but their sharply personal and often abrasive exchanges grate uncomfortably with his instincts as a compromiser and peacemaker. For all Damrosch's attempts to find common ground, the disagreements between his brilliantly opinionated friends are never resolved to anyone's satisfaction. *Meetings of the Mind* is haunted by the anxiety that when contemporary literary scholars talk among themselves, not only are they unable to agree, but they are unable even to arrive at meaningful disagreement.

For some commentators on the culture wars, however, the demise of 'consensus' is not necessarily an intellectual disaster. In *The University in Ruins*, for example, Bill Readings argues that the academic world must learn to think of itself as a '*dissensual community*', because 'Thought can only do justice to heterogeneity if it does not aim at consensus'.[7] But for all its admirable commitment to the irreducibility of difference, even such a radically anti-consensual model as Readings's seems to presuppose some 'agree-to-differ' moment as the inaugurating gesture of the University of Dissensus. Consensus survives in his scheme of things as a communal ideal even if it has been officially abandoned as an intellectual goal. Damrosch's novel, on the other hand, adopts a much more conventionally liberal view that consensus and collaboration are honourable goals of scholarly activity, even if it is becoming increasingly difficult to square them with commitment to difference and heterogeneity.

Damrosch's most obvious 'solution' to the intellectual problems dramatized in *Meetings of the Mind* is to be found in the names of his central characters, each of which is an anagrammatic variation of his own name: the narrator's conference sparring partners are, it seems, simply versions or projections of his own intellectual identity. Which suggests that we cannot, after all, read this novel as a 'realistic' account of the cut-and-thrust of the conference circuit; rather, it is a guided tour of the different intellectual agendas that compete for attention in the author's own mind. By *psychologizing* the culture wars in this way, *Meetings of the*

Mind does not necessarily put an end to the conflict, but it certainly makes things easier to manage. Vic, Marsha and Dov function not as life-like, free-standing 'characters' but as spokespersons for ostensibly irreconcilable intellectual positions that have always-already been resolved in the person of the author-narrator.

Symbolically, the novel ends with Damrosch receiving an unusual birthday present from his polymathic alter egos: four articles, on everything from Aztec poetry to Buster Keaton films, that will add much-needed lustre to his respectable but somewhat colourless curriculum vitae. This act of handsome intellectual generosity strikingly differentiates the heroes of *Meetings of the Mind* from the rogues' gallery of self-serving careerists in other recent academic fictions, where plagiarism and theft of intellectual property are everyday crimes. What this scene of gift-giving seems to exemplify is a model of an academic culture in which knowledge will be freely shared rather than squabbled over or aggressively monopolized. With Dov's philosophical gravitas, Marsha's ideological commitment and Vic's eclectic brilliance, the novel's diffident liberal humanist is re-born, on his birthday, as an interdisciplinary multiculturalist in whom the sharp divisions of the culture wars are 'contained' as just so many facets of one rich, many-sided intellectual personality. This ending is a consciously utopian one, all the more so because Damrosch is, impossibly, giving *himself* a birthday present via his fictive alter egos. The novel thus finds its panacea for the culture wars in the very object – the gift – that Jacques Derrida has described as 'The very figure of the impossible'.[8]

Though *Meetings of the Mind* arrives at an unconventionally utopian conclusion, the story that it tells – that of the plodding liberal humanist scholar struggling to keep up with the brilliant *wunderkinder* of critical theory – has been a familiar one in campus fiction ever since Philip Swallow first crossed paths with Morris Zapp. A common version of this story describes the career arc of the gifted young academic whose love of literature leads not to fame, prestige or even job security, but into the wilderness of short-term contracts and postdoctoral fellowships, a meagre professional life measured out in rejected journal articles, unsuccessful job applications and unpublished books. This is broadly the position of Dr Nelson Humboldt, the hero of James Hynes's *The Lecturer's Tale* (2001), whose prodigious knowledge of western literature fails to secure him tenure at the 'University of the Midwest', where he has been toiling as a visiting adjunct lecturer.[9] Humboldt's devotion to literature seems not just quaintly old-fashioned but downright suspicious in an environment where the department chair, Anthony Pescecane, delivers an MLA keynote entitled 'The Fuck Cares about Edmund Spenser?' (112), where self-styled intellectual *terroristes* burn copies of Aristotle during theory seminars (19), and where students who use words like 'beauty', 'truth', 'author' or 'literary' are immediately flunked (290). But it is not just Humboldt's lack of appetite for theory that makes him surplus to requirements at Midwestern: in an academic culture dominated by identity politics, he crucially lacks the fashionable kudos of marginality. Like Percival Everett's *Erasure*, which lampoons the critical esteem and commercial success enjoyed by exploitative 'ghetto fiction', *The Lecturer's Tale* takes the commodification of 'otherness' in contemporary literary culture as a primary satirical target. Hynes's novel is a multiple exposé of theoretical impostors who have knowingly capitalized on their own cultural marginality or even faked 'exotic' credentials as a career move. The 'vaguely gallic' (19) Foucault look-a-like Professor Jean-Claude Evangeline proves to be plain old Bobby Evangeline from Louisiana. Nelson's office-mate, the painfully shy feminist theorist Vita Deonne, is revealed to be a man in drag. Most outrageously, Midwestern's star theorist, the 'lycanthropically hirsute' (40) Serbian refugee Marko Kraljević, is unmasked as the Serbian war criminal Slobodan Jamisovich, aka 'the Butcher of Srebrenica'. In a novel that displays a consistently keen eye for the role of clothes in fashioning a critic's academic persona, Hynes's various theoretical impostors mount a veritable fancy dress parade of exotic costumes and cunning disguises, flamboyantly illustrating Jean-Michel Rabaté's wry suggestion that theory has always been a '*Sartor Resartus* in progress'.[10]

Though Hynes clearly views identity politics as a legitimate target for ridicule, he also takes a broadly satirical view of those who self-pityingly complain that 'the Really Good Jobs were no longer going to Guys Like Us' (26). Hynes's response to the notion that white, middle-class, heterosexual male graduates have been disinherited of their academic birthright is to tell an ironic 'what-if?' story. What if the most 'powerless' and 'disenfranchised' member of a literature department – the liberal white heterosexual male with an interest in traditional literature – were to be granted temporary omnipotence? On the day of his sacking, Humboldt's right index finger is severed in a tragicomic pratfall in the college quad, but after surgery he mysteriously acquires the power to bend people to his will with the slightest touch of his reattached finger. Though he attempts to wield this power benignly, to bring a little 'balm and sweet reason to the culture wars' (103), an increasingly corrupt Humboldt soon finds himself wreaking havoc on campus, exacerbating existing divisions and provoking new enmities in a plot of escalating violence and mayhem.

From the initial severing of Humboldt's finger through to an apocalyptic finale in which the university library goes up in smoke, *The Lecturer's Tale* is a campus comedy in which intellectual aggression leads constantly to outbreaks of physical violence. Sometimes theoretical texts are presented as the culture warriors' weapons of choice – *Of Grammatology*, for example, lands in academia 'like a Molotov cocktail' (101), while *Discipline and Punish* is used by the Department Chair to brain his PA (196–7). But the novel's most violent act is perpetrated by a theorist on canonical literary texts. When Kraljević firebombs the old library's collection of classic literature the theoretical attack on the old literary canon is escalated from propaganda into open warfare. Dominating the novel's finale, the burning library functions as a savagely overblown symbol of the demise of traditional literary culture and the eclipse of a centuries-old canon by an upstart theoretical anti-canon. In the end, however, both the canon *and* the anti-canon go up in flames when the old tower full of literary classics topples into the futuristic annex that houses Midwestern's collection of sleek theory paperbacks. Ironically, the interdependence of theory and literature is only discovered at the very moment that they collapse violently into one another. Not, however, that the literary tradition has been wholly obliterated: displaying a quite exceptional range of canonical intertextualities from Chaucer and Milton to Joyce and Borges – Elaine Showalter calls it 'a Norton Anthology of a novel'[11] – *The Lecturer's Tale* virtually qualifies as a portable library in its own right, a literary time-capsule designed to survive the worst ravages of the theory wars.

It is difficult to contemplate the scenes of devastation in the final chapters of *The Lecturer's Tale* without thinking of the title of Bill Readings's radical critique of modern university culture: *The University in Ruins*. But it is the institution that rises triumphantly from the ashes of Kraljević's inferno that most closely corresponds to Readings's vision of the modern university. Once the custodian of a nation's highest cultural values, the modern university has become, according to Readings, a 'transnational bureaucratic corporation' run for the benefit of student-consumers and dedicated to an (entirely meaningless) quest for 'excellence' in all areas of performance.[12] With its corporate logo, biannual performance reviews and NFL franchise, the slick corporate venture that is Midwestern™ is unmistakably a branch of what Readings calls the global 'University of Excellence'. Whether this adds up, as Showalter suggests, to a 'positive and even utopian ending'[13] seems doubtful. What is clear, however, is that in the end the invisible hand of free market capitalism is more powerful than even the uncanny energies in Humboldt's right index finger.

As Midwestern's literature professors try on their company blazers and settle into their new role as salarymen and -women for 'America's One-Stop Education Resource!' (376), Hynes grants us a vision of a possible future in which theoretical differences will simply be smothered by a new corporate uniformity. Other commentaries on the culture wars have presented notably different versions of what 'life after theory' might look like. In *The Western Canon*, Harold Bloom envisions a future in which 'Every teaching institution will have its department of cultural studies ... and an aesthetic underground will flourish, restoring something of the romance of reading'.[14] According to Bloom's triumphantly pessimistic prophecy, literature will thrive as a dissident, minority pursuit in a world where the moral high ground *is* the underground. You could scarcely ask for a better illustration of what Readings calls the 'relentless self-marginalization' of combatants in the culture wars – Bloom is annexing for literature the very marginal cultural territory on which his theoretical adversaries stake their claim for recognition. It is as though both sides are fighting it out for the right to be considered the underdog.[15]

If some accounts of the culture wars are to be believed, however, the 'aesthetic underground' is not a figment of Bloom's imagination but an everyday reality in English departments where classic literary texts have yielded pride of place to the new theoretical anti-canon. In John L'Heureux's *The Handmaid of Desire* (1996), for example, literature finds itself some surprising bolt-holes in a crisis-ridden department that is riven by an intergenerational conflict between the pleasantly torpid traditionalists (the 'fools') and the stroppy young theorists (the 'young Turks').[16] The latter's ringleader, Professor Zachary Kurtz, plans to dissolve the English Department and erect in its place a new Department of Theory and Discourse dedicated to subjecting 'all written documents' to the 'probing, thrusting, hard-breathing analysis of the latest developments in metaphilosophical transliterary theory' (43). Kurtz, however, is addicted to the very literature for which he has such public disdain; in private he likes nothing better than locking himself away in his study with one of his beloved Jane Austen novels. This arch-theorist's passion for canonical literature is his shameful little secret, a guilty pleasure that can only be furtively enjoyed behind closed doors. Unlike his notoriously depraved Conradian namesake, then, Professor Kurtz's hair-raising secret is that he is *civilized*, privately devoted to the very high culture of which he seems such a barbarous enemy.

L'Heureux's 'outing' of his theoretical firebrand as a closet Austenite suggests that if the republic of letters now has a flourishing 'aesthetic underground', then even diehard theorists might harbour an 'aesthetic unconscious', a zone of repression into which the modern scholarly mind consigns its taboo literary appetites. Everywhere in his novel there are signs of these repressed appetites welling up to the surface. For example, Kurtz is not the only one of L'Heureux's theorists who consumes literary fiction in secret. When his colleague Robbie Richter suffers a nervous breakdown – brought on, predictably enough, by a traumatic overdose of theoretical reading – he uses his spell in hospital to rediscover his love of literature. Surprisingly enough, his literary recidivism is aided by the feminist theorist Olga Kominska, who brings him four Barbara Pym novels disguised in 'paper jackets from Foucault's multi-volume *History of Sexuality'* (77). It as though, in contemporary academic culture, literature can only qualify as legitimate reading matter if it camouflages itself as critical theory. In L'Heureux's novel, literary fictions have become the samizdats of the modern republic of letters, dissident texts to be circulated and consumed in secret by the subversive enemies of an oppressive theoretical orthodoxy. Literature is thus constructed by L'Heureux as the repressed 'other' of theory, the guilty secret and illicit pleasure of career post-structuralists; it also functions therapeutically, as it were, 'curing' Richter from the debilitating effects of his theory-induced breakdown. The image of Richter enjoying Barbara Pym novels in his hospital bed unmistakably echoes that of Kurtz stretched out on his study couch, nursing a splitting headache that is gently soothed as he rereads *Emma* for the umpteenth time (55). Together, Kurtz and Richter stand for a profession in the grip of an acute but short-term case of 'theorrhoea' that nurses itself back to full intellectual health on a diet of classic literary fiction.

It is in the enigmatic person of Olga Kominska that *The Handmaid of Desire* constructs its most complex model of fiction–theory relations. A visiting professor of feminist drama and literary theory, Kominska is trailed by Kurtz as a personification of the radical new department he wants to build. But with her chameleon-like changes of clothing, appearance and accent, Kominska never quite settles into the role of iconoclastic European theory guru that Kurtz wants her to play. This constant shape-shifting extends also into her literary career, during the course of which she has adopted a cannily bipartisan stance in the culture wars, producing two theoretical studies and two novels. Increasingly, it becomes clear that when Kominska disguises those Pym novels as Foucault texts, she is gesturing towards the literary identity that she conceals behind her theoretical persona. What is more, in a knowingly metafictional gesture, L'Heureux's novel grants Kominska a number of 'authorial' privileges – she seems to know other people's secrets, to be conscious that she is a character in a novel, and even to have a say in decisions about how its storyline develops. It is as though she is not just *The Handmaid of Desire*'s central character, but its unacknowledged co-author. The metafictional complexity of L'Heureux's text is intensified when Kominska elects to rescue the career of the department's failing novelist Francis Xavier Tortorisi by counselling him to write a salacious *roman à clef* about his colleagues. Through the figures of Kominska and Tortorisi, then, *The Handmaid of Desire* presents itself as an act of mischievous literary retaliation against the young Turks of the culture wars. Throughout the novel theorists who write off fiction are being *written into* fiction, absorbed by the very literary discourses that they hoped to subject to the mastery of their 'probing, thrusting, hard-breathing analysis'.

For all its metafictional sophistication, however, *The Handmaid of Desire* is thoroughly conventional in at least one respect: that is, its representation of theory as a discourse of the young. It is almost an unwritten rule of campus fiction that the theory wars represent the struggle of radicalized young academics to seize control of literary studies from the arthritic grasp of ageing fogies and senescent gentleman-scholars. However, the idea of theory as a discourse of the past rather than the future is strikingly articulated by Richard Powers's novel of ideas, *Galatea 2.2* (1995).[17] The novel's hero, 'Richard Powers', is the 'humanist fly on the wall' (36) at the Centre for the Study of Advanced Sciences at an unnamed Midwestern university where a team of neuroscientists are attempting to build a self-aware computer. Theory appears in the novel as something that weighs heavily on Powers's mind – he does not understand it, and finds it imaginatively stultifying, whilst for his robustly sceptical scientist colleagues it is simply a joke, a form of lazy intellectual solipsism that contributes nothing to the quest for genuine knowledge. In the event, neuroscience and post-structuralist theory are brought into direct competition by an experiment that requires the 'self-aware' computer and a graduate literature student both to comment on the same two lines from *The Tempest*. The point of the exercise is to see if a machine can fake a 'human' response to literature, but one notable result of the experiment is a sharpened realization of the extent to which human responses have themselves been 'mechanized' by theory. The student produces a 'more or less brilliant New Historicist reading' that treats the play as 'a take on colonial wars, constructed Otherness, the violent reduction society works on itself' (326). The irony here is that this New Historicist/postcolonial reading of *The Tempest* is so predictable that it might as well have been produced by a machine, whereas the machine's response is much more quirky, personal and 'human' than that of the theoretically over-educated student. Like David Lodge's *Thinks ...*, then, Powers's novel broaches an exciting new dialogue between literature and science to which theory has precious little of interest to contribute. Though *Galatea 2.2* is by no means centrally concerned with critical theory, it does strikingly imagine a future in which theory will play no significant role, its achievements having been dwarfed by the continuing eminence of classic literature and the brave new world of cognitive science and artificial intelligence.

A very different take on the *passé* radicalism of theory is offered by Perceval Everett's outlandish postmodern fable, *Glyph* (1999). This novel's hero and narrator, Ralph Townsend, is a hyperintelligent toddler with an IQ of 475 and a photographic memory who can read and write from the age of ten months, but chooses not to develop or exercise the power of speech.[18] Having reached the grand old age of 4, Ralph takes the opportunity to review the ideas and personalities that dominated his singularly eventful babyhood, writing with measured scorn on Barthesian narratology, Derridean deconstruction and Lacanian psychoanalysis, but reserving special contempt for his father, a minor post-structuralist critic. In Ralph's private mental world, the story of post-structuralism and its discontents is played out as an engagingly preposterous variation on the Freudian family romance:

> My father was a poststructuralist and my mother hated his guts. They did not know – how could they have known? – that by the age of ten months I not only comprehended all that they were saying but that I was as well marking time with a running commentary on the value and sense of their babbling. (6)

Theory is mockingly personified in Everett's novel as an oppressive father figure with whom its infant narrator is locked in an Oedipal struggle. Reversing the conventional representation of theorists as the juvenile delinquents of the literary scene, *Glyph* represents theory as something that belongs to the discredited past rather than to some glorious and intimidating future. Ralph's 'poststructuralist pretender' (44) of a father thus stands for the all the pretences of post-structuralism that this infant prodigy is consigning to the scrap-heap of intellectual history. Another key reversal here is implied by the image of a literate baby eavesdropping on the 'babbling' of its mother and father. This surreal up-ending of the conventional linguistic relations between parents and children initiates the novel's running joke about the 'infantile' qualities

of supposedly grown-up, sophisticated discourses – not least the language of critical theory. As a form of presemantic babble or nonsensical
infantile chatter, post-structuralism thus represents everything that
Ralph has bypassed.

Conspicuous examples of such 'theory-babble' are to be found in the
cryptic sub-headings – many of them Derridean – that break up *Glyph*'s
narrative. Terms such as *'différance'*, 'pharmakon', and 'supplement'
interrupt the text in an apparently arbitrary and gratuitous manner,
whilst the linguistic and narratological diagrams from Barthes, Greimas,
Morris, Hjelmslev, Saussure – and Ralph himself – that appear at the
beginning of each new chapter seem like nothing more than ironic,
functionless decorations, background theoretical 'noise' that needs to be
filtered out, rather than amplified, if the reader is to make any headway
with Everett's storyline. It might however be added that some readers
have made resourceful attempts to unscramble the theoretical codes of
Glyph. In a perceptive discussion of the novel, Jacqueline Berben-Masi
speculates ingeniously on the links between the novel's theoretical
superstructure and its thematic content – but even she concludes that the
various theoretical models on display in *Glyph* need to be understood as
forms of 'metatextual prison', mental cages that constantly threaten to
close down on Ralph's prodigiously expansive intellectual development.[19]
Implicit in Berben-Masi's discussion is a recognition that theory is something to dwell on but not to inhabit, and that it is important not to let
our reading of *Glyph* be confined by the metatextual prisons from which
Ralph himself bids to escape.

But the novel does not promise any simple liberation from theory, not
least because of the fact that Ralph is in many ways a *product* of the
theoretical imagination, and that his situation seems irresistibly to
demand theoretical analysis. There is something curiously 'Derridean',
for example, about Ralph's choice of writing over speech as his preferred –
indeed sole – means of communication; it is as though Everett's infant
prodigy wants to throw his intellectual weight behind the critique of
voice-centred thinking launched in *Of Grammatology*. Except that Ralph
is no fan of 'that Derrida guy', branding *Of Grammatology* 'a sick discussion
at best' (110n3) in the course of a witheringly sceptical discussion of the
logic of the supplement. Elsewhere he rattles off a paragraph-long
parody of 'Différance' – '*Rin* instead of *run* ... neither a *word* nor a *concept*'
(159–60) – in a nonchalantly jaundiced display of fluency in a language
he cannot take remotely seriously.

If *Glyph* emphatically rebuffs its Derridean readers, it is even less hospitable to Lacanian analysis. Not that there is a shortage of raw material in

the novel for Lacanians to go to work on: after all, this is a story about the emergence of human subjectivity, the acquisition of language (but non-acquisition of speech) by an infant on the threshold of the symbolic order. Indeed, the first psychoanalyst to examine Ralph, one Dr Steimmel, hails him as nothing less than 'the link between the imaginary and symbolic phases' (51). Ralph himself is prone to the occasional Lacanian reflection on his own subjectivity, and at one point even launches into a detailed commentary on a well-known passage from 'The Agency of the Letter in the Unconscious':

> I am not wherever I am the plaything of my thought;
> I think of what I am where I do not think to think.[20]

> I had no problem with the Other, myself the Other, myself, or any bold line drawn between myself and the world, between signifier and signified and certainly, not for one second, was I troubled by a notion that in considering my conscious I-self that I was inhabiting or obscuring the line of any division between any of those things or my perception or conception of them. Blah blah blah. (145)

In Lodge's *Nice Work*, Robyn and Charles agree that this same passage of Lacan is 'marvellous' stuff (177–8), but Ralph is considerably less impressed – not because he violently disagrees but because he regards it as tediously obvious theory-babble. Lacan's anti-Cartesian one-liner is for Ralph nothing more than a mental plaything with which he quickly gets bored. On the whole, Lacanian thoughts only really preoccupy Ralph when he is on his potty, where he finds that meditating on desire, identification, lack and the phallus serves as the perfect mental laxative to facilitate his 'defecatory mission' (164). The novel is full of such cheerfully scatological associations between the hero's unpredictable bowel movements and what it represents as the mental diarrhoea of post-structuralism.

Lacan's position as the intellectual villain of the piece is consolidated when the Lacanian psychoanalyst Dr Steimmel kidnaps Ralph and takes him to a secret research laboratory where she plans to uncover the secrets of language acquisition by cutting open his brain. (In a nod to Lacan's essay on the mirror stage, which famously contrasts human infants with primates, Ralph discovers that one of his fellow inmates is a chimpanzee with a working knowledge of sign language.) But this is only the first episode of Ralph's adventures. He is subsequently kidnapped by a shadowy government agency, from whom he is in turn kidnapped by a childless couple desperate for a baby of their own; he then very nearly falls into the clutches of a pederastic priest who plans to perform an exorcism on him. Overall, Ralph's melodramatic ordeal rivals the one undergone by the long-suffering Text in *Masterpiece Theatre*, where abduction and hostage taking function as metaphors for violently unscrupulous forms of reading. Variously abducted, caged, strapped and restrained, Ralph is deprived of his liberty at every turn, reduced to the status of a scientific specimen to be experimented on, monitored, measured, analysed, tested and dissected. The ordeal of Everett's infant prodigy and serial abductee is thus a sustained exercise in 'textual paranoia', a bizarre allegory of the fate of the postmodern text that knows much, much more than its readers but is wholly powerless in their hands.

Shortly after the baby's abduction, Roland Barthes of all people begins to make a nuisance of himself by hanging around the Townsend house – almost in the capacity of a 'replacement' Ralph. He is portrayed as an exasperating poseur, in love with the sound of his own voice and oblivious to anyone else's, a master of long-winded digressions and hair-splitting equivocation on all matters. At various points in the novel he is on the receiving end of violence – kneed in the groin and brained with a coffee can by Ralph's mother, and later knocked unconscious by a wild blow from Dr Steimmel. Such moments of violence evidently function as displaced versions of the novel's fantasy of aiming a punch directly at post-structuralism. But elsewhere *Glyph* takes things out on Barthes in a more subtle parodic fashion by mimicking the voice and characteristic gestures of his criticism. In a critical vocabulary borrowed directly from the opening rationale of *S/Z*, Ralph explains that his fragmented narrative has been arbitrarily divided into 'lexia and sub-lexia' in order to transform it into a manageable set of 'reading units' (162). For Ralph, this strategy marks *Glyph* out as a systematic 'analysis of itself' (162), one that comprehensively exhausts its own interpretative possibilities:

> If I may, I say that I am a complete reading system. My meaning is exactly mine and I mean only those things I seek to mean, all other possible meanings having been considered and sifted from the material whole. I assert that no other reading than the one I intend is possible and I defy any interpretation beyond my mission. (163)

Ralph's hostility towards various celebrated post-structuralist readers is at this point being redirected squarely at his own reader. But he is clearly protesting all too much about his imagined monopoly on the meaning of his text – it is a fantasy of power that has its roots in his experience of powerlessness at the hands of his various captors. At this point in the novel his dream that every theoretical reading can be intellectually out-flanked, parodically deflated or simply laughed out of court has never seemed less plausible.

Ralph's claim that his text is an impregnably self-contained 'complete reading system' is clearly open to challenge – and it is intriguing to see that the challenge was indirectly taken up by Everett himself in his next novel, *Erasure* (2001).[21] This novel presents itself as the 'journal' of Thelonious Ellison, a Professor of English at UCLA who writes fiction that does not sell – 'retellings of Euripides and parodies of French post-structuralists' (4). Not only is this material impossibly highbrow, but it is crucially – as his agent explains – 'not black enough' (49). Ellison, who deploys terms like *black*, and *gritty*, and *real world* in wincing italics, is deeply suspicious of the commodification of 'authenticity' implied in his publisher's advice to write 'the true, gritty real stories of black life' (4), and initially prefers to concentrate on his latest experimental work, a novel entitled *F/V* that treats Barthes's *S/Z* exactly as Barthes's text treats Balzac's *Sarrasine*. At a meeting of the *Nouveau Roman* Society, he delivers the opening of this work, which subjects the title and the first one-and-a-half sentences of Barthes's text to microscopic structuralist analysis (18–22). It is certainly clever stuff, but you are also grateful to be spared the 1000-odd pages that a comprehensive Barthesian reading of Barthes's reading of Balzac would run to. Ellison's Barthesian novel promises to be an epic of postmodern unreadability, guaranteed to alien-ate what is left of his readership. So *Erasure* is in part a critical reflection on the vein of experimental self-indulgence in *Glyph*, though when Everett parodies his own parodies of Barthes, we have clearly come up against the dead-end of what Frederic Jameson calls 'blank parody' – literary imitation that has become somehow mechanical, perfunctory and uninflected by humour.[22]

If *Erasure* begins by presenting us with a writer who has been imagi-natively paralyzed by his theoretical obsessions, a broader view of recent US academic fiction reveals a generation of writers who have been energized by the theoretical controversies of the culture wars. By compar-ison with the campus fiction of David Lodge, recent US fiction has been broader in its intellectual range, in line with the broadening horizons of 'literary' studies. For example, whereas *Small World* dramatizes conflicting interpretations of canonical works, *Meetings of the Mind* covers silent movies, Barthes essays, children's fiction and Latin American poetry, and contains impromptu critical dissections of everything from Japanese museum architecture to Mexican folk art to the death cults of pharaonic Egypt. Even more striking than its expansion of the genre's intellectual range, however, have been the formal innovations of recent US campus fiction. Though these novels return frequently to the question of what life after theory might look like, they each provide evidence of an irrepressible literary creativity that will outlast the intellectual quarrels of the day. In the camp melodrama of *Masterpiece Theatre*, the split-personality *jeu d'esprit* of *Meetings of the Mind*, the Gothic fantasy of *The Lecturer's Tale*, the metafictional God-games of *The Handmaid of Desire*, the near-future science fiction of *Galatea 2.2* and the outlandish fabulation of *Glyph*, literary fiction has offered abundant proof of its vitality and variety at the height of the culture wars.

5
The Vanishing Author

'The story of an author', says Aleid Fokkema, 'is told again and again in postmodern texts'.[1] Citing examples of author-obsessed texts by Peter Ackroyd, Julian Barnes, Angela Carter, J. M. Coetzee and many others, she further points out that the author's emergence as *the* stock character of postmodern fiction occurs at a time when reports of the 'death of the author' are still echoing powerfully through the literary world. It seems that no sooner is the author pronounced dead by post-structuralist critics than s/he has been granted a stay of execution and a vibrant new lease of life in the pages of theoretically self-conscious fiction. On the face of it, the rise of the 'author novel' thus looks like a defiantly anti-theoretical gesture, emphatically at odds with the post-structuralist view that the author is an obsolete non-entity. But, then again, to reinvent the author as a *fictional* character is not necessarily the best way of proving that s/he is robustly alive: the author-as-character conceit could equally suggest that writers have *always* been simply figments of the literary imagination, that the author has always been nothing more than a plausible frontman for the quite impersonal operations of textuality. In this chapter I will explore these issues by considering the questions of authorship and authority as they are taken up by Malcolm Bradbury's *Mensonge* (1987), *Doctor Criminale* (1992) and *To the Hermitage* (2000), Gilbert Adair's *The Death of the Author* (1992) and John Banville's *Shroud* (2002). These novels are distinctive for their focus on the *critic* as author – or, to be more specific, the *post-structuralist* as author: Bradbury's Henri Mensonge, Bazlo Criminale and Jack-Paul Verso, Adair's Léopold Sfax and Banville's Axel Vander are all wedded to their particular models of authorial anonymity or non-being, while continuing to write, publish and be fêted as intellectual celebrities. Bradbury, Adair and Banville thus read post-structuralist theory back into the lives of its most enthusiastic

59

champions, and in doing so their novels oscillate between two versions of the 'story of an author'. On the one hand they offer variations on the theme of the 'return of the repressed' – the necessary recuperation or unavoidable resurgence of the old authorial self that recent critics have been far too eager to bury. On the other, the author in these stories tends to play the role of the 'man who wasn't there': time and again, the author-hero in Bradbury, Adair and Banville proves to be a ghost, a missing person with whom the postmodern reader will never be satisfactorily reunited. Incidentally, I use the gender-specific terms 'frontman' and 'man who wasn't there' advisedly in this context, because I am dealing with a cluster of novels that, for all their theoretical savvy, focus on the demise or disappearance of male authors without devoting any special attention to the fate of the female author in the age of post-structuralism. In the course of Chapter 6 I will discuss how Patricia Duncker's fiction shakes up traditional masculinist conceptions of authorship, and in Chapter 7 I will examine the question of female authorship as it is raised by the feminist fiction of Angela Carter and A. S. Byatt.[2]

The theoretical challenge to traditional models of authorship has been most influentially articulated in two landmark essays: Roland Barthes's 'The Death of the Author' (1968) and Michel Foucault's 'What is an Author?' (1969).[3] A calculated affront to literary-critical commonsense, Barthes's essay toys with the outrageously counter-intuitive idea that texts somehow write themselves or are retroactively ghostwritten by their own readers. The author – that flesh-and-blood individual with a pen, typewriter or word processor – does not come into it; the 'identity of the body writing' (142) is simply erased by the text to clear a space for the new arbiter of meaning, the reader. Now you could, if you wished, begin to pick holes in Barthes's arguments on the grounds of intellectual consistency. Seán Burke, for example, convicts post-structuralists of the '*folie circulaire* of *authoring* and *authorising* the disappearance of the subject, of *declaring* that no-one speaks'.[4] But there is precious little mileage in a literal-minded quarrel with Barthes on the question of whether authors really do exist as historical individuals, since he would scarcely deny this. Some three years after 'The Death of the Author', Barthes was already hailing the 'amicable return of the author',[5] and subsequently went on to produce a quirky autobiography, *Roland Barthes* (1975). 'The Death of the Author' does not deny the historical existence of authors, but rather aims to demolish a particular *version* of the author as it functions in the kind of literary criticism that subordinates work to life, achievement to intention, writing to psychology. Author-centred critics, those who speak of 'reading Shakespeare' or 'reading Proust', are for Barthes in the grip of a naïve anthropomorphic fallacy that misrecognizes a piece of writing as a human personality. To ground the act of reading in an appeal to the author's life, beliefs or intentions is simply a way of bypassing the complexities of textuality; the author-centred critic who claims access – however illusory – to the text's biographical prehistory always holds a spurious trump card in the game of interpretation. As Barthes says, 'To give a text an Author is to impose a limit on that text, to furnish it with a final signified, to close the writing' (147). For this reason the author – in the sense of the God-like figure who precedes, produces, controls and limits textual meaning – has become *persona non grata* in post-Barthesian criticism.

Foucault's 'What is an Author?', which reads like a wide-ranging sequel to Barthes's polemical essay, is framed by the provocative non-question 'What does it matter who is speaking?'. Like Barthes, Foucault regards the text as 'its author's murderer' (206) rather than a vehicle for self-expression or passport to literary immortality. He also echoes Barthes's argument that the author traditionally functions in critical discourse as the limit of the text, the 'regulator of the fictive' who controls and limits the 'proliferation of meaning' (222). But Foucault develops and challenges Barthes's position in two important ways. First, he does not share Barthes's confidence that the author can be eliminated from critical discourse at the stroke of a pen. Any shift of emphasis from the real-life author to 'the work' can only raise the question: 'the work by whom?'. Even in fashionable critical talk of '*écriture*', the author survives as a 'transcendental anonymity' (208), a nameless origin above or behind the text. Second, whereas Barthes perhaps too hastily installs the reader in the space vacated by the author, Foucault argues that we need to take the time to inspect the 'space left empty by the author's disappearance' (209). For Foucault, post-structuralist theory has created an author-shaped gap in the text that needs to be rigorously analysed rather than peremptorily filled with a new surrogate author.

It is tempting to read the 'author novel' as a genre that implicitly takes up Foucault's challenge to inspect the author-shaped gap in the text. The question that is asked time and again by novels in this tradition is not 'what is an author?' but 'where is the author?'. An entertainingly droll version of this 'man who wasn't there' narrative is offered by *Mensonge*, Malcolm Bradbury's spoof biography of the neglected French genius Henri Mensonge, the philosopher whose work has 'out-Barthesed Barthes, out-Foucaulted Foucault, out-Derridaed Derrida, out-Deleuzed-and-Guttaried Deleuze and Guttari'.[6] Mensonge is the unsung hero of modern critical theory, hugely influential – he seems to have inspired a whole generation of French structuralists and post-structuralists – but quite exceptionally self-effacing. This 'elusive non-author' (39) and 'laureate of absence' (81) has vanished from the public eye leaving behind nothing except the odd handkerchief, overcoat and unpaid bill. *Mensonge's* narrator, a breathlessly enthusiastic British academic, musters only a handful of biographical facts about his intellectual hero – he seems to have been born (like Kristeva and Todorov) in Bulgaria and educated in France, where he became a Barthes protégé and contributed to the journal *Qeul Tel* under a variety of pseudonyms. Apparently he has since taught classics at the little-known University of Paris XIV (clearly the Rummidge of French academe), but beyond that precious little is known of the great man, apart from occasional unverified sightings, rumours that he may have resurfaced in Munich, Wyoming or Provence, and unconfirmed reports of the appearance of a (non-)autobiography entitled *Non-Mensonge par Non-Mensonge*.

Mensonge's disappearance from public life in the late 1960s coincides, as the narrator points out, with the publication of the 'Death of the Author' – a retreat into self-imposed anonymity that seems to have been conducted in a spirit of fundamentalist obedience to the letter of Barthes's new theoretical law. The very personification of deconstructive thought, Mensonge has become a floating signifier, a human aporia, a non-self, the 'purest instance we have of *la mort de l'auteur*' (27). Whereas the personality of the famous literary recluse – a Pynchon or Salinger, say – might be characterized as an '*absent presence*', Mensonge has entered into the altogether more rarefied state of '*absent absence*' (26). The question of whether Mensonge ever existed in the first place is an open one. Nor does Mensonge's published work promise to occupy the stage he has vacated. He disowns his published writings and discourages people from reading them, claiming either that they are not his or that they do not exist. His masterwork, *La Fornication comme acte culturel*, runs to 39 pages in some versions, 115 pages in others, and 'constantly disputes with what may be previous or alternatively subsequent versions of itself' (67). Only a few copies of this reputedly untranslatable text were ever produced, full of possibly deliberate typographical errors and apparently printed on toilet paper treated with an acid that will cause all copies, sooner or later, to self-destruct. *La Fornication*, which the narrator hails as the 'greatest unread work of our times' (68), is evidently both unread and unreadable.

With his enigmatic life-story and unreadable texts, 'Mensonge' functions in the novella as a peg on which to hang a satirical history of structuralism and deconstruction; or, to be more precise, a satirical history of the credulously enthusiastic *reception* of those theories in Anglophone literary circles. The novel is less an attack on the *mensonges* of Parisian theorists than on the myths, fantasies and exaggerations that circulate among their admirers. Bradbury's wide-eyed narrator emerges as a supremely gullible champion of Mensongian theorizing, confident that the esoteric unreadability of his hero's writings is a sure sign of profundity – 'in the sphere of philosophy, as of everything else', he assures us, 'obscurity is there for a purpose, and not to confuse us' (3). The narrator's exaggerated sense of Mensonge's revolutionary impact on post-structuralism is rivalled only by his exaggerated sense of post-structuralism's revolutionary role in the history of ideas. '[N]ot since the Greeks first looked up from their ouzo and started to speculate about the meaning of the universe', he claims, 'has so remarkable a revolution in human thought occurred' (8). The narrator's grand overstatements typically stumble into bathos: structuralism and deconstruction, for example, are described as the natural correlates of 'our chiliasm, our apocalypticism, our post-humanist scepticism, our postmodernism, our metaphysical exhaustion, our taste for falafel' (5). With this characteristic slump from high seriousness to frivolous trend-spotting, the novel's prose ironically reproduces the banal *zeitgeist*-chasing rhetoric of the journalistic think-piece. 'Post-structuralism', to its popular consumers, is more a lifestyle accessory than a life-changing philosophy, a chic continental fad, on a par with experimental diets, ephemeral fashion trends, espresso coffee and *nouvelle cuisine*.

Bathos is a governing principle of *Mensonge*'s structure as well as its prose. It soon becomes clear that the novella is unlikely to grant us a face-to-face audience with its reclusive hero: what we are reading is a long-winded preamble to a quest that never gets properly underway. Mensonge is not referred to by name until chapter three of this ten-chapter novella; commentary on his work does not begin in earnest until chapter 9. Given Mensonge's legendary elusiveness, this is hardly surprising; but whereas the French philosopher craves anonymity, his English biographer evidently has designs on fame, carefully insinuating himself into the gaps left by his subject. Though he refers to himself as nothing more than a 'footnote to a footnote, a sub-sub-sub-librarian' (69), the narrator's performance is an exercise in coy self-promotion. He is, we learn, an 'old-fashioned scholar' (51) who works on obscure Elizabethan poetry, and is conducting an extra-marital affair with 'the girl in the post office' (which raises the suspicion that 'Mensonge' may be nothing more than an alibi for the occasional dirty weekend in Paris). *Mensonge* is thus a wry portrait of the amateurish efforts of an out-of-touch British don, who stumbles upon French theory almost by chance in the course of his ill-informed reading in twentieth-century literature, to reinvent himself as a post-structuralist. Or, more generally, it depicts the clumsy attempts of a generation of middle-aged British literary scholars to remain fashionable and up to date by having a fling with French theory. However, theory's appeal is seen in rather darker terms when we learn that the narrator witnessed a memorable lecture on – and possibly by – Mensonge at a conference deep in the Australian rain-forest, where he obtained a tattered copy of *La Fornication*, and subsequently joined the 'world network of devoted Mensongians' (60). The Conradian image of Mensonge as a charismatic voice in the jungle positions him as the Kurtz of post-structuralist theory – a name without a self, a disembodied voice at the centre of a sinister cult.

In the figure of Mensonge, the novel posits the existence of a writer who was *either* the great *ur*-theorist whose radical writings founded the very language of post-structuralism *or* a minor and possibly illusory side effect of that same movement. Both possibilities are exploited by Bradbury to poke fun at theory and its earnest disciples. The notion that post-structuralism might have an unacknowledged 'founding father' is, of course, quite alien to its own view that discourse has no *fons et origio*; but the cult of personality built up by Mensonge's disciples around their absent master amounts to an involuntary heresy against that key lesson of post-structuralism. On the other hand, the possibility that Mensonge may simply be an occasional *nom de guerre* for Derrida or one of Barthes's or Foucault's lesser-known epigones or even a collective figment of the imagination, fictitious even in the diegesis of the novel, suggests that even if the author is dead, it seems necessary – at least in the cultishly devoted minds of theorists – to reinvent him. For Bradbury's earnest narrator, the long-standing theory that there 'simply was *no Mensonge* – that he was a hypothetical figure or a convenient fiction, invented by some teasing journalist, hack writer or complex theoretician' (30) remains a source of nagging anxiety. Ultimately, Mensonge is the invention of a complex, teasing novelist, whose point is that theoreticians are still enslaved to the cult of the author. Except that Bradbury does not enjoy the last word on Mensonge – that privilege is reserved for another fictitious French theorist, David Lodge's narratologist Michel Tardieu, who contributes a 'Foreword/Afterword' to the volume. Or could this be Bradbury posing as Lodge posing as Tardieu? In this case Foucault's question – 'What does it matter who is speaking?' – is probably the best answer.

In *To the Hermitage*, Bradbury continues his fictional investigation into the fate of the authorial self in an age of deconstruction.[7] The narrator, an unnamed British novelist, is invited by an international committee to join various participants in the so-called 'Diderot Project' on an intellectual pilgrimage to St Petersburg, where the great French writer had been sage-in-residence to Catherine the Great. Bradbury's novel uses the theme of one writer's legacy to launch a broad meditation on the vagaries of history that grant some human personalities monumental permanence while scattering others to oblivion. The authorial self in *To the Hermitage* is somehow both imperishably solid and spectrally insubstantial; or, to borrow the novel's two central images, both a piece of grand public statuary and a face drawn in the sand.

To the Hermitage engages with theoretical arguments about the demise of authorship by closely examining actual deaths of authors. With time on his hands in Stockholm, where Descartes died of pneumonia, the narrator scours the city in a quest for the final resting place of 'the father of the cogito' (36). Though his quest is unsuccessful, he does learn the macabre story of the great philosopher's remains – he died in Stockholm where he was buried in an unconsecrated graveyard, before being dug up and reburied twice, first in Copenhagen, then in Paris. Each time Descartes' body was moved, bones went missing, and his skull was reportedly cut into pieces after the French Revolution – though an intact Descartes skull is apparently also on display in a Paris museum. Bradbury uses the mystery of Descartes' absence from his death-place as an allegory for the vanishing of the cogito, the eclipse of the Enlightenment self by postmodernist thought. The macabre scattering and doubling of Descartes' mortal remains, meanwhile, is like a gothic version of the demise of the unique, rational, coherent self in an era of postmodern fragmentation. In true gothic fashion, however, Descartes' death was simply the prelude to a hectic afterlife, since he was 'unquestionably much busier, better travelled, more argued over, more problematical, more celebrated, more entertained, in every respect far more attended to than he ever had been during his rather reclusive quiet life' (151). Nor, despite its grisly details, is Descartes' story an exceptional one in the history of authorship. Paradoxically, an author's life begins in earnest only when he or she dies; or, as the narrator puts it, 'Posterity' is 'the place where literature becomes literary' (153). If the author is never more alive and well than after s/he has been officially declared dead, then criticism must learn to think of itself as a form of 'postmortemism' or 'necrology' – a formal study of the dead (151). In proposing this new gothic model of the author as animated corpse, Bradbury's narrator both parodies and challenges ghoulish post-structuralist talk of the death of the author and the subject. His commonsense point is that there is something curiously redundant in proclaiming the 'death' of an author like Descartes or Diderot; the challenge for the critic is not to bury them all over again, but to find ways in which they might still be culturally alive.

The narrator's abortive quest for Descartes's remains functions in the novel as a dry run for his lengthier investigation into the legacy of Denis Diderot. The author to whom the novel dedicates its necrological curiosity was a man of limitless philosophical curiosity, interested, as one enthusiast puts it, in 'every who, which, why, what and however that existed or might exist in the world' (90). He was a voracious and polymathic reader, and a prolific novelist, essayist and correspondent – as well as author of a twenty-eight volume *Encyclopedia* that has been dubbed 'the Bible of the Age of Reason' (106). In short, Diderot was the author of the grandest of Enlightenment narratives, the architect of proud monuments to humanist rationality; as such, he might seem an eminently suitable target for a post-structuralist demolition job. But there is another side to this complex figure. Diderot was, as his successor at the Hermitage library explains, 'a writer with many faces – not only a thinker and a philosopher, but a trickster, a tease, a very modern writer ... He was a dreamer, a fantasist, a liar, a maker of the strangest stories' (320). Just as Descartes somehow acquires two skulls, Diderot seems to have two selves. From a distance, he looks like an Enlightenment encyclopedist, but if you look more closely he begins to resemble a postmodern anti-encyclopedist, an exponent of the intellectual playfulness that twentieth-century writers sometimes naïvely assume they have invented. Not that *To the Hermitage* canvasses earnestly for the idea of a 'postmodern Diderot'; rather, it invokes the tempting *possibility* of this idea as a rebuke to those postmodernists who, when they contemplate the literature of earlier centuries, can see only the fossils of dinosaurs.

To the Hermitage draws explicit attention to the 'doubleness' of its author-hero in the scene where two sculptors work simultaneously on statues of Diderot (369). Statues provide his novel with three-dimensional emblems of the aspirations of authors – and human beings in general – to outlive their allotted time on earth. 'In a godless world', says the narrator, 'statues are our one ideal Posterity – what we should be aiming for, an apotheosis, a final and complete granite selfhood ... life held in marble, biography done in bronze' (70). The problem with this dream of granite selfhood and bronze biography is that a sculpted self is alive only in the eyes of a sympathetic spectator. Étienne-Maurice Falconet's famous statue of Peter the Great, for example, comes to life in the imagination of the poets who celebrate its 'potent menace, its strange power to pass through the streets by night' (135). And Diderot momentarily takes a statue of Voltaire for the man himself (165–6) – though in the fame of his old age, Voltaire will indeed become 'his own statue' (478). Just as Voltaire proves that statuesque immortality can be achieved in one's own lifetime, Falconet proves that works of art are every bit as perishable as human beings when he takes a hammer to his plaster head of Diderot (375). Brooding over the contrary ideals of statues-as-people and people-as-statues, this novel works to unravel any neat opposition between the formal permanence of art and the precious transience of flesh-and-blood life. Statues and busts thus function throughout the novel as ambiguous icons of both immortality *and* lifelessness.

Bradbury's novel is deeply exercised by the question of 'life after death' – the survival of the author in his or her writings, or the survival of the individual *as* a work of art. These necrological preoccupations are linked to a wider anxiety over the reported demise of the 'grand and glorious self' (484) in the age of post-structuralism. *To the Hermitage* takes its refrain from the closing words of *The Order of Things*, where Foucault famously prophesies that the end of the present intellectual dispensation will witness the death of the subject – man will be 'erased, like a face drawn in sand at the edge of the sea'.[8] Cited or echoed frequently in Bradbury's novel (119, 131, 426, 436, 445, 456, 460), this image of the self as an all-too-erasable face in the sand acquires a pathos that it does not carry in Foucault. In a novel full of dreams of statuesque permanence, the face in the sand denotes the ephemeral insubstantiality of human life.

The one character who resists all nostalgia for the old humanist self is the American deconstructionist Jack-Paul Verso, Professor of Contemporary Thinking at Cornell. Verso styles himself an enemy of reason, is cheerfully scornful of the 'dear old cogito' (192), and cites Foucault's end-of-man prophecy with positive gusto. With his 'I LOVE DECONSTRUCTION' baseball cap and hedonistic appetites, Verso is the Morris Zapp of *To the Hermitage*, the flashy, extrovert theorist whose larger-than-life personality is conspicuously at odds with his austere theories of emptied selfhood. Also incongruous is the upbeat tone in which Verso spells out his frankly apocalyptic theories:

When he [Barthes] talks about the Death of the Author, he's telling us there are no writers, only writing, because writing is trapped in language and is not attached to a real world. So what he's talking about isn't the Death of the Author. It's the Death of Authority. In other words, he's doing for all of us. (194)

Leaping fearlessly from the death of the author to failure of linguistic reference to the death of the self, Verso lectures like a fast-talking sales-man running through a script he has pitched a thousand times before. Though his allegation that Barthes's essay represents a death-sentence for 'all of us' is preposterously exaggerated, Verso's lecture does never-theless seem to predict his own strange disappearance from the world of the novel. As the Diderot pilgrimage progresses, Verso drifts increasingly from center stage into obscurity: if he begins the novel in the Morris Zapp role, he ends it as an American Henri Mensonge. And when he mysteriously vanishes from St Petersburg – rumours place him in Moscow or maybe further east, no one knows for sure – he provides con-firmation of his own pet theory about the disappearance of the subject. As the narrator bids a thoughtful farewell to the 'funky professor, whose face was once so visible ... till it dissolved into the sand on the edge of the waves' (456), it seems as though *To the Hermitage* has banished the deconstructionist and his theories to permanent exile in some remote Siberia of the mind.

Although Verso's deconstruction is represented as a theoretical force that seems to cancel itself out, Bradbury's novel does nevertheless exhibit a broadly 'Derridean' fascination with the duplicity of the written word. On the one hand it is possible to think of writing in conventional terms as a medium in which authorial subjectivity expresses and preserves itself. But writing also has a life of its own – it can fend for itself in the arena of communication without an authorial chaperone keeping an eye on things. Paradoxically, then, texts seem both to monumentalize and to dissolve their authors, to endow them with granite selfhood yet erase them like faces in the sand. *To the Hermitage* involves itself know-ingly in these paradoxes of writing, most conspicuously in its representa-tion of grand literary monuments – archives, libraries, encyclopaedias – as prone to all the slipperiness of Derridean textuality. Not only has the Hermitage library been rocked by war, fire, revolution and the atten-tions of philistine Czars, but the Voltaire/Diderot collection has prolif-erated itself wildly across many languages and places. Copyists have produced many versions of Diderot's books; some of his papers are hidden or have disappeared for good; others have been officially copied and published; others have been scattered across Europe to resurface as 'forgeries' or unauthorized editions. The Diderot collection is riddled with 'blanks, apertures, elisions, or (as the theoreticians now like to say) aporias' (391). But it also contains surprising excesses. Diderot's copies of Richardson, Helvétius and Sterne are covered in underlinings, annotations and marginalia, scrawled with running commentary that often covers the printed type itself.

'So books breed books', the narrator concludes, 'writing breeds writing. The writer starts out as reader in order to become the new writer. In this fashion one book can actually become the author of a new one' (387). This is not quite the same as Verso's inflated claim that there are 'no writers, only writing'. Rather, it has become all but impossible to separate Diderot from his writings, or the real Diderot from his imitators, or indeed to separate Diderot from Sterne or Voltaire. 'Diderot', in short, spills over beyond the limits of both his 'own' texts and the institutional contexts in which his legacy is preserved and celebrated. In arriving at this realization, Bradbury's novel does not question the existence of authors but it does challenge Diderot Project-style efforts to monumentalize them. His 500-page monument to Diderot thus consciously subverts its own efforts to cast him in bronze. If history, as Foucault has remarked, is that which 'transforms *documents* into *monuments*',[9] then *To the Hermitage* transforms lifeless monuments into documents – or, rather, into living texts.

Like both *Mensonge* and *To the Hermitage*, Bradbury's *Doctor Criminale* concerns itself with the efforts of a British writer to track down an enigmatic giant of European letters.[10] Dr Bazlo Criminale has, in the course of a phenomenally prolific 40-year career, written fiction, philosophy, drama, travel writing, biography, aesthetics and history. He has produced challengingly sceptical readings of Marx, Nietzsche, Adorno and Heidegger, and is now mentioned in the same breath as 'Lacan and Foucault, Deleuze and Baudrillard, Derrida and Lyotard' (89). Though Criminale's reputation seems secure, his life-story is singularly murky territory. Born in 1921, or 1926, or 1927, or 1929 in Lithuania, or Moldova, or Bulgaria, he has studied in Berlin, Vienna, Moscow and Harvard, and has married at least three times. Somehow, this Eastern European intellectual managed to thrive as cosmopolitan intellectual in a climate that was anything but conducive to freedom of thought or travel. He has held posts in Budapest, Wroclaw, Leipzig, travels widely in Europe, Asia and the Americas, having effectively 'made homelessness into a postmodern art form' (43). He has also mastered the art of elusiveness. When Bradbury's narrator gets on the trail of Criminale, he rapidly discovers that his quarry is diabolically difficult to track down, and exasperatingly easy to lose. Fourteen of the novel's sixteen chapters end with the word 'Criminale', bringing the man into momentary focus before he disappears from our field of vision, slipping quietly into the next chapter – from which he will, in turn, unceremoniously absent himself. For all his monumentally palpable reputation, Criminale's life has been one long vanishing act.

The novel's narrator, Francis Jay, is a freelance journalist commissioned to research a television profile of Criminale. Like Lodge's Robyn Penrose, Jay read English at the University of Sussex – the anti-Oxbridge of British campus fiction – where he received formal training in literary-critical iconoclasm:

> we deconstructed everything: author, text, reader, language, discourse, life itself. No task was too small, no piece of writing below suspicion. We demythologized, we demystified. We dehegemonized, we decanonized. We dephallicized, we depatriarchalized; we decoded, we de-canted, we de-famed, we de-manned. (8–9)

The question of *which* writers or texts Jay and his contemporaries deconstructed seems beside the point, since all the emphasis is on the aggressive critical procedures that were drilled into them by their Sussex mentors. This is a literary education in which authors, canonical or otherwise, are conspicuous by their absence. However, we might pick up, in that final 'de-manned', a tell-tale echo of 'de Man', the guru of American deconstruction whose reputation was intact during Jay's undergraduate years but profoundly damaged by the time of this novel's publication. Though the novel does not address the de Man affair as directly as Adair's *Death of the Author* or Banville's *Shroud*, its story of a disgraced European philosopher-critic is nevertheless clearly inflected by the deconstruction, demythologization, and de-manning of de Man that took place in the late 1980s and early 1990s.[11]

On the face of it, Jay's assignment to research Criminale's life involves a certain intellectual regression from high theory into vulgar humanism, a return to the naïve pre-Barthesian days of man-and-his-work criticism. Except that the versions of deconstruction and post-structuralism that Jay has taken away from Sussex are scarcely characterized by highbrow rigour. What Jay finds in post-structuralist theory is the perfect language for the modern intellectual who believes in nothing in particular, a kind of Esperanto of contemporary liberal agnosticism. He is happy to characterize himself as a laid-back, non-committal 'late liberal humanist ... Liking my convictions soft, my faiths put to doubt, my gods upset, my statues parodied, my texts deconstructed' (169). Bradbury's narrator therefore personifies what might be termed the banalization of theory: he bandies its terms and ideas around with the slangy nonchalance of one for whom there is nothing terribly important at stake in contemporary intellectual debates. For Jay, deconstruction is a familiar mental habit rather than a wilfully counter-intuitive intellectual performance; similarly, he regards the 'death of the author' not as a scandal but a simple given. Typically, Jay is wholly incurious about the man behind Criminale's writings, perfectly happy with 'the word Criminale, the sign Criminale, the signature on the spine Criminale' (22), until his producer sends him looking for the 'living breathing, fallible human being' (28) of that name. Whereas the narrator of *Mensonge* is an old-fashioned scholar who witnesses an 'author' dissolve before his eyes, the narrator of *Doctor Criminale* is a blasé child of 'the Age of Deconstruction' (8) who witnesses an absent author slowly re-materialize into a complex human being.

Jay's interest in what he calls the 'who, who, who' (289) question of authorship is powerfully re-ignited when he learns that the official Criminale biography was written not by its nominal author Otto Codicil, but possibly by Criminale's estranged wife Gertla – or even by Criminale himself. Though this attributional controversy might be dismissed as a red herring in a world where *all* authors and selves are 'fictions', the possible discrepancy between Criminale's official and unofficial selves raises questions that are anything but academic. It seems, as Jay learns more about his past, that Criminale has every reason to retreat behind a smokescreen of misattributed and unreliable biographical narratives. For Jay, the key question is: how did Criminale obtain *carte-blanche* from the Marxist authorities to think, write, travel and publish on both sides of the Iron Curtain in 'a time of terror and error, of ideas imprisoned, books forbidden, thoughts silenced, people unpersoned, classes eliminated' (92)? The price of Criminale's intellectual 'freedom', Jay discovers, was to stifle any dissident impulses and make himself useful to party apparatchiks: he was an informer in the pay of the Hungarian secret police; he let his Swiss bank accounts be used by Eastern bloc powers to salt away vast sums of money; and he chose to look the other way when Soviet tanks crushed the 1956 Hungarian rising and carted his lover Irini off to a prison camp. This story of compromise and betrayal seems to take some of its inspiration from 'Georg Lukács and his Devil's Pact',[12] George Steiner's eloquent meditation on the predicament of the Eastern European intellectual in the twentieth century. Steiner's essay describes how Lukács became Minister of Culture in the liberalizing Nagy government but resigned on 3 November 1956, precisely one day before the Russians put down the October rising. On his return from a spell of exile in Romania, he was excoriated by his own comrades for the 'bourgeois idealism' of his work on such 'reactionary' authors as

Goethe and Balzac. Did Lukács ever manage to square his loyalty to the Marxist ideal with the reality of murderous oppression represented by the Soviet tanks? Or to sustain his dual loyalty to Marxism *and* literature in the face of ferocious philistine carping from his fellow Party members? As Steiner concludes, Lukács's story testifies to the fact that 'in the twentieth century it is not easy for an honest man to be a literary critic'.

Criminale's dishonesty, his secret history of compromise and betrayal, raises the enduringly intractable question of how far a thinker's moral failings can be said to weigh against his or her intellectual achievements. In this sense Criminale stands for all of those major modern intellectuals – Lukács, de Man, Heidegger – who consorted, reluctantly or otherwise, with totalitarianism. Bradbury is by no means intent on writing these figures off as just so many treasonable clerks, and his narrator is careful to describe Criminale as a 'moral disappointment' (318) rather than a monster. His novel forcefully implies that western intellectuals who have been fortunate enough not to live through such 'interesting times' should refrain from delivering premature verdicts on the case of Bazlo Criminale. Bradbury's novel is ultimately less interested in Criminale's disgrace than in what it reveals about the moral illiteracy of western postmodernism. As a survivor of the nightmare of contemporary Eastern European history, Criminale can scarcely be judged by those who have lived their intellectual lives in the comfort zones of western liberal democracy. The deconstructive and postmodernist theories that flourish in these zones seem entirely lacking in the kind of moral or political vocabulary needed to comment meaningfully on a case such as Criminale's. In Bradbury's satirical view, contemporary theory has, by virtue of its disengagement from history, simply disqualified itself from real-world debates. As the shifty Hungarian fixer Hollo Sandor acerbically remarks: 'Don't you know philosophy is dead? … Marxism-Leninism killed it here, Deconstruction in the west. Here we had too much theory of reality, there you had not enough' (103).

As Sandor's comment implies, the east–west divide in *Doctor Criminale* is as much intellectual as it is political. One useful way of reading the novel is as an intellectual travelogue that vividly maps the contrasts between the oppressively divided political geography of Eastern Europe and the privileged cultural spaces of western academe. Luxuriously insulated from the violent pressures of modern world history, the novel's various conference venues – the Isola Barolo in Lombardy, the Gothic hunting lodge in Schlossburg, the University of East Anglia campus – are a world away from the barbed-wire cityscapes of Eastern Europe. When Jay describes the UEA campus as 'a rather strange place, out of time … caught in a separate world that seems to have little to do with everyday history' (335), he could be speaking of any of the conference venues where 'radical' western academics – 'fat structuralists and thin deconstructors, denimed feminists and yuppified postculturalists' (336) – like to pamper themselves. Nor does Bradbury exclude himself from Jay's satirical take on the conference circuit – UEA was, after all, his home institution.

At the Schlossburg conference on 'The Death of Postmodernism', one notable absentee is Professor Henri Mensonge, who lives up to his self-effacing reputation by failing to turn up and deliver his paper, 'The Totally Deconstructed Self' (317). Behind Bradbury's joking reference back to his earlier novel, there is a serious point being made here about the currency that that language of death and deconstruction acquires in postmodern circles. Jay reiterates this point in his wryly disenchanted summary of Criminale's lecture at the same conference. The lecture begins with Criminale 'singing the song of the names that would always toll on these occasions: Habermas and Horkheimer; Adorno and Althusser; De Man and Derrida; Baudrillard and Lyotard; Deleuze and Guattari; Foucault and Fukuyama' (322). This lullaby-like invocation of the talismanic names of modern theory prepares Criminale's audience for an equally soothing excursion through pleasantly familiar theoretical territory: 'He reflected on all those things that cheer thinking spirits up these days – the end of humanism, the death of the subject, the loss of the great meta-narratives, the disappearance of the self in the age of universal simulacra, the depthlessness of history, the slippage of the referent, the culture of pastiche, the departure of reality' (322–3). The theory that Criminale blandly recycles here has precious little to do with the political and historical realities that he has lived through. Ultimately the problem with his lecture is not that it is iconoclastic, but that its iconoclasm is simply too *easy* – Criminale's apocalyptic talk of death and crisis is all too comfortably in line with what his audience of armchair nihilists wants and expects to hear. Bradbury's novel, by contrast, aims to make things uncomfortable, to challenge the facile iconoclasm of 'the Age of Deconstruction' by offering an ironic but humane account of the rise and fall of one of its own icons.

While *Doctor Criminale* gestures obliquely to the fall of Paul de Man, this major theoretical scandal is the central inspiration behind Gilbert Adair's postmodern whodunit, *The Death of the Author*.[13] This spry novella takes its cue from David Lehman's *Signs of the Times: Deconstruction and the Fall of Paul de Man* (1991), a book that tells the story of de Man's wartime journalism and posthumous disgrace with considerable anti-theoretical gusto. While he was an undergraduate student in wartime Belgium, de Man contributed some 170 articles on cultural and literary topics to *Le Soir*, a paper under the editorial supervision of the German authorities. De Man left Europe for America in 1948, where he rose to prominence as the leading US deconstructionist without ever publicly acknowledging his wartime activities, though he did privately discuss them with his employers. The *Le Soir* pieces did not come to light until four years after de Man's death, when they were discovered by the Belgian postgraduate researcher Ortwin de Graef. The consensus is that the content of most of these pieces is innocuous – though the very fact that de Man worked for a collaborationist paper is reason enough for some commentators to damn him. However, among de Man's contributions to *Le Soir* is one article that notoriously proposes the creation of a Jewish colony isolated from Europe as a '*solution du problème juif*'.[14] These patently anti-Semitic opinions, which de Man never publicly acknowledged or retracted, are the primary exhibits in the controversy that engulfed him after his death.

The discovery of de Man's wartime journalism was godsend to opponents of deconstruction and sparked off what Richard Klein calls the new science of 'DeManology'.[15] DeManological arguments usually centre on supposed continuities between the personal history that de Man buried and the wholesale repression of history that deconstruction allegedly involves. Deconstruction, so this argument goes, is a form of licensed scholarly amnesia that treats historical matters of life and death as just so many undecidable, endlessly misreadable linguistic constructs. Nowhere is this more notoriously exemplified than in de Man's remark that 'Death is a displaced name for a linguistic predicament'.[16] Detached from its original context – a discussion of Wordsworth's *Essays upon Epitaphs* – this remark has been cited countless times by de Man's detractors as chilling evidence of deconstruction's linguistic solipsism and moral bankruptcy. For them, de Man's deconstruction is the disreputable academic corollary of his lifelong evasion of the truth, while *Blindness and Insight* (1971), *Allegories of Reading* (1979) and *The Rhetoric of Romanticism* (1979) represent an ingenious alibi-in-instalments for his unacknowledged wartime offences. In particular, his essay on Rousseau, where he discusses the 'impossibility' of confession, can be read as a coded justification of his own guilty silence.[17] In the aftermath of de Graef's revelations and Lehman's popularizing exposé, deconstruction and its 'linguistic predicaments' seem to have been unmasked as the displaced names for a shabby politics of collaboration, anti-Semitism and historical cover-up. Lehman even quotes Jeffery Mehlman as saying that there are 'grounds for viewing the whole of deconstruction as a vast amnesty project for the politics of collaboration in France during World War II'.[18]

As Seàn Burke points out, the de Man scandal provoked an unavoidable resurgence of interest in the big questions of 'author-centred criticism' that had become so unfashionable during his lifetime. Terms like intention, authority, biography, accountability, oeuvre and autobiography became once more not merely respectable but indispensable in academic circles: the author was reborn, while de Man's theories were pronounced dead.[19] But what if de Man has been confronted with the damning evidence of his wartime journalism during his own lifetime? Would he have accepted that his youthful anti-Semitism had any bearing on his mature literary criticism? Would he have tried to disown or deconstruct the *Le Soir* articles? Though de Man's enemies would never have the ultimate satisfaction of seeing their bogeyman squirm in public, contemporary novelists have been mulling over these 'what if?' questions. One of the functions of works of fictional DeManology, like Adair's *The Death of the Author* and Banville's *Shroud*, is to fantasize a more satisfyingly dramatic downfall for de Man. No one was able to do in real life what the young *Village Voice* journalist does in *The Death of the Author* – after two brutal murders on the New Harbor campus, he doorsteps Léopold Sfax (Adair's de Man-figure), sarcastically quoting back at him his own morbid *bon mot* about death as a 'linguistic predicament' (120). But although this scene does seem to represent a gratifyingly straightforward comeuppance for de Man, in the end neither Adair's novel nor Banville's will settle for journalistic *schadenfreude* as an appropriate response to the scandal.

Adair's novel is narrated with preening self-regard by Professor Léopold Sfax, a Paris-born émigré whose brilliant works of theoretical criticism, *Either/Either* and *The Vicious Spiral*, have secured his reputation as 'by far the most celebrated critic in the United States' (24) in the 'heyday of the death of the Author' (23). His work revolves around recognizably de Manian themes – the irrelevance of the author, the inevitability of misreading, the undecidability of binary oppositions and the textuality of social experience. Like de Man, he has also achieved professional eminence in post-war America without any compromising information leaking out about the anti-Semitic journalism he wrote in wartime Europe. Sfax's nemesis is Astrid Hunneker, a graduate student and keen disciple, who announces her intention, out of the blue, to write his biography – or as she puts it (Hunneker is also a sculptor) to capture his likeness. When his would-be biographer pays him a visit, Adair's author-hero is thus confronted by two ironies – a sense in which the attentive reader is the author's worst enemy, and a worry that biography destroys the author by granting him an official 'life'.

Sfax seems to live in the company of death, and has a long-standing history of premonitions of his own demise. As a thirteen-year-old boy he succumbed to a screaming fit at his grandfather's funeral when he caught sight of the name on the coffin's plaque – 'Léopold Sfax' (5). He now walks to work through the City Burial Ground whose arched gateway carries the motto 'The Dead Shall Be Raised' (30). Shortly after Hunneker declares her intention to write a Sfax biography, his tweedy colleague Herb Gillingwater is bludgeoned to death with a bronze bust of Shakespeare. Hunneker meets a similar fate, though in her case the murder weapon is her own terracotta bust of Sfax. Like *To the Hermitage*, then, Adair's novel constructs the author in necrological terms as a creature of the graveyard, a figure whose funeral is always-already ongoing. But the use of iconic representations of authors in the murder of Gillingwater and Hunneker seems also to suggest that in this novel the afterlife of the author is achieved at the cost of the death of the reader.

The Death of the Author is narrated in such a way that these two brutal murders take place offstage. Throughout, we are confined to the fiercely introspective and diabolically unreliable mind of Léopold Sfax, as he mentally revisits the personal history that Hunneker wants to claim for the public sphere. Sfax's narrative spirals viciously back to the moment when Astrid Hunneker declares her intention to write his unauthorized biography, since this is also the moment when he begins to write and rewrite his own life-story, a wilfully incoherent mixture of cover-up and confession. Initially Sfax claims that he courageously declined the invitation to contribute to a 'collaborationist rag' (11) in wartime France, intimating also that he had links with the Resistance at the time. He then rewrites this story of noble resistance as one of abject collaboration. It seems that he had no connection at all with the Resistance, and that he did indeed write for the collaborationist press, producing some 150 pieces of 'putrid Nazi hackwork' (57) between 1941–3 under the pen-name Hermes (*Editions Hermès* was the name of the publishing house set up by de Man in Antwerp in 1945). Whether this second version of his life-story is any truer than the first is, of course, undecidable.

No less incoherent than Sfax's narrative structure is his convoluted attempt at self-exculpation. He blames everybody but himself – his anti-Semitic grandfather, his collaborationist father, his lack of an appropriate 'forum' for his genius – for his collaborationist journalism. He even erects an entire theory of literature that will convert his Nazi juvenilia into an array of empty, authorless, blankly self-referential signs. His detailed working-through of his position is a minor masterpiece of Freudian 'kettle logic', where a denial of guilt produces a sequence of contradictory assertions. Sfax asserts that Hermes simply does not exist, before going on to argue that his '*actual and historical existence*' should not concern us; he claims that the Hermes texts are wholly resistant to interpretation, before offering his interpretation of their self-subverting qualities; he denies that the Hermes texts refer to anything but themselves, and insists also that they engage with and undermine Nazi ideology (89–90). It is never clear just how far Sfax manages to persuade himself of the validity of this conspicuously faulty reasoning, but he seems to displace much of his self-doubt and self-disgust onto the 'lemming-like' (92) true believers who buy wholeheartedly into his theories. Surprisingly enough, Sfax is quite the most eloquent critic of theory in the novel, horrified as he is by the generation of young academics who take the opportunistic, self-serving nihilism of *The Vicious Spiral* and *Either/Either* as gospel.

Sfax, then, is an author who is both warily suspicious and roundly contemptuous of his readership. His most dangerous reader, it turns out, is the surly postgraduate Ralph MacMahon, who hacks into his Apple Mac and reads the signs that Sfax is almost certainly the campus killer. If the novel begins with an image of the reader-as-disciple, it ends with the reader-as-nemesis, though for Sfax the difference between the two has never been more than negligible. However, when MacMahon fulfils his nemesis role by shooting Sfax at close range, the novel plunges reader–author relations into even deeper uncertainty. Since Sfax could hardly have typed up this description of his own murder, we suddenly seem to be reading a text in search of a narrator. The novel's postscript, which purports to be narrated 'posthumously' by Sfax, claims that the entire text was in fact written by MacMahon. Is some or all of the novel by Sfax? Is some or all of it by MacMahon? These 'undecidable' questions promise to keep the deconstructionists busy for a good while yet, and in the meantime Sfax has been granted a loophole. He has disappeared, and we are left contemplating not a living author but an inscrutable machine, Sfax's word processor, on which the unattributable 'Apple Mac texts' are stored (132). Adair's novel thus enacts the same shift that de Man discerns in Rousseau's confessional writings, from the 'text as body' to the 'text as machine' – an arbitrary, unmotivated system that gratuitously churns out linguistic products to which we belatedly attach the illusion of personally authorized meaning.[20] The word processor thus presents us with a starkly depersonalized image of textuality: language stripped of what Foucault once called its 'psychological halo'.[21] And perhaps the greatest challenge of the textual machine, as Martin McQuillan points out, is that as a self-operating, self-regulating, self-deconstructing system it entails 'not the death of the author but the death of the reader'.[22]

The Death of the Author ends by implicitly posing the same question that opens John Banville's *Shroud*: 'Who speaks?'.[23] In many ways this is theory's great question, the one that keeps getting asked even, perhaps especially, when theorists have forbidden themselves from asking it. The official answer to the question, in the age of structuralism and post-structuralism, has been 'language'. Foucault, for example, says that the 'linguistic turn' of modern thought has brought us to 'the place that Nietzsche and Mallarmé signposted when the first asked: Who speaks? and the second saw his glittering answer in the Word itself'.[24] Like most novelists, however, Banville is not satisfied with this answer, and his novel is a searching attempt to reconstitute the human presences behind impersonal linguistic acts. One such presence in the novel is Paul de Man, whose life and writings provide much of the inspiration for its protagonist, Axel Vander. But Vander's exceptionally dark life-story is also partially derived from that of another fallen giant of post-structuralism, the French Marxist Louis Althusser.

Althusser, who had a history of manic depression, hallucinations and amnesia, was hospitalized as a psychiatric patient in November 1980 after strangling his wife Hélène. He subsequently offered detailed descriptions of his history of mental instability, and of the murder itself, in an autobiography whose candour is as disturbing in its own way as de Man's silence. In *The Future Lasts Forever*, Althusser describes himself as feeling on his release from hospital like a '*missing person* … neither alive nor dead'; his confessional autobiography is offered, in openly paradoxical fashion, as a bid for a '*definitive state of anonymity*'.[25] A leading theme of the book is Althusser's partly ironic sense of himself as an impostor, an academic fraud who has built a profound reputation on the basis of piti-fully shallow knowledge; he also confesses, disarmingly enough, to being an habitual and incorrigible liar whose 'totally inauthentic' life has 'consisted of nothing but endless artifice and deceit'.[26] He is, by his own admission, a less than trustworthy guide to the facts of his own life. Indeed 'The Facts' is the title of Althusser's 'autobiographical' narrative of 1976 which solemnly records for posterity the stories of his secret ecumenical negotiations with Pope John XXIII, his chance roadside encounters and intimate dinners with Charles de Gaulle, his 'first-rate non-violent hold-up in the Bank of Paris', and his audacious attempt – 'hushed up by the press' – to steal a French atomic submarine.[27] Althusser thus makes his bid for 'definitive anonymity' by playing the

Cretan liar in autobiographical narratives whose astonishing candour is everywhere qualified by disarming confessions of unreliability and surreally distorted by interludes of deadpan comic fantasy.

The hero of *Shroud* is a complex composite of de Man and Althusser. Axel Vander is an ageing European philosopher-critic who has enjoyed a distinguished academic career in America. His range of interests in nineteenth-century European poetry and philosophy – Shelley, Nietzsche, Rilke – closely resemble de Man's. His first major essay, 'Shelley Defaced', sounds like it could be a conflation of de Man's 'Shelley Disfigured' and 'Autobiography As De-Facement'. And his personal appearance – he is one-eyed, with a dead leg – inevitably recalls the de Manian conceits of blindness, defacement, disfiguration. Like de Man, Vander also harbours a decades-old secret. At the beginning of the novel, he relocates from California to Turin, there to confront a young woman who has uncovered evidence of his associations with the German-controlled press of wartime Belgium. But Vander also has Althusserian secrets: he returns continually to his sense of inauthenticity as a scholar and a human being; and he is haunted by the memory of his wife, whom he killed when her mind began to decay, feeding her tablets to make the murder look like a self-inflicted overdose.

Vander is thus haunted by some of the most troubling ghosts in the lives of modern critical theorists. But he is not simply the sum of de Man and Althusser's crimes. Rather, he stands in relation to them as the shroud does to the body of Christ – as a secondary representation or after-impression of dubious authenticity. The Holy Shroud of Turin has long been thought by believers to provide miraculous evidence of the physical resurrection of Christ; as such it might also function in Banville's novel as a symbolic promise of life after death for the contemporary author. However, the novel is significantly set in 1989, two years after the fall of de Man, and one year after radiocarbon dating revealed the Shroud to be of medieval provenance. The novel's associations between Vander and this mysterious artefact are thus charged with intense ambiguity. In the voices of passers-by in Turin, Vander repeatedly mis-hears the word *sindone* ('shroud') as *signore* (48, 87, 156) – which is to say that, in a moment of Althusserian 'interpellation', he misrecognizes himself in and as the shroud. When he obtains a souvenir replica – a copy of a copy, a fake of a fake – he is assured that 'It looks like you ... Just like you' (312). Though Vander is a kind of senescent Christ-figure, he is also, like the Shroud, a venerable relic that has been exposed as a fraud.

Banville's novel thus focuses its attention on desacralized icons, on crises of authenticity – not because it rejoices in demystification for its own sake, but in order to make some sense of a world from which authenticity seems to be slowly draining away. In any case, the narrative of demystification seems to be a gambit that *Shroud* consciously declines. The novel never quite becomes the exposé that it promises to be: in a sense it is a detective story that does not happen – there is no cat-and-mouse between Vander and nemesis Cass Cleave, no real sense of intellectual pursuit or sequence of escalating revelations. In part, this is because the investigation has long since got underway in Vander's mind, where he conducts a permanent inquest into his own past.

The 'authenticity' of Vander's narrative is, however, under constant suspicion. One sequence from his recollections, a childhood memory of attending a raucously friendly meal with local farmers at harvest time, is modelled in detail on a similar passage in Althusser's autobiography.[28] Althusser recollects being taken by his grandfather to see a spectacularly noisy threshing machine in action, followed by an uproarious meal for local farmers in a nearby farm kitchen where he gets caught up in all the drinking, singing and backslapping bonhomie. But Althusser concludes the anecdote by pulling back sharply to admit that it did not happen like this – 'I dreamt it ... I simply had an intense desire for it to be real'. Vander recalls involvement in a similarly festive scene but also confesses that it 'never happened'; it was, he confesses, 'a fantasy born of my longing to belong' (74). Banville's hero thus establishes himself as an Althusser-like narrator, a self-confessed liar and fantasist who owns up to his own unreliability. Vander has rewritten his own past in such painstaking detail that he has vivid memories of things that never happened. Indeed, he is so inauthentic than even his false memories are *Althusser's* false memories. His narrative thus represents a particularly vivid example of the unstable relationship between writing subject and written subject that de Man takes to be characteristic of all autobiographical discourse. When Vander confesses that 'mendacity is second, no, is first nature to me' (12), he seems to stumble upon a primal inauthenticity from which no amount of disarming confessional discourse can save him. As de Man says, in Nietzschean style, 'By asserting in the mode of truth that the self is a lie, we have not escaped from deception'.[29]

Vander has also built his academic life on lies. Like Althusser, he describes his intellectual career as a brilliant *performance* of brilliance. He quickly learns to manipulate his small repertoire of philosophical knowledge so as to give the impression of vast learning, discoursing with offhand omniscience on 'texts I had not got round to reading, philosophies I had not yet studied, great men I had never met' (61). Behind the mordant bravado of Vander's intellectual style, however, are precisely the same anxieties that preyed on Althusser, whose dread it was that *Reading Capital* and *For Marx* would expose him as 'a philosopher who knew almost nothing about the history of philosophy'.[30] *Shroud* thus functions as a case study in the psychology of charlatanism, and some of its keenest observations are on the logic of overcompensation that can breed delusions of grandeur from an intellectual inferiority complex. It is as though the very slenderness of Vander's learning emboldens him to exaggerate his intellectual status. 'Mine is the kind of commentary', he says with measured arrogance, 'in which frequently the comment will claim an equal rank with that which is supposedly its object; equal, and sometimes superior' (62). Despite these self-aggrandizing remarks, Vander's intellectual project is an emphatic assault on the myth of the human self. This at least has been his public position, though privately he cannot rid himself of 'the conviction of an enduring core of selfhood' (27). The very opposition that the novel constructs between the 'public' and 'private' Vanders presupposes the existence of the intimate core of subjectivity that he denies. But Vander's 'inner self' is more elusive than most, since Vander is not his real name. 'Vander', it turns out, was born into a poor Jewish family, and managed to escape the labour camps through his associations with the real Vanders – a cultured, prosperous, jauntily anti-Semitic Antwerp family by whom he was befriended as a young man. The narrator particularly hero-worships Axel Vander, an exquisitely handsome journalist of his own age, who contributes anti-Semitic broadsides to the *Vlaamsche Gazet*. When Axel disappears in mysterious circumstances, the narrator 'steals' his name and identity, concealing his Jewish self under the shroud of Vander's non-Jewish self.

A story of identify-theft narrated by a 'fake' de Man, *Shroud* thus counts as a semi-apocryphal entry in the canon of DeManological fiction rather than a simple *roman à clef*. Nor is Vander's identity the only item stolen by 'Vander' – Banville's light-fingered narrator candidly recalls helping himself to watches, books, pain-killers, money and sundry trinkets and knick-knacks while making his way to safety through wartime Europe. In one sense 'Vander' is not unlike Rousseau, who according to de Man's reading of *Confessions*, steals minor items because he secretly wants to be 'found out', to squirm satisfyingly in the exhibitionistic scene of shamed confession. But with its story of a writer who quietly purloins anything he can get his hands on, *Shroud* also seems to be implicitly formulating a new model of author-as-kleptomaniac according to which the authorial self is founded on a compulsive appropriation of the trappings of the other; it as though the authorial self can only ever be a *plagiarized* self. When the narrator steals Vander's identity, he also performs an act of retroactive plagiarism, illicitly assuming authorial responsibility for his friend's anti-Semitic journalism; he thus becomes a Paul de Man-figure as it were by default, in permanent dread at the prospect of a vengeful resurfacing of a past that was never his. 'Axel Vander' – or whatever his 'real' name might be – is indeed the 'man who wasn't there', but this does not prevent him from being exposed to a devastating return of the repressed.

It is a recurring theme of these novels that those who proclaim the death of the author may have their own sinister reasons for advocating voluntary amnesia over origins of texts. For Adair, Banville and Bradbury, post-structuralist theory has variously become a plagiarists' manifesto, an alibi for charlatans and impostors, a cover story for criminals. At the same time none of these novels proposes a return to a pre-Barthesian model of authorship, since the question of where textuality ends and authorial identity begins is one that none of them can resolve. Even in *The Death of the Author* and *Shroud*, where the first-person narratives might seem to promise some privileged access to the private subjectivity of the author-critic, we are left ultimately only with the images of the shroud and the word processor, sacred and secular relics of a vanished human presence. For all his apparent prominence in these novels, then, the author proves to a singularly elusive figure, never more so than when he seems to speak with confessional directness to the reader. This ability of authors to vanish into their own texts is teasingly commented on by Barthes when he suggests, in a droll essay on *Roland Barthes*, that the best pseudonym is the writer's own proper name.[31] But despite the author's constant retreat into anonymity, the case of de Man in particular has ensured that the questions Foucault wanted us to abandon – 'Who really spoke? ... what part of his deepest self did he express in his discourse?' – are being asked as urgently as ever in modern fiction.

6
Foucauldian Fictions

'Madness, death, sexuality, crime – these are the subjects that attract most of my attention'.[1] These may sound like the words of a Gothic novelist rather than a post-structuralist philosopher, but then Michel Foucault's work is always notable for its compelling engagement with the marginal, deviant and transgressive extremes of human experience: his (un)natural home seems to be the edgy territories of the creative writer rather than the innocuous haunts of the academic. It is perhaps for this very reason that a number of authors, including Hervé Guibert, Toby Litt and Patricia Duncker, have been drawn to Foucault's work as a source of creative raw material. Foucault himself emphasized the 'novelistic' qualities of *The Order of Things*, a comment that chimes in with Edward Said's remarks about the conscious 'extraterritoriality' of his work, its tendency to sprawl beyond the limits of any given intellectual genre or disciplinary specialism.[2] When Foucault traces the spiralling interplay of limit and transgression in the writings of Georges Bataille, for example, he seems to gesture also to the transgressive impulse that takes his own intellectual project to the 'uncrossable' limits between history, philosophy, theory and fiction.[3] Nor is his emphasis on madness, crime, sex and death the only source of potential inspiration for novelists. Of all the leading post-structuralists, Foucault is the most visibly engaged with the world 'outside the text'; his materialist credentials were never more proudly brandished than when he responded to Derrida's critique of *Madness and Civilization* with a furious denunciation of the solipsistic 'textualism' of deconstruction.[4] Not that Foucault clings to an old-fashioned humanist or empiricist position. Noam Chomsky was so freaked out by his outlandishly counter-intuitive views on liberty and human rights that he said debating with Foucault was like trying to communicate with a member of a different species.[5] It might be more accurate, however, to describe Foucault's thought not as creepily inhuman but as rigorously anti-humanist: for him, there is no free-standing 'human nature' outside of the powerful institutional contexts in which bodies are subjected to the legal, medical and moral regimes of 'normality'. Prisons, asylums, clinics and sanatoria thus stand as the sinister landmarks of his writings, behind whose blank edifices the old humanist self seems to have disappeared for good. Obviously the strains of pessimism and paranoia in this 'great conspiratorial epistemologist'[6] – as L'Heureux's Olga Kominska dubs him – were never likely to fill novelists with creative inspiration; instead, he has come to function as a source of 'negative inspiration' for a spate of mischievously anti-Foucauldian narratives by his literary followers.

The most obvious way in which Foucault's literary followers have flouted their master's teachings is by taking his life as a subject for their fiction. Hervé Guibert, Toby Litt and Julia Kristeva have all produced fictionalized portraits of Foucault, in the teeth of his forcible resistance to biographical curiosity. Pestered by an imaginary interlocutor in the Introduction to *The Archaeology of Knowledge*, Foucault famously describes himself as someone who 'writes in order to have no face'.[7] But his ambitions for literary self-effacement have been massively belied by the cult of personality that grew up around him in the 1970s and 1980s, and that was consolidated by the publication in quick succession of major biographies by Didier Eribon (1989), David Macey (1993) and James Miller (1993). With his unmistakeable shaved head and wire-rimmed glasses, Foucault fits the profile of 'postmodernist sphinx'[8] too perfectly for him to take refuge in anonymity. And with his high-profile political campaigning, his homosexuality, his immersion in the S&M subcultures of California, and his experiments with marijuana, cocaine and LSD, Foucault's very life seems to have been led in defiance of what he once called the 'universal reign of the normative'.[9] Both hieratic and *engagé*, Foucault inherited Jean-Paul Sartre's role as the iconic modern French intellectual, as well known for his public persona as for the content of his books; and the very fact that Patricia Duncker has published a novel entitled *Hallucinating Foucault* gives some idea of the exotic familiarity of his name in Anglophone literary circles.

Foucault appears in contemporary fiction in a number of guises – as 'Scherner' in Kristeva's *The Samurai* (1990), as 'Muzil' in Guibert's *To the Friend Who Did Not Save My Life* (1990), as an unnamed philosopher in the same author's 'Les secrets d'un homme' (1988), and as 'himself' in Toby Litt's 'When I Met Michel Foucault' (1996). His role in Kristeva's novel, though only a minor one, is instructively typical of the objectification of

Foucault in these narratives. The relevant passage is a rather cruel diary entry by the psychiatrist Joëlle Cabarus – a Kristeva *alter ego* – who catches sight of Scherner chuckling to himself in the Bibliothèque Nationale. *'Nothing is more revealing than a reader who thinks he's unobserved'*, she writes, *'His masturbating shows in his face'* (137). While the two share a companionable cigarette and a friendly word or two, Cabarus inwardly reviews and dismisses Scherner's work on psychiatry, on prisons and on sexuality. Though she acknowledges his genius, she deplores his nihilistic dream of *'a human race without a soul'* (139) and perceives in his *'absurd, corrupting, idiotic'* (137) laughter an unguarded revelation of the very private inner self whose existence he would deny. In its construction of 'Scherner' as the object of the psychiatric gaze, Kristeva's text exacts a certain kind of 'revenge' on Foucault by subjecting him to one of the mechanisms of power-knowledge that he demystifies in his writings.

A different kind of 'revenge' on Foucault is exacted by Toby Litt's 'When I Met Michel Foucault'.[10] This short story, whose epigraph is Foucault's line about writing in order to have no face, is a surreal *petit récit* that mocks the burgeoning Foucault industry of the 1990s and subverts the grand biographical narratives of Eribon, Macey and Miller. In terms that recall Chomsky's description of Foucault, the narrator describes him as *'one of the weirdest emanations our planet and species has ever put forth'* with a mind both *'poisonous and succulent, irresistible and hideous, freakish and generic, true and absurd'* (205). No Foucauldian of the narrator's acquaintance has ever said that they would like to have met him – a fact that he puts down to the veiled homophobia of academic culture. But our narrator gets introduced to the man himself – by his Great Aunt Edith, of all people – in the course of a surreal waking dream that takes them to Tunisia via San Francisco and Paris and climaxes with a scene of erotic torture in an S&M club.

Before recounting his adventures with Foucault, the narrator briefly outlines the main strengths and weakness of the Eribon, Macey and Miller biographies, and culls eight of the quirkiest details from Macey's text – including Foucault's childhood fantasy of being a goldfish, his inability to tell the difference between Mick Jagger and David Bowie, and the fact that he wet himself with excitement on a train to Jaruzelski's Poland (192–3). These entertainingly inconsequential items from the great philosopher's life story add up to a kind of Barthesian anti-biography, a self-consciously loose assemblage of 'biographemes' that make no claims to seize the essence of their subject. By deflecting the essentializing gaze of official biography, this catalogue of memorable trivia is as much a safeguard to Foucault's anonymity as the black leather catsuit and discipline hood that he wears on his visit to the S&M club. However, when Litt's narrator is invited to participate in the erotic torture of Foucault, he does so by reciting eight 'official' facts about his life – name, date and place of birth, education, published work, intellectual career, sexual adventures in California, time of death. He then uses a white-hot poker to brand Foucault with his own initials, and rips off the discipline hood to cry 'Behold the face of Michel Foucault!' (227). At this point the story reads like a deleted scene from Foucault's discussion of the tortured body in *Discipline and Punish*, where one of the primary functions of torture is 'to brand the victim with infamy'.[11] The narrator's unmasking of the 'Masked Philosopher' – as he once appeared in an interview for *Le Monde*[12] – is the final insult in a scene where Foucault has been tortured by his own biography, publicly branded by the very 'official' identity that he sought to disguise or efface.

Lengthier and more sympathetic fictional portraits of Foucault are offered by the fiction of Hervé Guibert, the photographer, journalist and novelist whom he befriended in 1977. Foucault's biographers disagree over whether they were lovers, but they were certainly intimate friends, and Guibert's Foucault-related fictions, 'Les secrets d'un homme' (1988), and *To the Friend Who Did Not Save My Life* (1990), derive in part from his contact with the philosopher during his dying days.[13] 'Les secrets d'un homme' centres on a hospitalized Foucault-figure who knows that his life and legacy are slipping out of his control. This unnamed philosopher is desperate not to become the centre of a scholarly industry that would feed on his biographical secrets and unpublished writings. But the story's central image, the surgical procedure of trephination, provides an all too vivid indication of the disturbingly intrusive scrutiny to which the philosopher is now prone. Just as the philosopher's dying body has been subjected once and for all to the expertise of *homo medicus*, so the contents of his mind are about to be laid bare to the *post mortem* gossip of scholars and biographers. What is more, brain surgery is also an implied metaphor for Guibert's own relationship with Foucault: 'Les secrets d'un homme' is an act of 'literary trephination' that gets us on appallingly intimate terms with the dying man. The story becomes a dreamlike journey into seam of buried childhood memories that may or may not shed light on the philosopher's later intellectual career. Three apparently unrelated memories stand out: 'le petit philosophe' being taken by his father to witness an amputation; the frisson of passing a house in Poitiers where a woman had once been confined; and his envious schoolboy rivalry with his gifted Jewish classmates. These episodes from the life of infant philosopher tantalize us with the possibility that Foucault's intellectual preoccupations may be traceable back to repressed childhood memories. It may possible to discern in these three memories the makings of Foucault's later preoccupations with bodies, medical discourse, confinement and otherness – though this of course is precisely the kind of post-Freudian psychologizing that his work systematically resists.[14] Whether or not the story is a 'betrayal' of Foucault's deathbed secrets, it certainly represents a betrayal of his intellectual methods.

As in 'Les secrets d'un homme', Guibert's autobiographical novel, *To the Friend Who Did Not Save My Life*, figures his relationship with Foucault as an intimate friendship tainted by a guilty betrayal. The novel takes the form of 100 diary entries written by an HIV-positive narrator whose friend and neighbour, the philosopher 'Muzil', is already hospitalized and dying from the effects of an AIDS-related illness. Moved from his apartment to the antiseptic anonymity of the intensive care unit, Muzil's illness is figured as a loss of identity at the hands of doctors and medical technology – a slide into terminal namelessness that cruelly grants him the one thing he craved but could never quite achieve in life. As the narrator points out, Muzil's attempt to 'make his face invisible' would never work in Paris, where 'the gleaming and self-contained enigma of that skull' (20) was instantly recognizable. If, as seems likely, Muzil's name is designed to echo that of the author Robert Musil, then this novel functions in part as a wry reflection on the philosopher's signal failure to be a 'man without qualities'. His instant and unwanted recognizability seems to have been behind Muzil's desire to 'obliterate' (18) his own name, and to have prompted his fantasy of entering a state-of-the-art hospice, from which people could slip out into anonymity – 'on the other side of the wall, in the alley, with no baggage, no name, no nothing' (17). The leather gear found in Muzil's apartment after his death – a huge bag of 'whips, leather hoods, leashes, bridles, and handcuffs' (21) – represents another expression of the quest for facelessness that preoccupied Foucault's life and work.

The paradox of Guibert's *roman à clef* is that it can pay its commemorative tribute to Foucault only by conferring additional visibility on this self-effacing philosopher. Rechristened 'Muzil', Foucault is 'nominally' faceless in this text, but its narrator is nevertheless conspicuously uneasy at completing the diary entries that spell out the degrading details of his friend's physical and mental deterioration. He feels both 'relieved and disgusted' (87) by these 'ignoble transcripts' (91), like a treacherous double agent secretly recording everything that his friend wanted to 'erase around the periphery of his life' (87–8). The narrator is at pains to justify his violation of Muzil's dream of a life circumscribed by absolute privacy. His narrative, he argues, is written not in a spirit of prurient curiosity but as an act of identification with the dying philosopher: 'it wasn't so much my friend's last agony I was describing', he remarks, 'as it was my own' (91). The novel's portrait of Foucault, then, is not a heartless *exposé* but an act of painfully close identification between one HIV-positive man and another. One might say that the novel's dominant emotion is not survivor's guilt but follower's anxiety – Guibert writes not because he has lived to tell the tale, but in order to use Foucault's fate to prenarrate his own death. 'Muzil' thus functions in the novel not simply as a fairly transparent alias for Foucault, but as a composite *memento mori* in whom the philosopher and the novelist are fatefully joined.

If Kristeva, Litt and Guibert's texts represent variously sympathetic or sadistic 'unmaskings' of Foucault, A. S. Byatt's *The Biographer's Tale* (2000) is a post-Foucauldian fiction that sticks much more faithfully to the principle of 'facelessness' that operates in his work. The novel originates not in his life story but in his writings: Byatt traces its origins back to specific paragraphs of *The Order of Things*. And although the novel's theme is the biography industry, its hero is a failed biographer and its theme is the failure of biography. *The Biographer's Tale* thus adheres closely both to the letter of Foucault's writing and to the spirit of his general resistance to subject-centred narrative. Intriguingly, however, Byatt's novel is ostensibly the story of a scholar's renunciation of post-structuralist theory. Its narrator, Phineas G. Nanson, is a postgraduate student working on 'personae of female desire' in modern fiction who experiences a moment of Damascene unconversion in the middle of a critical theory seminar. For Nanson, the problem with these seminars is that they purport to be exercises in rigorous demystification but soon settle into a pattern of mind-numbing intellectual *déjà vu*:

> All the seminars … had a fatal family likeness. They were repetitive in the extreme. We found the same clefts and crevices, transgressions and disintegrations, lures and deceptions beneath, no matter what surface we were scrying. I thought, next we will go on to the phantasmagoria of Bosch, and, in his incantatory way, Butcher obliged. I went on looking at the filthy window above his head, and I thought, I must have *things*. (1–2)

Nanson's devotedly Lacanian theory tutor, Gareth Butcher, is clearly an exponent of the hermeneutic of suspicion at its most monotonously predictable. As his name suggests, he also personifies a mode of violent theoretical reading that murders and dissects its literary illustrations.

The atmosphere of intellectual claustrophobia in Butcher's theory seminars leaves Nanson feeling starved of first-hand contact with things, facts and reality, and convinces him to find a new mentor in Professor Ormerod Goode, an Anglo-Saxon and Ancient Norse specialist. If Nanson's defection from Dr Butcher to Professor Goode seems an improbably neat switch of allegiance from theoretical villain to scholarly hero, he soon finds that old-fashioned scholarship does not necessarily provide effortless access to a world of palpable extra-theoretical realities. On the advice of Goode, Nanson begins to feed his new-found appetite for facts by reading Scholes Destry-Scholes' three-volume life of Sir Elmer Bole, the Victorian traveller, historian, civil servant, poet, naturalist, diplomat, soldier, polyglot, socialite, libertine and bigamist. Nanson soon gets hooked on Destry-Scholes' study, captivated by its 'almost impossible achievement of contact with the concrete world' (18). Inspired by the immense erudition of the *Life*, he undertakes to write a biography of Bole's biographer. Nanson's defection from the ranks of post-structuralist theorists thus promises to be a salutary shift of emphasis from deconstruction to reconstruction, from dismembered bodies to remembered lives, from empty textuality to full-blooded reality. But there seems to be an element of mischief, or possibly even malice, in Goode's attempt to convert this trainee Lacanian into a practitioner of antiquarian positivism. Once Nanson gets under the spell of Destry-Scholes' magisterial *Life*, he finds that the methodological problems of old-fashioned man-and-his-work criticism are much more gruellingly knotty than those raised by Butcher's painlessly routine deconstructions of over-familiar texts. Byatt's protagonist thus becomes an unwitting casualty of the sly revenge of traditional scholarship on critical theory.

When Nanson embarks on his new career as a biographer, he soon finds himself in the frustrating position of accumulating facts and things that refuse to tell a story. The extraordinarily colourful and intimate detail of Bole's life contrasts with the near-blankness that confronts the student of the exasperatingly self-effacing Destry-Scholes. Whereas the Victorian polymath seems to have lived the lives of a dozen men, his twentieth-century biographer has performed a vanishing act almost as baffling as that brought off by Bradbury's Henri Mensonge. It as though in the comparison between the larger-than-life Bole and the near-anonymous Destry-Scholes, we are being presented with an exemplary case study in the disappearance of the full-bodied human subject in the modern era. Destry-Scholes is rumoured to have perished in the

Maelstrøm, and this Nordic whirlpool is the novel's central image for the vortex of unreliable narratives that suck in and destroy the coherent biographical self. Not that Destry-Scholes has vanished entirely without trace. Nanson unearths some of his odd, factually unreliable biographical sketches of Linnaeus, Francis Galton and Ibsen, and also tracks down a suitcase containing some inscrutable odds and ends from the man's life, including a bag of marbles, and two boxes packed with index cards and photographs. But neither the biographical sketches nor the inscrutable memorabilia in the suitcase leave us any the wiser about Destry-Scholes personality or life story: Byatt's energetically inquisitive hero is left clutching a 'limp cache of unbegun and unended stories' (98). As Erin O'Connor has pointed out, *The Biographer's Tale* is like an inversion of the 'fantasy of scholarly wish fulfillment'[15] in Byatt's earlier novel, *Possession*, where diligent work in the archives produces one exhilarating revelation after another. By comparison, Phineas Nanson is that rare figure in a 'romance of the archive' – a tenacious, principled and painstaking researcher who discovers nothing because there is, apparently, nothing to discover.

When Nanson abandons the introverted theorizing of the Butcher seminars and immerses himself in the apparently untheorizable empirical data related to Destry-Scholes, he seems to have undergone a one-man 'epistemic shift'. But the post-structuralism that Nanson has banished to his intellectual prehistory is still powerfully present throughout this novel. In her Acknowledgements, Byatt traces the 'germ' of *The Biographer's Tale* to her reading of the 'remarks on Linnaeus and taxonomy in *Les mots et les choses*' (264). Elsewhere she has spelled out in more detail her interest in Foucault's work on the arbitrary principles of classification that have governed taxonomical thought since the renaissance, acknowledging him as a formative influence on her thinking about words and things.[16] Indeed, *Words and Things* – a literal English translation of the title of Foucault's book – would provide an apt alternative title for *The Biographer's Tale*. Nanson views his post-theoretical career as an opportunity to leave *a priori* system-making behind and rummage freely through the unclassifiable *bric-à-brac* of reality. Abundantly cluttered with quirkily unique *things* – Swiss Army knives, parakeets, corkscrews, glass marbles, fish-skeletons, battered shoes, stag-beetles – the world of Byatt's novel seems grant him this very opportunity, just so long as he can free himself from the systems, structures, patterns and codes of theory.

But Nanson does nevertheless have a lingering fascination with theoretical system-making, and comments appreciatively on Foucault's discussion of the impulse in Linnaean natural history to 'order and to name the world' (115). What troubles him is the question of whether such acts of naming and ordering can ever be anything but arbitrary. This question is raised by Nanson's comically futile efforts to match up each of the 366 glass marbles in the suitcase with one of the names that Destry-Scholes has listed separately. 'Originally, everything had a name',[17] Foucault observes in *The Order of Things*, but once proper names have become mere arbitrary signs there is no going back. As he sorts obsessively through Destry-Scholes's unnameable bits and pieces, Nanson begins to resemble the aphasiacs mentioned in the Preface to *The Order of Things* who are unable to arrange different skeins of wool into any coherent pattern on the basis of colour, texture, or size:

> [T]he sick mind continues to infinity, creating groups, then dispersing them again, heaping up diverse similarities, destroying those that seem clearest, splitting up things that are identical, superimposing different criteria, frenziedly beginning all over again, becoming more and more disturbed, and teetering finally on the brink of anxiety.[18]

These words provide an excellent summary of Nanson's ordeal in the Destry-Scholes archive. Though his desire for *things* has been abundantly fulfilled, he can discover no non-arbitrary basis on which to order and classify them, and becomes afflicted with an incurable taxonomical aphasia – the inevitable result, it seems, of his shift from a life without things to a life consisting *only* of things.

Not that Nanson ever manages to disentangle himself entirely from the language and ideas of Butcher's theoretical seminars. As the Destry-Scholes project begins to fall apart at the seams, his narrative becomes an involuntary autobiography that focuses on the question of how he classifies *himself* once he has decided that he is not a postgraduate student, or a postmodern theorist, or a scholar-detective. It becomes clear as the novel develops that Nanson is very much a 'theorist in denial', unconsciously obsessed with the language and ideas that he claims to have walked away from. This unacknowledged attachment to theory is evident in his repetitive insistence on the repetitiousness of post-structuralist thought, and in the way he protests too much about his clean break with theory. Paragraphs spelling out 'the reasons why I abandoned – oh, and I *have* abandoned – post-structuralist semiotics' (114) or 'the reasons I had given up post-structuralist thought' (144) cram the text with the very 'post-post-structuralist clutter' (165) that Nanson claims he wants to discard. *The Biographer's Tale* thus reads like the confessions of a lapsed post-structuralist who clings in spite of himself to the faith he has abandoned.

Engaging with Foucault's ideas rather than his life, *The Biographer's Tale* represents the polar opposite of the biographical fictions produced by Guibert, Kristeva and Litt. Between these two extremes of scholarly impersonality and biographical exposé lies an inventive novelistic treatment of Foucault's life and writings, Patricia Duncker's *Hallucinating Foucault* (1996). This work is a pseudo-*roman à clef* that deals with the Foucauldian themes of 'madness, death, sexuality, crime' in a fictional world where Foucault's influence is felt everywhere, but where the man himself never quite puts in an appearance. The novel is particularly indebted to James Miller's *The Passion of Michel Foucault*, the central theme of which is Foucault's lifelong pursuit of mental and physical 'limit-experiences'. *Hallucinating Foucault* dramatizes madness, obsession and transgression as powerful limit-experiences that shake up the blandly comfortable world of English academe and subvert the complacently self-validating norms of conventional knowledge. One of the questions that the novel raises is that of whether *reading* – never more innocuous than when practised by academics in libraries – can ever become a limit-experience. As Duncker's characters stalk one another through a maze of literary and sexual obsessions, the act of reading becomes an expression of the kind of violent desires and irrational fixations that conventional literary scholarship represses.

The novel's anonymous narrator is a Cambridge postgraduate working on a thesis on the *enfant terrible* of modern French letters, the novelist Paul Michel. A photogenic rebel who 'cherished the role of sexual outlaw, monster, pervert' (29), Michel has led a life touched by brilliance and insanity – and, increasingly, by mystery: his literary career flared into life during *les événements* of 1968 but he fell silent in the early 1980s. Some ten years after Michel's disappearance from public life, the narrator endeavours to track him down to the psychiatric hospital in which he has been sectioned. *Hallucinating Foucault* thus provides yet another variation on the theme of the 'vanishing author' that looms so large in theoretically self-conscious fiction. Like *To the Hermitage*, *The Death of the Author*, and *Shroud*, Duncker's novel is also notably rich in graveyard scenes and necrological conceits: Michel reads from *The Archaeology of Knowledge* in the Salpêtrière Hospital courtyard as Foucault's body is removed (31), and goes beserk in Père Lachaise cemetery the day after Foucault is buried in Poitiers (28). The narrator will later ride to Galliac in Michel's funeral cortege, where he undergoes his own harrowing psychological ordeal during and after the burial (171–5), images from which find their way into his recurring dreams of coffin-shaped rocks (3). But *Hallucinating Foucault* is not simply another literary tombstone over the grave of the unknown author, because the scholar-detective in this novel not only manages to track down his authorial quarry, but the two of them have a brief, passionate affair. In an age when modernist impersonality and New Critical anti-intentionalism have conspired with Barthesian post-structuralism to make author-centred reading the height of methodological incorrectness, *Hallucinating Foucault* savours the scandalous idea of an author, and a queer author at that, emerging from obscurity to disprove reports of his own demise, before seducing one of his own critics. Duncker's story of a Cambridge critic's sexual adventures with the subject of his doctoral dissertation has been aptly described by as Andrew Gibson as a 'powerful, feminist novel about the necessary queering of the contemporary bourgeois, *soi-disant* hetero-sexual and, above all, English, intellectual'.[19] One might also describe *Haullucinating Foucault* as a story about the necessary 'Frenchification' of the English critic: Duncker's narrator is soon playing the role of the café-haunting, chain-smoking, elegantly wasted Gallic intellectual, and when he shops for designer clothes with Michel, before heading south in a 2CV, his cultural makeover seems complete.

During the course of the novel's missing person enquiry, it becomes clear that Michel's madness, and the enigma of his decade of silence, are somehow bound up with his mysterious, obsessive relationship with Michel Foucault. The narrator explains that the thematic affinities between Michel and Foucault have long been evident: Foucault's list of core obsessions – 'Madness, death, sexuality, crime' – provides 'an excellent summary of all the themes in Paul Michel's fiction' (17). But the narrator soon unearths evidence, in the form of Michel's archived letters to Foucault, that there may also have been a *personal* relationship between the two. Like Byatt's *Possession*, Duncker's novel thus dramatizes the mildly disreputable pleasures imparted by documents that let scholars peer into authors' private lives. However, whereas the scholar-detectives in *Possession* discover concrete evidence of an illicit and long-suppressed relationship between two Victorian poets, the relationship between Michel and Foucault in *Hallucinating Foucault* is much harder to pin down – not least because of the uncanny skill with which Duncker's novel blurs fact into fiction. It is difficult to read *Hallucinating Foucault* without at times finding yourself thinking of the fictitious 'Paul Michel' as a figure drawn from real life or of 'Michel Foucault' as a figment of the imagination. This hallucinatory blurring of fact and fiction is intensified by the novel's sly intertextual relations with Hervé Guibert's life and work: the fictionalized account of Foucault's funeral in 'Les secrets d'un homme' provides Duncker with some distinctive details for her account of Michel's funeral (such as the heap of roses and anonymous letter on the coffin), whilst Michel is also in many ways a Guibert-figure, an ardent young devotee whose fate seems tragically interlinked with Foucault's.

However, whereas Guibert and Foucault were – at the very least – intimate friends, the same cannot be said of Foucault and Paul Michel. Whether Foucault and Michel ever genuinely knew one other, or even met one other, is one of the unresolved mysteries of this novel. Michel is on record as saying that his greatest influence was Michel Foucault, while Foucault has made only one passing reference to Michel. The two have been captured on film during a student protest in 1971, but this scarcely proves that they were on first-name terms. It seems possible that Duncker may have found some inspiration for the story of their curiously intimate non-relationship in Maurice Blanchot's essay 'Michel Foucault as I Imagine Him'. Blanchot remarks in this piece that he met Foucault only once, in May 1968, in the courtyard of the Sorbonne amid the impersonal camaraderie of *les événements*. '[D]uring those extraordinary events', Blanchot also recalls, 'I often asked: but why isn't Foucault here? Thus granting him his power of attraction and underscoring the empty place he should have been occupying … Perhaps we may simply have missed each other.'[20] Blanchot's question – 'why isn't Foucault here?' – might usefully be applied to the world of Duncker's novel, where he is a ubiquitous topic of conversation and point of intertextual reference but never appears *in propria persona*. When the narrator tries without success to find a single Foucault text in his girlfriend's flat he becomes a kind of proxy for the reader scouring *Hallucinating Foucault* for any trace of its title-character: although he is named on the front cover, Foucault scarcely qualifies as a 'character' in the pages of this novel. But then the title is, of course, mischievously double-edged: Is Foucault hallucinating, or being hallucinated? Is Foucault the subject or object of the hallucinations? If the latter, then by whom is he being hallucinated? By Paul Michel, certainly, who sees himself in Foucault's writings, and sees Foucault in his own. And perhaps also by the narrator, in a recurring nightmare in which he glimpses the 'shape of a man' (177) lurking enigmatically behind Paul Michel. But perhaps the most significant 'Foucauldian hallucinations' in this text are experienced by those of Duncker's readers who are tempted to imagine traces of Foucault in every paragraph of the novel.

Any temptation to imagine that the 'key' to this novel is to be found in the life and writings of Foucault is severely problematized by Duncker's portrayal of Paul Michel as a self-destructively Foucault-obsessed author. Michel's personal relationship to Foucault gradually emerges as a mixture of hero worship and fantasy. He claims that they moved in the same social circles, visiting the same bars and clubs and attending the same events, but somehow their paths never quite crossed: theirs was a Box-and-Cox relationship comprising one 'near miss' after another. Michel would additionally have the narrator believe that he struck a tacit agreement with Foucault never to acknowledge one another in public: if Michel is in the audience at one of his lectures, for example, Foucault will pretend not to notice. 'He never acknowledged me', says Michel, 'He always knew when I was there' (153). Between 1980 and 1984, Michel writes dozens of lengthy, impassioned letters to Foucault – 'love letters' (75), as the narrator describes them – but he never sends them. The more we learn about this 'relationship' the more it seems that we are dealing with a delusional admirer who fantasizes himself into a secret passionate rapport with Foucault that neither can ever publicly acknowledge. *Hallucinating Foucault* might almost be re-titled 'Michel Foucault as Paul Michel Imagines Him'.

The most striking of Michel's claims about Foucault is that although they studiously ignored each other in public, they conducted a secret dialogue through their published writings: 'We read one another with the passion of lovers', says Michel, 'Then we began to write to one another, text for text' (153). For Michel their published writings are like an almighty lovers' quarrel, a tit-for-tat exchange conducted in public but written in code. Of course, Michel's belief that Foucault wrote only for him sounds like the preposterous claim of a stalker, a fantasist. But this novel is not simply a case study in delusional obsession. Duncker uses the figure of Paul Michel to pose a fascinating 'what if?' question: what if, when we read *Discipline and Punish* or *The History of Sexuality*, we are hearing only one half of a passionate conversation? What if Foucault's published work was written as part of an ongoing dialogue with a brilliant novelist, a deranged *soixante-huitard* who matched him book for book? In pursuing this intriguing counterfactual logic, Duncker's invites us to rethink a central and controversial element of Foucault's work: his emphasis on those who have been silenced by history – the sick, the mad, the deviant, the other. These silencings are famously addressed in the opening to *Madness and Civilization*, which focuses on the 'broken dialogue' between reason and madness:

In the serene world of mental illness, modern man no longer communicates with the madman ... The language of psychiatry, which is

a monologue of reason about madness, has been established only on
the basis of such a silence.

I have not tried to write the history of that language, but rather the
archaeology of that silence.[21]

Foucault's project, then, is to rescue madness from its status as the silent –
or silenced – object of psychiatric discourse. But as Derrida famously
alleges, *Madness and Civilization* is still written *from* 'civilization' *about*
'madness'; it is yet another example of monologic reason applying itself
to the question of mental illness. Of course it is difficult to see how
things could have been any different. If Foucault were to speak for or on
behalf of madness, he would lay himself open to the charge of presump-
tuous cultural ventriloquism; whereas if he does not give the madness a
voice, if he chooses to write from the vantage point of Enlightenment
reason, he becomes complicit in its silencing. Either way, Foucault can
be accused of reproducing the very 'violent hierarchies' between reason
and madness, self and other, that he sets out to challenge. But Duncker's
novel opens a loophole for Foucault by re-imagining his writings as part
of a dialogic exchange with a novelist who speaks from and for everything – rootlessness, delinquency, homosexuality, madness – that is marginalized in the reign of the normative.

Michel's function in the novel, then, is as Foucault's countertype, his
mad novel-writing 'other'. When Michel sums up their relationship, he
characterizes it as one of uncanny doubling:

> He wanted to write fiction. He fretted that he was not handsome.
> That the boys would not flock to him, court him. I lived that life for
> him, the life he envied and desired. I had no authority, no position.
> I was just a clever charismatic boy with the great gift of telling stories.
> He was always more famous than I was. He was the French cultural
> monument. I was never respectable. But I wrote for him, petit, only
> for him. (154)

Michel and Foucault are caught in a relationship of reverse symmetry:
the philosopher writes about extreme experiences but leads an
apparently respectable life, whereas the novelist leads a disreputably
unconventional life but takes refuge in the order and clarity of writing.
This is a co-dependent model of literary relations in which theorist and
novelist are literary *doppelgängers* living vicariously through one other –
a notion that is given further weight by the symbolic significance of Paul
Michel's name. As Didier Eribon explains, Michel Foucault was known

to his mother and family as 'Paul-Michel Foucault', though he preferred to refer to himself simply as 'Michel' – perhaps because Paul was his father's name.[22] On a symbolic level, then, Duncker's 'Paul Michel' seems to borrow his identity from Foucault – he is the philosopher's creative *alter ego* or bastard son, the novelist he might have been. It would even be tempting to take this logic one step further and read *Hallucinating Foucault* itself as one of the unwritten novels that lurk in the pages of *Madness and Civilization* or *Discipline and Punish*.

However, although Michel likes to think of himself as the author of the novels Foucault could not write, there is also a sense in which he is both the product and the prisoner of the books that Foucault did write. Though Michel thinks of his literary relationship with Foucault as a mutual appreciation society, the truth is that it is more like a prison cell. Michel weds himself to the idea of having a readership of one – Foucault is his ideal reader, his only reader; Foucault's death therefore strands him in imaginative solitary confinement. He would have benefited from the advice scrawled by the narrator's girlfriend on her copy of one of his novels: 'BEWARE OF FOUCAULT' (13). However, it would always have been too late for Michel to receive this advice – since he was always-already a Foucauldian creature through and through. Whatever subjectivity he has seems to have been generated in the pages of Foucault's work on madness, deviance, otherness. Though his fiction returns obsessively to the theme of freedom – his titles include *Escape* and *The Prisoner Escapes* – the Michel whom Duncker's hero encounters is a long-term psychiatric patient, literally and imaginatively captivated by the world of *Madness and Civilization* and *Discipline and Punish*. In his numerous escape attempts and bids for freedom, meanwhile, Michel simply provides fresh case studies for the bleak subversion-containment dialectics that rumble on through Foucault's writings. We have already seen that in this novel 'Foucault' is in some important sense a figment of Michel's fantasy world; but it is equally possible to read 'Paul Michel' as a by-product of Foucault's writings. Foucault once described madness as 'the purest, most total form of *qui pro quo*; it takes the false for the true, death for life, man for woman'.[23] The 'mad' *qui pro quo* of Duncker's novel lies in the uncanny sense in which Michel and Foucault seem, impossibly, to have invented one another.

Hallucinating Foucault is quite the most mischievously inventive of the 'Foucauldian fictions' of recent years. *The Biographer's Tale* is a loyally 'Foucauldian' text, one that takes his ideas seriously and honours his desire for anonymity. The novels and stories by Guibert, Kristeva and Litt, meanwhile are unapologetically biographical narratives that display a shared fascination with the spectacle of a helpless Foucault, and take a certain sadistic pleasure in having the great philosopher secretly observed, dissected, infantilized, hospitalized and tortured. These anti-Foucauldian narratives thus expose him to all the mechanisms of observation and surveillance, psychiatric power and humanist gossip that he sought to demystify and evade in his writings. Though of course you could reverse this argument at the stroke of a pen by saying that because Foucault *has* demystified the discourses of panopticism, psychiatry and biography, he has therefore pre-emptively discredited the narrative strategies of Guibert, Kristeva and Litt. Duncker's novel is different, however, because it is not a Foucauldian but rather a *meta*-Foucauldian text – a novel about a Foucauldian novelist rather than about the man himself. In this sense, you could hardly ask for a better 'reading' of the Foucauldian narratives of Guibert, Kristeva and Litt than *Hallucinating Foucault*, since Duncker's novel provides us with a compelling portrait of a novelist locked in an inescapable power struggle with the 'great conspiratorial epistemologist'. Duncker's novel thus succeeds, uniquely, in maintaining an uncanny distance from the Foucauldian logic that limits and contains the transgressive gestures of his other delinquent literary aficionados.

7
Feminism *versus*
Post-structuralism

The relationship between feminism and post-structuralism has never been less than problematic. The pivotal debates of the latter – Lacan on Freud, Althusser on Marx, Derrida on Saussure – do after all look suspiciously like the latest chapter in the history of patriarchal thought, and the spectacle of a new generation of male philosophers wrestling with their intellectual fathers and grandfathers is hardly guaranteed to capture the imagination of female writers and academics. When Hélenè Cixous roundly derided 'the defenders of "theory", the sacrosanct yes-men of Concept, enthroners of the phallus',[1] she was referring specifically to male psychoanalytic discourse, but the note of defiant scepticism that she strikes here is broadly representative of feminist suspicions of contemporary male theorizing. It seems particularly problematic that many of the primary casualties of post-structuralism have been intellectual categories of obvious value to the feminist project. News of the death of the author, for example, seems to come at exactly the wrong time for those who bid to rescue female authors from the neglect they have suffered beyond the pale of a male-dominated canon: there is no advantage in having a room of one's own if there is no author to occupy it. Nor does the death of the subject seem an encouraging prospect in this context, given that autonomous subjectivity is another primary goal of the feminist project. Once upon a time, it seems, women were not entitled to certain cultural and ontological privileges; now that they are poised to seize their rightful share of truth, reality, authorship and subjectivity, those privileges have been declared null and void by the 'sacrosanct yes-men of Concept'. It might not be outlandishly paranoid, then, to think of post-structuralism as patriarchy's scorched-earth policy – a systematic obliteration of the age-old privileges of male subjectivity at the very moment that feminists are poised to inherit them.

However, to position post-structuralism in this way, as contemporary feminism's absolute 'other', would be something of an exaggeration; the writings of Derrida, Foucault and their contemporaries offer possibilities as well as problems for feminism. For example, when Foucault Prophesies the 'death of man', he seems strangely oblivious to the question of gender – for him, 'man' silently 'includes', which is to say excludes, 'woman'; but the idea that a post-Enlightenment reconstitution of the 'order of things' is likely to displace Man from the centre of the universe is not likely to provoke tremendous anxiety in feminist circles. Feminism need only take Foucault at his word, then, to read *The Order of Things* as an involuntary renunciation of the ancient privileges of male subjectivity. A similar kind of strategic alliance is possible between feminism and the post-structuralism of Barthes: if the notion of the 'death of the author' helps to do away with the literary cult of the lone male genius, then Barthes's essay would have done some considerable service to feminist revisions of the old patriarchal models of authorship.

The challenge for feminist theory, then, has been to think with and against post-structuralism, without itself becoming infected by the strains of demoralizing scepticism and patriarchal dogma to be found in the writings of Cixous's theoretical bogeymen. This challenge is articulated polemically by Cixous when she implies a wholesale gendering of theory as 'male', and non-theoretical discourse as 'female'. As 'The Laugh of the Medusa' memorably puts it, the subversive energies of *écriture féminine* are always liable to be wrongfully arrested by the cumbersome mechanisms of male theory:

> If the New Women, arriving now, dare to create outside the theoretical, they're called in by the cops of the signifier, fingerprinted, remonstrated, and brought into the line of order that they are supposed to know; assigned by force of trickery to a precise place in the chain that's always formed for the benefit of a privileged signifier. (263)

An obvious objection to this would be that Cixous's essay is an example of the very theorizing that it deplores; but of course 'The Laugh of the Medusa' could scarcely be further from the dreary academic discourse purveyed by the 'cops of the signified'. Indeed, Cixous's cops-and-robbers allegory, like her invocations of the power of the unconscious, laughter and the body, flamboyantly resists the bloodless protocols of conventional scholarly debate in order to strike out towards a no-man's-land between theory and creativity.

If 'The Laugh of the Medusa' represents a qualified breakthrough from theory into fiction, then contemporary feminist fiction might be said to move in the opposite direction. The two novels that I examine in this chapter represent powerful interventions by feminist authors in contemporary theoretical debates. Angela Carter's *Nights at the Circus* and A. S. Byatt's *Possession*, two of the most celebrated and sophisticated feminist novels of the late twentieth century, are conspicuously fluent in the language of post-structuralist theory, but notably ambivalent about its contribution to feminism; in different ways, their negotiations with post-structuralism are marked by a Cixousesque ambition to write 'outside the theoretical'. Of the two novels, Byatt's is much more obviously 'about' theory. *Possession* is a campus novel that deals directly with the tensions and intersections between post-structuralism and feminist literary scholarship in the sharply competitive academic climate of the 1980s, whereas Carter deploys language and imagery drawn from theoretical texts as part of the stylistic pyrotechnics of her fantastical, polyphonic novel. Lorna Sage, writing on Carter's debt to the French structuralist thinkers of the 1960s and 1970s, argues that they provided her with an 'armour of theory she could call on to protect her creative intuitions'.[2] *Nights at the Circus* certainly exudes a sense of theoretical self-consciousness. There is enough talk of signs, signifiers, simulacra, deconstruction, difference, panopticism, symbolic exchange and false consciousness in this novel to provoke a constant sense of theoretical *déjà vu*; it's very easy to think of *Nights at the Circus* as a hall of Lacanian mirrors, an archive of Derridean *écriture* or a raucous Bakhtinian carnival. But these tempting possibilities need to be viewed with a degree of scepticism. For example, this story of the riotous disintegration of a travelling circus in pre-revolutionary Russia seems so recognizably Bakhtinian that it is almost disappointing to learn that it was written before Carter had read *Rabelais and his World*; and it is also revealing to learn that when she did get round to reading Bakhtin, it was with some considerable scepticism.[3] We need to be wary of confusing this novel's *debts to* theory with its *affinities with* theory; with the exception of a chapter that is unmistakably modelled on a famous section from Foucault's *Discipline and Punish*, Carter's novel has covered its tracks. Whereas a novel like Burgess' *MF* leaves a trail of clues – surreptitious name-dropping, inconspicuous acrostics – for the reader to uncover its hidden structuralist agenda, *Nights at the Circus* does not flaunt traceable theoretical intertextualities, and it does not go in for theoretical name-dropping.

This chapter is necessarily speculative, then, in its account of the 'dialogues' between Carter and her theoretical sources and contexts. In addition to exploring her novel's Foucauldian intertextualities, I want to consider further its affinities with Cixous's 'Laugh of the Medusa', and with two further landmarks of 1970s theory: Derrida's work on mimesis in philosophy and literature, and Laura Mulvey's pioneering essay on cinema and the male gaze. The linguistic and thematic affinities between these texts and Carter's novel are often remarkably close – though never quite close enough to provide conclusive evidence of influence or intertextual overlap. What we certainly will not find in *Nights at the Circus* is any convenient symmetry between Carter and contemporary theory; as Alison Easton argues, her fiction represents 'an inventive, playful, sometimes critical and resisting use of these ideas in a fictional medium'.[4] But rather than saying that Carter 'uses' theory, or that her creativity inhabits a protective shell of theorists' words and ideas, it might be more appropriate to classify her as a theorist in her own right. 'She needed to *theorise*', says Lorna Sage, 'in order to feel in charge, and to cheer herself up'.[5] It is not a matter of Carter belabouring us with her pet theories; rather, she lets her garrulous characters theorize about their own predicaments like a cast of amateur philosophers displaying anachronistic fluency in the language of postmodernism. In a novel full of faulty clocks and watches, where events are often mysteriously out of step with the tick-tock of chronological time, it seems appropriate that Carter's *fin-de-siècle* whores and clowns should often sound as though they have been boning up on their twentieth-century philosophy.

The novel's heroine is Fevvers, a larger-than-life Cockney trapeze artist who claims to have been hatched from an egg in an abandoned laundry basket, and to sport a fully functioning pair of wings. 'Is she fact or is she fiction?' (7) is the question that tantalizes her admiring spectators – and engages the attention of Jack Walser, a young American journalist who makes it his business to expose Fevvers as a fraud. The novel opens in Fevvers' dressing room in the Alhambra Music Hall, where her first interview with Walser plays itself out as a lopsided power struggle in which the yarn-spinning circus performer runs rings around the truth-seeking journalist. Walser is outnumbered and overwhelmed from the start, not simply because Fevvers' monologue soon becomes a double act with her foster mother Lizzie, but also because he is confronted by multiple versions of Fevvers – there is her grinning reflection in a mirror and her picture emblazoned on a wall-size poster, not to mention the 'Fevvers' conjured up in the unverifiable tales of her outlandish past life as a *tableau vivant* in a whorehouse and exhibit in a museum of female monsters. Surrounded by Fevvers' specular, pictorial and linguistic doubles, and bamboozled by his loquacious interviewees, Walser is left feeling like 'a sultan faced with not one but two Scheherezades' (40).

Walser fails as an investigative journalist because he is hamstrung from the outset by his stubborn commitment to verifiable fact as the only form of truthful narrative. The nature of this failure is clarified later in the novel when, after a series of misadventures, he becomes apprenticed to a Siberian shaman, a village dream-reader who misreads his fragmented English as 'astral discourse' (260) full of prophetic visions. The Shaman functions in the novel as a kind of *alter ego* for Walser: if the journalist is addicted to fact, the dream-reader is immersed in a blend of mysticism and guesswork; together, they personify the contradictory extremes of male misreading. The Shaman's bungling attempts to interpret Walser's ramblings are like parodies of Walser's attempt to make sense of Fevvers, and when the Shaman treats Walser to glasses of his hallucinogenic urine, we might recall the image of Lizzie and Fevvers plying Walser with glass after glass of champagne; in both scenes, the text positions Walser as a professional sceptic who will swallow anything.

Nights at the Circus enjoys a great deal of irreverent fun, then, at the expense of incompetent male readers. In this sense it conforms to Cixous's definition of women's language as the 'anti-logos weapon' (250) that enters the zone of male writing in order to 'break up the "truth" with laughter' (258). Female laughter, for Cixous, is the only proper response to male myths of feminine monstrosity and lack: 'They riveted us between two horrifying myths: between the Medusa and the abyss. That would be enough to set half the world laughing, except that it's still going on' (255). *Nights at the Circus* certainly laughs long and hard at the clichés and category errors that bedevil male readings of women; and the epic laugh that concludes the novel – where the 'spiralling tornado of Fevvers' laughter' begins to 'twist and shudder across the entire globe' (295) – seems to echo and exceed the retaliatory laughter of Cixous's essay.

The captivating power of Fevvers' irrepressible voice and raucous laughter dominate the beginning and end of the novel: Walser feels from the outset that he has become a 'prisoner of her voice' (43), that she has 'lassooed him with her narrative' (60), and 'yarned him in knots' (89); and there is a corresponding devaluation of the power and authority of Walser's notebook and portable typewriter. As Fevvers will later taunt Walser, 'You mustn't believe what you write in the papers!' (294). But what we are not dealing with here is a naïvely phonocentric celebration of the female voice at the expense of a discredited male writing. Carter's novel does not attribute superior authenticity to the spoken word, nor does it regard the human voice as a short cut to the some inner region of genuine selfhood. *Nights at the Circus* reverberates with strangely displaced voices: the skeletal Madame Shreck is like a voice without a body; the circus singer Mignon is likened to 'fleshy phonograph' (247); Walser is schooled in ventriloquism by the Siberian shaman (263). Fevvers' own vocal performance strikes Walser as a piece of uncanny ventriloquism that originates 'not within her throat but in some ingenious mechanism or other behind the canvas screen' (43). If we recall that the novel's cast includes a voiceless manservant, literate chimpanzees, illiterate tribes-people, a professional writer who is reduced at one stage to unintelligible babble and a nonchalantly polyglot heroine who picks up foreign languages 'like fleas' (229), then we are evidently dealing with a formidably complex meditation on the acquisition, loss and recovery of language, on the shifting relations between speech and writing and on the permeability of the language barrier between different cultures – and even between different species.

Carter seems fascinated by the question of what it means to lose the power of speech and seize the power of writing, and this linguistic self-consciousness provides the context for the novel's engagement with the means by which women gain access to the written word. The novel frequently associates its female characters with revolutionary writings, like the anarchist pamphlets and newspapers half-concealed in Fevvers' dressing room; but it also concerns itself with the revolutionary impact of women gaining access to writing. When Fevvers briefly seizes Walser's notebook and pencil she performs a minor *coup d'état* in the republic of letters that is echoed elsewhere in the text. For example, Lizzie's letters from St Petersburg to exiled Russian comrades are smuggled via diplomatic channels that were earmarked for Walser's dispatches, while the female inmates of the Siberian prison prepare for their prison break by circulating notes written in bodily fluids on paper and rags. This theme of women taking subversive control of writing is replicated on a structural level in part three of the novel, where Fevvers, albeit in a patchy and unpredictable way, comes into her own as the novel's narrator.

Given this novel's complex variations on the themes of inscription and textuality, and on the supplementary relations between speech and writing, it seems reasonable to speculate on whether it might owe something to the writings of Jacques Derrida. Given also that Fevvers's real name is Sophie, and that she is 'a girl of philosophical bent' (185) whose ambiguous reality-status confounds the binary categories of western metaphysics, then it seems all the more tempting to associate *Nights at the Circus* with Derridean critiques of logocentric reason. So far, the question of Carter's knowledge and use of Derrida has been treated circumspectly. Robert Eaglestone says that questions of whether Carter read Derrida, or whether Derrida read Carter, are irrelevant, given the obvious affinities between the two; he concludes that it is enough to 'call Angela Carter a deconstructive writer or ... Derrida a Carteresque philosopher'.[6] Christopher Norris goes further by declaring his suspicion that *Nights at the Circus* may owe something to 'The Double Session', Derrida's long essay on mimesis in which he plays Mallarmé's short prose text 'Mimique' off against an excerpt from Plato's *Philebus*.[7] 'The Double Session' combs Mallarmé's writings on mime, theatre and dance for figures of in-betweenness – veils, fabrics, wings, feathers, curtains, mirrors – that might convey something of the 'undecidable' relationship between imitative art and imitated reality.[8] This repertoire of images displays a more than passing resemblance to those of *Nights at the Circus*; it is interesting moreover to notice the importance Derrida attaches to the figure of the 'hymen', which occurs at the heart of 'Mimique'. Signifying as it does both pristine virginity and consummated marriage, the hymen is taken by Derrida as another possible name for the undecidability that confounds any attempt to sort out presence from absence, identity from difference, original from copy; or, as he puts it, 'the hymen is the structure of *and/or*, between *and* and *or*' (268). The 'logic of the hymen' (223) articulated in Derrida's essay strongly invites comparison with the myth of Fevvers' virginity in the novel. It is only at the very end, after her first night with Walser, that Fevvers' claim to be 'the only fully feathered intacta in the entire history of the world' (71) is revealed to be unfounded. It is a revelation that changes everything and nothing. On one level it suggests that Walser has been asking the wrong question from the start, that Fevvers' sexual history rather than her reality-status might have been a more promising line of enquiry. But such an enquiry would of course simply trap Walser's understanding of Fevvers in the old virgin/whore dichotomy that occurs so often in male constructions of women. If the heroine of *The French Lieutenant's Woman* is a virgin posing as a fallen woman in order to expose the cruel double standards of Victorian gentility, Carter's heroine reverses the gambit by posing as a virgin in a community of fallen women. By performing innocence and fallenness, Fevvers and Sarah Woodruff are feeding masculine discourse back its own lies about women; in the case of Fevvers, the news of her non-virginity compounds one inadequate binarism (fact/fiction) with another (virgin/whore); or, to borrow Derrida's words, it places yet another *and/or* between the *and* and the *or*.

Derrida's essay also makes much of the image of the made-up face as an emblem of ungrounded representation, or what he will call 'mimicry imitating nothing ... reference without a referent' (217). When Derrida writes on the Pierrot who 'by simulacrum, writes in the paste of his own make-up upon the page he is' (208), and declares that the mime 'produces himself' (209), he could equally be describing the performative self-fashioning of Carter's clowns. Buffo, the Master Clown of Kearney's circus, similarly declares that 'We can invent our own faces! We *make* ourselves' (121). But the playful self-fashioning licensed by the clown's make-up is the corollary, for Buffo, of a troubling sense of inner hollow-ness: 'Take away my make-up and underneath is merely not-Buffo. An absence. A vacancy' (122). When Walser goes undercover as a clown, he experiences a comparable mixture of euphoria and anxiety:

> When Walser first put on his make-up, he looked in the mirror and did not recognise himself. As he contemplated the stranger peering interrogatively back at him out of the glass, he felt the beginnings of a vertiginous sense of freedom ... he experienced the freedom that lies behind the mask, within dissimulation, the freedom to juggle with being, and, indeed, the with the language which is vital to our being, that lies at the heart of burlesque. (103)

Walser here undergoes a kind of mirror stage in reverse, a moment of dizzying non-recognition rather than jubilant misrecognition, as he is absorbed into the very artifice that he sought to dispel. Though 'freedom' seems to be the byword of this passage, Walser will experience precious little freedom during his brief career in the circus. Like all of Carter's clowns, he seems to be caught between humanist and post-structuralist models of subjectivity, between an old model of selfhood as authentic interiority and a new one where the self is all surface and no depth. Though Carter's novel resists any simple nostalgia for the old humanism, it seems chary of new ideas of the self as sheer play of surfaces. Derrida writes very suggestively that 'the practice of "play" in Mallarmé's writing is in collusion with the casting aside of "being" ' (226). A similar suspension of being in play occurs when Buffo 'starts to deconstruct himself' (117) in the violent pirouettes that round off his performance; the master clown here provides a vivid corroboration of his pessimistic offstage philoso-phizing about the sense of absence and vacancy that lurks behind the clown's mask.

In true dialogic style, *Nights at the Circus* continually answers itself, chal-lenges its own intellectual positions, undermines its own 'truths'; rather than embodying the uproarious spirit of carnival, Carter's lugubrious clowns are there to offer downbeat counter-arguments to the euphoric versions of play and laughter that circulate elsewhere in the novel. As theorists of laughter, the clowns speak with the strange pathos of the professional laughing-stock who 'invites the laughter that would otherwise come unbidden' (119). They are attuned to the cruelty of laughter – 'The child's laughter is pure until he first laughs at a clown' (119) – and are mournfully aware of their tragicomic exclusion from the mirth that they provoke: as Buffo asks, 'who shall make the clown laugh?' (121). The cruelty of laughter is one element of Mallarmé's text that Derrida conspicuously fails to pick up on. 'Mimique' concerns a harlequinade in which a Pierrot straps his wife to a bed and proceeds to tickle her to death. Derrida's essay does not dwell on the unsavoury sexual politics of this uxoricidal fantasy, but if *Nights at the Circus* is a 'commentary' on 'The Double Session', it is one that reinstates the politics of sexual difference that Derrida elides. Men's murderous designs on women provide the novel with one of its more sinister motifs: Ma Nelson's brothel is in serial killer territory – 'tucked away behind the howling of the Ratcliffe Highway' (26) – whilst Fevvers narrowly escapes becoming a human sacrifice at the hands of Mr Rosencreutz. Matrimonial violence is also strikingly common in *Nights at the Circus* – Lizzie arranges for Jenny's wealthy husband to choke to death on a booby-trapped *bombe surprise* (46); the circus singer Mignon is the daughter of a wife-murderer (128); whilst the Siberian panopticon is full of unrepentant husband-killers (210). Apart from Fevvers and Walser, it would be difficult to find a single male–female relationship in *Nights at the Circus* that is not characterized by cycles of cruelty, exploitation and retaliation; sexual violence in this novel is obviously no laughing matter.

Just as the novel exposes the potential cruelty of laughter, it also dwells sceptically on notions of play and playfulness. Once again, the Master Clown provides an eloquently pessimistic commentary on what ought to be an upbeat theme. '[T]hose who hire us', says Buffo, 'see us as beings perpetually at play. Our work is their pleasure and so they think our work must be our pleasure, too, so there is always an abyss between their notion of our work as play, and ours, of their leisure as our labour' (119). Buffo's notion of play as oppressively hard work cuts powerfully against Colonel Kearney's marketing slogan, 'Welcome to the Ludic Game!' (103). This bombastic tautology strikes a false note in a novel whose disenchanted narrator at one point remarks that 'nothing is more boring than being forced to play' (109). With its insistent emphasis on the punishing economic necessity of working at the illusion of play, the novel is anything but a ludic free-for-all; it thus represents a significant problematization of the ideas of 'play' and 'freeplay' that achieved such inflated critical currency in the wake of Derridean deconstruction.[9] To the contention that *Nights at the Circus* makes direct use of Derrida's writings, we can only return the verdict 'not proven'; but what we can do is say that Carter's novel provides us with a sharply different angle on the matters of sadistic laughter and male violence; and it enables us to question whether the sense of compulsory playfulness that some readers find in deconstruction is really as liberating as it seems.

Liberation is something that *Nights at the Circus* dwells on quite obsessively: the novel is alive with emancipatory fantasies, but also sees prisons everywhere. Its freedom-loving characters are constantly menaced by nets, chains, cages, iron bars and strait-jackets; Fevvers, in particular, is in constant danger of having her liberty snatched away by any number of those sinister figures who aim, in Jago Morrison's words, to 'contain and police' her 'metamorphosing body'.[10] The novel registers and resists the claustrophobic forces that bear down on its flighty heroine by plotting an expansive narrative trajectory that begins in her oppressively cluttered dressing room but ends in the boundless wastes of Siberia. Except that somewhere deep in Siberia we stumble upon the novel's only real prison – a women-only prison, a female panopticon (210–18). Carter's panopticon is set up by one Countess P., who, having poisoned her husband, aims to assuage her sense of guilt by setting up a 'private asylum for female criminals' (210), specifically, for women who have been found guilty of killing their husbands. These women thus become her surrogate selves; they must experience penitential guilt because she has gotten away with murder. The Countess forces her murderesses to build a panopticon, and occupies the central viewing position to 'stare and stare and stare at her murderesses' whose cells were 'lit up like so many small theatres in which each actor sat by herself in the trap of her visibility' (210–11). This section of Carter's novel is obviously modelled on the famous section in Foucault's *Discipline and Punish* that explores Jeremy Bentham's design for the perfect prison with a central tower encircled by a ring of backlit cells whose solitary inmates are 'perfectly individualized and constantly visible'. In Foucault's panopticon, as in the Countess's, 'Visibility is a trap'.[11] For Foucault the major effect of the panopticon was 'to induce in the inmate a state of conscious and permanent visibility that assures the automatic functioning of power' (201). He defines the panopticon as a 'machine for dissociating the see/being seen dyad' (201), since it formally divides the all-seeing eye of the unseen centre from and the blindness of the permanently visible periphery.

While Foucault marvels at the seamless efficiency of Bentham's 'cruel, ingenious cage' (205), Carter is altogether less captivated by this perfect prison. Her first anti-Foucauldian move is to 'feminize' the panopticon. In Carter's novel, the brainchild of Bentham and Foucault is built, run and exclusively inhabited by women. But why would a feminist author want to lay claim to panopticism, or to fill a panopticon with women? In Carter's hands, Foucault's prison becomes a powerful image of false consciousness: although the institution is now run by and for women, it is still a male space, one that perpetuates imbalanced power relations in the name of a misguided project of moral rehabilitation. The place is 'manned' – Carter does not labour the obvious irony of the verb – 'exclusively by women' (214); which is another way of saying that the women-only panopticon is still a patriarchal environment. But the multiple *failures* of this patriarchal institution are what seem to capture Carter's imagination. She complicates the Foucauldian model of a one-way visibility with the image of inmates establishing intimate, erotic eye contact with their captors. She also presents the system's administrator as its most helpless victim: the Countess is 'trapped as securely in her watchtower by the exercise of her power as its objects were in their cells' (214). Moreover, whereas in Foucault the inmate is the 'object of information but never the subject of communication' (200), Carter's inmates begin to circulate passionate notes – a release of personal longing and desire into the impersonal machine that heralds a successful uprising against the Countess. In a sense these pages reveal Carter mobilizing against Foucault the very 'repressive hypothesis' that he tries to dismantle in *The History of Sexuality*. But it is perhaps for this very reason that the prison-break is, ultimately, something of a side issue in *Nights at the Circus*. If the Foucauldian model of society is too pessimistic to serve her feminist agenda, the image of the uprising as a glorious return of the repressed is too utopian for a novel that is full of narrow escapes but critical of escapism. In the figure of the 'Escapee', the fugitive anarchist whose dreams of 'a shining morrow of peace and love and justice' (239) are so trenchantly challenged by Lizzie, the novel satirizes any naïve equation between jailbreak and revolution; the idea that women are poised to escape from a hostile present into a glorious future glosses over their ongoing struggles with economic necessity and ideological oppression.

It is also significant that Carter places her panopticon on the very edge of the novel's world; with a telling irony, Foucault's model of power radiating out from some central vantage-point is consigned by Carter to an unsignposted corner of Siberia on the fringes of the text. *Nights at the Circus* reconstructs Foucault's monument to centralized power is in the middle of nowhere; none of its troupe of central characters pass through its gates or even catch sight of it. The panopticon is the only literal prison in the novel, and the only place in which Fevvers – so often caged and confined – is not imprisoned. Morrison suggests that Fevvers is not placed in the panopticon because 'the analysis of disciplinary society presented by Foucault seems to foreclose too radically on the possibility of personal autonomy ... fatally compromising the novel's emancipatory theme'.[12] It could alternatively be that Carter believes that Fevvers has always been the object of panoptical gazes, that modernity simply does not have any non-panoptical space left in which she might escape the faceless gaze of power. Joanne M. Gass argues along these lines when she links the panopticon with those other institutions in which society confines those whom it regards as 'deviant' – the whorehouse, the freak show and the circus. Fevvers' 'heroic role', according to Gass, is 'to be the instrument of destruction of panopticons': 'Just as the murderesses break the panopticon of their prison, so does Fevvers provide the means by which the panopticons of the whorehouse, the freak show, and the circus are ruptured'.[13] Gass is certainly right to suggest that there is more than one panopticon in the novel. To be imprisoned in some exquisite *objet d'art* – say, the tinsel bars of Fevvers' cage, or the Grand Duke's ornate Fabergé egg – is a form of ideological servitude every bit as oppressive as time in a prison cell. Throughout the novel, its female characters risk being confined in some 'cruel, ingenious cage' for the delectation of the male gaze; the Siberian panopticon is only a minor outpost of this ubiquitous system of surveillance.

The novel's sustained fascination with eyes and the gaze, with looking and being looked at, with spectacle, exhibitionism and visibility, invites comparison with Laura Mulvey's influential analysis of the operations of a sadistic and fetishistic male gaze on the female body in Hollywood cinema. For Mulvey, the visual pleasures afforded by the cinema are decidedly patriarchal:

> In a world ordered by sexual imbalance, pleasure in looking has been split between active/male and passive/female. The determining male gaze projects its fantasy onto the female figure, which is styled accordingly. In their traditional exhibitionist role women are simultaneously looked at and displayed, with their appearance coded for strong visual and erotic impact so that they can be said to connote *to-be-looked-at-ness*.[14]

Fevvers spends her career passing from one such 'exhibitionist role' to another – Cupid, Winged Victory, the Angel of Death, Cockney Venus. At Ma Nelson's brothel she serves her 'apprenticeship in *being looked at* – at being the object in the eye of the beholder' (23); as a young teenager, she 'existed only as an object in men's eyes' (39). This history of objectification leaves Fevvers in no doubt about the power of the gaze, but with some residual faith that not all eyes are cruel: 'is it not to the mercies of the eyes of others that we commit ourselves on our voyage through the world?' (39). Fevvers also learns to relish making a spectacle of herself: 'Look at me! With a grand, proud, ironic grace, she exhibited herself before the eyes of the audience ... LOOK AT ME!' (15). Her *to-be-looked-at-ness*, then, is anything but passive. To be sure, the male gaze that she captures so imperiously is often enough lasciviously possessive or even murderous, but Fevvers's constant gamble is that if she can keep her male admirers at a tantalizing look-but-don't-touch distance, she can fleece them for every penny. Quite how empowering such a strategy might be is disputed by a typically sceptical Lizzie: 'You must give pleasure of the eye', she says to her foster-daughter, 'or else you're good for nothing' (185). The troubling prospect that Fevvers might be not merely economically but *ontologically* dependent on the male gaze looms ever larger as she cuts an increasingly dishevelled figure in the novel's Siberian episodes, having apparently lost 'that silent demand to be *looked* at that had once made her stand out' (277). As Fevvers manages a defiant ripple of her plumage for the benefit of 'the eyes that told her who she was' (290), it seems that she can be herself so long as she manages to capture the right sort of attention; for her, there is all the difference in the world between being the centre of a spectacle and being an object of surveillance. But on the whole the novel's visual politics do not permit such an easy opposition between spectacle and surveillance; instead, we are invited to 'read' Fevvers with the enchanted eyes of the circus spectator *and/or* the degrading panoptical gaze of institutional power – equally unsatisfactory options that oblige the readerly gaze to turn back on itself and contemplate its own blindness and limitations. Carter's flamboyantly attention-seeking heroine thus turns out to be the blind spot of a novel where the crucial thing *to-be-looked-at* is the gaze itself.

Given Fevvers' craving for attention, it is perhaps surprising that the novel does not exactly grant us a ringside seat to enjoy the spectacle of her performances; she spends very little of the narrative airborne, and much more of it in the full flow of conversation, or monologue, as though her primary talent is as a *raconteuse* rather than an *aerialiste*. In part, the narrative keeps its distance from Fevvers in order to make the reader share Walser's uncertainty over the truth or otherwise of her wings; this also has the effect of making us think about what flight might signify more generally in the novel. As both John Brannigan and Sarah Gamble have observed, *Nights at the Circus* makes a series of associations between women and flight that are extremely suggestive of 'The Laugh of the Medusa'.[15] Given that 'woman has always functioned "within" the discourse of man', Cixous writes, 'the point is not to take possession in order to internalize or manipulate, but rather to dash through and to "fly" ' (257–8). She further claims that 'Flying is woman's gesture – flying in language and making it fly ... for centuries we've been able to possess anything only by flying; we've lived in flight, stealing away' (258). To 'fly', Cixous is suggesting, can mean to defy gravity; but it can also mean to flee – a play on words that encompasses a utopian dream of women soaring above oppression with a pragmatic recognition of women as permanent fugitives from patriarchal control. She further develops these ideas in a conceit that links aviation, escape and theft: '[Women] fly by the coop, take pleasure in jumbling the order of space, in disorienting it, in changing around the furniture, dislocating things and values, breaking them all up, emptying structures, and turning propriety upside down' (258). Cixous plays here on the French verb *voler*, which signifies both 'fly' and 'steal'. Women fly above, or flee from, or steal away from, or steal from, patriarchy; on the one hand, they soar free from its limits, on the other they stay close and siphon off its power. Feminism as imagined by Cixous is both spectacular and secretive; she refuses to choose between a dream of glorious emancipation and a reality of attritional resistance. Whether or not Carter is gesturing directly to Cixous – and the resemblances are certainly striking enough to foster that suspicion – her novel performs precisely the same balancing act between utopian dreaming and earth-bound pragmatism. Like Cixous, Carter tells a story of women whose relationship to male power is a matter of flying, fleeing and stealing; when Fevvers is not flying above or fleeing from men, she is fleecing them. And just as Carter's heroines leave a trail of devastation in their wake when they 'fly by the coop' – the whorehouse goes up in flames, the circus falls apart at the seams, the failed panopticon is left with a solitary occupant, the transsiberian express is blown off the rails by outlaws – so the novel itself 'flies' unpredictably beyond closed institutional structures and established routes towards an open, uncertain future.

Whereas *Nights at the Circus* takes the nineteenth century as its vividly realized historical 'present', Byatt's *Possession* dramatizes the scholarly reconstruction of the hidden lives of the Victorians by academics in the 1980s. The novel depicts a scramble between rival Victorianists to fathom the literary implications of an adulterous affair between two nineteenth-century poets, Randolph Henry Ash and Christabel LaMotte, details of which had been lost to history until a chance discovery in the London Library by a dogsbody research assistant, Dr Roland Michell. When Michell stumbles across two draft letters by Ash to an unidentified female addressee, curiosity gets the better of him, and he spirits them out of the library in an exemplary case of 'gamekeeper turned poacher'. Michell's thoroughly unprofessional act of academic delinquency abundantly redeems itself, however, by generating the kind of exhilarating literary–historical revelations that you would never get from his scholarly colleagues or theoretical rivals. Operating outside the jurisdiction of the 'Ash factory' (26), and in defiance of the one-size-fits-all models of post-structuralist theory, Byatt's hero not only discovers rich new seams of textual knowledge, but also *re*-discovers the intense excitements of reading itself. What seems to animate *Possession* from the outset, then, is a certain longing for the de-professionalization of reading, for its rediscovery as a powerful, individual human appetite rather than a factory operation.

Michell's readerly adventure takes place against the backdrop of the 'cut-throat ideological battles of structuralism, post-structuralism, Marxism, deconstruction and feminism' (311) that violently convulsed literary studies in the 1980s. On the face of it, Byatt's novel is a portrait of a profession that is riven by a clear generation gap between the elder statesmen of traditional scholarship and the unruly children of the theoretical moment. The distinguished Ash scholars James Blackadder and Mortimer Cropper are Byatt's representatives of the pre-theoretical old guard, veterans of a profession that has transformed itself beyond recognition within a single generation. The extent of these changes is registered by Blackadder's recurring nightmare in which he has to resit his final examinations 'at a moment's notice and with new papers on Commonwealth Literature and post-Derridean strategies of non-interpretation' (399). The idea of theory as a nightmare from which traditional literary scholarship is struggling to awake is one that *Possession* seems to take half-seriously, though Byatt's anti-theoretical satire styles itself as the voice of informed scepticism rather than defensive ignorance.

It seems unlikely that examinations on Commonwealth literature and Derrida would provoke much nightmarish anxiety in the novel's primary theoreticians, the swaggering deconstructionist Fergus Wolff and the radical feminist Leonora Stern. As his name suggests, Wolff is a blood relative of the lycanthropic Marko Kraljević in Hynes's *The Lecturer's Tale*, a shape-shifting predator in the field of literary studies. His ventures into the territory of feminist criticism also reveal him as an exponent of 'critical cross-dressing', to borrow Elaine Showalter's term for the bad faith of male critics who opportunistically borrow the garb of feminist radicalism.[16] Strong on Parisian flair and dazzle, Wolff is obviously weak on the kind of gruelling archival spadework performed by the novel's scholarly journeymen and -women. For all his critical cross-dressing and shape-shifting, Wolff learns and develops less than any of the other scholars and critics in the course of the novel.

The problem with Leonora Stern's theorizing, meanwhile, is not bad faith but wishful thinking. Generously excerpted in Byatt's narrative, Stern's monograph on LaMotte and female subjectivity traces far-fetched links between the evasive landscapes of women writers from the Brontës to Woolf, female auto-eroticism in Irigaray and Cixous, and the 'mythemes [*mitemi*] of the vegetable cycle of lettuce' (246) in contemporary anthropology. These efforts to plumb the anthropological and mythological secrets of LaMotte's poem seem, in the end, to land us back in the bad old days when scholars sought the 'answer' to *The Waste Land* in obscure vegetation ceremonies. Stern's reading of *Melusina* is less a rigorous interpretation than a new feminist mythopoeia, a cross-disciplinary fiction of huge ambition and unintentional bathos. On reading these paragraphs from Stern, it is difficult not to recall Byatt's description of Monique Wittig's Amazonian fantasies as 'both unforgettable and boring'.[17]

Unlike many novels of the theory wars, however, *Possession* does not resolve itself in to a simplistic stand-off between the old guard and the Young Turks. Positioned somewhere between these two extremes are Michell himself and the LaMotte specialist Maud Bailey, with whom he collaborates and eventually falls in love. Michell and Bailey have none of Blackadder and Cropper's phobic incomprehension of theory, but neither do they exhibit much of an appetite for the language and ideas of post-structuralist thought. They belong to a *post*-theoretical generation, fluent in the language of post-structuralism but impatient with its limitations and resentful of its oppressive ubiquity. For Michell and Bailey, theory is not the lifeblood of critical debate but a distracting source of background intellectual noise that drowns out the voices of the literary past. It is ironic in this context that Roland Barthes threatens to overshadow Browning's Childe Rolande as Michell's most obvious literary namesake and precursor. But then again, what significance Michell and Bailey attach to theory tends to be personal rather than literary – that is, they use their training in the 'post-structuralist deconstruction of the subject' (9) to read *themselves* rather than to read the texts of Ash or LaMotte. Roland, for example, is capable of deriving 'precise postmodernist pleasure' (421) from the sense of *déjà vu* provoked by his re-enactment, with Maud, of the Ash–LaMotte affair. Postmodernism and post-structuralism provide them both with a surprising degree of pleasure and even comfort. Roland and Maud seem fond of their deconstructed selves, reasonably happy with the idea of the subject as a 'illusion' (424), a 'crossing-place for a number of systems' (424) or a 'sussuration of texts and codes' (251). The model of the deconstructed self certainly accords nicely with a style of critical reading in which the critic tactfully melts into the background so that the author can occupy centre stage. But part of the appeal of post-structuralism is also that it translates Maud and Roland's English reserve into a language they can understand: it is easier to think of oneself as illusory, fractured and decentred than as awkwardly diffident and self-effacing.

In other respects, however, theory seems to offer a model of the self that is oppressively knowing rather than comfortingly vague:

> They were children of a time and culture which mistrusted love, 'in love', romantic love, romance *in toto*, and which nevertheless in revenge proliferated sexual language, linguistic sexuality, analysis, dissection, deconstruction, exposure. They were theoretically knowing: they knew about phallocracy and penisneid, punctuation, puncturing and penetration, about polymorphous and polysemous perversity, orality, good and bad breasts, clitoral tumescence, vesicle persecution, the fluids, the solids, the metaphors for these, the systems of desire and damage, infantile greed and oppression and transgression, the iconography of the cervix and the imagery of the expanding and contracting Body, desired, attacked, consumed, feared. (423)

As this flood of theoretical logorrhoea washes back and forth through his mind, Roland finds himself in an intellectual world where knowingness has replaced knowledge. Theory has had too much to say about the self, and too much of what it has said pathologizes the body as a place of oppressive anxieties and perverse desires or fragments it into impersonal orifices and erogenous zones. The question is whether, after ' "all the *looking-into*" ' (267) by these peeping Toms of the psyche, such claustrophobically intimate 'knowledge' of the self can be unlearned. Maud's quiescent answer to this question is that 'In every age, there must be truths people can't fight ... We live in the truth of what Freud discovered' (254). For Roland, the answer increasingly lies in a shift from the rebarbative lexicon of post-Freudian theory to 'the words that named things, the language of poetry' (473).

Roland's attempt to escape from theory into literature represents a defiant attempt to fight the 'truths' of post-structuralist and post-Freudian thinking; in many ways his story is *Possession*'s story, since Byatt's novel mounts its own forceful resistance to theory. But unlike its unaligned hero, the novel does have a set of complex and ambivalent theoretical allegiances, most significantly to various strands of feminism and post-structuralism, though these allegiances do not always leap off the page. For example, Byatt has described *Possession* as a 'very, very feminist book',[18] but as we have seen in the case of Leonora Stern, she does not grant her feminists any special privileges or exempt them from her wide-ranging satire of hyper-specialized approaches to literature. For Byatt, feminism is as capable as any other theoretical approach of producing selective, flawed and distorted readings. She has voiced her disquiet, for example, over the fate of those women writers 'who are not taught because they do not address "women's issues" ',[19] and is staunchly reluctant to be 'ghettoized by modern feminists into writing about women's problems'.[20] Which makes it all the more intriguing to learn that LaMotte's fairy epic *Melusina* – lengthy excerpts from which are 'reproduced' in *Possession* – was inspired by Luce Irigaray's work, in *Divine Women*, on powerful women who were neither virgins nor mothers. '[*Melusina*] was written', says Byatt, 'to conform with a feminist interpretation of the imaginary poem – an interpretation I had in fact written before writing the text itself'.[21] What Byatt traces here is a remarkable reversal of traditional 'literary causality'. Ordinarily, you would expect the literary text to produce the theoretical interpretation, but in this case the feminist interpretation has produced the literary text: LaMotte's poetry is a side effect of feminist theory rather than its origin or pretext.

In the character of Christabel LaMotte, Byatt has thus created a nineteenth-century woman poet whose life and work tally faultlessly with the concerns of contemporary feminism. Reclusive, unmarried and possibly lesbian, LaMotte cannily shelters herself from the patriarchal question with which Irigaray says women are constantly bullied:

> 'Who are you in love with?' 'Are you a virgin?' 'Are you married?' 'Do you have any children?' These are the questions which one always asks and which position a woman. They only position her in relation to a social *function* and not in relation to feminine identity and autonomy. With this function as a starting point, how can a woman

keep for herself a margin of singularity, of non-determinism which would permit her to become and remain herself?[22]

It is precisely in a bid to 'become and remain herself' that LaMotte behaves so elusively in this novel, disappearing from view during her pregnancy and rebuffing Ash's attempts to discover whether the child he fathered survived. And it is a measure of her success that nearly a century later literary historians are still labouring under the misapprehension that she was virgin rather than a mother. Like Fowles's Sarah Woodruff and Carter's Fevvers, LaMotte emerges as a feminist heroine who successfully confounds reductive efforts to classify her as a mere 'social function'. It is LaMotte's *writing* in particular that secures her a certain 'margin of singularity' in a claustrophobically patriarchal society. Every bit as elusive as its author, LaMotte's poetry locates itself in the wild zones of the female unconscious where women are figured as 'monstrous' hybrids, singular creatures of the margins where they can escape the voyeuristic male gaze. The neglect of LaMotte's poetry by the male literary establishment has only made it more attractive to feminist critics, though as we have seen in the case of Leonora Stern, the female poet has not always been well served by her feminist readers. Not only does Leonora's reading seem flawed on its own terms, but the novel's scholarly revelations about LaMotte bring all sorts of discordant new biographical information into the picture. It seems, for example, that the fantastic landscapes of *The Fairy Melusina* may derive as much from a walking tour of Yorkshire as from some collective female unconscious. More broadly, the long-delayed revelation that LaMotte participated in at least one heterosexual relationship, from which she bore a child, is awkward news for those who want her to be a closet lesbian or proto-feminist. So whilst Byatt has taken her cue from Irigaray, *Possession* is less an obediently 'Irigarayan' text than a mischievous exploration of what happens when theoretical readings are seriously inconvenienced by historical facts.

While *Possession* is broadly satirical in its representations of feminist *readings*, it attaches considerable value to feminism's involvement in archival and editorial labours that have none of the cachet of postmodern theorizing. As Louise Yelin remarks, the novel is a 'rewriting of the history of post-war criticism that restores to prominence scholarly labors regarded as feminine and accordingly undervalued or, conversely, deemed of little value and accordingly assigned to women'.[23] *Possession* begins with Michell poring over Ash's copy of Vico's *Principj di Scienza Nuova* – that is, with a male critic reading a male philosopher for signs of his influence on a male poet. But this exclusively male textual environment is disrupted when Roland stumbles upon the draft letters concealed within Ash's Vico, and speculates about their unidentified female addressee. This unexpected female presence in this world of male textuality prompts Roland to call upon the expertise of Maud Bailey, who will eventually discover that LaMotte is her great-great-grandmother. In this shift of emphasis, the novel rehearses in fictional terms the gestures of those feminist critics who attempt to reconstruct the matrilineal traditions obscured by patriarchal culture. As such, it functions as a novelistic tribute to the ongoing recuperation of neglected traditions of women's writing and the feminist rehabilitation of certain genres – the letter, the private journal, the fairly tale – that have been gendered as 'female' and therefore deemed to be sub- or extra-canonical. Broadly speaking, then, if *Nights at the Circus* resonates most closely with the 'French feminism' of Cixous, *Possession* is a piece of fictionalized gynocritics, in the tradition of scholarship on marginalized nineteenth-century women writers by such critics as Gilbert and Gubar, Elaine Showalter and Byatt's dedicatee, Isobel Armstrong.

Feminism is, however, by no means the only critical theory with which the novel engages: Byatt has remarked that *Possession* is 'a post-modernist, poststructuralist novel and it knows it is'.[24] Its credentials as such are evident from the opening scene, when Roland opens Ash's Vico to find the letters to LaMotte: we are immediately positioned in a world of texts about texts and texts within texts. The narrative is interspersed by thousands of words of quotation from real and fictitious authors – lavish excerpts from poetry, fiction, diaries, letters, biographies, theory and criticism that transform *Possession* into a kind of pseudo-anthology of nineteenth-century prose and poetry 'framed' by a miscellany of twentieth-century criticism. The novel's 'tour-de-force of manufactured evidence',[25] its patchwork of invented quotation and fictionalized scholarship, transforms the scholarly archive into a postmodern labyrinth from which there are no obvious openings onto historical 'reality'. Although the novel begins with the image of a scholar striking gold in the archives, it displays less than whole-hearted confidence in ability of scholarship to reconstruct the past in any comprehensive or accurate fashion. Historical 'evidence' in *Possession* is necessarily incomplete and endlessly misreadable – which is good news if you want to set about debunking existing patriarchal versions of 'official' literary history, but rather more problematic if you want to construct a feminist counter-narrative as the 'correct' alternative. To oversimplify slightly, we might say that the novel's feminist content is at odds with its post-structuralist form – the aspirations of gynocriticism to set the record straight is every-where problematized by the effects of textuality, indeterminacy, unde-cidability. The relationship between feminism and post-structuralism in Byatt's novel might therefore be characterized as a dialogue between a hermeneutic of repossession (the feminist recuperation of a suppressed chapter of literary history) and a hermeneutic of dispossession (a sense of truth as irrecoverably dispersed among endless textual traces).

Possession's narratives of dispossession begin with a pair of stolen letters – or 'purloined letters', as the text repeatedly calls them (30, 40, 124). The literary reference here is of course to 'The Purloined Letter', Edgar Allen Poe's classic detective story about an unnamed Minister's audacious theft of a compromising letter from under the very eyes of its royal addressee, and the same letter's reappropriation by the brilliant Dupin, who finds it casually hanging in plain view in a letter rack in the Minister's apartment (where it had gone completely unnoticed by police search teams). Byatt's novel is not only an ambitious rewriting of 'The Purloined Letter' as a 'romance of the archive', but also a disguised commentary on the quite extraordinary amount of theoretical attention that Poe's story has attracted. When Lacan published his hugely influ-ential 'Seminar on "The Purloined Letter" ' he initiated an ongoing debate that has made the text a *locus classicus* of post-structuralist controversy.[26] For Lacan, the key point about Poe's tale is that its pattern of intersubjective relationships – between King, Queen and Minster, and between the Police, the Minister and Dupin – is entirely determined by the whereabouts of the letter; this story of a stolen and re-stolen letter can thus be read as an allegory of 'the decisive orientation that the subject receives from the itinerary of a signifier' (40). Crucially, we never get to learn what the Queen's letter is *about*; it functions, as Lacan puts it, as a 'pure signifier' (45) with no signified content. In tracing the effects of a content-free signifier that's 'hidden' in plain view, Lacan is arguing against a model of content-obsessed depth psychology that he implicitly associates with the 'realist's imbecility' (55) of the police in Poe's story, who naively assume that a systematic probe into every inch of the Minister's apartment will reveal the purloined letter's secret hiding place. What they fail to appreciate is that 'nothing, however deep in the bowels of the earth a hand may seek to ensconce it, will ever be hidden there, since another hand may always retrieve it, and that what is hidden is never but what is *missing from its place*' (55). The 'Seminar on "The Purloined Letter" ' thus represents a decisive move away from a model of psychoanalytic reading that aims to plumb the depths of psychic interiority in search of buried content or hidden signifieds.

Lacan's 'Seminar' was only the first intervention in what has become an increasingly involved debate. In an ingenious critique of the 'phallogocentrism' of Lacan's argument, Derrida points out that the 'Seminar' focuses primarily on the 'content and meaning' of 'The Purloined Letter' rather than 'the writing itself', and that Poe's floating signifier has therefore become Lacan's secure signified.[27] Barbara Johnson would subsequently trump Derrida by examining the moments in his argument where he reproduces the very intellectual fallacies that it claims to critique in Lacan, though she also shrewdly observes that like Lacan and Derrida (and the Minister and Dupin), she is playing an interpretative game that 'seems to turn one-upmanship into inevitable one-downmanship'.[28] And sure enough, Poe's commentators have continued to outflank one another in this apparently never-ending game of one-upmanship/one-downmanship.[29] But despite the formidable intricacy of the arguments and counter-arguments involved, what the debate between Lacan, Derrida and Johnson boils down to is an almost comically protracted wrangle over meaning and validity of Lacan's slightly enigmatic claim that a letter 'always arrives at its destination' (72). If Lacan believes that the trajectory of the signifier can furnish us with reliable map of intersubjective relationships, Derrida argues that things are never quite so predictable. Linguistic messages do not always stick to their 'proper' course, the signifier does not always coincide dependably with the signified – the force of dissemination means that 'a letter can always *not* arrive at its destination' (65; emphasis mine).

As it weighs into the debate over 'The Purloined Letter', Byatt's novel exhibits a keen sense of the exciting and exasperating 'metatextual vertigo'[30] generated by any attempt to think back through Johnson's reading of Derrida's reading of Lacan's reading of Poe. *Possession* is a novel of epistolary theft and disruption in which letters are constantly going astray; in the course of the action, linguistic messages are variously intercepted, stolen, destroyed or forgotten both by its secretive Victorians and its hungrily inquisitive contemporary scholars. Unlike Lacan, however, Byatt conceives of the letter not as a 'pure signifier' but as a text rich in signified content – we get to read dozens of revealing letters in the course of the novel; and whilst Poe's detective recovers a letter that's paradoxically 'hidden' in plain view, the lost letters of *Possession* are retrieved by its scholar-detectives from the depths of secret hiding places. Whereas Poe's policemen find nothing when they riffle through the pages of the Minister's books, Roland finds emotionally revealing letters in Ash's Vico, while Maud Bailey finds the Ash–LaMotte correspondence in a secret compartment in a four-poster bed in the poet's childhood home, Seal Court (83–4). Christabel's final letter to Ash is subsequently discovered in a sealed box in the Ash grave (498) – not quite the 'bowels of the earth', but certainly an example of the kind of secret spatial interiority that Lacan scornfully dismisses. With its sealed boxes and intimate nooks and crannies harbouring all sorts of Victorian literary treasures and sensational family secrets, the narrative space of *Possession* is richly three-dimensional and unapologetically 'realist', quite unlike the flattened-out space mapped by Lacan in 'The Purloined Letter'.

Possession also seems to part company from Lacan on the question of whether letters always reach their destination. Towards the end of the novel we learn of two key messages that never arrived – Christabel's unopened letter to Ash confirming that his daughter is alive and well (499–503), and Ash's verbal message to Christabel, confirming that he has met their daughter (511). It seems that when Byatt joins the Lacanian-Derridean epistolary paper-chase, she does so on the side of Derrida, constructing her novel like a postal system gone haywire or a huge dead-letter office. There is, however, one privileged channel of communication in the novel through which messages always get through – the relationship between author and reader. In the novel's remarkable, vaguely dream-like 'Postscript', Byatt takes us directly to 1868 to witness the meeting between Ash and his daughter, whom he entrusts with a message for Christabel that is promptly forgotten by the carefree young girl. Unlike Christabel, and unlike Byatt's ensemble of grave-robbing Victorianists, Byatt's readers know that Ash knew he had a daughter; the novel thus seems to end on a note of emphatic literary one-upmanship by forging a bond of shared omniscience between author and readers from which scholars and critics are pointedly excluded.

We have seen, then, that this novel values hard-won archival knowledge over glib theoretical knowingness; but it also discloses the limitations of even that knowledge in comparison with the full-bodied recuperation of the past that seems possible only in fiction. The omniscient author's surprising comeback in this postmodern text is evidently designed to point up just how much of what passes for rigorous scholarship and well-informed criticism is really only guesswork. The melodrama of the novel's grave-robbing scene – the definitive scene of authorial necrology in modern fiction – thus assumes its full significance as a comic-gothic allegory for Byatt's sly resurrection of the long-buried conventions of nineteenth-century literature. In laying claim to the old privileges of authorial omniscience, *Possession*'s Postscript makes its readers privy to secrets beyond the grasp of her novel's army of critics, theorists, biographers, editors, collectors and archivists; what the novel celebrates here is the vital capacity of literature to resist and exceed the schematic designs of the professional reader. The Postscript therefore represents the novel's most formal attempt to stake out an imaginative territory 'outside the theoretical', an extra-archival narrative space that cannot be rummaged through by scholars or peered into by prurient theorists. But as Steven Connor argues, in a subtle discussion of the novel's ending, the status of the Postscript is nevertheless highly problematic; it is a teasingly ill-defined piece of 'virtual history', an undocumented episode that the novel 'both includes … and omits'.[31] What is more, by concluding with the image of a letter 'which was never delivered' (511), the novel reaches its destination by entrusting to the reader an ambiguous message about the non-arrival of a message. The 'metatextual vertigo' is as strong as ever: Byatt's secret dialogue with Lacan is conducted through to the very end of a section that aims to transcend the theoretical – which is to say that *Possession*'s crowning gesture of anti-theoretical one-upmanship is, perhaps inevitably, also its most revealing moment of one-downmanship.

8
Criminal Signs: Murder in Theory

When detectives in Norman N. Holland's *Death in a Delphi Seminar* (1995) scan the bookshelves of a brutally murdered graduate student, they are surprised to find novels by Amanda Cross, Kirby Farrell, Sarah Paretsky and Q. Patrick 'alphabetized in with his copies of Barthes and Derrida and Lacan and Foucault'.[1] This image of detective thrillers interleaved with highbrow theoretical texts provides us not simply with a glimpse of the victim's eclectic literary tastes, but also with a memorable clue about how to read Holland's own novel – that is, as a poststructuralist whodunit in which theoretical enquiry is explicitly associated with the procedures of a criminal investigation. If this seems like an improbable conflation of the mandarin with the mainstream, it is worth remembering that critical theorists have a long-standing interest in crime fiction – Barthes, Derrida and Lacan have all written on the genre – and that the critic-as-detective conceit is sufficiently commonplace to be dropped into informal conversation in both *Possession* and *The Biographer's Tale*. The affinities between theory and crime fiction are strong enough for novelists to have been tempted by the idea of the detective as a kind of hard-boiled Derrida, or the theorist as a Dupin of the conference circuit. Like the detective, the theorist is a tenacious reader of signs, frequently unconventional in his or her methods and prone to arrive at counter-intuitive conclusions that provoke the disdain of those (the regular police, traditional critics) who prudently confine themselves to 'commonsense' interpretation. If a certain 'hermeneutic of suspicion' is the default position of post-structuralist epistemology, then so too does detective fiction display an instinctive distrust of the 'self-evident'. Nothing is 'obvious' for the detective or the theorist: they inhabit a world of equivocal signs, red herrings, hidden agendas, aporetic narratives, missing persons. As Gilbert Adair has shown, the question *whodunit?* applies as much to an unattributable post-Barthesian text as it does to an unsolved murder. In the theoretically self-conscious fiction of writers like Adair, Byatt and Holland, the site of reading has been reinvented as the scene of a crime.

Where detectives and theorists part company, however, is on the question of determinate meaning. Detective fiction, at least in its more conventional forms, displays a generic confidence in the legibility of signs. We can be confident, in a conventional whodunit, that all those telltale signifiers at the crime scene – the fingerprints, bloodstains and so forth – will be reunited by the detective with their hidden signifieds, prior to the identification of the tale's ultimate hidden signified, the murderer. In this sense you could say that the detective is a professionally logocentric reader whose investigations, however idiosyncratically they are conducted, plot a predictable course towards determinate meaning and interpretative closure. As Julia Kristeva points out in one of her decidedly unconventional whodunits, what detective fiction promises is 'the eternal return of lucidity'.[2] From a theoretical perspective, on the other hand, questions of readerly interpretation are not susceptible of dependably lucid resolution; the case can never be closed, because any definitive connection between the signifier and the signified has been placed on permanent hold. You can see how, in contradistinction to the efficient problem-solving of the whodunit, the discourse of post-structuralism might strike the average private eye as quite phenomenally indecisive, both in its language of 'indeterminacy', 'undecidability', and 'open-endedness', and in the have-it-both-ways gestures that characterize its arguments. Despite their intriguing affinities, then, post-structuralist theory and detective fiction are, as this chapter will show, mutually problematizing forms of intellectual narrative. Umberto Eco's *The Name of the Rose* and Kristeva's Stephanie Delacour novels represent the investigator as a privileged but not infallible semiotician bringing his or her expertise to bear on bafflingly enigmatic crimes. In other examples of the post-structuralist whodunit, theory is itself the guilty party. Adair's *The Death of the Author*, as we have seen, is a fictive inquest into deconstruction, its shady origins, guilty secrets, and the crimes against truth that are committed in its name. Campus murder stories like *Death in a Delphi Seminar* or D. J. H. Jones's *Murder at the MLA* follow Adair's lead by placing theory itself under investigation, turning the detective's forensic gaze on the misdemeanours – criminal and intellectual – of post-structuralism and its practitioners.

Murder at the MLA revolves around the violent deaths of four professors of literature at a convention hotel in Chicago thronged with ambitious, rivalrous and backbiting critics.[3] Baffled by the background noise of theoretical chatter that accompanies his investigation – talk of polyvocal narrativities, representativity, alterity, nonlinear commodification and the like – the lead detective, Boaz Dixon, enlists the help of Nancy Cook, an Assistant Professor from Yale, as his interpreter and unofficial side-kick. Their 'partnership', like the one between Lodge's Robyn Penrose and Vic Wilcox, is designed to demystify theory by exposing it to non-academic savvy; the far-fetched claims and *avant garde* logic of post-modernism may go down well at the convention, but are unlikely to cut much ice with a streetwise homicide cop. As in Lodge's novel, however, the odd-couple scenario does lead to modest degree of role-reversal: Cook gets to play detective while Dixon receives an accelerated educa-tion in the controversies that dominate contemporary literary theory. The academic culture to which Cook introduces him is acrimoniously polarized between the old-fashioned 'Tweeds' and the hyperproductive, sharply factionalized 'Trendies', whose lunatic fringe, as she sees it, are the literature-hating deconstructionists for whom language has absolutely no semantic content and no secure basis in reality. The satire of deconstruction here is fairly crude stuff, and the same is true of Jones's pot shots at political theories – the Marxist delegates at the conference are obviously hypocritical because they wear leather jackets and expensive gym shoes. More interestingly, the novel also launches a critique of the *commerce* in theoretical ideas. Aggressively marketed by sidewalk 'hucksters' and 'snake oil' merchants (73–4), the latest theories are eagerly snapped up by gullible 'idea-shoppers' (113) like so many brands, fashions and lifestyle options. Commodified in this way, theory provides the impatient modern intellectual, the don with articles to pub-lish and deadlines to meet, with a shortcut to knowledge; it offers precisely the kind of instant intellectual gratification sought by the conference delegate who 'hated to read and only wanted to *know* things' (151).

But if this tawdry theoretical bazaar satisfies the modern demand for instant knowledge, it also ministers to much darker appetites. Theory, as represented by Jones, exhibits an unsavoury fascination with historical representations of violence; the New Historicism, in particular, seems to have an almost pornographic interest in narratives of cruelty, degradation and murder. One conference delegate, Sarton P. Mudge, laces his work on early modern witch-hunts with accounts of eighteenth-century child abuse by starvation and pigtail strangulations in nineteenth-century China – gratuitously nasty anecdotes that find their way into his work 'evidently by free association of the professor's mind around the numi-nous nexus of blood' (109). The title of Mudge's book, *Learning to Parse*, is evidently meant to bring to mind Stephen Greenblatt's *Learning to Curse*, which reproduces in its introduction a detailed account of the torture and execution of a Chinese goldsmith in seventeenth-century Java – an opening gambit whose calculated shock-value is itself indebted to the spectacularly gruesome public execution scene at the outset of Foucault's *Discipline and Punish*.[4] It seems, at least in Jones's eyes, that nothing excites the contemporary theorist more than stumbling upon episodes of inhuman cruelty that can be served up for the delectation of an audience whose moral sensitivities have long since been numbed by a steady diet of Foucauldian and Derridean nihilism.

One such professorial sociopath in Jones's novel is Malcolm Gett, a Derridean-Foucauldian expert on serial killers who takes the sensationalist view that murder is 'the ultimate human freedom' (174); predictably enough, Gett is brutally killed by the MLA murderer. Another, Michael Alcott, who writes obsessively on 'dismemberment, body distortion, deformity' (152), is pushed from a tenth-floor balcony to end up resembling the very mutilation photos that adorn his publications. The 'irony' here is that deaths of Gett and Alcott serve as graphic illustrations of their morally unhinged scholarship; in a sense, they are killed by their own theories. Indeed, all four of the novel's murders represent forms of vicious poetic justice served up by an embittered young academic, Deborah Rames, who lost her job at the University of Arizona because of her ignorance of critical theory. The convention is Rames's opportunity to settle a score with the fashionable intellectual community that rejected her, though there is a perverse sense in which her killing spree is also a belated attempt to 'prove' her credentials as a postmodernist. One victim, named Irene, is killed as a grisly pun on Irene, irenic and ironic; another dies a ' "postmodernist death" ' (179) because she is unlucky enough to choose a coffee pot laced with poison – a victim who 'creates' her own murder in the same way that, for postmodern theorists, the reader 'creates' the text. Paradoxically, then, Rames's retribution on theory and theorists takes the form of murderous theoretical one-upmanship: she revenges herself on postmodernism by committing acts of postmodern revenge. And of course exactly the same goes for the novel itself: for all its disgust at the amoral obsessions of theory, *Murder at the MLA* orchestrates a killing spree worthy of the attention of the most bloodthirsty professorial mind, and leaves a scene littered with corpses that would not look out of place in the gore-spattered pages of the latest post-Foucauldian article on dismemberment and mutilation.

A more ambitious variation on the theme of 'literary killings' and 'postmodern deaths' is offered by *Death in a Delphi Seminar*, a metafictional whodunit that amplifies the critique of post-structuralism articulated in

Norman N. Holland's non-fictional work on reader-response theory. *The Critical I* is his disparaging conspectus of the major figures and trends in post-Saussurean linguistics and literary interpretation; for him, the cardinal error of modern criticism has been its willingness to grant language a life of its own, independent of the creative involvement of writers or readers. Holland is especially critical, in this regard, of the gurus of post-structuralist thought – Derrida, Barthes, Foucault, Lacan – whom he dubs the 'New Cryptics'; he is impatient also with critics like Iser and Eco who, despite their ostensibly reader-oriented theories, nevertheless set out to 'de-pscyhologize the process of meaning'.[5] Holland's criticism thus involves a bid to re-psychologize the process of meaning; it is a forceful reassertion of the role of flesh-and-blood individuals in the dynamic of literary creativity and interpretation.

Holland's novel revolves around the deaths of a series of students associated with an innovative graduate seminar run by 'Dr Norman Holland' at Buffalo University. The 'Delphi Seminar' requires students to circulate 'squibs' (off-the-cuff, non-academic, jargon-free feedback) in response to a given literary excerpt, and then to analyse one another's responses. The point of the seminar is that the reader – the real-life reader, that is, as opposed to some hypothetical 'implied reader' – is always the unknown quantity in the business of literary interpretation: by attempting to 'read' readers and to 'read' reading, Holland and his students are thus reintroducing a problematic variable that is conveniently ignored by mainstream critical theory. Post-structuralism and deconstruction are the obvious methodological villains of this piece. Holland's students are liberal in their contempt for 'all that French crap' (38), 'Decockstruction' (38), and 'deconstructive bullshit' (50); their tutor is himself politely dismissive of the 'dreadful litcrit jargon' (128) associated with these theories. Unsurprisingly, then, the seminar's two zealous deconstructionists, the Yale-educated Patricia Hassler and Christian Aval, prove to be the trouble-making nihilists at the heart of the mystery. The investigation begins when the truculently disruptive Hassler dies after sitting on a poisoned tack that she herself has planted in a bid to frame Aval for her murder. The fact that there is 'history' between Aval and Hassler – a failed relationship at Yale that broke down amidst unresolved allegations of plagiarism – demonstrates the irrepressible intrusion of extra-textual reality in the arena of literary debate. When further deaths violently disrupt the peaceable world of the Delphi Seminar – Aval brutally murders Hassler's accomplice and confidant, before fleeing and apparently committing suicide – the novel emphatically reiterates this core theme.

The feud between Hassler and Aval originates in the allegation that Aval stole her senior thesis together with all her notes and drafts, and passed it off as his own work. This messy unfinished business from the headquarters of American deconstruction raises all the questions of authorship, history and psychology that Yale has trained Hassler and Aval to ignore. In particular, it shows deconstruction to be grievously lacking in the language of ethical responsibility that the plagiarism case obviously calls for. In a sense, post-structuralism licenses the very act of intellectual fraud that Aval seems to have committed: if there is no genuine author then there can be no false author, no plagiarist – the text 'belongs' to everyone and no one. Similar paradoxes bedevil the concepts of death and murder in the novel. If, as Hassler brutally puts it, 'The subject is dead. I'm dead, and so are you' (114), then the question of what counts as 'murder' becomes a vexed one. How can you kill what is already dead? To a certain extent, the novel is a case of 'life imitating theory', because Hassler is literally dead from the outset. However, the shock of her death is designed not to validate her theoretical position, but to expose it as just so much nihilistic schoolroom rhetoric. In Holland's novel, proclamations of the death of the human subject are true only to the extent that they reveal the theorist as sorely lacking in humanity. *Death in a Delphi Seminar* represents deconstruction as the misanthropist's theory of choice, a heartlessly dehumanizing celebration of pure textuality at the expense of literature's historical origins, experiential content and affective power. Naturally, Holland's deconstructionists are themselves distinctly lacking in full-blooded humanity. Everyone else in the seminar is endowed with colourful non-academic life experience – the Vietnam veteran, the former air hostess and prostitute, the actress – but Hassler and Aval are 'dead subjects' in the sense that they are creatures of the text rather than the world. Hassler's proud claim to be nothing more than 'words, themes, publishing, argument' (113) is strikingly indicative of the repression of humanity that Holland obviously regards as the hallmark of deconstruction.

Though the dramatic content of *Death in a Delphi Seminar* is designed to present deconstruction in a most unflattering light, the novel's complex structure seems in many ways to invite deconstructive analysis. It is constructed as a dossier of texts relating to the three deaths – letters transcripts of police interviews, squibs, student papers, department memos, newspaper reports, journal excerpts. There is no 'external' narrator to arbitrate between these different linguistic constructions of reality: in the absence of any such editorial metalanguage, or any secure position 'outside the text', Holland's readers are left to fend for themselves as they leaf through his bulging case-file. Much of the case also revolves around absences – missing computer files, vanishing squibs, purloined letters and a 'phantom student' who never attends seminars; there are even references to a minor character named 'Abe Poria' (who naturally proves to be a no-show in the storyline itself). On the face of it, the novel's string of tempting references to textuality and aporias seems to play obligingly into the hands of the very deconstructive theory that it aims to debunk. But what we are really dealing with here is a series of canny pre-emptive strikes against the theoretical reader. For Holland, reading *begins* rather than *ends* with the identification of the aporia; in this sense detective work, rather than deconstruction, provides Holland with his preferred model of literary interpretation. The detective's task gets underway at the very point where the post-Derridean reader gives up – the point of where signs have become mysteriously, inscrutably unreadable. So in *Death in a Delphi Seminar*, as in *Murder at the MLA*, it is hardly surprising that the anti-theoretical critic proves to be a remarkably effective amateur detective. A career of dedicated reading, of sifting evidence and interpreting signs, has obviously prepared Holland well for the rigours of forensic enquiry. As he pores over his students' squibs late into the night to search for clues to the identity of the killer, the techniques of the Delphi seminar come into their own as methods of criminal investigation. It seems appropriate at this point to recall Nancy Cook's acerbic comment in *Murder at the MLA* that the success of deconstruction can be put down to 'English academics wanting to feel empowered for a change' (68). A similar kind of impulse seems to be at work in the scholar-detective fantasy of Jones's and Holland's novels. Nothing could be more 'empowering' for the traditionalist literary scholar than to join forces with the police on an enquiry that has all the gravity of a life-or-death drama and all the intellectual satisfaction of an anti-theoretical manhunt.

In both *Murder at the MLA* and *Death in a Delphi Seminar*, various acts of violent crime are traced back to the malign influence of post-structuralist thought on the modern campus. Umberto Eco's *The Name of the Rose* (1980), which stages contemporary theoretical debates in a fourteenth-century setting – Steven Connor calls it a 'mediaeval campus novel'[6] – offers a strikingly different version of the story of murder in a closed intellectual community. Whereas Jones and Holland position theory as the object of investigation, Eco treats investigation as itself a theoretically self-conscious process. And whereas Jones and Holland focus on the interpretation of violence, *The Name of the Rose* explores the violence of interpretation, the fatal distortions that can be created by even the most scrupulous acts of reading – not to mention the singularly unscrupulous acts of reading performed by the papal inquisitor Bernard Gui, whose brutal methods of getting at the 'truth' are so strikingly counterpointed to those of Eco's detective, William of Baskerville.

Prefaced by a tongue-in-cheek assurance that its story is 'gloriously lacking in any relevance for our day', *The Name of the Rose* smuggles a whole range of modern and postmodern themes into its fourteenth-century setting.[7] Most conspicuously, there is a string of references to Conan Doyle and Borges: William of Baskerville and his mildly obtuse sidekick/narrator Adso of Melk function as the Holmes and Watson of the piece, while Jorge of Burgos is a malevolent Borges-figure at the heart of the abbey's labyrinthine library. The rich intertextualities of Eco's novel thus effect a creatively anachronistic intermingling of modern literature and medieval history. More subtly, the novel also takes the opportunity to rehearse in a fictional setting the arguments that preoccupy Eco's extensive work on reader-response, semiotics and the limits of interpretation. This work, which is rooted in the theories of the American semiotician Charles Sanders Peirce, has always stood somewhat apart from the radically playful strands of contemporary theory. Eco is notably sceptical of any theory that grants the reader limitless interpretative freedom or throws the text open to a potentially infinite range of signification. His second novel, *Foucault's Pendulum* (1989), where a clique of conspiracy theorists misidentify a laundry list as a key to all mythologies, powerfully satirizes the frenzy of over-reading and misreading that post-structuralism seems to license. As a medievalist, Eco is also critical of contemporary thinkers who congratulate themselves for having 'invented' theories that have been around since the Middle Ages. *The Name of the Rose* does not export twentieth-century ideas to the middle ages; rather, it shows modern semiotics to be the *product* of a medieval world whose intellectual culture was dominated by debates over the operation and interpretation of signs.[8] As Theresa Coletti observes, it is not a matter of 'medievalizing' theory, but of revealing that theory is 'already medievalized'.[9] The difference, of course, is that contemporary semioticians do not share their medieval counterparts' faith in a divine source and guarantee of all signs. Capitalizing on this tension between medieval faith and postmodern doubt, Eco's novel is, according to Walter E. Stephens, 'a semiotic duel, a "showdown" between medieval theocentric semiosis and a version of Peircean unlimited semiosis'.[10] This is true as far as it goes, but there is a crucial third term that Stephens overlooks: Derridean dissemination is obliquely invoked by Eco's text as a process that radically undermines both the theocentric *and* the Peircean models of signification to produce a world 'tormented by the problem of difference itself' (196).

Theresa Coletti has aptly described *The Name of the Rose* as Adso's 'semiotic *Bildungsroman*'.[11] Brother William's investigation into a series of murders at a Benedictine abbey in northern Italy is a sustained and often bravura exercise in semiotic interpretation that gives Adso, and by implication the reader, a compelling insight into the theory and practice of semiotics. William's teacherly utterances, rich as they are in pithy generalizations about signs, rarely let us forget that his creator is a Professor of Semiotics. Adso is particularly taken by his master's observations on the *duality* of the sign. 'A book is made up of signs', William observes at one point, 'that speak of other signs, which in their turn speak of things' (396). The idea that signs can lead both to things and to other signs is implied by the enigmatic title of Eco's novel, which associates a signifying label (the *Name*) with a signified object (the *Rose*) that is itself also, as Eco has observed, an enormously versatile signifying label.[12] It is in the nature of language that every signified is potentially also a signifier: or, as Peirce puts it, 'The meaning of a representation can be nothing but a representation'.[13] The term coined by Peirce for this model of language as a potentially endless relay of cross-referring signs is 'unlimited semiosis' – a term that might appear to suggest that signs can speak *only* of other signs and never of things. But Eco is careful to differentiate Peirce's position from what he characterizes as a Derridean semiosis 'of infinite play, of difference, of the infinite whirl of interpretation'.[14] He does so by distinguishing between the unlimited *system* (which grants the theoretical possibility that signs may refer to other signs *ad infinitum*) and the finite *process* (the acts of meaningful communication that do nevertheless happen between language users).[15] For Eco, unlimited semiosis does not preclude relatively determinate acts of interpretation, any more than the fact that an orbital motorway has no end point prevents people from getting anywhere on it.

The Name of the Rose might usefully be characterized as a novel about the limits of unlimited semiosis. The problem of getting from signs to things – or from books to life – is, in this text, literally a matter of life and death. In this regard, a key phase of Adso's semiotic education is his dawning realization that 'books speak of books: it is as if they spoke among themselves' (286). The novel's privileged image for this endless criss-crossing of quotation and allusion within and between books is, of course, the labyrinth. Borrowed from the Borges of 'The Library of Babel' and 'The Garden of Forking Paths', Eco's library-cum-maze is an intertextual image of intertextuality that implicates his novel in the great bookish conversation that Adso overhears. For Eco, there are three kinds of labyrinth. The 'classical labyrinth' is eminently negotiable: it is 'the Ariadne's-thread of itself'. The 'mannerist maze' is more difficult, with many blind alleys and only one exit. Finally, there is 'what Deleuze and Guattari call "rhizome" ... so constructed that every path can be connected with every other one. It has no centre, no periphery, no exit, because it is potentially infinite'.[16] Eco's novel seems to be both master and prisoner of just such an endless rhizomatic labyrinth, and dramatizes its predicament through the story of a detective searching for a lost text in a labyrinth who comes to realize that he is lost in a labyrinthine text.

The narrative of textual loss is central to *The Name of the Rose*. It opens with an unnamed editor-narrator introducing his version of the 'terrible story of Adso of Melk', a narrative that has been translated, supplemented, modernized, rewritten, lost and rediscovered many times in its long and eventful journey from the fourteenth century to the present day. The version that has come into his hands is of doubtful authenticity, but the question marks over its provenance soon become irrelevant when he is permanently separated from his copy in tragic-comic circumstances. This lost-and-found-and-lost pattern also applies to the key textual artefact in the novel, the second book of Aristotle's *Poetics*, a lost manuscript of incalculable cultural significance which also proves to be the key to the murders. This priceless literary artefact is briefly rediscovered and tantalizingly skim-read by Brother William, only to be trebly destroyed at the end of the novel: dismembered, eaten, and burned. The novel thus ends as it began, with the image of a reader clutching fragmented leftovers from a precious text whose original version has vanished or been destroyed. When Adso revisits the ruined Abbey years after it was consumed by fire, he roots through the 'disiecta membra' of the old library in order to construct a new one 'made up of fragments, quotations, unfinished sentences, amputated stumps of books' (500). Intriguingly, Adso's post-apocalyptic library resembles nothing so much as the multilingual gibberish of the demented monk Salvatore, whose outlandish babble recycles the 'disiecta membra of other sentences' (47). This abject figure is the holy fool or idiot savant of the novel, a walking, talking representation of Eco's dictum that 'every period has its own postmodernism'.[17] It is Salvatore, after all, who appears to Adso during a dream of fragmenting bodies to cry, in a moment of uncanny postmodern clairvoyance, 'Fool! Can't you see this is the great Lyotard?' (434). There is certainly a sense in which the demise of the greatest library in Christendom prefigures the fragmentation of grand narratives into *petits récits* that, for Jean-François Lyotard, characterizes the 'postmodern condition'. It is as though Eco is giving his characters a foretaste of what it feels like to be excluded from the world of things and left to scavenge through the *disjecta membra* of postmodern intertextuality.

One possible motto for this novel might therefore be 'There nothing outside the library'. The 'outside world' in *The Name of the Rose* is every bit as textualized and sign-ridden as the library's holdings. A snowfall, for example, is described by William as 'an admirable parchment on which men's bodies leave very legible writing' (105). Similarly, hoof-prints, snapped twigs and hairs snagged on bushes tell Eco's detective all he needs to know about the size, appearance and whereabouts of the Abbot's missing horse, Brunellus (23–4). William also knows how the monks will describe Brunellus because he knows the qualities that the *auctoritates* attribute to a supposedly excellent horse. In other words, William not only reads the world like a text, but can also second-guess the habitual errors of less gifted readers. The Brunellus episode resembles one of those moments where Sherlock Holmes performs a casually brilliant act of 'deduction' – such as inferring the life-story of Watson's brother from the scratches on his pocket-watch – as a dress rehearsal for the major investigation to follow. But it would be a mistake to take Conan Doyle as our *auctoritas*, and to read this scene as secure evidence of William's Holmesian infallibility. In the event, the novel's first mystery proves to be William's finest hour; the remainder of the novel shows him to be altogether more fallible than the Brunellus episode might lead us to believe.

William's gravest error is in taking seriously Alinardo of Grottaferrata's hunch that the murderer is dispatching his victims in a pattern that resembles the seven trumpets of the Apocalypse. When word of this misapprehension gets back to Jorge, he consciously plays along with it, having persuaded himself that he is indeed an instrument of apocalyptic retribution. At this point in the novel its formal opposition between the violence of inquisition and the finesse of detection begins to break down. If 'inquisitors create heretics' (50), as Adso thoughtfully remarks, then there is a sense in which detectives create criminals. Eco's detective becomes the unwitting co-author of his arch-enemy's murderous narrative, supplying his rationale, his pretext, his divine alibi. The investigation that brings William face-to-face with Jorge thus takes the form of a conspicuously faulty process of what Peirce calls 'abduction', or reasoning from a 'Case' to a 'Rule'. In an essay that relates Peircian abduction to Borges's anti-detective stories, Eco states that at its highest level ('third-level abduction') the process is one in which 'the Rule does not exist, and one must invent it'.[18] This form of abduction requires the detective to imagine a general scenario (the 'Rule') that might plausibly accommodate and explain enigmatic local details (the 'Case'). Third-level abduction therefore requires the detective to indulge in educated guesswork, to play storyteller – which is to say that the detective's quest for the truth becomes structurally dependent upon an arbitrary fiction. In the case of Brother William's investigation, the murderer's plot is actually *produced* by the detective's hunch: 'There was no plot', he ruefully concedes, 'and I discovered it by mistake' (491).

Eco characterizes William's 'failure' as a detective by relating it to his three-fold typology of literary labyrinths. What William belatedly realizes is that he is not living in a 'mannerist maze' but a 'rhizome space' – one that 'can be structured but is never structured definitively'.[19] It is intriguing that Eco should invoke Deleuze and Guattari as the architects of his rhizomatic world, given that his novel contains numerous sly digs at the clever sophistry of the 'masters of Paris' (153). But there is another master of Paris in the text whose presence is obliquely invoked by the central image of the poisoned text. When Jorge coats the Aristotle text with poison he literalizes the conceit of writing-as-poison that Derrida elicits in his extended discussion of relations between speech, writing and memory in Plato.[20] Eco's herbalist points out that 'the line between poison and medicine is very fine; the Greeks used the word "pharmacon" for both' (108). *Pharmakon* is the word that Derrida homes in on in his discussion of the problematic devaluation of writing in the *Phaedrus*. Writing, in this text, is frequently described as a *pharmakon* – a term that signifies both medicine and poison. Writing can be both beneficial and harmful for speech and memory: it records and preserves the living voice, but only in the form of a lifeless mechanical substitute; it serves as a prosthetic *aide mémoire* that helps us to remember precisely because it lets us forget.

The lost Aristotle text is the *pharmakon* of *The Name of the Rose*, playing the structurally incompatible roles of poison and cure. As a theory of comedy, of laughter, the text seems to provide a much-needed antidote to the world of Bernard Gui and Jorge of Burgos; not simply in the banal sense that William's adversaries are entirely lacking in humour, but in the spirit of William's philanthropic desire to '*to make truth laugh*' (491). A world where truth cannot call itself into question through laughter will be one of paranoia, censorship and permanent inquisition; this is why William describes laughter as 'a good medicine' (131). Jorge, meanwhile, poisons the book because for him its contents are already poisonous – not least because they promise to become a 'dangerous supplement' to the teaching of the Bible. William and Jorge both know that the gospels are silent on the question of whether Christ ever laughed, but the rediscovery of Aristotle's theory of comedy raises the possibility that Greek philosophy may supply answers that are missing from the scriptures. The second book of the *Poetics* thus strikes Jorge as a singularly dangerous 'supplementary parasite' (to borrow Derrida's description of the *pharmakon*), one that threatens to decentre all truth and authority. '[O]n the day when the Philosopher's word would justify the marginal jests of the debauched imagination', he warns, 'or when what has been marginal would leap to the centre, every trace of the center would be lost' (475). Shortly after uttering these definitively logo-centric words, Jorge begins to stuff pages of the manuscript into his mouth, as though by ingesting the text he can use his own body as a *cordon sanitaire* to prevent the toxic effects of the Aristotelean *pharmakon* disseminating themselves any further through the Abbey.

Meditating on the 'undecidability' of the *pharmakon*, Derrida refers to it as 'the differance of difference' that can never be pinned down as a name, a substance, or a stable concept: 'We will watch it infinitely promise itself and endlessly vanish through concealed doorways that shine like mirrors and open onto a labyrinth' (130). Here we recognize, in the heart of an essay whose intertextual presences include Borges himself, the very mirrored doorways and endless corridors of Eco's novel. And as a final twist in the labyrinthine relationship between Derrida, Borges and Eco, one might speculate that Borges's role in the novel is not as Eco's villain but as Derrida's patsy. Though it is certainly plausible to read *The Name of the Rose* as the story of the defeat of Peircian semiotics at the hands of Borgesian playfulness, there are other, less obvious suspects in the background. On reviewing the evidence – the centre invaded by the margins, logocentric thinking tormented by the problem of difference, a *pharmakon* concealed in a rhizomatic space, the fragmentation of grand narratives into *petits récits* – it seems that the answers to this case may lie not with the blind Hispanic librarian after all, but in the writings of William of Baskerville's *bêtes noires*, those shadowy masters of Paris.

A very different model of the Parisian intellectual is at the centre of *The Old Man and the Wolves* (1991), the first of Julia Kristeva's sequence of crime stories which follows the adventures of the Paris-based journalist and amateur sleuth, Stephanie Delacour. Described by Kristeva as a 'gothic *roman noir*',[21] the novel sees Delacour dispatched to investigate human rights abuses in the Eastern European city of Santa Varvara, where she grew up as the daughter of the French ambassador. Her inves-tigation focuses the suspicious death of the 'Old Man' of the novel's title, whom she associates with her own recently deceased father. The novel is a self-consciously problematic attempt to articulate some of Kristeva's central theoretical preoccupations – paternity, barbarism, otherness, abjection and the erosion of frontiers in the modern world – as a murder mystery. The difficulties arise because the complexity of this material defeats the problem-solving mechanisms of the conventional whodunit. In the end the novel is about reading the abject signs of criminality rather actually solving crimes; or, in other words, it is a novel about *being a detective* rather than doing detection.

The Old Man and the Wolves seems to take its cue from the Freudian idea, frequently invoked in Kristeva's theoretical writings, that society is 'founded on a common crime', the murder of the father.[22] This Oedipal theme is developed in *Totem and Taboo*, where Freud traces the birth of civilization to the moment when primitive men rise up against the dominant male of their group, kill him and eat him. By forging bonds of guilt, remembrance and repentance, this primal act of revolt transforms a world that happens to be male-dominated into a society that is properly patriarchal.[23] If this 'totemic fable', as Kristeva characterizes it, figures murder as the inaugural gesture of civilization, elsewhere in her writings crime is represented as an altogether more corrosive force. In *Powers of Horror*, for example, Kristeva declares that 'Any crime, because it draws attention to the fragility of the law, is abject'.[24]

The 'abject', for Kristeva, is made up of those vilely fascinating objects of disgust and fear that populate the hinterlands of the psyche. It represents material that is emphatically banished from sight, only to linger queasily in our peripheral vision. Abjection manifests itself in the spasms of nausea and disgust provoked by sewage or rotting food; but the 'utmost of abjection', according to Kristeva, is the corpse. 'In that compelling, raw, insolent thing in the morgue's full sunlight', she writes, 'I behold the breaking down of a world that has erased its borders'.[25] These words might almost have been spoken by Delacour of the various abject lifeless bodies that she inspects – such as the bloated, slime-covered body of an unidentified woman in *The Old Man and the Wolves*, or the decapitated corpse of the translator Gloria Harrison in *Possessions*. Though these texts obviously belong to the murder-mystery tradition of novel-as-autopsy, their emphasis on the 'borderline anxieties' associated with abjection makes things difficult for any detective who would patrol the boundaries between crime and legality, self and other, life and death. In her conclusion to *Powers of Horror*, Kristeva argues that literature's natural home is on just such problematic borderlines:

> all literature is probably a version of the apocalypse that seems to me
> rooted, no matter what its socio-historical conditions might be, on
> the fragile border (borderline cases) where identities (subject/object,
> etc.) do not exist or only barely so – double, fuzzy, heterogeneous,
> animal, metamorphosed, altered, abject.[26]

Leaving aside the question of whether *all* literature conforms to this definition, we can certainly say that these words capture the themes and
motifs of *The Old Man and the Wolves* so aptly that they could well stand
as its blurb. Both apocalyptic and abject, the novel teems with imagery
of collapsing borders, doubled identities and uncanny metamorphoses.

The Old Man of the novel's title is a Professor of Latin whose fate it is
literally to 'cry wolf' – to sound the alarm among Santavarvarans about
lupine invaders taking over towns and villages and passing themselves off
as human. The question of the wolves' reality-status is never satisfactorily
resolved: prowling the margins of the text, they could be real predators, or
they could be allegorical creatures – or they could be nothing more than
the figments of a dying man's nocturnal paranoia. Even the Professor has
trouble separating the wolves that haunt the outskirts of the city from the
ones that are 'tearing him to pieces from within' (5). And even if we do
accept that the wolves are symbolic, their meanings are still disconcert-
ingly multiple. According to Kristeva, the wolves stand for three things:
first, 'the invasion of the Red Armies, the establishment of totalitarianism';
second, 'everyone's barbarity, everyone's criminality'; third, 'the invasion
of banality' and the rise of 'racketeering, corruption, wheeling and dealing'
in post-communist Eastern Europe.[27] But the gravest danger represented
by the wolves seems to lie not in the specifics of these different threats, but
in their capacity to represent contradictory threats *simultaneously*. The
wolves are deadly not because they represent the oppressiveness of com-
munism, the amorality of capitalism, or the banality of evil – but because
they can stand for all three at one and the same time. Wolfishness in the
novel ultimately represents a breakdown of the boundaries between
symbol and reality, human and non-human, inside and outside, Eastern
totalitarianism and Western decadence, civilization and barbarism – that
is, for a bloodcurdling metamorphosis of every concept into its opposite.

Like the Professor's beloved Latin poetry, Kristeva's novel presents a
world slouching towards a new barbarism of which the place-name
'Santa Varvara' (or 'Santa Barbara' in the French original) is an oblique

warning. As Kathleen O'Grady points out, this resonantly symbolic name invites comparison with Kristeva's remarks on barbarians and barbarism in *Strangers to Ourselves*.[28] The word 'barbarian', Kristeva observes, was coined in Homeric times by uncomprehending Greeks who could hear only *bla-bla* or *bara-bara* in the voices of foreigners and outsiders. To label someone a 'barbarian' is therefore to turn an expression of incomprehension into a gesture of mastery. For Kristeva, this exclusion of the 'barbarian' to a position outside the *logos*, beyond the pale of Greek language, philosophy and civilization, typifies the xenophobic logic of narratives of cultural self-definition.[29] Following Freud, she argues that the designation of some persecuted sub-group as 'other', 'foreign' or 'barbaric' occludes the truth that 'we are our own foreigners'[30] – the demonized not-self is never anything but a projection of the self. The prospect of civilization being engulfed by barbarism can therefore never be anything more than a scare-story invoked by those who self-identify as civilized; which is to say that Kristeva's Santa Varvarans are waiting for a barbarism that will never come because it has always-already arrived.

Positioned against the backdrop of the fall of the Iron Curtain, *The Old Man and the Wolves* takes the collapse of frontiers as its central motif. What the novel cannot seem to decide is whether the necessary permeability of borders should be cause for celebration or for concern. On the one hand the deconstruction of the civilization/barbarism antithesis is a necessary step in the dismantling of xenophobic ideology. Parochial nationalism is also challenged by the positive value that Kristeva's fiction attaches to border-crossing intellectuals – ambassadors, translators and foreign correspondents. And of course Kristeva's own novelistic practice intermingles fiction and philosophy in a bid, as the narrator of *The Old Man and the Wolves* puts it, to violate 'the frontiers once drawn up between the different genres for the benefit of lazy schoolboys' (65). On the other hand, as Stephanie Delacour asks herself in the same novel, 'Is crime inevitable when there are no more frontiers?' (183). Once upon a time differences were policed with fanatical vigilance, but the modern world is now witnessing a slide into moral and geographical *indifference*. Symptomatically, Santa Varvara and its neighbouring cities, towns and villages are merging into one endless, nondescript suburban sprawl – 'one continuous Santa Varvara' (68).

Indifference is also the keynote of the city's moral atmosphere. All the Professor's attempts to publicize the threat of the wolves fall on deaf ears among Santavarvans. Nor does his death – apparently by natural causes, though Stephanie suspects a cover-up – do anything to ruffle the town's zombie-like citizens. For all Stephanie's suspicions of foul play, it seems that the Professor was not killed but simply written off, the victim of a conspiracy of silence among Santavarvarans for whom his tales of lupine invasion were a matter of sheer indifference, as irrelevant as his knowledge of Ovid and Tibullus. The death of the Old Man thus represents a rewriting of Freud's 'totemic fable' of primordial patricide. Rather than marking some epoch-making shift from nature to culture, the Professor's death is merely one episode in the contemporary banalization of evil. The death of the novel's patriarch does not provoke guilt, commemoration or repentance, merely a hollow sense of business as usual. The citizens of Santa Varvara thus bring to mind Kristeva's description of what people without Oedipal guilt and responsibility might look like: 'mechanized, roboticized, lobotomized, a sorry and embarrassing version of the human'.[31] The question that increasingly comes to haunt this text is not whether crime is inevitable but whether it is *possible* in a world without frontiers. 'Where's the Crime?', the title of the final chapter, confronts Kristeva's detective not merely with the epistemological question *whodunit?* but with the ontological question *who-did-what?* The town certainly 'reeks of murder' (80). Stephanie knows that her friend Vespasian dreams of killing his wife Alba, and that she in turn is lacing his food and drink with tranquilizers and sleeping tablets. The couple are murdering each other one day at a time, but as yet there is no victim. If in the case of Vespasian and Alba we have a murder without a victim, in the case of the Professor we have a victim without a murder. The novel has an atmosphere of rank criminality, but with no crime for Stephanie to solve. Ultimately, Stephanie is not a reporter in search of a story but 'a detective in search of the void' (135). It is an unwrittten law of detective fiction that the truth is what is hidden, but for Kristeva's post-structuralist sleuth, what is hidden is the absence of truth.

With its inconclusive investigation into an insoluble non-crime, *The Old Man and the Wolves* emphatically resists the 'eternal return of lucidity' that characterizes the traditional detective story. It also represents the antithesis of theoretically self-conscious murder stories like *Death in a Delphi Seminar* and *Murder at the MLA* where theory is made to investigate itself, to own up to its crimes against lucidity. Like Jones and Holland's novels, *The Name of the Rose* also 'criminalizes' post-structuralism, though not in a way that grants an easy victory to the non-theoretical reader-detective. In the end, when we set them alongside texts as intricately ambiguous as *The Name of the Rose* and *The Old Man and the Wolves*, Jones and Holland's anti-theoretical whodunits recall nothing so much as the scene in Charlie Kaufman's film *Adaptation* (2002) where a screenwriter flippantly pitches an idea for a serial killer film about a literature professor who cuts his victims to pieces and calls himself 'The Deconstructionist'.

9
The Novel in Hyperreality

In the course of an influential and controversial discussion of the changing status of signs in industrial and post-industrial culture, Jean Baudrillard remarks, almost in passing, that 'art is dead'.[1] This casually apocalyptic comment refers in the first instance to the demise of ideals of inspired solo craftsmanship or lone genius in an age driven by the conveyor-belts of mass production. Cultural artefacts that once enjoyed the priceless cachet of inimitability are now prone to endless replication by the technologies of advanced capitalism; the signature of a given artist's 'unique' creative style can be instantaneously forged by something as banal as a machine. Baudrillard was by no means the first cultural theorist to speculate that the era of mass production might put paid to the ideal of the aesthetic masterpiece as a sublime one-off, and he duly acknowledges Walter Benjamin's celebrated essay, 'The Work of Art in the Age of Mechanical Reproduction' (1938), as the ground-breaking intervention in this area of debate. For Benjamin, the consequences of such a revolution need to be understood in political terms. If the work of art has lost its numinous 'aura' of uniqueness and unapproachability, then that can only be a good thing, because it satisfyingly dispels the atmosphere of privilege and mystique in which high culture shrouds itself from democratic participation.[2] Baudrillard, on the other hand, is less interested in the political than the ontological consequences of the 'death of art'. For him, Benjamin has merely identified one symptom of a much wider phenomenon, the death of reality itself – or, rather, its vertiginous 'implosion' into hyperreality.

For Baudrillard, 'reality' in the age of mechanical, electronic and digital reproduction has somehow been absorbed by its own hi-tech self-representations. Saturation media coverage of 'current affairs', fly-on-the-wall documentaries, pollsters' guides to the fluctuations of 'public opinion', museums stocked with flawless replicas – in each case the gap between original and copy, reality and representation, dissolves before your eyes. Perhaps Baudrillard's most well-known illustration of hyperreality, however, is given in his account of the enchanted crowds that flow through the 'frozen, childlike world' of Disneyland. But it is not Walt Disney's fairytale theme park that Baudrillard labels as 'hyperreal'; rather, it is the America that lies beyond its magical frontiers. Disneyland's function is to be such a delightfully artificial world of make-believe that the rest of non-Disneyfied America can only seem drably, reassuringly authentic by comparison. 'Disneyland exists', Baudrillard explains, 'in order to hide that it is the "real" country, all of "real" America that *is* Disneyland'.[3] In Baudrillard's postmodern world, then, what counts as 'real' is never more than a 'simulacral' by-product of endless copies, fakes, replicas and media illusions.

On two occasions Baudrillard has produced helpfully schematic accounts of the emergence of the simulacral. The first of these maps successive phases in the history of the sign onto major periods of socio-economic history:

- The *counterfeit* is the dominant schema in the 'classical' period, from the Renaissance to the Industrial Revolution.
- *Production* is the dominant schema in the industrial era.
- Simulation is the dominant schema in the current code-governed phase.[4]

In 'The Precession of Simulacra', Baudrillard lays down a revised version of this scheme that distances itself from the residual Marxism of its predecessor by abandoning its historical subdivisions. Now 'the successive phases of the image' unfold according to an internal logic that seems to have no socio-economic determinants:

- it is the reflection of a profound reality;
- it masks and denatures a profound reality;
- it masks the *absence* of a profound reality;
- it has no relation to any reality whatsoever: it is its own pure simulacrum.[5]

The key question raised by all of this is that of how Baudrillard has managed to climb free from the quicksand of the simulacral in order to spread the news about its treacherously beguiling properties. It seems contradictory for Baudrillard to claim, albeit implicitly, to have seen the 'truth' of what he represents as an inescapable media hallucination. If there really is no getting outside the global Disneyland of postmodern simulation then surely Baudrillard's essays are simply another attraction in the theme park? To a certain extent, ambiguous 'answers' to these questions are built into structures of Baudrillard's intellectual narratives. Tony Thwaites has pointed out, for example, that there is a curious tension between his story on the chronological *succession* of the 'phases of the image', and his broader emphasis on the *precession* of the real by the simulacral. In Baudrillard's history of the sign, it is as though the emergence of the simulacral is the grand finale that has always-already happened. Which means, as Thwaites suggests, that the distinction he draws between 'basic reality' and simulation is *itself* simulacral: 'Baudrillard's account of the simulacrum thus has a quite indeterminate status as the simulation of a theory of simulation: it is the very simulacrum it fears'.[6]

The one detail on which I would demur from Thwaites is his remark about Baudrillard's *fear* of the simulacrum. Baudrillard's extensive writings on simulation and hyperreality strike me as angst-free, sometimes to the point of nonchalance. Other commentators might denounce hyperreality as a media-induced epidemic of false consciousness, an ideological daydream that we urgently need to snap out of, but Baudrillard will have none of this. He remains studiedly 'cool' in his writings on the topic, declining all opportunities to polemicize against the dominance of the simulacral, and refusing to indulge in any nostalgia for lost authenticity. There is no vocabulary of resistance or opposition in his theorizing; rather, he seems prepared to play along with his subject matter, even to raise the stakes by generating hyperreal narratives of his own, as part of a strategy that Steven Connor describes as a constant 'outbidding of simulation'.[7] The risks involved in such a strategy are notoriously exemplified by Baudrillard's trilogy of essays on the Gulf War of 1991, in which he describes the conflict as a media event that was not going to happen, that was not happening, and that had not happened.[8] Unsurprisingly, these essays attracted widespread condemnation, most notably from Christopher Norris, who furiously castigates Baudrillard for his meek acquiescence in a postmodern culture of illusion and disinformation.[9] For Norris, Baudrillard's intellectual position amounts to a 'systematically inverted Platonism: a fixed determination to conceive no ideas of what life might be like outside the cave'.[10]

It was perhaps to pre-empt such scathing critiques as Norris's that Baudrillard remarked, half-jokingly, that his book on the Gulf War is actually a novel.[11] If *The Gulf War Did Not Take Place* is indeed a work of fiction, then its 'arguments' cannot be falsified; novels are under no obligation to meet the standards of intellectual consistency or documentary accuracy that are expected of the discourses of philosophy or official history. Now clearly Baudrillard's text cannot qualify for literary status simply by virtue of its author's say-so, but there is certainly a sense in which he is operating as an *agent provocateur* whose feigned indifference to the Gulf War is precisely designed to whip up a storm of controversy about the conflict and its media representations. All of which suggests that the most appropriate response to his outrageous overstatements and hyperreal fantasies might take the form of *another fiction*, a calculated 'outbidding' of Baudrillard in his own high-stakes game of intellectual provocation. It is in these terms that we might address a cluster of recent novels that engage, often in explicitly Baudrillardian terms, with questions of reality, hyperreality and simulation in a media-saturated age. Christine Brooke-Rose's *Textermination* (1991), Julian Barnes's *England, England* (1999), A. N. Wilson's *A Jealous Ghost* (2005), and Mark Z. Danielewski's *House of Leaves* (2000) represent a series of fictive journeys into hyperreality that engage both playfully and sceptically with Baudrillardian ideas on his own territory.

Before I discuss these works in detail, however, I would like briefly to consider a tricky question of reading raised by the compound unrealities of post-Baudrillardian fiction. When Julian Barnes imaginatively re-creates a hyperreal theme park, or when Christine Brooke-Rose simulates an ensemble of simulacral characters, we seem to have strayed beyond the limits of even Baudrillard's maps of the hyperreal – perhaps into an unthinkable fifth phase in his four-phase model, a kind of hyper-hyperreality. On the other hand, it could be that novelistic illusion and hyperreal simulation simply cancel one another out, and that Barnes and Brooke-Rose's readers are ultimately landed back at the square one of 'basic reality'. Such questions come usefully into focus in a memorable comic episode from Hynes's *The Lecturer's Tale*, where David Branwell, a sottish professor of Celebrity Studies, delivers a lecture on Elvis Presley's 'lost masterpiece' (213), the little-known musical *Viva Vietnam!*, directed by Howard Hawks with a soundtrack by Brian Wilson and Kurt Weill. Branwell develops his *jeu d'esprit* with ingeniously perverse Baudrillardian logic, defiantly asserting that, whether or not this film technically 'exists', it assuredly 'plays nightly in the multiplex of the American consciousness' (216). Quibbles about its place in the Presley canon are supremely irrelevant, since of course there never was a 'real' Elvis, and in any case the digital technology exists to create the film retroactively – and once it ' "exists", it will be as if *it had always existed*' (217–18).

Branwell's lecture is self-evidently a piece of frivolous postmodernist whimsy, the work of a critic who believes that if theory-friendly texts do not exist then it is necessary to invent them. And in a sense the film *does* now 'exist' – as part of the fictional world of *The Lecturer's Tale*, where its function is broadly equivalent to that of Disneyland in America: *Viva Vietnam!* is there to make the rest of Hynes's novel seem more real. The novel thus neither outflanks nor punctures Baudrillardian hyperreality; rather, it reproduces the very logic of simulation that it sets out to lampoon in the person of its cranky postmodernist professor.

Part of the joke with Hynes's postmodernist is his name: Branwell is named after the boozy underachiever of the Brontë siblings, as though he is himself a simulacral by-product of literary history rather than a free-standing character in his own right. But it is not only career Baudrillardians whose subjectivity is undermined in this way in contemporary fiction. Indeed, Christine Brooke-Rose has devoted an entire novel, *Textermination*, to the fate of ideas of rounded novelistic 'character' in a world where represented selves are increasingly confined to the flickering, two-dimensional screens of cinema and television. In a striking variation on the 'conference novel' of Lodge and Bradbury, *Textermination* follows not a group of professional critics but a host of classic literary characters as they converge on San Francisco for an annual convention at which they offer up prayers for their continued existence in the mind of the reader.[12] As Sarah Birch points out, if Brooke-Rose's *Thru* 'plagiarizes' texts from other authors, *Textermination* 'abducts'[13] their characters: Emma Woodhouse, Josef K., the Wife of Bath, Captain Ahab, Clarissa Harlowe, Leopold Bloom and hundreds of others attend the convention, which takes place at a uniquely perilous time for their endangered literary species. *Textermination* dwells on two main reasons for what Brooke-Rose has elsewhere described as the 'dissolution of character' in the modern novel.[14] For one thing, the notion of 'character' has never been less fashionable in academe, where theoreticians have been busy dissolving fictional personalities into 'constellations of semes' (63), or breaking them down into 'schemata, structures, functions within structures, logical and mathematical formulae, aporia' (26). At the same time, literature's heroes and heroines can no longer count on the devoted attention of a non-academic readership, who are increasingly being lured away from their books by the spectacles of Hollywood and popular culture: symptomatically, one of the novel's convention papers on 'The Art of Telling' is continually interrupted by talk of 'The Art of Tele' (83).

The mass-media threats to Brooke-Rose's ensemble of literary heroes and heroines become strangely 'real' when the convention is over-run by an influx of *cinematic* characters demanding their right to participate, a throng of 'flat, filmy people' that includes 'Heathcliff as Laurence Olivier, Captain Ahab as Gregory Peck, Jean Valjean as Jean Gabin' (116–7) and dozens of others. What is slightly uncanny about this roll-call of film stars is that fictional characters appear *as* real-life actors: Olivier *as* Heathcliff would sound fine, but Heathcliff *as* Olivier sounds odd, as though the role is playing the actor rather than *vice versa*. In some cases, a single character-role 'plays' multiple actors: Zorro appears 'as' Douglas Fairbanks but also 'as' Alain Delon, whilst Sherlock Holmes appears 'as' Raymond Massey, Basil Rathbone, Christopher Lee and Peter Cushing. In other cases, different character-roles 'play' the same actor: Dr Zhivago and Professor Stavroguin, for example, appear 'as' Omar Sharif, whilst Valmont, Julien Sorel and Fabrice appear 'as' Gérard Philippe (117–8). This influx of mass-cultural gatecrashers thus exacerbates the reality-crisis that is already plaguing the novel; it as though their vivid onscreen existence is acquired at the expense of both their literary originals and the actors who brought them to life. As Brooke-Rose's beleaguered characters are confronted by this plague of their own cinematic *doppelgängers*, classic literature seems to be in imminent danger of being swallowed by the hyperreal – or, as Pynchon's Oedipa Maas puts it, over-run by 'one helluva set of non-events and non-persons' (148). Perhaps the closest that this novel of non-events and non-persons gets to a 'hero' might therefore be in the figure of Italo Calvino's 'Non-Existent Knight', an empty suit of armour that is indefatigably committed to its chivalric duties. Calvino's knight thus neatly 'personifies' the empty concept of fictional character bravely soldiering on in the modern world, long after it has been exposed as 'non-existent'.

The prospect of novelistic character being emptied out or 'flattened' into two dimensions seems to prompt a curious shift in the text's generic affiliations. At the same time that *Textermination's* literary characters find themselves apparently outnumbered by their cinematic equivalents, the novel itself takes a decidedly cinematic turn. When the Hilton Hotel is consumed by fire and coastal California is ripped away from the mainland by a violent earthquake, *Textermination* seems to be consciously rewriting itself as a 1970s disaster movie. Brooke-Rose's novel threatens, in the end, to become a postmodern *Towering Inferno* in which its own credentials as highbrow *nouveau roman* will go up in flames.[15] In the event, however, her ensemble of literary characters seem fairly indestructible – one by one, they emerged unscathed from the wreckage, and the novel ends as it began with Emma Woodhouse finding herself, for perhaps the billionth time, trapped in a carriage for an uncomfortable *tête-à-tête* with Mr Elton. As Emma finds herself once again imprisoned in a plot that she thought she was stage-managing, Brooke-Rose's circular novel seems to imply that that those spectacular hyperreal threats to its characters' well-being and survival were simply escapist distractions from a more mundane literary truth: that 'characters' are serving life sentences in narratives from which no reader can ever liberate them

If the strange reality loops of *Textermination* are designed to plot the lives and afterlives of fictional characters as they are lived out in the minds of readers, Julian Barnes's *England, England* (1998) explores the ways in which an entire culture might be assimilated to the world of the hyperreal.[16] The novel concerns itself with the creation on the Isle of Wight of a huge theme park of English culture, heritage and national identity, the monstrously successful brainchild of a megalomaniac media tycoon, Sir Jack Pitman. Crammed into this Anglo-Saxon Disneyland are reproductions of all of the mainland's chief tourist attractions, from the White Cliffs of Dover and Hampton Court maze to Brontë Country and the National Gallery. The Isle is populated by scores of actors impersonating everyone from Sherlock Holmes and Nell Gwyn to Robin Hood and his Merrie Men. 'Great British Breakfasts' are served up by Beefeaters while Manchester United play regular fixtures at Wembley Stadium and Dr Johnson holds court at the Cheshire Cheese Inn. *'England, England'* clearly has no pretensions to scholarly or museum-like accuracy: it is an offshore replica of an England that does not exist, or that exists only in the minds of the international focus groups whom Sir Jack asks to list the 'characteristics, virtues or quintessences' suggested to them by the word 'England'. Their responses in this game of cultural word-association are drawn up into a list (one of many in the novel) grandly entitled 'The Fifty Quintessences of Englishness', a colourful inventory of picturesque clichés that includes '2. BIG BEN/HOUSES OF PARLIAMENT', '6. A ROBIN IN THE SNOW', '9. WHITE CLIFFS OF DOVER', '27. TV CLASSIC SERIALS', and '36. ALICE IN WONDERLAND' (83–4). Clearly we are not dealing here with the 'raw material' of Englishness – if there could be such a thing – but with a *simulated* Englishness, gleaned at second-hand from picture postcards, TV screens and literary fantasies. The whole focus group exercise distinctly recalls Baudrillard's comments on the culture of polling and market research: 'We live in a *referendum* mode precisely because there is no longer any *referential'*.[17]

'England', in this novel, is thus always-already an insubstantial fiction rather than a secure referent. Sir Jack's alternative England therefore functions not as a cheap imitation of the genuine article, but rather as a high-profile decoy to distract attention from the fraudulence of the 'original'. However, the very success of the theme park and its exhibits means that the borderline between the old England and its kitsch postmodern double becomes increasingly difficult to police. The frontier between reality and representation is first seriously blurred when the real King and Queen are persuaded to relocate to the Isle of Wight and become part of the exhibit. Gradually, *'England, England'* acquires a life of its own – the actors in the smugglers' villages bring real contraband onto the island; the Dr Johnson lookalike proves as irascible and melancholic as his eighteenth-century counterpart; Robin Hood's outlaws are found to be poaching wildlife from the island's Animal Heritage Centre. Ironically, these outlaws are altogether more 'real' than the mythical heroes of medieval folklore whom they impersonate. As the old oppositions between authentic and counterfeit reality are undermined, 'England' is absorbed in hyperreality as a living facsimile of itself. As Randall Stevenson remarks, you could scarcely ask for a more perfect illustration of the 'narrative of inversion' spelled out in Baudrillard's work on the simulacral.[18]

The influence of Baudrillard on *England, England* is unmistakable, though never explicitly acknowledged. Barnes prefers, appropriately enough, to present one of his characters as a thinly veiled simulacrum of the author of *Simulacra and Simulation*. Barnes's Baudrillard-figure is an unnamed French philosopher, drafted in by Sir Jack as part of the planning process, who bestows his intellectual blessing on the project by favourably quoting Guy Debord's famous comment that all lived experience 'has become mere representation' (54).[19] But whereas Debord's remark is tinged with sentimental regret, Barnes's Gallic philosopher pours scorn on cultural nostalgia:

[L]et me state that the world of the third millennium is inevitably, is ineradicably modern, and that it is our intellectual duty to submit to that modernity, and to dismiss as sentimental and inherently fraudulent all yearnings for what is dubiously termed the 'original'. We must demand the replica, since the reality, the truth, the authenticity of the replica is the one we can possess, colonise, reorder, find *jouissance* in, and, finally, if and when we decide, it is the reality which, since it is our destiny, we may meet, confront and destroy. (55)

Too polished to be disturbing or even particularly radical, these sentiments come across as the well-rehearsed postmodernist *shtick* of a superficially brilliant intellectual-for-hire. The philosopher's brief cameo appearance in the novel – he is soon off to a conference in Frankfurt, after a quick shopping spree in London – establishes him as its foil rather than its trustworthy *raisonneur*. Barnes's novel resists his enthusiastic submission to modernity, and unapologetically harbours the 'yearnings' for truth and authenticity that its Baudrillard figure places under taboo. For all its postmodern playfulness, then, *England, England* exudes a certain impatience with theories of the simulacral, and applies itself to the task of envisioning a reality beyond and outside of the world of glossy Baudrillardian slogans.[20]

It is through the career of his complex heroine, Martha Cochrane, that Barnes explores the simulatedness of England and probes the limits of simulation. We first encounter Martha through her recollections of herself as a young girl assembling her Counties of England jigsaw puzzle. This puzzle establishes 'England' from the outset as a man-made construct or self-assembly kit rather than an expanse of natural landscape. Martha's childhood pastime is thus a perfect rehearsal for her adult role as in-house sceptic on the team who design and run the giant jigsaw puzzle that is *'England, England'*. Martha's cynicism is presented as a defensive habit she developed in childhood after her father disappeared, with a piece of the jigsaw puzzle in his pocket, leaving behind him an incomplete puzzle and a daughter affected by a profound sense of loss. Behind Martha's cynicism is a secret hankering after authenticity that emerges most clearly in one notable passage of extended soul-searching where she muses regretfully over love, happiness, self-knowledge, and the problem of being 'true to your heart' (226–7). All those intimate qualities of authentic human subjectivity, which might seem to have no place in postmodern hyperreality, are revealed as having been poignantly lacking from Martha's make-believe England. 'Reality', in this novel, is thus figured as the missing piece of the jigsaw, the priceless item that cannot be contained, catalogued, reproduced, commodified, bought or sold.

The final section of the novel sees Martha undertake a symbolic return from *'England, England'* to old England – or 'Anglia', as it has been re-named – which has become an impoverished backwater of Europe. Whereas in Baudrillard's scheme of things, California's theme parks are 'imaginary stations that feed reality, the energy of the real'[21] into Los Angeles, in Barnes's novel the theme park seems to sap the life out of its real-world neighbour. Anglia's advanced capitalist infrastructure is crumbling to bits, and the entire nation is drifting slowly back into a pre-industrial culture centred on village communities. With its bicycling policemen, thatched cottages and village fêtes, Anglia looks suspiciously like a sentimental version of an old – or 'olde' – authentic England; in this deeply ambiguous ending, 'neither idyllic nor dystopic' (256), we seem to have entered into the hyperreality that prevails beyond the limits of the theme park. Despite its sceptical treatment of Baudrillard, then, the novel seems to chime in with his sceptical comments about what he calls '*demuseumification*' – the futile attempt to restore museum exhibits to some lost space of original authenticity.[22] The final section of *England, England* might well be described as a narrative of 'failed demuseumification', in which the novel's heroine quits the museum of Englishness only to find that England has become a museum. As Martha contemplates the uncanny postmodern heritage site that is Anglia, she might be reminded of Baudrillard's remark that 'Five hundred years after the discovery of America we now have to discover England'.[23]

Martha's status as the disenchanted architect of a hyperreal environment from which she can never quite free herself contrasts intriguingly with the fate of Sallie Declan, the disturbed postmodernist heroine of A. N. Wilson's Jamesian novella, *A Jealous Ghost*.[24] Sallie is an American graduate student who comes to London to pursue a PhD on *The Turn of the Screw* that focuses on the fortunes of James's celebrated ghost story during the 'postmodern revolution in theory' (23). The thrust of her work is that Baudrillardian theorizing can liberate James's readers from the sterile old debates about whether his story's ghosts are 'real' or simply figments of the heroine's over-active imagination. James's novella, according to Sallie, demands to be read as 'a classic example of Baudrillard's "hyperreality" (53) several decades *avant la lettre*, a text in which 'real' and 'unreal' have imploded into one another. It soon becomes clear that Sallie's interest in a theory that blurs fact and fiction into one another is connected to her own shaky hold on reality. Harbouring a profound horror of sexuality and the body, she takes refuge in literary and theoretical narratives where bodies are dematerialized, transformed into ghosts or clusters of signs. Particularly in times of heightened stress or pressure, she is also prone to confuse fact with fiction, to get her rich fantasy world mixed up with her mundane everyday experiences; naturally, such tendencies are only exacerbated when she accepts a job as a nanny in circumstances that seem precisely to replicate those of *The Turn of the Screw*. Sallie's feeling on accepting her new post – that she is somehow 'walking into her own thesis subject' (13) – seems to echo that of Patricia Duncker's student-hero when embarks on his quest for Paul Michel. But whereas *Hallucinating Foucault* takes its hero on an adventure beyond the limits of his own timid bookishness, Wilson's heroine encloses herself more and more deeply in her favourite James text, re-enacting the heroine's ordeal, imagining that she has seen ghosts, and ultimately killing one of her own charges. 'Hyperreality' in *A Jealous Ghost* is thus pathologized as a telltale symptom of the violent paranoia that produces Sallie's misreadings of both of literature and life – or, rather, that prompts her tragically to misread one as the other. As Toby Litt concludes, 'given the right circumstances, frigidity plus literary theory equals murder'.[25] Wilson's heroine thus takes her place alongside Holland's Christian Aval, Jones's Deborah Rames and Adair's Léopold Sfax in the ranks of the postmodernist killers who have stalked the pages of recent campus fiction.

Though *A Jealous Ghost*'s treatment of Baudrillardian theory is both cursory and unsympathetic, it nevertheless raises questions about hyperreality and reading that are worthy of further reflection. For Wilson's heroine, the concept of hyperreality is both an element of her protocol of reading, and an attribute of the text that she is studying; it is something that she brings to the text from an external source, yet claims to discover *inside* the text. Not that such an ambiguity should be terribly surprising in this context; after all, these kind of fuzzy boundaries between subject and object, text and reader are the very stuff of postmodern theory. But the question of whether we can ever differentiate securely between hyperreality as methodological tool and as textual object – between 'hyperreal reading' and 'reading hyperreality' – is worth bearing in mind when we confront a vastly more sophisticated example of the postmodern ghost story, Mark Z. Danielewski's *House of Leaves* (2000).[26]

Danielewski's novel purports to be a scholarly edition of an annotated collation of a sprawling, fragmented commentary on a mysterious documentary film, *The Navidson Record*, shot by the photojournalist Will Navidson in his new family home in the Virginia countryside. Nothing in Danielewski's labyrinthine narrative is securely 'real', 'authentic' or 'genuine': the documentary footage of the bizarre supernatural qualities of Navidson's house may have been digitally enhanced or simply faked; both Navidson and his film may be preposterous fictions conjured up in the 'commentary' obsessively accumulated by the blind octogenarian recluse Zampanò or both Zampanò; and *The Navidson Record* may be the products of the febrile imagination of the L.A. tattoo artist Johnny Truant, who claims to have found and edited the Zampanò archive, but who also insists that *The Navidson Record* does not exist. The question of whose story to trust in this world of unreliable narrators and suspect artefacts seems both urgent and unanswerable. Truant is a Cretan liar of a narrator, proud of his gift for improvising tall tales, and disarmingly honest about his editorial interference in Zampanò's narrative. Howerever, as Truant approvingly reports, 'Zampanò knew from the get go that what's real or isn't real doesn't matter here' (xx); the old man regards any debate conducted around 'the antimonies of fact or fiction, representation or artifice, document or prank' (3) as a waste of time and energy. The either/or logic of 'authenticity' seems conspicuously irrelevant in this context. Even though *House of Leaves* seems to be dealing with an elaborate hoax, it is impossible to guess who is hoaxing whom, or to determine a point in the text where mischievous simulation ends and trustworthy reality begins. In any case, hoaxes are typically perpetrated in the service of reality, of realism – they function as Emperor's New Clothes-style reminders of our collective gullibility, whereas in Danielewski's novel we are dealing with an endless interplay of simulated realities rather than a one-off prank or self-limiting illusion. In other words, hoaxes belong to reality whereas *House of Leaves* belongs to hyperreality.

The novel's reality-crisis is intimately associated with the effects of film and photographic technology. As Larry McCaffery and Sinda Gregory point out, *House of Leaves* is a reflection on the ways in which 'technologies of reproduction have already profoundly transformed our relationship to memory, to ourselves, and to 'reality' itself'.[27] One such transformation, as Baudrillard has noted, involves strenuous attempts at the 'exhumation of the real in its fundamental banality, in its radical authenticity'. By way of illustration he cites *An American Family*, the pioneering fly-on-the wall documentary about a supposedly typical US household that was first broadcast in 1973. Pointing out that the family in question disintegrated during the process of filming, Baudrillard declares that 'Because heavenly fire no longer falls on corrupted cities, it is the camera lens that, like a laser, comes to pierce lived reality in order to put it to death'.[28] We might expect photography and documentary footage to consolidate our grasp of the world around us by producing indisputably objective records of concrete events; instead, they somehow seem to leach reality out of the real. As Susan Sontag argues, the powers of photography have 'de-Platonized our understanding of reality' since the photograph is both image and object, copy and original.[29] Sontag here seems to approximate the Baudrillardian sense of the world as a product of its own copies – a position that grants uncanny power to the apparatus of mechanical reproduction, and casts an intriguing light on the vein of technophobia in Danielewski's novel. When Navidson rigs his house with motion-sensitive Hi 8 cameras to record the day-to-day dramas of a low-key domestic idyll, his technology instead captures events that would not be out of place in a Stephen King horror. It is as though the very presence of recording technology is enough to generate uncanny transformations in the house; the fly-on-the-wall cameras that were meant passively to record the *heimlich* seem actively to conspire in the production of the terrifyingly *unheimlich* events that engulf the Navidson house.

The uncanny events on Ash Tree Lane develop through a rhythm of escalating shocks familiar from countless horror films. Navidson's house appears, impossibly, to be fractionally bigger on the inside than on the outside, and it mysteriously acquires a new doorway opening onto an endless hallway, a 'twisting labyrinth extending into nowhere' (99). Unlike his claustrophobic partner Karen Green, Navidson is fascinated by the 'empty rooms, long hallways, and dead ends' (109) of this 'all consuming ash-walled maze' (318). The labyrinth seems to harbour some hidden and malevolent forces: any equipment – food rations, markers, lights – left in there is destroyed, and the place echoes to the sound of an ominous 'growl' whose source is never identified. This unearthly subterranean environment, whose shape and proportions are liable to vertiginous and unpredictable change, is forbiddingly hostile but irresistibly fascinating; the challenge of plumbing its depths, probing its limits or finding its secret, is compelling precisely to the extent that it seems dangerously unfeasible. Given that the labyrinth is evidently a metaphor for Danielewski's text, and for textuality in general, then it seems that the novel is challenging us to succeed where its heroes fail by finding a way to navigate through its impossible spaces. At times the novel begins to resemble a Borgesian garden of forking paths, with competing columns and mirror writing, passages that loop back on themselves, and others that need to be read back-to-front or upside-down. Everything in the novel seems either incomplete – dozens of its pages are near-blank, whereas others are apparently missing or stained beyond legibility – or off-centre, as though *House of Leaves* is only a series of digressions winding around one another. The Escher-like architecture of the Ash Tree Lane labyrinth, which seems to correspond to Eco's third type of labyrinth, the net or 'rhizome space' with infinite ramifications and no centre, periphery or exit, thus becomes our best visual shorthand for the novel's own maze-like structure.

Given that the Ash Tree Lane labyrinth brings out the worst in its would-be explorers and conquerors – it elicits obsessive, irrational behaviour, and attempts to explore it culminate in three violent deaths – then it might be fair to describe this novel as a map of its own misreadings. *House of Leaves* exhibits a sustained fascination with the enormous energies that are poured into obsessive, misguided quests for meaning. Zampanò was, according to Truant, a 'graphomaniac' (xxii) who devoted his life to scribbling fragments of his unfinishable masterpiece, the definitive study of *The Navidson Record*. Nor is Zampanò the only one of Danielewski's characters to exhibit symptoms of graphomania; if the old man is to be believed, an improbably vast body of critical material has been generated by *The Navidson Record* in 'trendy academic circles' (6), and Truant himself writes furiously on and around the subject once his interest is piqued. Navidson's film seems to have addictive properties; it has captured the obsessive attention of critics, musicologists, psychoanalysts, psychologists, film theorists, semioticians, structural engineers, explorers and architects. It has resonated with practitioners of everything from 'Biosemiotics' and 'Neo-Minimalism' to 'New Age spirituality' and 'Neo-Plasticism' (4). It has inspired dissertations, conferences, magazine articles, journalistic think-pieces, scholarly publications (including one that runs to 4000 pages), short stories, jokes and even an opera.

House of Leaves is thus a satirical case study of academic graphomania in all its fashionable, pedantic, pretentious, earnest and cranky manifestations. Its treatment of academic discourse, as Christine Brooke-Rose has observed, is funny but also 'very profound in miming the constantly fed animal growth of all obsession; indeed, of all discourse'.[30] Critical theory is just one voice in this babel of interpretations, but it does not fare much better than any of the other intellectual frameworks that the novel satirizes. Danielewski studied at Yale in the 1980s, and *House of Leaves* bears the impress of the writings of leading theoretical figures associated with his *alma mater* – Bloom, de Man, and, in particular, Derrida, whose language and texts are significant reference points throughout the novel. Its layout seems to owe something to the innovative typography of *Glas* (545, 654); it invokes the auricular and labyrinthine conceits of 'Tympan' (401); it plays with, and puns on, the notion *différance* (48, 515, 637); and it quotes at some length from 'Structure, Sign, and Play in the Discourse of the Human Sciences' as it wrestles with the paradoxes of structure and centrality raised by the Navidson labyrinth (111–2). It seems tempting therefore to think of *House of Leaves* as a 'Derridean' novel – not least because Derrida also appears as a talking head in Karen Green's documentary, *What Some Have Thought*, which appears in some versions of *The Navidson Record*. But Green's film, in which Derrida's cryptic remarks on interiority, exteriority and otherness (361, 365) appear alongside Bloom's discourse on the uncanny (358–60), places the guru of deconstruction, with comic incongruity, alongside various novelists, scholars and celebrities in a chattering classes *vox pop* whose soundbites are drained of any great intellectual credibility. It is tempting but futile to posit a 'Derridean' reading of *The House of Leaves*, because that would be to force to Derrida to the centre of the text, or to place him at the centre of a reading that claims that the text is unreadable and decentred.

In the midst of the novel's most taxing chapter, Zampanò helpfully cites a citation of Pascal in de Man's *Allegories of Reading*: 'If one reads too quickly or too slowly, one understands nothing' (115). *House of Leaves* certainly functions as an allegory of reading, perhaps most vividly in those moments when the book makes a paradoxical appearance as a 'character' in its own story. On one of these occasions, a musician in a bar in Arizona hands Truant a well-thumbed and -annotated copy of the first edition of *House of Leaves* (513). *House of Leaves* is also the book that Navidson takes with him on his final expedition into the labyrinth, where he burns pages he has already read to illuminate the pages he is reading. In the end he lights the very last page, and reads it as it burns; the book is thus doubly consumed – by the flame and by the reader, as though the now-empty-handed reader has created meaning by destroying the text. These paradoxical scenes in which the novel stages its own reading focus on the uncanny space of textuality that yawns between the covers of that familiar hand-held object, the book – a space of recessive secretiveness and maze-like intricacy that echoes other texts, and whose openness to other readers and to endless re-reading means that it can never be definitively mapped or measured. In a sense the theme of *House of Leaves* is the question of how to read *House of Leaves*; its main clue is in its superabundance of examples of how *not* to read such a text, those instances of totalizing, essentialist or logocentric reading that aim to fix a text's meaning once and for all. The novel tempts us to over-read its symbolism, or to skip forward over its more taxing digressions; this way, we find out what kind of readers we are – whether we prefer the pace of the slow-moving pedant edging cautiously through the labyrinth, or the breakneck reading swept forward by a hungry sense of what-happens-next curiosity. The novel's efforts to make us read our own reading habits might help account for its mania for lists, which far exceeds the cataloguing mentality of Barnes's *England, England*. Danielewski's narrative is interrupted, often at suspenseful moments, by epic lists – the names of hundreds of photographers, buildings or architects, for example. It musters encyclopaedic resources of knowledge that do or say very little beyond transforming the text's postmodern labyrinth into a Chinese wall of fact. The novel thus puts us through a kind of ordeal by information that tempts us either to skim-read or pore over its every detail for 'clues'. In this context, the professional explorer Holloway Roberts functions as our unreliable proxy in the world of the novel, a bad reader, impatiently blundering into the depths of the labyrinth in a tragically misguided quest for the outside or the centre that leads to madness, violence and death.

The novel is designed to provoke abnormal degrees of readerly self-consciouness, to keep readers aware that they make the meanings that they think they have found. Zampanò seems to chime in with this eye-of-the-beholder theory of meaning and perception when he speculates that the house may be an 'absurd interactive Rorschach test' (179). If Navidson's house is a place where people come face-to-face with their own repressed fears and desires, and *The Navidson Record* is a film that viewers will re-write in the language of their preferred critical methodology, then *House of Leaves* must also be seen as a warped mirror in which readers misrecognize their own obsessions. But if there is something for everyone in this text, then it also seems curiously empty, a vacuum that sucks in vast intellectual energies, or to quote Eco, a mindless 'machine for generating intepretations'.[31] The novel thus confronts the professional reader with its sense of academic discourse as an obsession in search of an object, or an obsession so violent that is prepared to invent its own object, to create a McGuffin worthy of its frenzied pursuit. According to this logic, criticism is not contaminated but *constituted* by the fictive; critical reading thus emerges in *House of Leaves* as an obsessive quest for the 'truth' of its own lies. And, having confronted its academic readers with this revelation, Danielewski's novel seems to have exceeded their grasp. Its teasing non-dedication – 'This is not for you' (ix) – might therefore serve as an appropriate warning that critical readers ought to abandon hope of discovering anything about the novel that it does not already know about itself. Indeed, Danielewski has publicly congratulated himself on the fact that 'I have yet to hear an interpretation of *House of Leaves* that I had not anticipated'.[32] *House of Leaves* is probably as close as you are ever going to get to a text that is an exhaustive 'analysis of itself': clairvoyantly mindful of the obsessive hermeneutic activity that is will provoke, Danielewski's novel predicts and lampoons its own feverish critical reception, and parades its knowledge of critical and theoretical methodologies with a self-explicating candour that seems to leave the reader curiously passive – as though the final secret of this superlatively *scriptible* text is that it is, in the end, just another mundanely *lisible* novel.

10
Conclusion: Fiction after Theory

In *The Future of Theory*, Jean-Michel Rabaté declares that 'Theory reigned supreme between 1975 and 1991'.[1] But if theory's finest hour really did pass a decade and a half ago then does it still make sense to speculate about its future? Or should we now be talking about it in the past tense? Rabaté's book takes a surprisingly upbeat line on the continuing relevance and vitality of theoretical debate,[2] but it is worth setting his optimism against the disenchanted portrait of life after theory offered in a memorable comic sequence from Jonathan Franzen's *The Corrections* (2001). When the disgraced academic Chip Lambert falls on hard times, he begins to sell off the collection of theoretical texts that he assembled during his brief career as an Assistant Professor of Textual Artifacts. Beginning with the Marxists – two heavy bags of Adorno, Habermas and Jameson fetch him a mere $64 – he begins to work his way through the collection, one -ism at a time:

> By the beginning of October [...] he'd sold his feminists, his formal-
> ists, his structuralists, his post-structuralists, his Freudians, and his
> queers. ... [A]ll he had left was his beloved cultural historians and his
> complete hard-cover Arden Shakespeare; and because a kind of magic
> resided in the Shakespeare – the uniform volumes in their pale blue
> jackets were like an archipelago of safe retreats – he piled his Foucault
> and Greenblatt and Hooks and Poovey into shopping bags and sold
> them all for $115.[3]

As Elaine Showalter points out, this is a version of the classic fictional scene where 'emblems of a treasured past, objects laden with nostalgic emotions, historical meaning, and sentimental value are sold to unfeeling strangers'.[4] More specifically, Lambert's tragicomic clearance sale positions theory as yesterday's controversy; sooner rather than later, Franzen suggests, the hallowed writings of the great theory gurus will be gathering dust on the neglected shelves of second-hand bookshops having been sold for a fraction of their original cost, whilst ordinary readers will continue to gravitate towards the magical archipelagos of priceless classic literature.

The possibility that the whole theoretical enterprise may dwindle to the status of an arcane footnote to the history of ideas, as quaintly obscure as geomancy or theosophy, has certainly troubled some of its adherents. Reflecting on the rise and fall of theoretical methodologies, David Lodge once remarked that 'structuralism may be the first such movement to go through the complete life-cycle of innovation, orthodoxy and obsolescence, without ever touching the popular consciousness'.[5] And even if structuralism was the first movement to undergo such a brutally compressed life-cycle, it now seems that each successive theory is entitled to fifteen-odd minutes of academic fame or notoriety, before vanishing into obscurity without troubling any non-specialist audience beyond the conference circuit or seminar room. If we are indeed currently witnessing the 'aftermath' of theory, then it is tempting to ask whether Lodge's judgement on structuralism is true also of Theory in general: has Theory itself passed through the cycle of innovation, orthodoxy and obsolescence without troubling the 'popular consciousness'?

It seems reasonable to suppose that whatever contact theory has made with the 'popular consciousness' in recent years has been substantially achieved via the fiction of Lodge and his fellow theoretical novelists. Not that all of the writers I have been discussing here share Lodge's popularizing instincts. For example, the English translation of Kristeva's *The Samurai* confidently promises us that 'Readers will instantly recognize ... Lacan, Derrida, Barthes, Althusser'. The possibility that some readers may *not* be on intimate terms with Kristeva's post-structuralist cronies is clearly too far-fetched to have occurred to her blurb-writer. Similarly, it is difficult to imagine quite what headway the 'general reader' might ever make with the cryptic theoretical riffs of a text like Federman's *Take It Or Leave It* (1976), with its 'crashup of confusionism masturbatory telquelism drifting on the lacanian raft derridian barge shipwrecked in other words on the sea of fucked up literature'.[6] However, the insularity of Kristeva and the hyper-experimentalism of Federman are reassuringly uncommon in this field. Far from confining itself to some highbrow ghetto, the novel of theory has been surprisingly hospitable to the non-specialist reader. For all their fascination with intellectual radicalism, these novels tend to be constructed with a keen sense of the pleasures of convention, even if those conventions are being playfully reinvented – as is the case with the metafictional ghost stories of Danielewski and Wilson, the philosophical murder mysteries of Holland and Eco or the postmodern Victoriana of Byatt, Fowles and Lodge. Theoretical novelists like to operate within the rubrics of popular genres, such as romance, or heroic quest, or criminal investigation, where there are lovers to be paired off, missing persons to be tracked down, crimes to be investigated and enigmas to be resolved; the alien language and bizarrely counter-intuitive thinking of theory are thus safely contained for the novice reader within reassuringly familiar horizons of expectation.

Behind all these user-friendly narrative strategies is what looks like a concerted effort to *humanize* theory, to endow it with a face, a personality and a life-cycle. If we think back to the name-checking of Barthes in *The French Lieutenant's Woman* or Lévi-Strauss in *MF* or, especially, the frenetic theoretical name-dropping of *Thru*, it is clear that for most readers in those early days theorists were *only* names – albeit exotic continental ones – culled from the precocious interdisciplinary reading of Fowles, Burgess and Brooke-Rose. Structuralists, post-structuralists and post-modernists would only come to acquire personalities when Lodge and Bradbury created the likes of Morris Zapp, Robyn Penrose, Henri Mensonge and Bazlo Criminale, when Sollers and Kristeva populated their *romans à clefs* with lightly disguised theorists, and when Adair and Banville re-imagined the secret lives of Paul de Man. In recent years, with the comic turns of Barthes in *Glyph* and Derrida in *House of Leaves*, the novel seems to have entered a new phase of gossipy familiarity in its relationship with the theorists who were such unknown quantities in *Thru*. After thirty-odd years of theoretical fiction, we should now begin to recognize the cluster of different 'types' to which fictional theorists are assigned – there is the questing protagonist of a mock-heroic academic romance (Byatt's Roland Michell; Lodge's Persse McGarrigle); the macho careerist (Lodge's Morris Zapp; Hynes's Anthony Pescecane); the terminally self-effacing deconstructionist (Bradbury's Mensonge and Jack-Paul Verso); the faintly sinister European philosopher-critic (L'Heureux's Olga Kominska; Adair's Léopold Sfax; Bradbury's Bazlo Criminale; Hynes's Marko Kraljević; Banville's Axel Vander); the androgynous feminist (Lodge's Robyn Penrose; Hynes's Vita Deonne); and the predatory dissector of literary texts (Byatt's Fergus Wolff and Gareth Butcher).

The colourful 'humanizations' of theory in these novels are obviously produced in defiance of the efforts of structuralism and post-structuralism to erase every trace of human subjectivity from discourse. If theorists choose to write 'in order to have no face', then the novel of theory has reversed this gambit by dragging self-effacing theorists into direct public scrutiny. In previous chapters we have seen disgraced theorists variously unmasked as bandwagon-chasing careerists, as obnoxious womanizers and bullshitters, as intellectual charlatans, impostors and plagiarists, as child snatchers and grave robbers, as money-launderers, murderers, closet Nazis and fugitive war criminals. This adds up to a quite extraordinary charge sheet, but unquestionably the most damning allegation that is repeatedly levelled against these prophets of anti-humanism is that they are as human as anyone else. Even more than all those fraudulent and obnoxious theorists, it is the affable Marxists, diffident post-structuralists and reluctant postmodernists who function in these novels as living, breathing 'disproof' of all this alarming talk of the death of the subject.

The further chief advantage of 'humanizing' theory in these ways is that it enables sceptical novelists to think reassuring thoughts about the mortality of theory, and to look forward expectantly to the moment when it reaches the end of its natural life-span. There is a strong tendency in fiction to associate theory with sickness and death – not just the grisly murders witnessed in Eco, Jones or Holland, but also the kind of curious intellectual malaise experience by Dr Nicholas Page in Raymond Tallis's *Absence* (1999).[7] If you were looking for an alternative title for *Absence*, you might well choose *Theorrhoea and After*, the title of one of Tallis's pungent critiques of recent critical trends, since his novel constructs theory as an intellectual disease from which its hero struggles to recover. Page is a gifted young physician who, during a spell of lovesick *angst*, becomes addicted to post-structuralist theories of absence, lack and desire, and finds in the writings of Derrida and Lacan 'not only a mirror in which to view the senselessness of his condition but also the hint of a cure that was worse that the disease' (7). The novel thus pathologizes theory by presenting it as a symptom of indulgent self-pity fuelled by Page's dilettantish flirtation with continental philosophy – though the idea of theory as both 'disease' and 'cure' seems to flirt with the very Derridean logic of the *pharmakon* that the novel officially despises. In any case, Page's addiction to theory is an acute but not chronic condition, and he is eventually restored to full intellectual health when he rediscovers 'presence, meaning and truth' (189) in the arms of Sister Janet Parker, herself a literature graduate who has long since outgrown her youthful theoretical enthusiasms. Page's story is thus clearly offered by Tallis as an optimistic allegory of what he hopes will be our prompt collective recovery from the acute case of 'theorrhoea' that has been gripping contemporary intellectual culture in recent years.

If Page's case of theorrhoea was hardly life-threatening, we have already seen theory figured as a poisonously deadly force in *Murder at the MLA, Death in a Deadly Seminar* and *The Name of the Rose*. In Kristeva's *The Samurai* and Philippe Sollers' *Women*, on the other hand, theory itself seems to be dying off. Kristeva's novel becomes increasingly funereal in its later stages as it narrates the deaths of Lacan ('Maurice Lauzun'), Barthes ('Armand Bréhal'), and Foucault ('Scherner'). *Women* is also an a novel of cultural bereavement, an elegy for the *Tel Quel* generation whose end-of-an-era poignancy is tempered by the cynicism of the narrator, who regards the deaths of Althusser ('Laurence Lutz'), Barthes ('Jean Werth'), and Lacan ('Paul Fals') as evidence of the failure of post-structuralism's 'vast attempt to destroy the "Subject"'.[8] In what is now a most familiar gesture in the novel of theory, Sollers rewrites the 'death of the author' and 'death of the subject' as the 'death of the theorist' – that is, he presents theorists as victims of their own theories. Of course in doing so, Sollers's narrator is simply playing the same necrological games as the post-structuralists whose theories he ridicules; nothing is more theoretical than proclaiming the 'death of theory'. Like all those novelists who have fantasized the end of theory, Sollers is contributing to what Derrida calls the 'multiplication of necrologies' in the rhetoric of contemporary literary pundits:

> I've heard this for at least twenty-five years: it [deconstruction] is finished, it is dying. Why do I say dying? It is dead! I tell you it's dead! And, every time I hear this I say, well, that's interesting, because usually when someone (for, in order to die, it must be 'someone', something cannot die, deconstruction cannot die) dies, you read in the newspaper 'So and so Died'. Now, if the next day, you read 'He or she died,' and, then, on the third, and the fourth, days, you read this yet again, after a year you would start asking the question, 'What's happening with this dead person'? Because s/he goes on dying for years and years and years![9]

Novelists have been imagining the death of theory for 'years and years and years' now, but the tremendous energies they have devoted to envisioning its demise or disappearance have only served to grant it a rich and indefinitely prolonged afterlife in the pages of contemporary fiction.

Notes

1 Introduction: Theory in(to) Fiction

1. See 'Novels come out of life, not out of theories: An Interview with Julian Barnes', in Rudolf Freiburg and Jan Schnitker, eds, *'Do You Consider Yourself a Postmodern Author?' Interviews with Contemporary English Writers* (Münster: Lit Verlag, 1999), p. 52.
2. Paul de Man, 'The Resistance to Theory', in *The Resistance to Theory* (Manchester: Manchester University Press, 1986), pp. 3–20 (10).
3. Mark Currie, *Postmodern Narrative Theory* (Basingstoke: Macmillan, 1998), p. 33.
4. Julia Kristeva, 'Concerning *The Samurai*', in *Nations without Nationalism*, trans. Leon S. Roudiez (New York: Columbia University Press, 1993 [1990]), p. 77.
5. See Raymond Federman, 'Critifiction: Imagination as Plagiarism', in *Critifiction: Postmodern Essays* (Albany: State University of New York Press, 1993 [1976]), pp. 48–64.
6. Currie, *Postmodern Narrative Theory*, p. 70.
7. See Imre Salusinszky, *Criticism in Society* (New York: Methuen, 1987), p. 22.
8. Roland Barthes, 'Réponses', *Tel Quel* 47 (1971), 89–107 (102); Roland Barthes, *Roland Barthes*, trans. Richard Howard (Berkeley, CA: University of California Press, 1977 [1975]), p. 120.
9. Michel Foucault, 'The Discourse of History' [1967 interview with Raymond Bellour], in Sylvère Lotringer, ed., *Foucault Live: Collected Interviews, 1961–84*, trans. Lysa Hochroth and John Johnston, (New York: Semiotex(e), 1996), p. 24; Jean Baudrillard, 'This Beer Isn't a Beer' [1991 interview with Anne Laurent], in Mike Gane, ed., *Baudrillard Live: Selected Interviews* (London: Routledge, 1993), p. 188.
10. 'The problem', says Connor, 'seems to be partly in the assumption that a text can be dialogic or monologic as a matter of simple authorial or stylistic choice. But if the condition of all texts is to be only partly aware and in charge of the conditions of possibility that make them readable in different contexts, then to embrace that condition of partial mastery as part of a conscious programme is always going to be futile'. 'Post-Modesty: Renunciation and the Sublime', in *Postmodernist Culture: An Introduction to Theories of the Contemporary* (Oxford: Blackwell, 1997), pp. 227–50 (247).
11. Geoffrey H. Hartman, 'Literary Commentary as Literature', in *Criticism in the Wilderness: The Study of Literature Today* (New Haven, CT: Yale University Press, 1980), pp. 189–213 (212–2).
12. Jonathan Culler, 'The Literary in Theory', in Judith Butler, John Guillory and Kendall Thomas, eds, *What's Left of Theory?: New Work on the Politics of Literary Theory*, (New York: Routledge, 2000), p. 286.
13. Niall Lucy, *Postmodern Literary Theory: An Introduction* (Oxford: Blackwell, 1997), p. 153.

14. Seán Burke, *The Death and Return of the Author: Criticism and Subjectivity in Barthes, Foucault, and Derrida* (Edinburgh: Edinburgh University Press, 1999), p. 179.

15. Patricia Waugh, 'Postmodern Fiction and the Rise of Critical Theory', in Brian Shaffer, ed., *A Companion to the British and Irish Novel 1945–2000* (Oxford: Blackwell, 2005), pp. 65–82 (67).

16. Elaine Showalter, 'Towards a Feminist Poetics', in *The New Feminist Criticism: Essays on Women, Literature, and Theory* (London: Virago, 1986), pp. 125–43; Hélène Cixous, 'The Laugh of the Medusa', in Elaine Marks and Isabelle de Courtivron, eds, *New French Feminisms: An Anthology* (Sussex: The Harvester Press, 1981), pp. 245–64.

17. Nicolas Tredell, 'Post-Theory', in *The Critical Decade: Culture in Crisis* (Manchester: Carcanet, 1993), pp. 32–6; Thomas Docherty, *After Theory* (Edinburgh: Edinburgh University Press, 1997); Martin McQuillan, Robin Purves, Graeme Macdonald, Stephen Thomson, eds, *Post-Theory: New Directions in Criticism* (Edinburgh: Edinburgh University Press, 1999); Raymond Tallis, *Theorrhoea and After* (Basingstoke: Macmillan, 1999); Valentine Cunningham, *Reading After Theory* (Oxford: Blackwell, 2002); Michael Payne and John Schad, eds, *life.after.theory* (London: Continuum, 2003); Terry Eagleton, *After Theory* (London: Allen Lane, 2003).

18. John Sturrock, *The Word from Paris: Essays on Modern French Thinkers and Writers* (London: Verso, 1998).

19. Barthes, *Roland Barthes*, p. 54.

20. Dominic Head, *The Cambridge Guide to Modern British Fiction, 1950–2000* (Cambridge: Cambridge University Press, 2002), p. 4; Cunningham, *Reading After Theory*, p. 46.

21. Jonathan Coe, *The House of Sleep* (Harmondsworth: Penguin, 1997), pp. 282–95.

22. De Man, 'The Resistance to Theory', pp. 19–20.

2   The Structuralist Novel

1. Ferdinand de Saussure, *Course in General Linguistics*, trans. Wade Baskin (London: Fontana, 1974 [1916]), p. 14.

2. Saussure, *Course in General Linguistics*, p. 122.

3. Roland Barthes, *S/Z*, trans. Richard Howard (Oxford: Blackwell, 1990 [1973]), p. 21.

4. Anthony Burgess, *MF* (New York: Knopf, 1971), p. 10.

5. Anthony Burgess, 'Oedipus Wrecks', in *This Man and Music* (London: Hutchinson, 1982), pp. 162–79 (163).

6. David Lodge, *How Far Can You Go?* (Harmondsworth: Penguin, 1980).

7. The phrase is Roland Barthes's. See 'The Reality-Effect', in *The Rustle of Language*, trans. Richard Howard (Oxford: Blackwell, 1986 [1984]), pp. 141–8.

8. Gérard Genette, *Narrative Discourse: An Essay in Method*, trans. Jane E. Lewin (Ithaca, NY: Cornell University Press, 1980 [1972]), pp. 114–16.

9. Its status as a canonical work of British postmodernism is confirmed by discussions in Patricia Waugh, *Metafiction: The Theory and Practice of Self-Conscious Fiction* (London: Routledge, 1984), pp. 32–4, 123–7; Linda Hutcheon, *A Poetics*

of Postmodernism: History, Theory, Fiction (New York: Routledge, 1988), where it is adduced as the first example of 'historiographic metafiction', p. 5.

10. John Fowles, *The French Lieutenant's Woman* (London: Pan, 1987 [1969]), p. 9.
11. See, for example, Robert Siegle, 'The Concept of the Author in Barthes, Foucault, and Fowles', *College Literature* 10 (1983), 126–38.
12. Burgess, 'Oedipus Wrecks', p. 163.
13. Claude Lévi-Strauss, 'The Scope of Anthropology', in *Structural Anthropology*, vol. II, trans. Monique Layton (London: Allen Lane, 1977 [1960]), pp. 3–32.
14. Suzanne Keen, *Romances of the Archive in Contemporary British Fiction* (Toronto: University of Toronto Press, 2001). See p. 35 for a useful breakdown of the recurring characteristics of the genre.
15. Keen, *Romances of the Archive*, p. 231.
16. Burgess, 'Oedipus Wrecks', p. 177.
17. See Frank Kermode, '*M/F*', *Anthony Burgess Newsletter* (December 2000), 23–6.
18. Frank Kermode, 'The Use of the Codes', in *Essays on Fiction 1971–82* (London: Routledge and Kegan Paul, 1983), pp. 72–91 (81).
19. See Karen R. Lawrence, 'Dialogizing Theory in Brooke-Rose's *Thru*', *Western Humanities Review* 50–1 (1996–97), 352–8, for discussion of the interaction of theories in the novel.
20. Christine Brooke-Rose, *Stories, Theories and Things* (Cambridge: Cambridge University Press, 1991), p. 11.
21. Malcolm Bradbury, *The Modern British Novel 1878–2001* (London: Penguin, 2001), p. 393.
22. Ellen J. Friedman and Miriam Fuchs, 'A Conversation with Christine Brooke-Rose', in Ellen J. Friedman and Richard Martin, eds, *Utterly Other Discourse: The Texts of Christine Brooke-Rose* (Normal, IL: Dalkey Archive Press, 1995), p. 31.
23. Waugh, *Metafiction*, p. 145.
24. Friedman and Fuchs, 'A Conversation with Christine Brooke-Rose', p. 36.
25. Brian McHale, 'The Postmodernism(s) of Christine Brooke-Rose', in Friedman and Martin, eds, *Utterly Other Discourse*, pp. 192–213 (200).
26. Roman Jakobson, *The Framework of Language* (Ann Arbor, MI: University of Michigan, 1980), pp. 81–92.
27. Shlomith Rimmon-Kenan, 'Ambiguity and Narrative Levels: Christine Brooke-Rose's *Thru*', *Poetics Today* 3 (1982), 21–32 (28); Glyn White, ' "YOU ARE HERE": Reading and Representation in Christine Brooke-Rose's *Thru*', *Poetics Today* 23 (2002), 611–31 (624).
28. Christine Brooke-Rose, 'Is Self-Reflexivity Mere?', in *Invisible Author: Last Essays* (Columbus, OH: The Ohio State University Press, 2002), pp. 63–108.
29. Umberto Eco, *The Role of the Reader: Explorations in the Semiotics of Texts* (London: Hutchinson, 1979), p. 9.

3 From Structuralism to Dialogics: David Lodge

1. For examples of Lodge's 'self-analysis', see *The Novelist at the Crossroads and Other Essays on Fiction and Criticism* (London: Routledge and Kegan Paul, 1971), ch. 4 and *Working With Structuralism: Essays and Reviews on Nineteenth- and Twentieth-Century Literature* (London: Routledge and Kegan Paul, 1981), ch. 4.
2. David Lodge, *After Bakhtin: Essays on Fiction and Criticism* (London: Routledge, 1990), pp. 7–8.

3. David Lodge, *The Modes of Modern Writing: Metaphor, Metonymy, and the Typology of Modern Literature* (London: Arnold, 1977), p. 52.
4. Bernard Bergonzi, *David Lodge* (Plymouth: Northcote House, 1995), p. 54; Terry Eagleton, 'The Silences of David Lodge', *New Left Review* 172 (1988), 93–102 (97).
5. See *The Modes of Modern Writing*, pp. 73–81, for Lodge's account of Jakobson on metaphor and metonymy.
6. Robert A. Morace, *The Dialogic Novels of Malcolm Bradbury and David Lodge* (Carbondale and Edwardsville, IL: Southern Illinois University Press, 1989), p. 203.
7. See Siegfried Mews, 'The Professor's Novel: David Lodge's *Small World*', *MLN* 104 (1989), 713–26.
8. Steven Connor, *The English Novel in History 1950–95* (London: Routledge, 1996), p. 82.
9. Lodge, *After Bakhtin*, p. 4.
10. See especially Mikhail Bakhtin, *Rabelais and His World*, trans. Hélène Iswolsky (Bloomington, IN: Indiana University Press, 1984 [1965]), ch. 5.
11. Mikhail Bakhtin, 'Forms of Time and the Chronotope in the Novel', in *The Dialogic Imagination: Four Essays*, trans. Caryl Emerson and Michael Holquist (Austin: University of Texas Press, 1981), pp. 84–258.
12. Mikhail Bakhtin, *Problems of Dostoevsky's Poetics*, trans. Caryl Emerson (Minneapolis, MN: University of Minnesota Press, 1984), p. 6.
13. David Lodge, *Thinks ...* (Harmondsworth: Penguin, 2001), pp. 224–6.
14. Eagleton, 'The Silences of David Lodge', p. 102.
15. Bakhtin, 'From the Prehistory of Novelistic Discourse', in *The Dialogic Imagination*, p. 49.

4   The 'Culture Wars' and Beyond: Theory on the US Campus

1. Sandra M. Gilbert and Susan Gubar, *Masterpiece Theatre: An Academic Melodrama* (New Brunswick, NJ: Rutgers University Press, 1995).
2. Kenneth Womack, *Postwar Academic Fiction: Satire, Ethics, Community* (Basingstoke: Palgrave, 2002), p. 133; Ihab Hassan, 'Prometheus as Performer: Toward a Posthumanist Culture? A University Masque in Five Scenes', in *The Right Promethean Fire: Imagination, Science, and Cultural Change* (Urbana, IL: University of Illinois Press, 1980), pp. 187–207.
3. Karen R. Lawrence, 'Saving the Text: Cultural Crisis in *Textermination* and *Masterpiece Theatre*', *Narrative* 5 (1997), 108–16 (112).
4. See Gerald Graff, *Professing Literature: An Institutional History* (Chicago, IL: The University of Chicago Press, 1987).
5. David Damrosch, *We Scholars: Changing the Culture of the University* (Cambridge, MA: Harvard University Press, 1995).
6. David Damrosch, *Meetings of the Mind* (Princeton, NJ: Princeton University Press, 2000).
7. Bill Readings, *The University in Ruins* (Cambridge, MA: Harvard University Press, 1996), pp. 127, 187.
8. Jacques Derrida, *Given Time: 1. Counterfeit Money*, trans. Peggy Kamuf (Chicago: The University of Chicago Press, 1992), p. 7.
9. James Hynes, *The Lecturer's Tale* (New York: Picador, 2001).

10. Jean-Michel Rabaté, *The Future of Theory* (Oxford: Blackwell, 2002), p. 7.
11. Elaine Showalter, *Faculty Towers: The Academic Novel and Its Discontents* (Philadelphia, PA: University of Pennsylvania Press, 2005), p. 110.
12. Readings, *The University in Ruins*, p. 172.
13. Showalter, *Faculty Towers*, p. 110.
14. Harold Bloom, *The Western Canon: The Books and School of the Ages* (London: Macmillan, 1995), p. 15.
15. Readings, *The University in Ruins*, p. 114.
16. John L'Heureux, *The Handmaid of Desire* (New York: Soho Press, 1996).
17. Richard Powers, *Galatea 2.2* (London: Abacus, 1995).
18. Percival Everett, *Glyph* (Saint Paul, MN: Graywolf Press, 1999).
19. Jacqueline Berben-Masi, 'Perceval Everett's *Glyph*: Prisons of the Body Physical, Political, and Academic', in Monika Fludernik and Greta Olson, eds, *In the Grip of the Law: Trials, Prisons and the Space Between* (Frankfurt: Peter Lang, 2004), pp. 223–39 (234).
20. Ralph's quotation is from Jacques Lacan, 'The Agency of the Letter in the Unconscious or Reason since Freud', in *Écrits: A Selection*, trans. Alan Sheridan (London: Routledge, 1977[1957]), p. 166.
21. Percival Everett, *Erasure: A Novel* (London: Faber, 2003).
22. Frederic Jameson, 'Postmodernism, or the Cultural Logic of Late Capitalism', *New Left Review* 146 (1984), 53–92 (65).

5 The Vanishing Author

1. Aleid Fokkema, 'The Author: Postmodernism's Stock Character', in Paul Franssen and Ton Hoenselaars, eds, *The Author as Character: Representing Historical Writers in Western Literature* (Madison, WI: Farleigh Dickinson University Press, 1999), pp. 39–51 (49).
2. See Mary Eagleton, *Figuring the Woman Author in Contemporary Fiction* (Basingstoke: Palgrave, 2005), for a wide-ranging study of (re)constructions of the woman author in the post-Barthesian novel.
3. Roland Barthes, 'The Death of the Author', in *Image-Music-Text*, trans. Stephen Heath (London: Fontana, 1977 [1968]), pp. 142–8; Michel Foucault 'What Is an Author?', in James Faubion, ed., *The Essential Works Volume 2: Aesthetics*, trans. Robert Hurley *et al.* (London: Allen Lane, 1998 [1969]), pp. 205–22.
4. Burke, *The Death and Return of the Author*, p. 99.
5. Roland Barthes, *Sade Fourier Loyola*, trans. Richard Miller (Berkeley, CA: University of California Press, 1976 [1971]), p. 8.
6. Malcolm Bradbury, *My Strange Quest for Mensonge: Structuralism's Hidden Hero* (London: Deutsch, 1987), p. 27.
7. Malcolm Bradbury, *To the Hermitage* (London: Macmillan, 2000).
8. Michel Foucault, *The Order of Things: An Archaeology of the Human Sciences* (London: Routledge, 1970 [1966]), p. 387.
9. Michel Foucault, *The Archaeology of Knowledge*, trans. A. M. Sheridan Smith (London: Routledge, 1989 [1969]), p. 7.
10. Malcolm Bradbury, *Doctor Criminale* (London: Secker & Warburg, 1992).
11. One potentially de Manian detail in the novel is the presence of Criminale's estranged wife, Gertla Riviero, in Argentina. The novel's South American

episodes are probably a means of amplifying its already strong Borgesian intertextualities, but Argentina is also where de Man's estranged wife, Anaide Baraghian, ended up with their three children after the war while he pursued his academic career – and re-married – in the United States. See David Lehman, *Signs of the Times: Deconstruction and the Fall of Paul de Man* (London: Deutsch, 1991), pp. 188–91, for details of de Man's alleged bigamy.

12. George Steiner, 'Georg Lukács and his Devil's Pact', in *Language and Silence: Essays 1958–1966* (London: Faber, 1967), pp. 355–70 (367–8).

13. Gilbert Adair, *The Death of the Author* (London: Minerva, 1992).

14. Paul de Man, 'Les Juifs dans la Littérature actuelle', *Le Soir*, 4 March 1941, in Werner Hamacher, Neil Hertz and Thomas Keenan, eds, *Wartime Journalism, 1939–43* (Lincoln, NE: University of Nebraska Press, 1988), p. 45. For a range of responses, see Werner Hamacher, Neil Hertz and Thomas Keenan, eds, *Responses: On Paul de Man's Wartime Journalism* (Lincoln, NE: University of Nebraska Press, 1989).

15. Richard Klein, 'DeMan's Resistances: A Contribution to the Future Science of DeManlogy', in Hamacher, Hertz and Keenan, eds, *Responses*, pp. 285–97.

16. Paul de Man, 'Autobiography as De-Facement', in *The Rhetoric of Romanticism* (New York: Columbia University Press, 1984), p. 81.

17. Paul de Man, 'Excuses (*Confessions*)', in *Allegories of Reading: Figural Language in Rousseau, Nietzsche, Rilke, and Proust* (New Haven, CT: Yale University Press, 1979), pp. 278–301.

18. Lehman, *Signs of the Times*, p. 213. Mehlman has subsequently distanced himself from this comment. See his 'Perspectives: on De Man and *Le Soir*', in Hamacher, Hertz and Keenan, eds, *Responses*, p. 330.

19. Burke, *The Death and Return of the Author*, pp. 4–6.

20. De Man, 'Excuses (*Confessions*)', p. 298.

21. Foucault, *The Archaeology of Knowledge*, p. 98.

22. Martin McQuillan, *Paul de Man* (London: Routledge, 2001), p. 122.

23. John Banville, *Shroud* (London: Picador, 2002).

24. Foucault, *The Order of Things*, p. 382.

25. Louis Althusser, *The Future Lasts Forever: A Memoir*, trans. Richard Veasey (New York: The New Press, 1993), pp. 23, 210.

26. Althusser, *The Future Lasts Forever*, p. 277.

27. See 'The Facts', in *The Future Lasts Forever*, pp. 346–50.

28. See Banville, *Shroud*, pp. 71–4; Althusser, *The Future Lasts Forever*, pp. 79–81.

29. Paul de Man, 'Rhetoric of Tropes (*Nietzsche*)', in *Allegories of Reading*, p. 112.

30. Althusser, *The Future Lasts Forever*, p. 148.

31. Roland Barthes, 'Barthes to the Third Power', in Marshall Blonsky, ed., *On Signs: A Semiotics Reader* (Oxford: Blackwell, 1985), pp. 189–91 (191).

6 Foucauldian Fictions

1. Michel Foucault, cited in James Miller, *The Passion of Michel Foucault* (London: HarperCollins, 1993), p. 158.

2. Edward W. Said, 'Michel Foucault, 1926–1984', in Jonathan Arac, ed., *After Foucault: Humanistic Knowledge, Postmodern Challenges* (New Brunswick, NJ: Rutgers University Press, 1991), p. 3.

3. Foucault, 'A Preface to Transgression' [1963], in *Aesthetics*, pp. 69–87.
4. Foucault, 'My Body, This Paper, This Fire' [1972], *Aesthetics*, pp. 393–417.
5. See Miller, *The Passion of Michel Foucault*, p. 203.
6. L'Heureux, *The Handmaid of Desire*, p. 71.
7. Foucault, *The Archaeology of Knowledge*, p. 17.
8. Miller, *The Passion of Michel Foucault*, p. 320.
9. Michel Foucault, *Discipline and Punish: The Birth of the Prison*, trans. Alan Sheridan (Harmondsworth: Penguin, 1979 [1975]), p. 304.
10. Toby Litt, 'When I Met Michel Foucault', in *Adventures in Capitalism* (Harmondsworth: Penguin, 2003 [1996]), pp. 189–228.
11. Foucault, *Discipline and Punish*, p. 34.
12. See 'The Masked Philosopher' 1980 interview with Foucault in *Le Monde* in Paul Rabinow, ed., *Ethics: The Essential Works of Foucault 1954–84*, vol. I, trans. Robert Hurley *et al.* (London: Allen Lane, 1997), pp. 321–8.
13. Hervé Guibert, 'Les secrets d'un homme', in *Mauve le Vierge: Nouvelles* (Paris: Gallimard, 1988), pp. 101–11; *To the Friend Who Did Not Save My Life: A Novel*, trans. Linda Coverdale (London: Quartet Books, 1991 [1990]).
14. See Miller, *The Passion of Michel Foucault*, ch. 11, for discussion of the biographical 'accuracy' of these revelations.
15. Erin O'Connor, 'Reading *The Biographer's Tale*', *Victorian Studies* 44 (2002), 379–87 (380).
16. A. S. Byatt, 'Still Life/Nature Morte', in *Passions of the Mind: Selected Writings* (London: Chatto and Windus, 1991), pp. 16–17.
17. Foucault, *The Order of Things*, p. 113.
18. Foucault, *The Order of Things*, p. xviii.
19. Andrew Gibson, 'Crossing the Present: Narrative, Alterity and Gender in Postmodern Fiction', in Roger Luckhurst and Peter Marks, eds, *Literature and the Contemporary: Fictions and Theories of the Present* (Essex: Longman, 1999), p. 191.
20. Maurice Blanchot, 'Michel Foucault as I Imagine Him', in Michel Foucault and Maurice Blanchot, eds, *Foucault/Blanchot*, trans. Brian Massumi and Jeffrey Mehlman (New York: Zone Books, 1990), pp. 63–4.
21. Michel Foucault, *Madness and Civilization: A History of Insanity in the Age of Reason*, trans. Richard Howard (London: Routledge, 1989 [1961/4]), p. xii.
22. Didier Eribon, *Michel Foucault*, trans. Betsy Wing (London: Faber, 1991 [1989]), pp. 4–5.
23. Foucault, *Madness and Civilization*, p. 30.

7 Feminism *versus* Post-structuralism

1. Cixous, 'The Laugh of the Medusa', p. 262.
2. Lorna Sage, *Angela Carter* (Plymouth: Northcote House, 1994), p. 2.
3. For a discussion of Carter, carnival and Bakhtin, see Linden Peach, *Angela Carter* (Basingstoke: Macmillan, 1998), ch. 5. Peach argues that for Carter carnivalesque 'is a theme and not necessarily a position from which she writes' (p. 144).
4. Alison Easton, 'Introduction: Reading Angela Carter', in Alison Easton, ed., *Angela Carter: Contemporary Critical Essays* (Basingstoke: Macmillan, 2000), pp. 6–7. See also Susan Watkins, *Twentieth-Century Women Novelists: Feminist*

Theory into Practice (Basingstoke: Palgrave, 2001), pp. 132–45, for an illuminating discussion of *Nights at the Circus* as an exploration of Carter's ambivalent relationship with postmodernist theory.

5. Sage, *Angela Carter*, p. 35.
6. Robert Eaglestone, in 'The Fiction of Angela Carter: The Woman Who Loved to
   Retell Stories', in Richard J. Lane, Rod Mengham and Philip Tew, eds,
   Contemporary British Fiction (Cambridge: Polity Press, 2003), pp. 195–209 (203).
7. Christopher Norris, *Derrida* (London: Fontana, 1987), pp. 51–2.
8. Jacques Derrida, 'The Double Session', in *Dissemination*, trans. Barbara
   Johnson (London: Continuum, 2004 [1972]), pp. 187–316.
9. See Lucy, *Postmodern Literary Theory*, pp. 99–103, for a careful restatement of
   what Derrida means by 'play'.
10. Jago Morrison, *Contemporary Fiction* (London: Routledge, 2003), p. 175.
11. Foucault, *Discipline and Punish*, p. 200.
12. Morrison, *Contemporary Fiction*, p. 177.
13. Joanne M. Gass, 'Panopticism in *Nights at the Circus*', *The Review of
    Contemporary Fiction* 14 (1994), 71–6 (75).
14. Laura Mulvey, 'Visual Pleasure and Narrative Cinema', in Anthony Easthope,
    ed., *Contemporary Film Theory* (London: Longman, 1993), pp. 111–24 (116).
15. John Brannigan, *Orwell to the Present: Literature in England, 1945–2000*
    (Basingstoke: Palgrave, 2003), pp. 130–1; Sarah Gamble, *Angela Carter:
    Writing from the Front Line* (Edinburgh: Edinburgh University Press, 1998),
    pp. 160–1.
16. Elaine Showalter, 'Critical Cross-Dressing: Male Feminists and the Woman of
    the Year', in Alice Jardine and Paul Smith, eds, *Men in Feminism* (New York:
    Methuen, 1987), pp. 116–32.
17. A. S. Byatt, 'Monique Wittig: *The Lesbian Body*', in *Passions of the Mind*, p. 276.
18. A. S. Byatt, in Nicolas Tredell, ed., *Conversations with Critics* (Manchester:
    Carcanet, 1994), p. 60.
19. A.S. Byatt, 'Reading, Writing, Studying: Some Questions about Changing
    Conditions for Writers and Readers', *Critical Quarterly* 35 (1993), 3–7 (5).
20. Byatt, in Tredell, ed., *Conversations with Critics*, p. 60.
21. A. S. Byatt, 'Forefathers', in *On Histories and Stories: Selected Essays* (London:
    Chatto & Windus, 2000), p. 47.
22. Luce Irigaray, *Divine Women*, trans. Stephen Muecke (Sydney: Local
    Consumption Publications, 1986), p. 12.
23. Louise Yelin, 'Cultural Cartography: A. S. Byatt's *Possession* and the Politics of
    Victorian Studies', *The Victorian Studies Newsletter* 81 (1992), 38–41 (39).
24. Byatt, in Tredell, ed., *Conversations with Critics*, p. 62.
25. Keen, *Romances of the Archive in Contemporary British Fiction*, p. 32.
26. Jacques Lacan, 'Seminar on "The Purloined Letter" ', *Yale French Studies* 48
    (1972), 38–72.
27. Jacques Derrida, 'The Purveyor of Truth', *Yale French Studies* 52 (1975),
    31–113 (48).
28. Barbara Johnson, 'The Frame of Reference: Poe, Lacan, Derrida', *Yale French
    Studies* 55–6 (1977), 457–505 (465).
29. See John P. Muller and William Richardson, eds, *The Purloined Poe: Lacan,
    Derrida and Psychoanalytic Reading* (Baltimore, MD: Johns Hopkins University
    Press, 1988) for further contributions to the debate.

30. Jean-Michel Rabaté, *Jacques Lacan* (Basingstoke: Palgrave, 2001), p. 42.
31. Connor, *The English Novel in History 1950–1995*, p. 150. Connor further argues that 'If the completion of the past in the present is imaged as the final delivery of a letter, its solidification into an event achieved by its eventual arrival in the present, this final episode postulates a more indefinite kind of occurrence, which may never arrive in memory or narrative, or achieve the completeness of an event' (150).

8 Criminal Signs: Murder in Theory

1. Norman N. Holland, *Death in a Delphi Seminar: A Postmodern Mystery* (Albany: State University of New York Press, 1995), p. 282.
2. Julia Kristeva, *The Old Man and the Wolves*, trans. Barbara Bray (New York: Columbia University Press, 1994 [1991]), p. 65.
3. D. J. H. Jones, *Murder at the MLA* (Albuquerque, NM: University of New Mexico Press, 1993).
4. Stephen J. Greenblatt, *Learning to Curse: Essays in Early Modern Culture* (New York: Routledge, 1990), pp. 11–15.
5. Norman N. Holland, *The Critical I* (New York: Columbia University Press, 1992), p. 182.
6. Connor, *The English Novel in History 1950–95*, p. 69.
7. Umberto Eco, *The Name of the Rose*, trans. William Weaver (London: Vintage, 1983 [1980]), p. 5.
8. See Umberto Eco, 'Towards a New Middle Ages', in Blonsky, ed., *On Signs*, pp. 500–1, for a brief discussion on the affinities between the 'intellectual games' of medieval scholasticism and the linguistic theories of Barthes, Chomsky and Jakobson.
9. Theresa Coletti, *Naming the Rose: Medieval Signs and Modern Theory* (Ithaca, NY: Cornell University Press, 1988), p. 167.
10. Walter E. Stephens, 'Ec(h)o in Fabula', *Diacritics* 13 (1983), 51–64 (51).
11. Coletti, *Naming the Rose*, p. 40.
12. '[T]he rose is a symbolic figure so rich in meanings that by now it hardly has any meaning left'. Umberto Eco, *Reflections on 'The Name of the Rose'*, trans. William Weaver (London: Secker & Warburg, 1985 [1983]), p. 3.
13. Charles Sanders Peirce, cited in Umberto Eco, 'Unlimited Semiosis and Drift', in *The Limits of Interpretation* (Bloomington and Indianapolis, IN: Indiana University Press, 1990), p. 28.
14. Eco, 'Unlimited Semiosis and Drift', p. 34
15. Eco, 'Unlimited Semiosis and Drift', p. 28.
16. Eco, *Reflections on 'The Name of the Rose'*, p. 57.
17. Eco, *Reflections on 'The Name of the Rose'*, p. 66.
18. Eco, 'Abduction in Uqbar', in *The Limits of Interpretation*, pp. 153–62. Eco applies a more intricate model of abduction to Conan Doyle in 'Horns, Hooves, Insteps: Some Hypotheses on Three Types of Abduction', in Umberto Eco and Thomas A. Sebeok, eds, *The Sign of Three: Dupin, Holmes, Peirce* (Bloomington, IN: Indiana University Press, 1983), pp. 198–220.
19. Eco, *Reflections on 'The Name of the Rose'*, pp. 57–8.
20. Derrida, 'Plato's Pharmacy', in *Dissemination*, pp. 67–186.

21. Julia Kristeva, in Bernard Sichère, 'An Interview with Julia Kristeva', trans. Leon S. Roudiez, *Partisan Review* 61 (1994), 120–31 (122).
22. Kristeva, 'Open Letter to Harlem Désir', in *Nations Without Nationalism*, p. 50.
23. Julia Kristeva, *The Sense and Non-Sense of Revolt: The Powers and Limits of Psychoanalysis*, trans. Jeanine Herman (New York: Columbia University Press, 2000 [1996]), pp. 11–15.
24. Julia Kristeva, *Powers of Horror: An Essay on Abjection*, trans. Leon S. Roudiez (New York: Columbia University Press, 1982 [1980]), p. 4.
25. Kristeva, *Powers of Horror*, pp. 3–4.
26. Kristeva, *Powers of Horror*, p. 207.
27. Kristeva, in Sichère, 'An Interview with Julia Kristeva', 121.
28. Kathleen O'Grady, 'The Tower and the Chalice: Julia Kristeva and the Story of Santa Barbara', in Morny Joy, Kathleen O'Grady and Judith L. Poxon, eds, *Religion in French Feminist Thought: Critical Perspectives* (London: Routledge, 2003), pp. 85–100.
29. Julia Kristeva, *Strangers to Ourselves*, trans. Leon S. Roudiez (Hemel Hempstead: Harvester Wheatsheaf, 1991 [1988]), p. 51.
30. Kristeva, *Strangers to Ourselves*, p. 181.
31. Kristeva, *The Sense and Non-sense of Revolt*, pp. 86–7.

9   The Novel in Hyperreality

1. Jean Baudrillard, *Symbolic Exchange and Death*, trans. Iain Hamilton Grant (London: Sage, 1993 [1976]), p. 75.
2. Walter Benjamin, 'The Work of Art in the Age of Mechanical Reproduction', in *Illuminations*, trans. Harry Zohn (London: Cape, 1970), pp. 211–44.
3. Jean Baudrillard, in *Simulacra and Simulation*, trans. Sheila Faria Glaser (Ann Arbor, MI: The University of Michigan Press, 1994 [1981]), p. 12.
4. Baudrillard, *Symbolic Exchange and Death*, p. 50.
5. Baudrillard, *Simulacra and Simulation*, p. 6.
6. Tony Thwaites, 'Miracles: Hot Air and Histories of the Improbable', in Niall Lucy, ed., *Postmodern Literary Theory: An Anthology* (Oxford: Blackwell, 2000), p. 273.
7. Connor, *Postmodernist Culture*, p. 247.
8. Jean Baudrillard, *The Gulf War Did Not Take Place*, trans. Paul Patton (Sydney: Power Publications, 1995).
9. See Christopher Norris, *Uncritical Theory: Postmodernism, Intellectuals, and the Gulf War* (London: Lawrence & Wishart, 1992), pp. 11–31, 192–6.
10. Christopher Norris, *What's Wrong with Postmodernism? Critical Theory and the Ends of Philosophy* (New York: Harvester Wheatsheaf, 1990), p. 180.
11. Jean Baudrillard, 'This Beer Isn't a Beer', p. 188.
12. Christine Brooke-Rose, *Textermination* (Manchester: Carcanet, 1991).
13. Sarah Birch, *Christine Brooke-Rose and Contemporary Fiction* (Oxford: Clarendon Press, 1994), p. 137.
14. See Christine Brooke-Rose, 'The Dissolution of Character in the Novel', in Thomas C. Heller, Morton Sosna and David E. Wellbery, eds, *Reconstructing Individualism: Autonomy, Individuality, and the Self in Western Thought* (Stanford, CA: Stanford University Press, 1986), pp. 184–96.

15. For more on the *Towering Inferno* connection, see Lawrence, 'Saving the Text', 109.
16. Julian Barnes, *England, England* (London: Cape, 1998).
17. Baudrillard, *Symbolic Exchange and Death*, p. 62.
18. Randall Stevenson, *The Last of England?* (Oxford University Press, 2004), p. 65.
19. See Guy Debord, *Society of the Spectacle* (Detroit, MI: Black and Red, 1983 [1967]), chapter I, section 1.
20. Barnes 'Novels Come Out of Life, Not Out of Theories', p. 64, for a brief discussion of the novel's Baudrillard connection.
21. Baudrillard, 'The Precession of Simulacra', in *Simulacra and Simulation*, p. 13.
22. Baudrillard, 'The Precession of Simulacra', p. 11.
23. Baudrillard, '*Amor Fati* (a letter from Baudrillard)', in Gane, ed., *Baudrillard Live*, p. 208.
24. A. N. Wilson, *A Jealous Ghost* (London: Hutchinson, 2005).
25. Toby Litt, 'Screwed by the Turn', *The Guardian* 30 April 2005.
26. Mark Z. Danielewski, *House of Leaves* (London: Doubleday, 2000).
27. Larry McCaffery and Sinda Gregory, 'Haunted House – An Interview with Mark Z. Danielewski', *Critique* 44 (2003), 99–135 (100).
28. Baudrillard, 'The Precession of Simulacra', pp. 27–8.
29. Susan Sontag, *On Photography* (New York: Farrar, Straus and Giroux 1977), p. 179.
30. Brooke-Rose, *Invisible Author*, p. 166.
31. Eco, *Reflections on 'The Name of the Rose'*, p. 2.
32. McCaffery and Gregory, 'Haunted House', 106.

10 Conclusion: Fiction after Theory

1. Rabaté, Jean-Michel, *The Future of Theory* (Oxford: Blackwell, 2002), p. 4.
2. See *The Future of Theory*, pp. 147–9, for Rabaté's breakdown of the 'schools', 'agendas' and 'projects' that he expects to dominate theory in forthcoming years.
3. Jonathan Franzen, *The Corrections* (London: Fourth Estate, 2001), pp. 106–7.
4. Showalter, *Faculty Towers*, p. 114.
5. David Lodge, 'Structural Defects', in *Write On: Occasional Essays '65–'85* (London: Secker & Warburg, 1986), p. 115.
6. Raymond Federman, *Take It Or Leave It* (New York: Fiction Collective, 1976), ch. 14.
7. Raymond Tallis, *Absence: A Metaphysical Comedy* (London: The Toby Press, 1999).
8. Philippe Sollers, *Women*, trans. Barbara Bray (New York: Columbia University Press, 1990 [1983]), p. 92.
9. 'As *if* I were Dead: An Interview with Jacques Derrida', in John Brannigan, Ruth Robbins and Julian Wolfreys, eds, *Applying: To Derrida* (Basingstoke: Macmillan, 1996), pp. 224–5.

Bibliography

Primary Texts

Adair, Gilbert, *The Death of the Author* (London: Minerva, 1992).

Banville, John, *Shroud* (London: Picador, 2002).

Barnes, Julian, *England, England* (London: Jonathan Cape, 1998).

Bradbury, Malcolm, *Doctor Criminale* (London: Secker & Warburg, 1992).

——, *My Strange Quest for Mensonge: Structuralism's Hidden Hero* (London: Deutsch, 1987).

——, *To The Hermitage* (London: Picador, 2000).

Brooke-Rose, Christine, *Textermination* (Manchester: Carcanet, 1991).

——, *Thru* (London: Hamish Hamilton, 1975).

Burgess, Anthony, *MF* (New York: Knopf, 1971).

Byatt, A. S., *The Biographer's Tale* (London: Chatto and Windus, 2000).

——, *Possession: A Romance* (London: Vintage, 1990).

Carter, Angela, *Nights at the Circus* (London: Vintage, 1984).

Coe, Jonathan, *The House of Sleep* (Harmondsworth: Penguin, 1997).

Damrosch, David, *Meetings of the Mind* (Princeton University Press, 2000).

Danielewski, Mark Z., *House of Leaves* (London: Doubleday, 2000).

Duncker, Patricia, *Hallucinating Foucault* (London: Picador, 1996).

Eco, Umberto, *Foucault's Pendulum*, trans. William Weaver (London: Secker & Warburg, 1989 [1988]).

——, *The Name of the Rose*, trans. William Weaver (London: Vintage, 1983 [1980]).

Everett, Percival, *Erasure: A Novel* (London: Faber and Faber 2003 [2001]).

——, *Glyph* (Saint Paul, Minnesota: Graywolf Press, 1999).

Federman, Raymond, *Take It Or Leave It* (New York: Fiction Collective, 1976).

Fowles, John, *The French Lieutenant's Woman* (London: Pan, 1987 [1969]).

Franzen, Jonathan, *The Corrections* (London: Fourth Estate, 2001).

Gilbert, Sandra M., and Susan Gubar, *Masterpiece Theatre: An Academic Melodrama* (New Brunswick: Rutgers University Press, 1995).

Guibert, Hervé, 'Les secrets d'un homme', in *Mauve le Vierge: Nouvelles* (Paris: Editions Gallimard, 1988), pp. 101–11.

——, *To the Friend Who Did Not Save My Life: A Novel*, trans. Linda Coverdale (London: Quartet Books, 1991).

L'Heureux, John, *The Handmaid of Desire* (New York: Soho Press, 1996).

Holland, Norman N., *Death in a Delphi Seminar: A Postmodern Mystery* (State University of New York Press, 1995).

Hynes, James, *The Lecturer's Tale* (New York: Picador, 2001).

Jones, D. J. H., *Murder at the MLA* (Albuquerque: University of New Mexico Press, 1993).

Kristeva, Julia, *The Old Man and the Wolves*, trans. Barbara Bray (New York: Columbia University Press, 1994 [1991]).

——, *Possessions*, trans. Barbara Bray (New York: Columbia University Press, 1998).

——, *The Samurai: A Novel*, trans. Barbara Bray (New York: Columbia University Press, 1992).

Litt, Toby, 'When I Met Michel Foucault', in *Adventures in Capitalism* (Harmondsworth: Penguin, 2003 [1996]), pp. 189–228.

Lodge, David, *How Far Can You Go?* (Harmondsworth: Penguin, 1980).

——, *Nice Work* (Harmondsworth: Penguin, 1988).

——, *Small World: An Academic Romance* (Harmondsworth: Penguin, 1984).

——, *Thinks ...* (Harmondsworth: Penguin, 2001).

Powers, Richard, *Galatea 2.2* (London: Abacaus, 1996).

Sollers, Philippe, *Women*, trans. Barbara Bray (New York: Columbia University Press, 1990 [1983]).

Tallis, Raymond, *Absence: A Metaphysical Comedy* (London: The Toby Press, 1999).

Wilson, A. N., *A Jealous Ghost* (London: Hutchinson, 2005).

Secondary Texts

Althusser, Louis, *Essays on Ideology* (London: Verso, 1984).

——, *The Future Lasts Forever: A Memoir*, trans. Richard Veasey (New York: The New Press, 1993).

Arac, Jonathan, ed., *After Foucault: Humanistic Knowledge, Postmodern Challenges* (New Brunswick, New Jersey: Rutgers University Press, 1991).

Bakhtin, Mikhail, *The Dialogic Imagination: Four Essays*, trans. Caryl Emerson and Michael Holquist (Austin: University of Texas Press, 1981).

——, *Problems of Dostoevsky's Poetics*, trans. Caryl Emerson (Minneapolis: University of Minnesota Press, 1984).

——, *Rabelais and His World*, trans. Hélène Iswolsky (Bloomington: Indiana University Press, 1984 [1965]).

Baldick, Chris, *Criticism and Literary Theory, 1890 to the Present* (London: Longman, 1996).

Barthes, Roland, *Critical Essays*, trans. Richard Howard (Evanston, Illinois: Northwestern University Press, 1972 [1964]).

——, *Empire of Signs*, trans. Richard Howard (London: Cape, 1983 [1970]).

——, *Image–Music–Text*, trans. Stephen Heath (London: Fontana, 1977).

——, *Mythologies*, trans. Annette Lavers (London: Paladin, 1973 [1957]).

——, 'Réponses', *Tel Quel* 47 (1971), 89–107.

——, *Roland Barthes*, trans. Richard Howard (Berkeley: University of California Press, 1977 [1975]).

——, *The Rustle of Language*, trans. Richard Howard (Oxford: Blackwell, 1986 [1984]).

——, *Sade Fourier Loyola*, trans. Richard Miller (Berkeley: University of California Press, 1989 [1971]).

——, *S/Z*, trans. Richard Miller (Oxford: Blackwell, 1990 [1973]).

Baudrillard, Jean, *Baudrillard Live: Selected Interviews*, ed. Mike Gane (London: Routledge, 1993).

——, *The Gulf War Did Not Take Place*, trans. Paul Patton (Sydney: Power Publications, 1995).

——, *Simulacra and Simulation*, trans. Sheila Faria Glaser (Ann Arbor: The University of Michigan Press, 1994 [1981]).

Baudrillard, Jean, *Symbolic Exchange and Death*, trans. Iain Hamilton Grant (London: Sage 1993 [1976]).

Benjamin, Walter, *Illuminations*, trans. Harry Zohn (London: Fontana, 1973).

Berben-Masi, Jacqueline, 'Perceval Everett's *Glyph*: Prisons of the Body Physical, Political, and Academic', in Monika Fludernik and Greta Olson, eds, *In the Grip of the Law: Trials, Prisons and the Space Between* (Frankfurt: Peter Lang, 2005), pp. 223–39.

Bergonzi, Bernard, *David Lodge* (Plymouth: Northcote House, 1995).

Birch, Sarah, *Christine Brooke-Rose and Contemporary Fiction* (Oxford: Clarendon Press, 1994).

Bissell, Elizabeth Beaumont, ed., *The Question of Literature: The Place of the Literary in Contemporary Theory* (Manchester University Press, 2002).

Blonsky, Marsall, ed., *On Signs: A Semiotics Reader* (Oxford: Blackwell, 1985).

Bloom, Allan, *The Closing of the American Mind: How Higher Education Has Failed Democracy and Impoverished the Souls of Today's Students* (New York: Simon and Schuster, 1987).

Bloom, Harold, *The Western Canon: The Books and School of the Ages* (London: Macmillan, 1995).

Bloom, Harold, Paul de Man, Jacques Derrida, Geoffrey H. Hartman, and J. Hillis Miller, *Deconstruction and Criticism* (London: Routledge & Kegan Paul, 1979).

Bouchard, Norma, ' "Critifictional" Epistemes in Contemporary Literature: The Case of *Foucault's Pendulum*', *Comparative Literature Studies* 32 (1995), 497–513.

Brannigan, John, *Orwell to the Present: Literature in England, 1945–2000* (Basingstoke: Palgrave, 2003).

Brannigan, John, Ruth Robbins and Julian Wolfreys, eds, *Applying: To Derrida* (Basingstoke: Macmillan, 1996).

Brooke-Rose, Christine, 'The Dissolution of Character in the Novel', in *Reconstructing Individualism: Autonomy, Individuality, and the Self in Western Thought*, eds. Thomas C. Heller, Morton Sosna and David E. Wellbery (California: Stanford University Press, 1986), pp. 184–96.

——, *Invisible Author: Last Essays* (Columbus: The Ohio State University Press, 2002).

——, *Stories, Theories and Things* (Cambridge University Press, 1991).

Burgess, Anthony, *This Man and Music* (London: Hutchinson, 1982).

Burke, Seán, *The Death and Return of the Author: Criticism and Subjectivity in Barthes, Foucault and Derrida* (Edinburgh University Press, 1999).

Byatt, A. S., *On Histories and Stories: Selected Essays* (London: Chatto & Windus, 2000).

——, *Passions of the Mind: Selected Writings* (London: Chatto & Windus, 1991).

——, 'Reading, Writing, Studying: Some Questions about Changing Conditions for Writers and Readers', *Critical Quarterly* 35 (1993), 3–7.

Carter, Ian, *Ancient Cultures of Conceit: British University Fiction in the Post-War Years* (London: Routledge, 1990).

Childs, Peter, *Contemporary Novelists, 1970–2003* (Basingstoke: Macmillan, 2004).

Cixous, Hélène, 'The Laugh of the Medusa', in *New French Feminisms: An Anthology*, eds. Elaine Marks and Isabelle de Courtivron (Sussex: The Harvester Press, 1981), pp. 245–64.

Coletti, Theresa, *Naming the Rose: Medieval Signs and Modern Theory* (Ithaca: Cornell University Press, 1988).

Connor, Steven, *The English Novel in History 1950–1995* (London: Routledge, 1996).
——, *Postmodernist Culture: An Introduction to Theories of the Contemporary* (Oxford: Blackwell, 1997).
Conradi, Peter J., *John Fowles* (London: Methuen, 1982).
Culler, Jonathan, 'The Literary in Theory', in *What's Left of Theory?: New Work on the Politics of Literary Theory*, eds Judith Butler, John Guillory and Kendall Thomas (New York: Routledge, 2000), pp. 273–92.
Cunningham, Valentine, *Reading After Theory* (Oxford: Blackwell, 2002).
Currie, Mark, ed., *Metafiction* (London: Longman, 1995).
——, *Postmodern Narrative Theory* (Basingstoke: Macmillan, 1998).
Damrosch, David, *We Scholars: Changing the Culture of the University* (Cambridge, MA: Harvard University Press, 1995).
Davis, Colin, 'Psychoanalysis, Detection, and Fiction: Julia Kristeva's Detective Novels', *Site: The Journal of Twentieth Century Contemporary French Studies* 6 (2002), 294–306.
Debord, Guy, *Society of the Spectacle* (Detroit: Black and Red, 1983 [1967]).
Deleuze, Gilles, and Félix Guattari, *A Thousand Plateaus: Capitalism and Schizophrenia*, trans. Brian Massumi (London: Athlone Press, 1988 [1980]).
Derrida, Jacques, *Archive Fever: A Freudian Impression*, trans. Eric Prenowitz (Chicago, IL: The University of Chicago Press, 1995).
——, *Dissemination*, trans. Barbara Johnson (London: Continuum, 2004 [1972]).
——, *Given Time: 1. Counterfeit Money*, trans. Peggy Kamuf (University of Chicago Press, 1992 [1991]).
——, *Of Grammatology*, trans. Gayatari Chakravorty Spivak (Baltimore: The Johns Hopkins University Press, 1976 [1967]).
——, *The Post-Card: From Socrates to Freud and Beyond*, trans. Alan Bass (University of Chicago Press, 1987 [1980]).
——, 'The Purveyor of Truth', *Yale French Studies* 52 (1975), 31–113.
——, *Writing and Difference*, trans. Alan Bass (London: Routledge, 1978 [1967]).
Docherty, Thomas, *After Theory* (Edinburgh University Press, 1997).
Eaglestone, Robert, 'The Fiction of Angela Carter', in *Contemporary British Fiction*, eds. Richard J. Lane, Rod Mengham and Philip Tew (Cambridge: Polity Press, 2003), pp. 195–209.
Eagleton, Mary, *Figuring the Woman Author in Contemporary Fiction* (Basingstoke: Palgrave, 2005).
Eagleton, Terry, *After Theory* (London: Allen Lane, 2003).
——, 'The Silences of David Lodge', *New Left Review* 172 (1988), 93–102.
Easton, Alison, ed., *Angela Carter: Contemporary Critical Essays* (Basingstoke: Macmillan, 2000).
Eco, Umberto, *Faith in Fakes: Travels in Hyperreality*, trans. William Weaver, 1998 [1983]).
——, *The Limits of Interpretation* (Bloomington: Indiana University Press, 1990).
——, *Reflections on 'The Name of the Rose'*, trans. William Weaver (London: Secker & Warburg, 1985 [1983]).
——, *The Role of the Reader: Explorations in the Semiotics of Texts* (London: Hutchinson, 1979).
——, *Semiotics and the Philosophy of Language* (Basingstoke: Macmillan, 1984).
Eco, Umberto and Thomas A. Sebeok, eds, *The Sign of Three: Dupin, Holmes, Peirce* (Bloomington: Indiana University Press, 1983).

Eribon, Didier, *Michel Foucault*, trans. Betsy Wing (London: Faber, 1991 [1989]).

Federman, Raymond, 'Critifiction: Imagination as Plagiarism' [1976], in *Critifiction: Postmodern Essays* (New York: State University of New York Press, 1993), pp. 48–64.

Fokkema, Aleid, 'The Author: Postmodernism's Stock Character', in *The Author as Character: Representing Historical Writers in Western Literature*, eds. Paul Franssen and Ton Hoenselaars (Madison: Farleigh Dickinson University Press, 1999), pp. 39–51.

Foucault, Michel, *The Archaeology of Knowledge*, trans. A. M. Sheridan Smith (London: Routledge, 1989 [1969]).

——, *Discipline and Punish: The Birth of the Prison*, trans. Alan Sheridan (Harmondsworth: Penguin, 1979).

——, *The Essential Works*, 3 vols., ed. James Faubion, trans. Robert Hurley *et al.* (London: Allen Lane, 1998).

——, *Foucault Live: Interviews, 1961–1984*, ed. Sylvère Lotringer, trans. Lysa Hochroth and John Johnston (New York: Semiotext(e), 1996).

——, *The History of Sexuality 1: An Introduction*, trans. Robert Hurley (London: Allen Lane, 1979 [1976]).

——, *Madness and Civilization: A History of Insanity in the Age of Reason*, trans. Richard Howard (London: Routledge, 1989 [1961/4]).

——, *The Order of Things: An Archaeology of the Human Sciences* (London: Routledge, 1970 [1966]).

——, *Politics, Philosophy, Culture: Interviews and Other Writings 1977–84*, ed. Lawrence D. Kritzman, trans. Alan Sheridan *et al.* (Routldge: New York, 1988).

Foucault, Michel and Maurice Blanchot, *Foucault/Blanchot*, trans. Jeffrey Mehlman and Brian Massumi (New York: Zone Books, 1990).

Freiburg, Rudolf and Jan Schnitker, eds, *'Do You Consider Yourself a Postmodern Author?': Interviews with Contemporary English Writers* (Münster: Lit Verlag, 1999).

Friedman, Ellen J. and Richard Martin, eds, *Utterly Other Discourse: The Texts of Christine Brooke-Rose* (Illinois: Dalkey Archive Press, 1995).

Fuller, David, and Patricia Waugh, eds, *The Arts and Sciences of Criticism* (Oxford University Press, 1999).

Gamble, Sarah, *Angela Carter: Writing from the Front Line* (Edinburgh University Press, 1997).

Gass, Joanne M., 'Panopticism in *Nights at the Circus*', *The Review of Contemporary Fiction* 14 (1994), 71–6 (75).

Genette, Gérard, *Narrative Discourse: An Essay in Method*, trans. Jane E. Lewin (Ithaca, NY: Cornell University Press, 1980 [1972]).

Graff, Gerald, *Beyond the Culture Wars: How Teaching the Conflicts Can Revitalize American Education* (New York: Norton, 1992).

——, *Professing Literature: An Institutional History* (Chicago, IL: The University of Chicago Press, 1987).

Greenblatt, Stephen J., *Learning to Curse: Essays in Early Modern Culture* (New York: Routledge, 1990).

Haffenden, John, *Novelists in Interview* (London: Methuen, 1985).

Hamacher, Werner, Neil Hertz, and Thomas Keenan, eds, *Responses: On Paul de Man's Wartime Journalism* (Lincoln: University of Nebraska Press, 1989).

Hanson, Clare, ' "The Red Dawn Breaking Over Clapham": Carter and the Limits of Artifice', in *The Infernal Desires of Angela Carter: Fiction, Femininity, Feminism* eds. Joseph Bristow and Trev Lynn Broughton (London: Longman, 1997), pp. 59–72.

Hartman, Geoffrey H., *Criticism in the Wilderness: The Study of Literature Today* (New Haven: Yale University Press, 1980).

Hassan, Ihab, *Paracriticisms: Seven Speculations of the Times* (Urbana: University of Illinois Press, 1975).

——, *The Right Promethean Fire: Imagination, Science, and Cultural Change* (Urbana: University of Illinois Press, 1980).

Hayles, N. K., 'Saving the Subject: Remediation in *House of Leaves*', *American Literature* 74 (2002), 779–806.

Head, Dominic, *The Cambridge Introduction to Modern British Fiction, 1950–2000* (Cambridge University Press, 2002).

Holmes, Frederick M., 'The Reader as Discoverer in David Lodge's *Small World*', *Critique* 32 (1990), 47–57.

Hutcheon, Linda, *A Poetics of Postmodernism: History, Theory, Fiction* (New York: Routledge, 1988).

Irigaray, Luce, *Divine Women*, trans. Stephen Meucke (Sydney: Local Consumption Publications, 1986).

Jameson, Frederic, 'Postmodernism, or The Cultural Logic of Late Capitalism', *New Left Review* 146 (1984), 55–92.

Johnson, Barbara, 'The Frame of Reference: Poe, Lacan, Derrida', *Yale French Studies* 55–6 (1977), 457–505.

Keen, Suzanne, *Romances of the Archive in Contemporary British Fiction* (University of Toronto Press, 2001).

Kermode, Frank, *Essays on Fiction 1971–82* (London: Routledge and Kegan Paul, 1983).

——, 'M/F', *Anthony Burgess Newsletter* (2000), 23–6.

Knapp, Steven and Walter Benn Michaels, 'Against Theory', *Critical Inquiry* 8 (1982), 723–42.

Kristeva, Julia, *In the Beginning Was Love: Psychoanalysis and Faith*, trans. Arthur Goldhammer (New York: Columbia University Press, 1987 [1985]).

——, *Nations Without Nationalism*, trans. Leon S. Roudiez (New York: Columbia University Press, 1993).

——, *Powers of Horror: An Essay on Abjection*, trans. Leon S. Roudiez (New York: Columbia University Press, 1982).

——, *The Sense and Non-sense of Revolt: The Powers and Limits of Psychoanalysis*, trans. Jeanine Herman (New York: Columbia University Press, 2000 [1996]).

——, *Strangers to Ourselves*, trans. Leon S. Roudiez (New York: Columbia University Press, 1991).

——, *Tales of Love*, trans. Leon S. Roudiez (New York: Columbia University Press, 1987 [1983]).

Lacan, Jacques, *Écrits: A Selection*, trans. Alan Sheridan (London: Routledge, 1977 [1966]).

——, 'Seminar on "The Purloined Letter" ', *Yale French Studies* 48 (1972), 38–72.

Lawrence, Karen R., 'Saving the Text: Cultural Crisis in *Textermination* and *Masterpiece Theatre*', *Narrative* 5 (1997), 108–16.

——, 'Dialogizing Theory in Brooke-Rose's *Thru*', *Western Humanities Review* 50–1 (1996–67), 352–8.

Lehman, David, *Signs of the Times: Deconstruction and the Fall of Paul de Man* (London: Deutsch, 1991).

Lévi-Strauss, Claude, 'The Scope of Anthropology', in *Structural Anthropology*, vol. II, trans. Monique Layton (London: Allen Lane, 1977), pp. 3–32.

Litt, Toby, 'Screwed by the Turn', *The Guardian* 30 April 2005.

Lodge, David, *After Bakhtin: Essays on Fiction and Criticism* (London: Routledge, 1990).

——, *Consciousness and the Novel: Connected Essays* (London: Secker & Warburg, 2002).

——, *The Modes of Modern Writing: Metaphor, Metonymy, and the Typology of Modern Literature* (London: Arnold, 1977).

——, *The Novelist at the Crossroads and Other Essays on Fiction and Criticism* (London: Routledge and Kegan Paul, 1971).

——, *Working With Structuralism: Essays and Reviews on Nineteenth- and Twentieth-Century Literature* (London: Routledge, 1981).

——, *Write On: Occasional Essays '65-'85* (London: Secker & Warburg, 1986).

Lotringer, Sylvère and Sande Cohen, eds, *French Theory in America* (New York: Routledge, 2001).

Luckhurst, Roger and Peter Marks, eds, *Literature and the Contemporary: Fictions and Theories of the Present* (Essex: Longman, 1999).

Lucy, Niall, *Postmodern Literary Theory: An Introduction* (Oxford: Blackwell, 1997).

Lyotard, Jean-François, *The Post-Modern Condition: A Report on Knowledge*, trans. Geoff Bennington and Brian Massumi (Manchester University Press, 1984 [1979]).

——, *Postmodern Fables*, trans. Georges van den Abbeele (Minneapolis: University of Minnesota Press, 1997).

Macey, David, *The Lives of Michel Foucault* (London: Vintage, 1993).

De Man, Paul, *Allegories of Reading: Figural Language in Rousseau, Nietzsche, Rilke, and Proust* (New Haven: Yale University Press, 1979).

——, *Blindness and Insight: Essays in the Rhetoric of Contemporary Criticism* (London: Routledge, 1983).

——, *The Resistance to Theory* (Manchester University Press, 1986).

——, *The Rhetoric of Romanticism* (New York: Columbia University Press, 1984).

——, *Wartime Journalism, 1939–1943*, eds Werner Hamacher, Neil Hertz, and Thomas Keenan (Lincoln: University of Nebraska Press, 1988).

Mews, Siegfried, 'The Professor's Novel: David Lodge's *Small World*', *MLN* 104 (1989), 713–26.

MacCabe, Colin, *Theoretical Essays: Film, Linguistics, Literature* (Manchester University Press, 1985).

McCaffery, Larry and Sinda Gregory, 'Haunted House – An Interview with Mark Z. Danielewski', *Critique* 44 (2003), 99–135.

McHale, Brian, *Postmodernist Fiction* (New York: Methuen, 1987).

McQuillan, Martin, *Paul de Man* (London: Routledge, 2001).

McQuillan, Martin, Robin Purves, Graeme Macdonald, Stephen Thomson, eds, *Post-Theory: New Directions in Criticism* (Edinburgh University Press, 1999).

Miller, James, *The Passion of Michel Foucault* (London: HarperCollins, 1993).

Miller, J. Hillis, *Fiction and Repetition: Seven English Novels* (Oxford: Blackwell, 1982).

Morace, Robert A., *The Dialogic Novels of Malcolm Bradbury and David Lodge* (Carbondale: Southern Illinois University Press, 1989).

Morrison, Jago, *Contemporary Fiction* (London: Routledge, 2003).

Mulvey, Laura, 'Visual Pleasure and Narrative Cinema', in *Contemporary Film Theory*, ed. Anthony Easthope (London: Longman, 1993), pp. 111–24.

Norris, Christopher, *Derrida* (London: Fontana Press, 1987).

——, *Uncritical Theory: Postmodernism, Intellectuals, and the Gulf War* (London: Lawrence & Wishart, 1992).

——, *What's Wrong With Postmodernism: Critical Theory and the Ends of Philosophy* (New York: Harvester Wheatsheaf, 1990).

O'Connor, Erin, 'Reading *The Biographer's Tale*', *Victorian Studies* 44 (2002), 379–87.

O'Grady, Kathleen, 'The Tower and the Chalice: Julia Kristeva and the Story of Santa Barbara', in *Religion in French Feminist Thought: Critical Perspectives*, eds. Morny Joy, Kathleen O'Grady and Judith L. Poxon (London: Routledge, 2003), pp. 85–100.

Payne, Michael and John Schad, eds, *life.after.theory* (London: Continuum, 2003).

Peach, Linden, *Angela Carter* (Basingstoke: Macmillan, 1998).

Rabaté, Jean-Michel, *The Future of Theory* (Oxford: Blackwell, 2002).

——, *Jacques Lacan* (Basingstoke: Palgrave, 2001).

Readings, Bill, *The University in Ruins* (Cambridge, Massachussetts: Harvard University Press, 1996).

Rosso, Stefano, 'A Correspondence with Umberto Eco', trans. Carolyn Springer, *Boundary 2* 12 (1983), 1–13.

Sage, Lorna, *Angela Carter* (Plymouth: Northcote House, 1994).

Salusinszky, Imre, *Criticism in Society* (New York: Methuen, 1987).

Saussure, Ferdinand de, *Course in General Linguistics*, trans. Wade Baskin (London: Peter Owen, 1960 [1916]).

Selden, Raman, Peter Widdowson, and Peter Brooker, *A Reader's Guide to Contemporary Literary Theory* (Harlow: Pearson Education Limited, 2005).

Shaffer, Brian W., ed., *A Companion to the British and Irish Novel 1945–2000* (Oxford: Blackwell, 2005).

Shiller, Dana, 'The Redemptive Past in the Neo-Victorian Novel', *Studies in the Novel* 29 (1997), 538–60.

Showalter, Elaine, 'Critical Cross-Dressing', in *Men in Feminism*, eds. Alice Jardine and Paul Smith (New York: Methuen, 1987), pp. 116–32.

——, *Faculty Towers: The Academic Novel and Its Discontents* (Philadelphia: University of Pennsylvania Press, 2004).

——, ed. *The New Feminist Criticism: Essays on Women, Literature and Theory* (London: Virago, 1986).

Sichère, Bernard, 'An Interview with Julia Kristeva', trans. Leon S. Roudiez, *Partisan Review* 61 (1994), 120–31.

Siegle, Robert, 'The Concept of the Author in Barthes, Foucault, and Fowles', *College Literature* 10 (1983), 126–38.

Sokal, Alan and Jean Bricmont, *Intellectual Impostures: Postmodern Philosophers' Abuse of Science* (London: Profile, 1998).

Sontag, Susan, *On Photography* (New York: Farrar, Straus and Giroux, 1977).

Stafford, Andy, *Roland Barthes, Phenomenon and Myth: An Intellectual Biography* (Edinburgh University Press, 1998).

Steiner, George, *Language and Silence: Essays 1958–66* (London: Faber, 1967).

Stephens, Walter E., 'Ec(h)o in Fabula', *Diacritics* 13 (1983), 51–64.

Stevenson, Randall, *The Last of England?* (Oxford University Press, 2004).

Sturrock, John, *The Word from Paris: Essays on Modern French Thinkers and Writers* (London: Verso, 1998).

Tallis, Raymond, *In Defence of Realism* (London: Arnold, 1988).

Tallis, Raymond, *Not Saussure: A Critique of Post-Saussurean Literary Theory* (Basingstoke: Macmillan, 1988).

——, *Theorrhoea and After* (Basingstoke: Macmillan, 1999).

Tew, Philip, *The Contemporary British Novel* (London: Continuum, 2004).

Tredell, Nicolas, ed., *Conversations with Critics* (Manchester: Carcanet, 1994).

——, *The Critical Decade: Culture in Crisis* (Manchester: Carcanet, 1993).

Vipond, Dianne L., ed., *Conversations with John Fowles* (Jackson: University Press of Mississippi, 1999).

Waters, Lindsay, and Wlad Godzich, eds, *Reading De Man Reading* (Minneapolis: University of Minnesota Press, 1989).

Watkins, Susan, *Twentieth-Century Women Novelists: Feminist Theory into Practice* (Basingstoke: Palgrave, 2001).

Waugh, Patricia, *Metafiction: The Theory and Practice of Self-Conscious Fiction* (London: Routledge, 1984).

White, Glyn, ' "YOU ARE HERE": Reading and Representation in Christine Brooke-Rose's *Thru'*, *Poetics Today* 23 (2002), 611–31.

Widdowson, Peter, 'The Anti-History Men: Malcolm Bradbury and David Lodge', *Critical Quarterly* 26 (1984), 5–32.

——, *Literature* (London: Routledge, 1999).

Womack, Kenneth, *Postwar Academic Fiction: Satire, Ethics, Community* (Basingstoke: Palgrave, 2002).

Yelin, Louise, 'Cultural Cartography: A.S. Byatt's *Possession* and the Politics of Victorian Studies', *The Victorian Studies Newsletter* 81 (1992), 38–41.

Index

Adair, Gilbert, 3, 5, 60, 123, 124, 158
  The Death of the Author, 3, 5, 7, 59,
    73, 75–8, 82, 92, 124
Althusser, Louis, 3, 78–81, 99
Armstrong, Isobel, 118

Bakhtin, Mikhail, 7, 25, 34, 35–40, 101
Banville, John, 5, 60, 158
  Shroud, 5, 59, 75, 78–82, 92
Barnes, Julian, 1, 6
  England, England, 6, 143, 146–9
Barthes, Roland, 2, 3, 4, 6, 7, 9, 10, 14,
    15, 25, 30, 56, 57, 60–1, 82, 100,
    123, 158
Baudrillard, Jean, 2, 4, 140–3, 146,
    147, 148, 149, 151
Benjamin, Walter, 140
Bennett, William J., 42
Berben-Masi, Jacqueline, 54
Bergonzi, Bernard, 25
Birch, Sarah, 144
Blanchot, Maurice, 94
Bloom, Allan, 41, 42
Bloom, Harold, 41, 50, 153
Borges, Jorge Luis, 5, 130, 131, 133,
    135, 152
Bradbury, Malcolm, 3, 5, 60, 158
  Doctor Criminale, 5, 59, 69–73
  My Strange Quest for Mensonge, 18,
    59, 61–4, 71, 89
  To the Hermitage, 59, 64–9, 76, 92
Brannigan, John, 112
Brooke-Rose, Christine, 2, 5, 6, 11,
    20, 153
  Textermination, 6, 143, 144–6
  Thru, 5, 11, 20–3, 144, 158
Burgess, Anthony,
  MF, 3, 5, 10, 16–20, 101, 158
Burke, Seán, 4, 75
Byatt, A.S., 3, 6, 60, 124, 158
  The Biographer's Tale, 18, 88–92,
    97, 123
  Possession, 6, 90, 93, 101, 112–22, 123

Carter, Angela, 3, 6, 7, 60
  Nights at the Circus, 3, 6,
    101–12
Chomsky, Noam, 83, 85
Cixous, Hélène, 6, 7, 99, 100, 102,
    103, 112, 118
Coe, Jonathan, 8
  The House of Sleep, 8
Coletti, Theresa, 130, 131
Connor, Steven, 4, 33, 122, 129, 142,
    161n10, 169n31
Culler, Jonathan, 4
Cunningham, Valentine, 7
Currie, Mark, 2, 3

Damrosch, David, 41, 45–7, 58
  Meetings of the Mind, 45–7
Danielewski, Mark Z., 6
  House of Leaves, 6, 143,
    149–55, 158
Debord, Guy, 147
Deleuze, Gilles, and Félix Guattari,
    132, 134
Derrida, Jacques, 2, 3, 4, 6, 7, 39,
    41, 47, 54, 99, 100, 102, 104–8,
    120, 123, 130, 131, 134–5, 153,
    154, 160
Duncker, Patricia, 3, 60, 83, 84
  Hallucinating Foucault, 3, 7,
    92–8, 149

Eaglestone, Robert, 105
Eagleton, Mary, 165n2
Eagleton, Terry, 25, 39
Easton, Alison, 102
Eco, Umberto, 2, 6, 23, 152, 155,
    158, 159
  Foucault's Pendulum, 130
  The Name of the Rose, 7, 124,
    129–35, 139, 160
Everett, Percival, 5, 41
  Erasure, 48, 57
  Glyph, 53–7, 58, 158

Federman, Raymond, 161n5
Take It Or Leave It, 157
Fokkema, Aleid, 59
Foucault, Michel, 2, 3, 6, 7, 60, 61, 64,
    67, 69, 77, 78, 82, 83–98, 100,
    101, 108–10, 126
Fowles, John, 5, 11, 158
The French Lieutentant's Woman, 5,
    11, 13–16, 105, 158
Franzen, Jonathan,
The Corrections, 156–7
Freud, Sigmud, 115–16, 130, 138, 139

Gamble, Sarah, 112
Genette, Gérard, 9, 12
Gilbert, Sandra M. and Susan Gubar,
    3, 5, 41, 118
Masterpiece Theatre, 42–5, 56, 58
Graff, Gerald, 41, 45
Greenblatt, Stephen, 125–6
Greimas, A. J., 9, 22
Gubar, Susan, *see* Sandra M. Gilbert
Guibert, Hervé, 6, 83, 84, 93–4, 97, 98
'Les secrets d'un homme', 86–7
*To the Friend Who Did Not Save My
    Life*, 86–8

Hartman, Geoffrey, 4
Hassan, Ihab, 42
Head, Dominic, 7
L'Heureux, John, 41, 84, 158
The Handmaid of Desire, 50–2, 58
Holland, Norman N., 6, 124, 158,
    159, 160
Death in a Delphi Seminar, 123, 124,
    126–9, 139
Hutcheon, Linda, 162n9
Hynes, James, 3, 5, 41, 158
The Lecturer's Tale, 47–50, 58, 114,
    143–4

Irigaray, Luce, 116–17

Jakobson, Roman, 9, 22, 26
James, Henry, 5
Jameson, Frederic, 57
Johnson, Barbara, 120
Jones, D. J. H., 6, 159, 160
Murder at the MLA, 124–6, 129, 139

Kaufman, Charlie, 139
Keen, Suzanne, 18
Kermode, Frank, 19
Klein, Richard, 74
Kristeva, Julia, 3, 6, 7, 42, 97, 98, 124
The Old Man and the Wolves, 135–9
Possessions, 136
The Samurai, 84–5, 157, 160

Lacan, Jacques, 6, 7, 8, 54–5, 99,
    119–22, 123
Lawrence, Karen R., 44
Lehman, David, 73, 74
Lévi-Strauss, Claude, 9, 16–17, 19,
    20, 158
Litt, Toby, 6, 83, 84, 97, 98, 130
'When I Met Michel Foucault', 85–6
Lodge, David, 3, 5, 24–40, 41, 57, 64,
    125, 157, 158
Changing Places, 5, 24, 25
How Far Can You Go?, 5, 11–13, 24,
    25, 26
Nice Work, 24, 30, 32–40, 55
Small World, 5, 24, 26–32, 36,
    40, 57
Thinks..., 5, 25, 37–8, 53
Lucy, Niall, 4
Lukács, Georg, 71–2
Lyotard, Jean-François, 2, 132–3

Man, Paul de, 2, 5, 8, 44, 70, 73–82,
    153, 154, 165n11
McCaffrey, Larry and Sinda
    Gregory, 151
McQuillan, Martin, 78
Mehlman, Jeffrey, 74
Morace, Robert A., 29
Morrison, Jago, 108, 110
Mulvey, Laura, 102, 110–11

Nabokov, Vladimir, 5
Norris, Christopher, 105, 142

O'Grady, Kathleen, 138

Peirce, Charles Sanders, 130, 131,
    133–4, 135
Powers, Richard, 5, 41
Galatea 2.2, 52–3, 58

Rabaté, Jean-Michel, 48, 156
Readings, Bill, 46, 49, 50
Rimmon-Kenan, Shlomith, 22
Robbe-Grillet, Alain, 14, 15

Sage, Lorna, 101, 102
Said, Edward W., 42, 45, 83
Saussure, Ferdinand de, 9, 10
Showalter, Elaine, 6, 49, 114, 118, 156
Sollers, Philippe,
    Women, 3, 160
Sontag, Susan, 151
Steiner, George, 71–2
Stephens, Walter E., 130
Stevenson, Randall, 147
Sturrock, John, 7

Tallis, Raymond, 3
    Absence, 3, 159–60
Thwaites, Tony, 142
Todorov, Tzvetan, 9

Watkins, Susan, 167n4
Waugh, Patricia, 4, 20,
    162n9
White, Glyn, 22
Wilde, Oscar, 5
Wilson, A. N.,
    A Jealous Ghost, 6, 143,
    149–50
Womack, Kenneth, 42

Yelin, Louise, 117